THE HYBRIDS

Name	Lineage	Date of Transformation	Area of Earth charged with protecting from the Nergal
Marodeen Present day = Joshua Arieil Present day = Cassandra Nasir Present day = Nathaniel	Assyrian	705 BC Battle with Cimmerians @ Tushpa	Southern Half of N. America
Regulus Present day = Reggie			******
Avinash Pravit	Indian	321 BC Battle for Pataliputra	India continent & Middle East
Gamba Salina	Egyptian	30 BC	African continent
Valfind Bjorn	Vikings	793 AD	European continent
Tomor Khun (Khūnbish)	Mongolian	1239 AD (Genghis Khan) 1253 AD (Kublai Khan)	Asia
Tupac Itzcali	Aztecs	1386 AD Mercenary Wars	S. America's & Pacific islands
Shamas Nevan	Irish	1651 AD Confederate War	European & American continents
Tyree Coorain	Australian	1830 AD Black War	Australia & Pacific Islands
Ki "Kisomm" (sun) Ko "KoKo" (night)	Blackfoot	1837 AD Raiding Party Wars	Northern half of N. America
Katherine Chambers	American	2012	Southern Half of N. America with the Assyrians

OF BLOOD AND LIONS

By Karen Ann

Martin Sisters Publishing

Published by

Martin Sisters Publishing, LLC www.

martinsisterspublishing. com

ISBN: 978-1-937273-83-5
Editor: Kathleen Papajohn
Literary
Cover Art: Danielle Festa
Printed in the United States of America
Martin Sisters Publishing, LLC

DEDICATIONS

I wish to thank my family and friends who have nurtured and shaped my personality and made me who I am today.

I also give thanks to Christine and Jennifer, who have shown me how to love unconditionally.

I dedicate this book to my husband Jim, who has given me a life that would not have been worth living without him, and who taught me that one of the most important lessons in that life is to accept people for whom they are.

Maureen,

   Thanks for all
the lovely years
of wonderful
friendship that
I hope will
continue forever.

            Kan Am

ACKNOWLEGDEMENTS

Thanks to all the wonderful people at Martin Sisters Publishing for giving me the opportunity of a lifetime.

Nikki Andrews is best known for her novels Framed, Chicken Bones, and A Windswept Star.

The book cover is a watercolor rendition by Danielle Festa of the "The African and the Lioness" carving c 899-700 B.C. Danielle may be reached at www.DanielleFesta.com.

I give additional special thanks to my friend Kassim, for helping me understand and describe my Assyrian.

PROLOGUE

Before *Of Blood and Lions*, if I had been asked to list the characteristics that best describe me, my answer would have read like this: scientist, recycler, gardener, animal lover, stitcher, daughter, sister, mother, wife-, anything but a writer. My novel appeared from out of nowhere like in a transporter scene from Star Trek. During my thirty plus years in the biomedical industry I've written hundreds of memos and reports that follow a standard scientific outline, consisting of page after page of tables and graphs. The drafts were passed from me to my supervisor for one or two re-writes, and then on to the next level for the next set of re-writes. Each reviewer made an effort to add some flair to the reports, but it was a challenge to make words like dilution points, linearity or precision as exciting as being chased down by a demon or as romantic as a first kiss.

Even now, when I look back on the events that led to this new path in my life, I'm astounded at the many twists and turns that might have accidently strayed my course. It had to be fate! The main character *Of Blood and Lions* may scowl at the thought of fate, but there's no doubt in my mind that it exists.

It all began in 2008, on a visit to the Boston Museum of Fine Arts. My parents, Richard and Joan Chelman, members of the museum for over twenty years, invited my husband and me to join them to see the latest exhibit "Art and Empire: Treasures from Assyria in the British Museum."

As Dad drove us from the restaurant through the slow moving Boston traffic, my only thought was getting through the Assyrian exhibit as quickly as possible, my ultimate goal being the museum's collection of mummies. Uncovering the secrets of a three-thousand-year-old preserved body is an undeniable lure for any biologist. I was bored and anxious as we made our way to the Assyrian exhibit, past hall after hall of famous paintings. I was pleasantly surprised, and instantly fascinated, by the numerous relief carvings of lions in the main exhibit. However, it wasn't until I came across a small wooden carving titled "The Lioness and the African" that I forgot all about the mummies. The powerfully sensual way in which the lion held the man's neck, as if to kiss rather than kill him made the image whirl in my head for the rest of the night.

The only souvenir I purchased during that visit was a postcard size picture of the lion carving, but that 6 x 6 piece of paper was the catalyst that changed my life, and I treasure it to this day.

At first, I tacked the postcard over my desk at work. Whenever I was having trouble getting through one of my technical reports I would look to the ancient masterpiece for inspiration and dream about the possibilities of the story surrounding the events in the carving (please don't tell my boss). Finally, with my husband's encouragement, I sat down on one particularly snowy January day, using my daughter's discarded laptop that was as slow as molasses, and began to compose my story.

Nikki Andrews, my first editor, has the patience of a saint. She spent most of her time fixing my horrendous punctuation, but the subtle comments she put in throughout the revisions were enough to point me in the right direction. Before I knew it, the jumble of pages actually began to resemble a genuine novel.

The Assyrian Empire (2400 to 608 BC) was one of the greatest kingdoms of the ancient world, and, like Sparta, Rome and Greece, it flourished mostly due to its great military prowess. This advantage also gave it the means to become the cultural center of its time. Assyrian King Ashurbanipal (685-627 BC) is most famous for his magnificent library in which he employed an academy of scribes to record history on his library's forty thousand clay tablets. Archeologists found one of the very first "super-human" stories, the Epic of Gilgamesh, among these tablets.

The great respect Assyrians had for lions can be seen throughout their extensive carvings. They considered lions to be the fiercest of all animals. To kill a lion was a remarkable feat reserved mostly for the Assyrian monarchs.

"The Lioness and the African" is one of two identical jewel-inlaid carved ivory panels, thought to be part of a throne from around 859 BC. The carvings are Phoenician in style and were most likely a tribute or a spoil of war. One of the carvings is presently held by the British Museum. Unfortunately, the second carving was looted from the National Museum of Iraq in 2003 during the US attacks on that country, and has not been found to this day.

The Assyrians' assessment of lions is spot-on. These magnificent animals have a difficult life, a life that's getting more challenging with each passing day. Whether life on this planet happened by cosmic chance or as the result of some intricate planning, I believe everyone can agree that our existence on this Earth is a gift not to be squandered.

The natural world is made up of thousands of checks and balances. When one species is disturbed or disappears, the whole balance of our planet is put in jeopardy. Big cats such as lions, tigers, leopards, jaguars and cheetahs are part of that circle of life and need large tracts of land on which to live and raise their families. The fact is that their populations have been in steep decline since the beginning of the twentieth century and are now at critically low levels (see lion map).

As the human race continues to increase in numbers, to the point where, just recently, the world population hit seven billion, there is less and less room for these magnificent beasts of the jungle. Your purchase of this book will help to stem that decline, because fifty percent of the book's proceeds will be donated to the National Geographic "Big Cats" Wildlife Conservation Program. Please visit National Geographic's website at ww.nationalgeographic.com and consider an additional donation to one of their conservation programs.

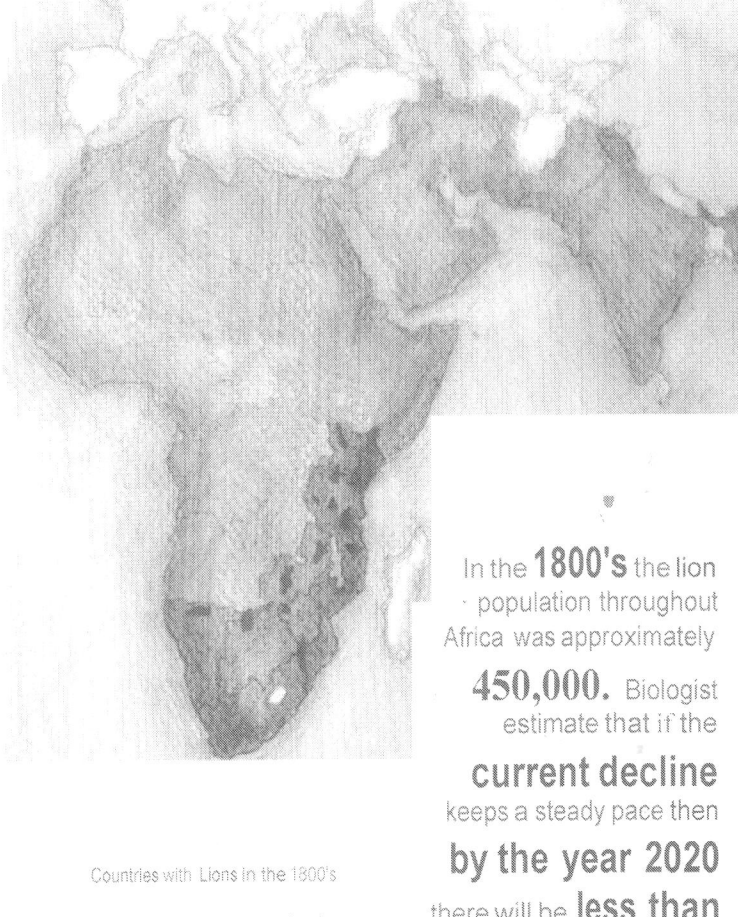

In the **1800's** the lion population throughout Africa was approximately **450,000.** Biologist estimate that if the **current decline** keeps a steady pace then **by the year 2020** there will be **less than 20,000 wild lions** and those will be found only on protected preserves

Countries with Lions in the 1800's

Estimated Countries with Lions in 2020

Estimated Lion Ranges in 2020

Chapter 1

THE DEPARTURE

Cowards die many times before their death;
The valiant never taste of death but once.
Of all the wonders that I have yet heard.
It seems to me most strange that men should fear:
Seeing that death, a necessary end,
Will come when it will come.

~ *William Shakespeare, Julies Caesar, A2, S2*

The moon hung low on the horizon, kissing the far edge of the desert. My personal oracle assured me that its colossal size was a good omen. The color of the magnificent orb, more yellow than white tonight, lit up the vast expanse surrounding me and could have made me fail to remember that it was nighttime. I had walked with my sandals in hand to the highest dune overlooking our sleeping camp. A cozy blanket of sand, still warm from the day's ample amount of sunlight, engulfed my feet with each step. While I waited, I prayed to several of our most important gods for success in our upcoming endeavor. We were poised on the edge of what I hoped would be one of our ultimate victories. I loved war. It excited me more than anything else in this life did. Even more than making love to a beautiful woman. That type of pleasure weakened a man, whereas war strengthened him. If Assyria were to make peace and never fight again, I would cease to exist. I could not imagine life without the thrill of battle. I reveled in it.

My younger siblings, who had accompanied me on this campaign, did not agree. They had deluded themselves into thinking that we were working towards a final peace.

Sennacherib and I, the first born of the king's children, had other ideas. Next to our father, Sargon, we would be the greatest rulers Assyria had ever seen and we would accomplish that by expanding our empire.

Dark figures ghosting across the farthest dune caught my eye and refocused my attention. They would be the scouts returning from the surveillance mission that Sennacherib, the leader of our security forces, had arranged. Their report would help me, the leader of my father's tactical force, in determining the execution for the morning's assault. I alone would have the final say.

When I arrived, the strategy room was crowded with the upper echelon of our military. Sargon, weak from his most recent illness, sat lazily in his chair at the head of the table. The findings from the reconnaissance mission were encouraging. The enemy had fortified their forces in the center of their main line. Without difficulty, we would be able to split our forces, striking with unbridled vengeance at their weakest points. Then coming in from behind, we would easily encircle and crush them.

Sennacherib would lead the eastern barrage while I led the main assault to the west. Sargon was too weak to ride today. My brother had insisted that he remain behind.

As I dressed for the coming battle, I could feel the energy pumping through me, filling me with courage. It was exhilarating, the feel of metal slicing into flesh, the air saturated with the smell of fresh blood, knowing I had the authority over life and death. My arms filled with goose bumps in anticipation. When my wardrobe was complete, I went to find my other siblings. All bowed to me when I entered their tent. Even though I didn't demand this gesture of them in private, protocol in public required it out of respect for my station as next in line for the throne.

"Are you ready, brother?" I asked, directing the question towards Marodeen.

He frowned. "Yes, just about."

Marodeen's response didn't surprise me. He and Arieil were only half Assyrian. Their blood was weak. A Nordic tribe gave their mother as a peace offering to my father and explained why they had no taste for war. What I couldn't understand was why my younger full-blood brother, Nasir, felt the same. I was furious sometimes, as I believed Marodeen and Arieil had poisoned his mind with all their talk of peace.

Regardless, I didn't want to argue with them now. All of us needed to have our minds clear if we were to survive the coming onslaught.

"Great." I put out my hand toward them, palm down. They placed their hands in the same manner on top of mine. I was the only one that added our usual bolster for good luck before a battle. "Live well...Love well...Fight well." I could tell that they were lacking in enthusiasm, but I knew they would fight or our father would disown them as cowards, even Arieil, who in any other family would have been attending to household chores and preparing for marriage.

Sargon had known Arieil would be different from his other female children ever since the night of her birth. That night a mired of shooting stars had crossed the hunter moon, signaling that a warrior had been born.

The battle began at dawn with the enemy launching arrows so thick they covered the sun akin to a black cloud. I chuckled quietly to myself as I noted the sheer waste of this first maneuver. My soldiers easily deflected the projectiles, which found no mark against the smooth metal of our protecting shields.

"Fools, we'll easily overrun them." My second in command nodded in agreement.

Column after column of men with weapons drawn, moved towards us, followed by a line of horse-drawn chariots. In spite of the frantic looks from my generals, I ordered our line to hold. Underestimating the direction and strength of the wind was my opponent's second mistake. Their commandeer most likely had not walked barefoot last night. If he had, he would have realized why the ever-increasing speed of the horse's hoofs and rolling wheels was stirring the soft dry sand into a dust storm of tremendous proportion, blinding their front line, and causing utter chaos among their ranks. I saw our opportunity and gave the signal for the attack.

Bodies on both sides clashed with a thunderous, deafening sound. Shields and swords clanged and buckled, followed by the sound of gurgling, as the screams cut off. My arms didn't stop moving as I hacked my way through the crushing throng.

Time seemed endless when I was in battle. Minutes materialized into hours. I was unaware of the lull in the fighting until the sight of Marodeen and Arieil across the field, swords raised, distracted me. I stepped cautiously through the piles of twisted and disfigured corpses as I made my way towards them, in case any of the enemy soldiers were feigning death to ambush me.

"What's wrong?" I scowled as I reached their position, irritated by their interruption.

"We need to move fast," Marodeen said grabbing my arm, forcing me to follow. As we ran, he explained. "An enemy regiment on the far side of the field has broken through our defenses and is headed for Sargon's tent."

I put all my remaining energy into my legs, arriving at my father's tent well ahead of them. A sons worst fears were before my eyes as I walked through the through the entrance. Sargon was lying on the ground, his clothing bright red. A contingent of enemy soldiers stood over the king's body. The anger that flooded through me at that moment was overwhelming. It propelled me forward, all reason gone, causing me to do something only an unskilled warrior would attempt. I charged the devils, attacking them full on, alone, not knowing how far behind the others where. As I fell to the ground, I heard Marodeen's voice in the distance, but I knew it was too late. One after another, cold steel blades slid into my chest, arms and legs. Despair overtook me as I fell into unconsciousness.

*

"It's about time," I heard as I opened my eyes to see Nasir standing over me, his posture relaxed. I quickly examined myself. Except for feeling extremely fatigued, I was fine. No injuries. The battle in the king's tent must have ended better than I could recall.

"Has the lion got your tongue?" Nasir asked winking at Marodeen.

"Very funny," Marodeen retorted. "I'm telling you it really happened. How else would you explain the fact that we're still alive and our injuries have healed in less than a day and...?"

Nasir's laughter interrupted Marodeen. "Maybe Sargon's oracle actually does know what he's talking about and one of the gods that he forces us to pray to sent the animal."

Marodeen flung something at Nasir who dodged out of the way with lightning speed, at the same time catching the object before it hit the ground.

I was beginning to get aggravated at their cryptic sentences. "What are you all going on about?"

In between bursts of laughter, Nasir explained, "Marodeen thinks we were bitten by a mystical lion and that's what saved us from death,"

I stared at Marodeen. I knew my siblings were not as convinced of the presence of the gods as I was. Every day, upon awakening, I gave thanks to the Ilu for giving me the life that I had. Our people considered us descendants of the gods, at least I was. My father had named me Regulus after the great lion in the heavens where he assured me I would ascend to in death to join Assyria's other great kings. "Was the lion one of the gods?"

"I don't know. The animal didn't speak to me. It just bit us and left. Be thankful that you were all unconscious for that part. It was horribly painful, more painful than any wound I've ever sustained."

"How did it heal us?"

Marodeen shrugged. "A strange amber fluid dripped from its fangs. Maybe the fluid was a magical potion."

"Did anyone else see the lion besides you?"

Marodeen frowned. "No. The animal disappeared from right in front of me as soon as the guards entered the tent."

That was disappointing. If it had been one of our Ilûtu, I would have liked to know which one. It would be appropriate for me to send an offering of thanks. I wouldn't want them to think me ungrateful for their gift.

"How long have I been out?"

"Two days. We were only out for one. Your wounds were massive and took longer. We could see the wounds closing up as we watched." Marodeen shuddered at the memory.

"We haven't let anyone in to see you. We were concerned that their reaction might lead to negative rumors." Marodeen was always thinking, which is why I trusted him as I did.

"You were right to do that. We'll think of something to explain it after I speak to the king." I would make sure this would be used to my advantage. Play up the fact that we healed very quickly because we were more god-like than mortal.

"The king is dead," Nasir said in a grave tone.

I nodded and could feel my frown deepen. We all suspected that Sargon would die soon. His death at the hands of our enemy, although not ideal, was still a good death. It is always better for a soldier to die in battle than to waste away in sickness.

"Sennacherib has broken encampment and gone back to Nineveh. He is making arrangements for his coronation." Marodeen's voice was shaky. He knew this news would upset me more than the news of my father.

18

"Sennacherib left without me?"

"He wasn't sure you were going to live and he didn't want to waste time taking charge in case there were any uprisings at the news of Sargon's death."

"Oh, that makes sense." Whenever a king dies there's always renegades who will challenge the new ruler, testing his steadfastness. "Is there something else?"

"I... I'm not sure. Some of the circumstances surrounding the events on the day of the battle are a little disturbing. I'm afraid they might trouble you."

Arieil and Nasir were both looking at the floor while Marodeen spoke, unwilling to meet my gaze.

"You three are my most trusted friends and siblings. If there is something I should know you must tell me."

"We've come to suspect that someone inside the camp conspired to have the king killed."

"No," I screamed, my hands balled into fists in front of me. Marodeen backed a few inches away.

"This could not be, who... who would do such a thing? Someone will pay dearly for this." I began to leave the tent determined to speak to the king's guards.

Marodeen grabbed my arm. I glared at him and he released me immediately. "Please listen to us, brother," he pleaded, "one of the guards, a man I would trust with my own life, told me that Sennacherib highest ranking general ordered them to leave the king's tent, to head off a would-be attack, but when they arrived at the eastern end of the camp, there was no one. They realized quickly that it must have been a ruse. By the time they returned it was too late."

"I want to speak to that general myself." I was furious.

Nasir cautioned me. "We need to tread carefully on this matter, my brother. Sennacherib's generals report directly to him. We're concerned that he might have had a hand in this and if it's true then we are all in danger. Rumors are circulating through the camp."

I rocked back on my feet. Marodeen grabbed my arm to steady me.

Sennacherib was the other half of my being. Not only were we physically connected from sharing a womb together, but also spiritually. I knew Sennacherib was jealous of my popularity with the masses but I assured him we would be equals in all respects once we were king.

"No, No, No," I shook my fists at them. "Sennacherib would never betray me. To speak of this is treason. Don't any of you ever breathe a word of this conspiracy again or I will have you imprisoned. Do you understand?"

They nodded in unison but their eyes remained wary and troubled.

"Have our horses brought around. We ride for Nineveh." Rumors and conspiracy were all part of palace life. Marodeen and Nasir were wrong on this one... so wrong.

I pushed my companions hard for two long days. Something in the pit of my stomach didn't sit well with me. On the way, Marodeen and Nasir filled me in on what I had missed while I slumbered. Sargon had died quickly, which comforted me. Our enemies might have considered him brutal, but from a warrior's point of view, he was a great man. Sennacherib had halted the fighting after it was apparent that the battle, without me to lead, would be a draw.

The desert was a quiet place, most sounds absorbed by the dunes and I didn't detect anything unusual with my hearing until after we had arrived back in the crowded city. I could hear one of Sennacherib's messengers speaking to him from inside the palace when we approached the courtyard.

"Regulus is alive."

My twin did not reply.

Was he not elated that I was well? Maybe he didn't want to show his emotion and look weak in front of his underlings.

Nasir, Marodeen and Arieil followed close by as we made our way to the throne room, their posture resembling that of an attacking army, their swords ready for use at the first sign of danger.

Sennacherib showed no emotion nor did he acknowledge us as we entered. None of his soldiers lining the room bowed to me. My guard went ahead reminding them of their duty. They all turned to Sennacherib for advice. Why were they turning to him? It was known far and wide that we would be co-reagents as per my father's wishes.

My three siblings were scanning the room nervously. I refused to entertain their paranoia. Sennacherib would have certainly heard the same rumors as me and was perhaps equally concerned about my intentions. I would do my best to reassure him that he had nothing to fear from me.

Sennacherib's secretary ran towards me, his hands up to stop me from approaching. I removed my sword in a blinding movement, the speed surprised and froze me for a split second. The sword raked across the man's chest tearing his clothing and drawing a line of blood.

"Think carefully about your next step, clerk. If you are not on your knees the next time I blink, you will have lost your head."

I moved past the sniffling man putting my hand out to greet Sennacherib. "Brother, I am most elated that you are well and survived the battle unscathed."

"Thank you. I am well and I can see that you have healed quickly from your wounds and are also well." Sennacherib made no move to greet me.

I tried again putting slightly more authority into my tone. "We must speak in private. There is much to discuss."

"Yes," Sennacherib agreed. "Later perhaps? I have urgent matters at the moment."

Marodeen and Nasir moved to my flanks, both hands wrapped around the hilt of their swords. I knew they would die to protect me, but I didn't want a fight. I put my hand up, ordering them to hold. I loved my twin brother deeply but this behavior towards me was unacceptable. I growled a reply and moved closer. "No, we will speak now."

The guards along the wall moved in to block me, this time Sennacherib put out his hand while his eyes scanned the room assessing the situation.

Even though my contingent was outnumbered, we were by far the better swordsmen and would no doubt devastate his guard. We waited quietly, for Sennacherib's next move would surely determine who lived or died.

"You're right, brother. Please forgive me."

Sennacherib's guard relaxed.

Then Sennacherib ordered everyone out of the room. Marodeen, Nasir and Arieil made no move to leave.

Sennacherib glowered at them.

"Leave," I snapped.

Marodeen began to protest but I put my hand on his shoulder and walked him to the door. "Sennacherib and I are bound by more than just blood. I trust him."

Marodeen nodded but I could see the worry in his distorted features. "Please wait outside and listen for any trouble." Marodeen's eyes widened with awareness and I knew that even through the thick walls they would be able to hear my conversation with Sennacherib. Though none of us had spoken of it on the journey home, I suspected that they had also begun to experience the same heighted sense of hearing and sight.

Once we were alone, Sennacherib hugged me tightly. "I'm relieved to see that you are well, my dear brother. I hope you understand that I had to act coolly toward you in order to show a certain amount of strength for my men. The palace is full of conspiracies. I wanted to give each of us an edge to play to."

I knew it must have been something like that. Marodeen was wrong.

"Of course. I suspected such. Are our plans in place?"

"Yes. Preparations for our coronation have begun. My oracle has set the date for six months from now. It will be the grandest celebration Assyria has ever seen. You must be exhausted from your journey, though. We can discuss the details at some other time."

"Yes, I am," I lied. I felt surprisingly good. "If you will excuse me then I'm anxious to see my children and my wife."

"Yes, I'm sure your family is eager to see you also." Sennacherib continued to stare at me intently. "It's amazing how quickly you've healed. I was told by the physicians that your wounds were deadly." He sounded disappointed.

I shook my head. No rumors, I reminded myself. "Yes, it was a miracle from the gods." A warning in my head told me that for the moment I should keep quiet about the lion.

Marodeen, Nasir and Arieil were still waiting for me when I had finished my talk with Sennacherib. I commanded them to go about their duties. "You were wrong," I told Marodeen as I walked away. I didn't turn to see his expression.

My children, Domara and Leja, ran into my arms when they spotted me coming down the long entranceway to my quarters. Domara, who was only ten years old, was already a man by Assyrian standards. My daughter Leja was eight, with long silky dark hair and a sparkling set of teeth. She was a mirror image of her mother. I pulled them tightly to me and kissed them both on their cheeks.

"So you survived," the snarled voice said from behind. Try as I might I had not been able to make any improvements in my relationship with my wife.

I turned to meet the voice that didn't fit the beauty of the face. "I'm sorry it couldn't have turned out differently for you."

Nagia shrugged, unaffected by my mockery. "Go play," she ordered the children.

"No, we want to stay and see father. He's been gone for so long," my son protested.

"Do as your mother asks. I'll see you both later tonight." I tried to keep my tone civil but failed as I anticipated the upcoming argument.

As soon as the children were out of sight, Nagia started. "You will become king now that your father is gone."

"Yes."

"That means I will become queen?"

"Yes, you are my wife." I didn't add that it was fortunate for her that she had given me two children. It was for their sake only that I kept her around.

"I'll need new clothing that's befitting of my station."

Nagia was always thinking about herself of course. Normally, I would have enjoyed not giving her what she wanted but I had other important matters to think about now. "Order what you need and try not to bankrupt the kingdom at the same time."

"I will also require more servants. I want young men. The women are not strong enough to assist with the renovations that will need to be done."

I laughed. "Sure you do."

Nagia tried to glare at me but I could see the smile underneath her facade. She already knew that she would get what she wanted. I turned and left without any further arguing. I hated to make her happy. Tonight, though, I would make myself happy in the arms of my consort.

The first month after the battle at Tushpa, Marodeen, Nasir, Arieil and I all suffered from the same mysterious cramps. It was difficult to hide anything in such a large palace.

Sennacherib came by only once to visit during that time. He seemed more aloof than ever but I was too preoccupied with the affairs of the kingdom to be concerned. Surprisingly our health returned once again a short time later and the four of us reveled in our new appearance and abilities, until the rumors started.

One week before the coronation ceremony, Marodeen came to me at dawn and his appearance was frightening even for a seasoned soldier such as me.

"What...what happened to your eyes? Can you still see?" I could hear the revulsion in my tone.

"Better than an eagle I suspect." Marodeen grabbed the shiny metal plate from my dresser. My eyes were not as bright as his were, but they were definitely a lighter color than the brown they had always been.

"What's happening to us?"

"Nasir and Arieil's eyes are the same. The whole palace is alarmed and gossip is spreading about us being cursed or possessed by a demon." Marodeen frowned deeply. "It's not just the slaves and workers. Today I heard Sennacherib discussing what to do about us with some of his ministers. Us, his own flesh and blood."

"We must tell them the story of the lion."

"I don't think that's a good idea." Marodeen said quietly.

"Why?"

"Sennacherib is plotting our destruction, even yours. It would only be more evidence against us."

"I told you to never speak of this." I put my hands up to my ears, not wanting to hear any more of his lies just as Nasir and Arieil walked in. They closed the heavy doors behind them and engaged the locks.

"The soldiers are coming for us." Nasir announced. "Sennacherib wants to have us investigated for plotting with witches." As Nasir spoke, the doors began to shake and moments later, splintered at the lock. Sennacherib's guard leaped in, their swords raised high to attack. I could see that some of mine had joined them.

I reached for my weapon. "How dare you enter my chambers!"

"His highness has sent for you." The lead guard shouted. "You are to be arrested for conspiring with the necromancers."

"I am also your king." The soldier ignored me and moved closer, his eyes glinting in anticipation of a kill. Nasir and Marodeen immediately flung themselves in front of me, easily defeating the attackers one by one.

"We need to leave the palace, Regulus, without delay. Our families have already been sent to safety. We have a carriage waiting to take us to Dumah to join them," Nasir said.

I quickly packed a few things from my room and headed down the hall with Marodeen in tow, to retrieve my sleeping children. I knew they would be in danger as well. I couldn't leave without them or my unloving wife.

As I entered my family's chambers, Nagia was there, blocking my way. She looked surprisingly relaxed considering the commotion that was now ensuing in the hallway.

"What are you still doing here?" she said in the familiar tone that she usually reserved just for me.

"We must leave. We are all in danger from Sennacherib."

"You can leave and I suggest that you do so quickly if you want to live. We're staying. Sennacherib would never hurt me or the children."

"My brother is trying to force me out of power and the first thing he will do is dispose of you and my children."

Nagia looked straight at me, her cold emotionless eyes piecing my being and said, "They're not your children."

Neither Marodeen nor I moved for a long moment. Then Marodeen grabbed my arm as the knowledge of what Nagia was telling us finally sank in.

"Regulus, we must leave. We're out of time."

I couldn't fight him. Nagia had killed my resolve. She might just as well have stabbed me in the heart with my own knife. I let Marodeen tow me towards the door that would lead us out of the palace and away from my kingdom forever—away from a life and time that I would never know again.

Chapter 2

ORIGINS

I shall be telling this with a sigh
Somewhere ages and ages hence:
Two roads diverged in a wood, and I--
I took the one less traveled by,
And that has made all the difference

~ *Robert Frost*

I've had this dream many times before and it's always the same. Row after row of round white tents hug the ground snugly, following the curve of the massive dunes to the horizon. The scene is reminiscent of a Hollywood movie depicting a great epic battle. An urgent need propels me onward, down the narrow corridors of the encampment. Swirling eddies of sand guide my way.

The sun, at its zenith, reflects off the desert floor, making it impossible to open my eyes fully. I must fight against the breeze as I push forward, and although it is hot and dry, it raises goose bumps along my exposed arms.

I search frantically for my sunglasses or a hat or something to relieve the blinding light and stinging airborne particles, but come up empty. My quest does reveal a wet spot on my shirt below my left breast and I'm shocked to see that a thick red fluid has stained my hand with what looks like blood, but I don't feel injured. Actually, I feel numb.

More important than the mystery of the red fluid, though, is my need to get inside, but none of the tents has an opening. I call out in desperation, "Is anyone there? Please, I need help."

Then I see it and I know this is what I have been searching for. With a splendor reserved for kings and ten times bigger than any of the others, it looms ominously among the sea of white. A repeating symbol that I don't recognize decorates the mustard yellow walls of the tent.

Standing by the regal enclosure is a young girl. At first, her face is hidden, but as my steps bring me closer, she turns and I can see that she's my daughter.

"Lindsey?" I call out.

Lindsey's eyes meet mine and her answering smile is so infectious that I smile back, in spite of my confusion. She waves to me before disappearing through the entrance. I try to follow but two sentinels appear suddenly, blocking my way.

"Please," I implore, "I must get inside out of the sun." They ignore me. I try again. "Please, I must find my daughter," but still, the bulked up brutes pay me no attention. Without uttering a sound, they push me back. Raising their arms in unison, they signal for me to leave. I walk away, dejected, but turn back quickly to the unusual growling that's out of place in this desert environment.

The enormous lion emerges from in between the guards who pay no attention to the beast. It looks directly towards me with eyes equally as brilliant as the overhead sun. A sparkling amber fluid drips from its mouth. Incised on the lion's forehead is the same symbol as decorates the colorful tent.

The animal's powerful gaze holds a hint of recognition that does nothing to alleviate my desperate worry for my daughter's safety. The lion crouches into a hunting position and stalks slowly toward me, claws extended.

Fear for my own life freezes me in place. As futile a gesture as it might be, I instinctively put out one hand to stop the approaching predator and can feel its soft silky fur brush my fingers. As its hot moist breath pours over me, the intoxicating smell of sweet honeysuckle fills my senses. I watch in horror as the animal's lips pull back, revealing its huge fangs, and then it lunges.

*

My heavy lids opened wide as the sound of Alex's voice pulled me from the dream. "Wake up, sleepyhead." Alex's lips touch the top of my head. "Time to get up. I hope you won't be too disappointed to know it's Saturday and we won't be going to work today."

"Terribly." My laugh sounds groggy. "I'll be up in a minute." I work to calm my breathing. I didn't want Alex to notice my panic. I have enough crazy problems as it is.

I sat up, fighting off the exhaustion and aggravation within myself for having had such a terrible dream. It was ruining my euphoria after the wonderful night I had had with Alex.

I slid off the bed and my injured knee sent me a painful reminder.

"Oh," I moaned, louder than I had intended.

Alex's voice is anxious. "What's wrong?"

"Oh, nothing. It's just my knee."

A few weeks earlier, I had tripped over my flip-flops and my knee broke the fall. I was fortunate enough not to have done any permanent damage. It had been taking a long time to heal.

Still in a fog, I stumbled into the kitchen. I wasn't sure if I was having trouble focusing because of the nightmare or Alex's lovemaking. I hoped it was the latter. I found Alex staring out the window enjoying the antics of the birds at one of his many feeders. I wrapped my arms around him, burying my face in between his collar blades, and began kissing his back. "Did you have fun last night, Mr. Chambers?"

It had been the end of the work week and we had spent several hours at our favorite Italian restaurant, sipping wine, and watching the world go by from the wide-open windows that faced Groton's main street. This particular night was a double celebration. Josephine, the younger of my two daughters, had moved to her own apartment. The house was empty now and Alex and I were looking forward to having time to ourselves.

After we were home, I had put on one of my favorite sci-fi movies. Half way through, Alex began kissing my ear, trying to distract me. Even after twenty years together, he still made my heart flutter. Needless to say, we hadn't seen the end of the movie.

The timer on the stove began to beep, pulling me from my reverie. Alex shut off the burner, turned, and deftly slipped his hand up under the front of my pajama top.

I shrieked. "Alexander, I can't breathe and your hand is all wet."

"Hmm ... too bad." He pressed his lips to mine. The passionate kissing made me dizzy and I forgot all about his cold hand that had now warmed against my skin. When Alex released me from the kiss, he had a smug look on his face. "See? I knew I could have my way with you."

"Ugh, you are such a cheater," I grumbled, hitting his back ineffectually with my fist.

"Would you like me to stop?"

"No!" I buried my face in his chest.

"Umm, that's what I thought." Alex raised my chin to his face and continued where he had left off.

My head was still floating when Alex finally answered my earlier question. "Last night was great, Mrs. Chambers but we had better be careful," he warned, "we might get carried away."

I shrugged. "I don't mind. You realize, that we can get carried away anywhere at any time now."

"Hold that thought. I need to finish getting breakfast ready." As Alex scrutinized my face he noted, "You look tired. Didn't you sleep well? *I* certainly did." Both his eyebrows moved up and down in a jerky motion like a villain.

I laughed at his clowning around. Alex always made me laugh.

"I had that dream again. That's the fifth time in two weeks. What's wrong with me?" Usually I didn't remember my dreams. If I did, it was mostly only short cloudy clips, nothing clear, with the memory fading soon after waking. "The dream is so real. I can feel myself sweating, feel hot sand in between my toes and smell stuff."

Alex raised both eyebrows in unison, "Katherine, how many times have you watched *Lord of the Rings* or *Underworld* this year? You watch too many of those scary movies. I think they're starting to get to you."

I frowned. Alex was right. I had been a Sci-Fi addict ever since I was a child and had begun watching *Star Trek* and *Lost in Space*. I could daydream endlessly about being in many of the same situations as the characters in the movies. It was amazing that I was able to keep the fantasy part of my life from spilling over into my real life.

"Was Lindsey in your dream again?" Alex asked as I tried to refocus on our conversation.

"Yes, and she was in the same Arabian princess outfit."

"Umm," Alex mused, "maybe it means she'll marry a rich oil sheik. That would be cool. We could winter in Dubai."

Being a mother, I was always worried about my children, but Lindsey was the one that I fretted about the most. She had been out of college now for four years and although she had a great job, I knew it wasn't inspiring enough for her. Lindsey hadn't really found her place in life yet nor anyone to share it with.

"No thanks. I'd rather we stay poor than have her move away."

Alex chuckled, releasing me. "Lindsey will be fine. Can I pour you a cup of coffee?"

"Yes, please." I struggled to clear the now formed lump in my throat as Alex held open the screen door that led out onto the back deck. Our house w a s just y o u r a v e r a g e ranch situated in Townsend, a small town an hour north of Boston, but it was our own private paradise.

After we were seated, I heard Alex take a deep breath before saying, "Now, promise me you won't get mad."

"Okay," I replied in a wary voice, "no getting mad. What's up?"

"Well, I know that I was to help you with the quilt show setup, but there's an auto event up at the Budweiser plant today. Would you mind terribly if I went? It's actually not going to rain and the Viper Club will be there today."

I could see that Alex was worried. My daughters were always telling me that I overreacted to everything. I dragged Alex to enough of my events and he was always extremely pleasant about going. He never complained about anything, the total opposite of me.

"It's fine," I said, looking away. "You don't have to go." I hoped he wouldn't hear the disappointment in my voice. I really didn't want to keep Alex from his fun.

"We'll spend time together this afternoon," Alex promised. "We can go for a late afternoon walk. The doctor did say to keep your knee exercised, right?" I could see the patience on Alex's face as he locked gazes with me. "Now don't be upset with me, you go places with your girlfriends all the time."

"You're right," I agreed sourly, forcing a smile. Alex looked more than happy about the change in the day's plans.

I watched through the living room window as Alex drove away. As soon as his car was out of sight, I sat down on the couch to sulk. I told myself it was irrational for me to be this possessive about him. As my mom use to point out, Alex never looked at other women. He still looked at me the way he had when we first married.

They weren't expecting me at the Reed House until 11 a.m. It was only eight and I wasn't in the mood to do anything but put on a movie. Nothing like seeing the world coming to an end to cheer me up!

After I was dressed, another idea came to me. Maybe I would go for a walk myself. Townsend had an overabundance of state parks for hiking but Alex and I most often went to Pearl Hill. It was the only one of the parks that had a paved road that doubled as a walking loop. That meant there were no branches or logs for someone like me, who lacked any coordination, to trip. After my walk, I would drop off the quilts and be back in time to see Alex when he returned.

I knew I was going for this walk without Alex just to be a brat. I felt a twinge of guilt knowing he would be disappointed. Even so, it wasn't enough to stop me. I couldn't suppress the strange, compelling urge to go on my solo adventure.

As I was packing up the car, I noticed Nutmeg, our new cat, sleeping on the exact spot where we had buried our previous cat. Cinnamon had been with us for twenty years and her death had been very traumatic for me. As I stared at the memorial plaque that my father had engraved with her name, I was sure I could still hear her cat cries even now. I knew it sounded like something from a science fiction movie and I was too embarrassed to tell anyone about it, even Alex. I ignored the creepy cat cries and left for the park.

The parking lot at Pearl Hill was empty except for a Ford Mustang that had inconveniently parked in the only shady spot under the spreading branches of an ancient Hemlock. I pulled in next to the shiny sports car, trying to keep my quilts in as much shade as possible. I put my cell phone in the glove box. No sense taking a chance of losing it on the walk, which I embarrassingly had to admit had happened several times before.

I stood for a few minutes ogling the brand new Mustang. Alex would have loved to see this. The deep blue metallic paint was eye catching. I'm sure it cost a pretty penny, more pennies than I had but that was all right. Alex and I were not rich, but considered ourselves fortunate in many other aspects and we lived comfortably.

The ranger station had not opened for the season, but the clear acrylic box that hung on the door had complimentary maps of the park. I unfolded one and proceeded to get my bearings. There was no need to risk getting lost. If Alex were with me, I wouldn't have to worry about that. I swear he had compass built into his head.

With every breath, I could feel the crisp cool spring air, still saturated with the morning dew. The musty odor from the composting forest litter was a comforting familiar smell. The sun shone through the branches of the tall pines, lighting up the particles in the air that danced in a ballet of colors. The emerging leaves on the deciduous trees blew slightly in the soft breeze, creating a rustling that soothed me. The melody of rushing water echoed in the distance.

The canopy began closing in on me as the paved road narrowed to the size of a cart path. I felt free of all the burdens of life as I reveled in the peacefulness. Only the scurrying of small animals and songbirds calling to their companions interrupted the solitude.

About twenty minutes into the walk, I came upon a neatly cut passage that veered off to the right of the paved road. According to the map, this trail, named "Narrows Way," made a short loop that eventually came back out onto the paved road. The ingress beckoned me. Emerald colored lichen enveloped the tree trunks in random patterns. Fiddlehead ferns stretched as far as the eye could see. Every few feet, patches of princess pine, superbly delicate and charming, popped up along the trail's edge.

So enchanting was the scene before me that I expected to see Snow White and the seven dwarfs skipping happily along. Even though I was normally not the adventurous type unless Alex was with me, I decided to proceed down the new-found path. Today, I would be an explorer.

Strolling down the moss-covered trail was akin to walking on a giant green sponge. I had to watch every step, especially when I came to the mounds of fallen pine needles but I didn't regret my decision to take this route. Nature was truly magnificent. A sense of melancholy overwhelmed me and I speculated that this might have been how Robert Frost felt when he penned the *Road Less Travelled*. I wondered if this choice would make a difference for me, as it had for Mr. Frost.

When I was about halfway down the new route, small rodents began darting out from the underbrush in front of me and running away. I didn't think much of it at first. Most likely, I had disturbed them with my noisy footsteps.

The sound of rustling silk drew my attention upwards as a flock of jet-black ravens flew by, calling out a chorus of deep-throated alarms. Then a large groundhog dashed out from under a thick stand of ferns and slammed into my leg, instantly giving me an eerie feeling that the perhaps the animals were hurrying to get away from a greater threat than I posed.

Townsend did have occasional sightings of potentially dangerous animals. A bear or coyote might wander into someone's back yard but there had never been any attacks. The logical part of my mind told me that it was just my imagination causing my now escalating wariness. As a biologist, I knew that most wild animals would avoid contact with humans unless directly threatened.

My head turned reflexively to the sound of breaking branches and crackling leaves echoing from somewhere behind me. "Hello," I yelled softly, hesitantly, "is someone there?" but there was no response to my question. I could feel the tears welling up, ready to spill out in a torrent.

Suddenly the solitude, at first welcoming, had become frightening. A spasm of fear gripped me as I realized the similarity to my recent dream and I found myself walking at a faster pace than was good for my injured knee. I would certainly be paying for this, in all probability spending the rest of the day on the couch with an icepack. Alex would be upset with me.

As I moved further down the path, I became aware of an unnatural shrieking far off in the distance. It had the same unnerving effect as someone scrapping a nail across a chalkboard.

Calm overtook me for a short moment when I noticed a sign posted up ahead and I assumed that it would direct me back to the main road. The panic returned as I read the white hand painted words "Fallen Log Trail" and realized that I must have taken a wrong turn. Adding to my discomfort, the shrieking noise was getting louder, getting closer.

My sense of bearing was horrendous; I could get lost in a department store. How did I ever imagine that I would be able to get out of the woods by myself? I wished I had waited for Alex. I tried to think about what he would do and I reached into my back pocket for the map but it wasn't there. I took a deep breath and wiped the tears from my face. I told myself that I needed to keep moving and focused on seeing Alex and being home. This would be over soon and I would probably look back at the whole day and laugh.

As I rounded the next turn, the menacing sound had become deafening. I fell to the ground, holding my hands over my ears. The noise vibrated through me. Kneeling frozen on the ground, I realized that I did recognize the sound. It was the sound that I had heard every alien make in every sci-fi movie I had ever seen. Honestly, I told myself. Get a grip! I was letting my imagination run amok as usual. Only I could take a pleasant walk in the park and turn it into a horror story.

Then, as quickly as it had begun, the noise faded and stopped.

Still down on my knees, I lifted my head and looked around cautiously, trying not to draw attention to myself. My injured knee was screaming in protest from having been slammed onto the ground. I couldn't think about that pain right now.

Not far away I could hear the snapping of large branches again, but I didn't want to find out what was causing the commotion. I got to my feet and in that instant my attention came to a pause on two shimmering orbs. They appeared to be attached to something big that was making its way through the trees in my direction. I tried to recall what I had seen on the National Geographic Channel about surviving a bear attack. I knew I should fall to the ground and roll up into a ball but I couldn't wrench myself free from the sight before me.

As the figure moved closer I could see that it wasn't a bear. It was certainly as large as a bear, a grizzly bear maybe but it had neither fur nor hair anywhere on its massive form. Instead, it was covered entirely by reddish membrane that had a worn leathery appearance, similar to an Egyptian mummy. The body was solid-looking, akin to a weight lifter, with huge muscles that ran in rippled formation along its arms, chest and legs. Its eyes, which I now realized were the shiny objects that I had first spotted, were a shockingly bright amber and extremely reflective.

As beautiful as the monster's eyes were, they could not distract from the horribly distorted face that framed them. Cavernous lines running in twisted patterns covered the entire surface from its brow down into its neck. It wouldn't have surprised me to find out that this anguished-looking being had been making that awful noise.

The forest had become deathly quiet. Even the breeze had stopped. Considering how frightened I was, it was surprising that I was able to notice such outside influences. As the abomination and I stood not thirty feet apart, I heard a small voice in my head, over the pounding of my blood that told me not to move. The warning was unnecessary, because I doubted that I would have been able to run if I wanted to. My legs were cemented to the ground.

The monster arched its neck and sniffed the air, like a wolf. I involuntarily blinked and when my eyelids reopened, it took my brain a few seconds to realize that the creature was gone. I would have questioned my sanity if not for the swaying of the sapling and fluttering leaves that delineated its passage away from me.

I took a few moments to memorize the creature's details. When I returned home I might send a picture of the ghoul to Joss Whedon. Maybe he could use it in his next TV show.

I closed my eyes tightly and took a deep breath. Even though I was scared and lost, all I was thinking about was the Buffy DVD set that my daughter Josephine had bought me. We had spent hours together watching the series. Josephine and I shared many of the same interests. She was virtually a mirror image of me, except she knew the difference between fantasy and reality.

Speaking of reality, I shook my head again, hoping to keep a hold on my present circumstances. "Geesh! Katherine, get a grip, will you?"

The sound of my voice dislodged me from my petrified state and I grabbed onto a nearby tree to keep from falling. I patted myself over, searching for my cell phone until it hit me that I had left it in the car. That realization caused me to blunder forward aimlessly, desperately hoping to stumble out into the lot where the Honda was parked. Although there was little chance of that outcome. I was nearly blind from the streaming tears and had no idea of the direction I was headed.

Without warning, that awful shrieking noise began again. This time I ran at a furious pace, not caring which way my feet took me. I knew I had strayed from the trail when I found myself slashing at branches and small trees, trying to clear a new passage for myself, cutting my hands and face in the process. My stomach began to churn and I was sure I would throw up at any moment.

Then miraculously, thankfully, there was a slight change in the brightness of the sky and I could tell that I was nearly out of the woods. The white of the Honda and the blue of the Mustang peaked from between the tree trunks on the other side of the clearing.

In my haste, I didn't see the fallen tree trunk that my shin banged into. My arms reached out instinctively but I didn't fall. I felt something akin to a vise grab hold of me. I turned, afraid to look, afraid not to look.

What I did see took my breath away and also brought relief. It was a man, a beautiful man. He was olive-skinned with a scruffy beard. His blond hair hung ruler straight to his shoulders. The sparkle of the man's amber eyes added further to his stunning beauty. When he blinked, there was an odd layer of skin that peeked out from the corners of his eyes, like the nictitating membrane in a cat's eye.

I shook my head. Something familiar about all of this was playing around at the edges of my memory but I couldn't make the lines of thought connect. I was too befuddled by his exquisiteness.

"Do I know you?" I asked, perplexed, my concentration locked on his face.

The man's answering voice rang like a stringed instrument. "No, but I know you."

His reply only further confused me and I tried to ask how he knew me, but before I could get the words out he said, "It's a long story." At the same time his free hand stroked my cheek. I knew that I should flinch away from his touch and moreover that I should be troubled, alone in the woods with this stranger yet his presence was extraordinarily comforting. His skin was as soft as the finest spun wool and his touch just as warm. I realized at one point that I was actually leaning into his hand, giving in to the overwhelming bliss.

Time stopped. When I was finally able pull myself from his touch, I opened my eyes and flushed red at my bewildering behavior. The man's features were bright, pleased with my reaction. Without thinking I blurted out, "Your, your eyes are beautiful. What color are they?"

The man chuckled, running his hand threw his stringy hair, pushing it out of his face. "Thank you. We can talk about the color later. Right now, Katherine, we need to get you out of here."

He tugged at my arm but I didn't respond. How did he know my name?

He tried again to shake me from my trance. "Katherine, you need to focus. Clear your head. There is much danger here, please come with me."

"Danger?" I said in puzzled tone. "What danger?"

"The danger is from the Nergal that you saw a few minutes ago."

"Ner... what?" I asked, but without further explanation the stranger wrapped his arm around my waist, lifting me off my feet. There was no resistance. I wanted to be in his arms. We ghosted across the football size clearing in seconds.

The unexpected movement however gave me motion sickness. "I feel sick. Please put me down," I pleaded.

"Sorry, take a few deep breaths," he suggested as he sat me gently on the grass.

When the nausea was alleviated he tried to pick me up again.

By now my head had cleared and I was determined to find out what was happening "Where are you taking me?"

"To your car."

"Let go of me," I demanded. Surprisingly the man did as I requested. He immediately released me and I stumbled to the ground, landing on my side. I heard a crack as my watch hit something.

"Ugh," I complained getting back on my feet. "Why did you do that? Are you crazy?" Before I could finish scolding him his arm reached for me, and in a blinding movement placed me behind him in a protective position.

"Too late! It's…it's…found us!" His voice choked on the last few words.

I looked up in time to see the same aberration coming out of the woods, holding onto a long thin object. The tip of the object resembled a Fourth of July sparkler. Like a participant in a javelin-throwing contest, the creature ran forward and launched the rod into the air, towards the blond-haired man and me. I couldn't imagine how the object would reach us here on the opposite side of the field, but somehow it did.

The man stepped away from me and raised his right arm as the rod split into several projectiles. That was when I noticed the sword with which he intercepted four of the oncoming objects. The last one twirled around on itself and rather than spiraling away as the others had, it bounced off the man's arm and struck me instead.

Like a hot knife slicing into butter, the foot-long long shaft tore into me. I could hear the crack when the tip hit my back rib. My hands automatically wound around the stem as the impact threw me to the ground.

In spite of the searing pain I gritted my teeth and pushed myself up on my good side, struggling to see. The rod dug itself deeper into my flesh and I whimpered uncontrollably in response. The blond-haired man knelt down and he looked like he was going to cry. Before either one of us could speak, the monster screamed and began moving in our direction.

Like heat rising from a hot tarmac, the empty space surrounding the monster shimmered, opening an invisible door through which came another man with a young woman by his side. They positioned themselves directly in the path of the monster, which was now only about fifty feet away from where I lay injured.

The girl looked to be in her early teens. Her blond hair was braided into a long rope. I winced as I realized how much she reminded me of my daughters. The second man was very similar in appearance and age to the first man who had tried to defend me.

I was filled with both horror and awe as the beast continued its attack. While the second man watched with indifferent concern, the girl jumped into the air, lifted her right leg and kicked the monster square in the middle of its chest. The mammoth creature flew away in the opposite direction from the two warriors. Several loud cracks filled the air as it hit a stand of trees on the edge of the clearing.

I shivered uncontrollably while watching the now expanding pool of blood by my side. Certain that I would die this day, pictures of my family began filling my mind. Lindsey and Josephine were just getting started in life and even though I had wished earlier in this ordeal that Alex had been with me, I was eternally grateful now that he wasn't.

I hadn't even left Alex a note. What if my body was never found? How could my family deal with never knowing what happened to me? I deeply regretted not bringing my cell phone. At least that way I could have left them a message, told them how much I loved them. Remorse swept over me as I realized how selfish and reckless I had been to come here today.

While I was considering my family's reaction to my disappearance, my protectors launched several arrows from a complicated looking bow into the air toward the now startled beast. More hair-raising, spine-chilling screeches filled the air when one after another hit their mark.

Undiscouraged, the creature grasped at the sunken arrows with both hands, tearing them from its chest, a glistening amber fluid gushing out with each pull. Another screech filled the air as the thing charged again. In a movement so quick I would have missed it if I had blinked, the man and the young girl pulled swords from behind their heads. The black blades glinted with such brilliance that the sunlight bouncing from them was blinding.

With the grace of a ballet dancer, the second man intercepted the onrushing monster. Jumping into the air, he swung his sword across the vertical plane at the height of the monster's shoulders, severing the distorted head from its torso. The hideous orb fell to the ground with a thump followed by the lifeless body. In that instant, the grand battle was over.

I heard the girl scold the man. "It was my turn, Nathaniel. You promised. I'm not coming with you anymore." She folded her arms across her chest.

The man chuckled. "You weren't fast enough, Cassie. Maybe next time. Besides, that was the strongest one yet. It might have been too much for you to handle, being a girl and all." His tone was teasing.

"You know, Nathaniel, considering that I am your only sister, you need to treat me with more regard." She frowned, like a child having had an ice cream cone snatched from its hands.

Nathaniel kissed the top of her head. "I promise, next time it will be your turn." He chuckled again, seeming unable to control his laughter.

Hopefully, this whole ordeal was one of my nightmares and hopefully, I wouldn't be having this dream over and over again. Why hadn't Alex shaken me awake yet? I must be screaming by now.

Then like before, when the other two strangers had appeared from out of a wavy image, now an animal appeared and I felt my heart stop. I was absolutely positive that this animal was the same one that had been the prominent star in my most recent re-occurring dream with the tents and my daughter Lindsey. How did the lion get out of my dream and into the State Park?

"Wow," I said aloud. I had to admit I was certainly impressed with the depth of my imagination. I had only seen real lions once during a trip to Lion Country Safari in Florida. This certainly was not one of those lions.

Words couldn't do justice to the majesty surrounding this big cat. The man named Nathaniel bent down and petted the animal's enormous backside.

In response to some unforeseen prompt, the two people on the other side of the field plus the lion shot a quick glance in my direction, and then with astonishing swiftness, moved to stand next to me in a half circle.

Close-up I finally realized what it was that had felt so familiar. Their eyes, even the eyes of the now-dead demon, were the same color as the lion's eyes in my dream. The dream began re- playing itself in my head as I tried to work out the connection.

My absolute attention was diverted momentarily to the round stone object positioned on the animal's huge forehead. The two opposite-facing crescent moons chiseled into the surface of the unusual feature were the same as the decoration on the tent in my dream. As I continued to scan the animals head, I took in the fact that although it was lion like, its face was devoid of the usual tactile hair around the mouth and eyebrows found on most felines. The thick golden fur that covered the remainder of the animal's body hung to the ground, giving its physique an extra fluffy look.

"I won't lose her," my original protector, who was still beside me, said to the others. His voice was stern and demanding.

The man and young girl didn't answer him. They stood perfectly still, staring at me.

The lion shook its head back and forth gesturing a no. Could the animal understand him?

Why not? I thought grudgingly to myself.

The same man continued to speak. "We don't have enough time to get her to the hospital. The humans wouldn't be able to deal with this type of wound, anyway."

Humans? Maybe I had fallen and hit my head. That was something I would be apt to do.

Though chattering teeth I asked, "What are you people? Aliens?"

The man named Nathaniel answered, apparently insulted by my question. "Certainly not!"

Ignoring Nathaniel's response, my protector turned and spoke in a pleading voice to the lion, "Surely you can see that she is the woman from my dream. Please, I've been searching for her forever."

"Dream?" I asked. "Did you say something about a dream?"

No one answered. It looked like the three of them, including the lion, were carrying on a conversation by the way they moved their heads back and forth, but there was no lip movement.

Finally, when I was unable to take the silence anymore, I shrieked at them, "Hey, if you people are done with your staring contest, could we move along to the wounded person?"

Nathaniel gave me a disparaging look, but remained silent and the staring contest continued. I groaned loudly in protest.

My protector knelt down, cradling my upper body in his arms. I screamed involuntarily as the movement jostled the rod that had impaled me. After a minute, the pain faded to a tolerable level and I was able to look up.

When my protector spoke next, the potent honeysuckle from his breath stunned my mind. It was the same smell as in my dream. The heat coming off his skin raised goose bumps on my ice-cold flesh. "We're going to fix this, but you must trust us. My name is Joshua. This is my brother Nathaniel and our sister Cassandra. The lion is our friend…" Joshua stopped short of giving the animal a name.

"Of course," I said. Perhaps if I turned onto my back I would start snoring and wake myself up, since apparently Alex wasn't going to wake me up.

"You're not dreaming," Joshua confirmed, softly stroking my cheek.

Nathaniel barked out a stern warning. "You shouldn't do this, Joshua, it's very dangerous. You know what could happen to her without guidance and you won't be able to offer any assistance during her transformation. This one will be the most complicated of all."

Joshua shook his head violently. "This is not going to go down like that, Nathaniel. Stop thinking that."

Nathaniel took off his hat, ruffled his hair with his hand and said, "You know, there are times when I question your sanity. You could have any woman you wanted but you only want this one? The image in the dream is still hazy. She may not be the one."

Nathaniel walked away, shaking his head, still complaining. "Well, whatever you're going to do, do it quickly please. I want to go home; it's been a long day."

I watched Nathaniel return to where the creature had fallen but there was nothing left. He picked up the arrows, and began to shake the amber liquid away.

"Where did the monster go?" I asked, struggling in Joshua's arms to see.

I don't know why I was even concerned about it. The numbness that was now overtaking me was most likely due to the heavy loss of blood. I didn't have much life left in me.

"I'll explain it all to you another time."

"Another time? If I live through this I don't ever want to run into you people again," I grumbled.

Joshua's face fell, seeming unhappy at my response. "Right now we need to attend to your injury. How much do you weigh, Katherine, 140 pounds?"

"No, one thirty five."

Joshua laughed lightly. "All right, 135." Considering the state I was in I guess it was comical that I was concerned over such a minor detail.

Cassandra chimed in next, answering an unspoken question. "I don't have any problem with this, Joshua. I think you're right. She is similar to the woman in your dream. Of course, the woman in your dream is much younger. Obviously, she'd been bitten. This would make sense, considering the circumstances of the dream."

Cassandra shrugged and after a few seconds continued. "In any case, if we're to save her life we need to get the serum into her before her heart stops."

Joshua bent closer and his lips touched my ear. His breath sent a flutter of pleasure throughout my body that for an instant overrode the excruciating lack of feeling. A powerful attraction flowed between us. It felt like we were lovers, or could be lovers.

"Katherine," he cooed. His voice was soft now, all the tension reigned in. "Don't be afraid."

How did he know my name? I shook my head again in a futile effort to clear the fog. "Don't be afraid, right…tooooo… late for that." I crossed my arms tightly over my chest, trying to keep the spasms from tearing me apart.

Joshua motioned to the lion. The animal shuffled toward me and I instinctively tried to back away but Joshua held me tightly in place.

Joshua grabbed a stick from the ground and put it across my mouth, locking it between my hammering teeth. "Bite down on this while I remove the weapon."

Before I could protest he grabbed onto the rod and in one swift pull, it was out.

The ensuing pain put me on the edge of unconsciousness. My head bobbed listlessly as a deluge of warm blood gushed down my side.

The lion positioned its massive body directly over me, placing a front leg on each side of my torso, directly below my arms. The spasms stopped instantly.

"The lion's serum has healing properties," Joshua explained. "Please hold very still. The bite will hurt at first but the pain will fade as the solution spreads throughout your body."

With my last ounce of energy I whimpered, "There's going to be more pain?"

"Katherine, I promise it will be over in seconds. I will return for you," Joshua hesitated "after your human life is over."

Again with the human stuff. "I don't understand." I knew Joshua heard me but he didn't clarify his comment. He leaned down and kissed the top of my head.

Joshua turned toward the lion. "Yes, I am very sure. Bite her! Do it, now, before it is too late, before I lose her forever."

The animal placed one of its huge paws around my neck, holding my head with the gentlest of touches. Joshua released me, the warmth on my back replaced by the warmth from the lion in front. Lips as soft as silken fabric brushed past my ear, producing a feeling of euphoria as sensual as the anticipation of a first kiss. The lion did not kiss me, though. The glorious beast opened its mouth wider, exposing my skin to its teeth, and bit into me.

The four red hot fangs slid with ease through the muscle and sinew, only stopping when the sharp points hit upon bone. My echoing screams gurgled then cut off as I struggled to free myself from the iron weight that held me in place.

As my racing heart pumped the morphine-like substance from limb to limb, the pain faded and moments later ended. The lion released me and stepped back.

Warm arms caught me in that same instant, lifting me up off the ground, embracing me securely.

I peered through heavily clouded tears at the lion's muzzle stained red with my blood. The king of the beasts opened its mouth to roar and I knew what I would see next. Bright amber-colored ooze dripped from its fangs, sparkling in the sunlight.

Then, whether from the terror or the anesthetizing effect of the bite, I slid willingly into unconsciousness.

Chapter 3
SHOW ME YOUR TEETH

The king of beasts hunts mostly by night, its eyes reflecting like two beacons in the night. The lion is most skilled at hiding and is phenomenally patient. It pursues with cunning skill, from cover to cover with a final burst of speed at the end, bringing a quick and merciful death to its victim. Its teeth are perfectly sculptured for ripping and tearing. Flesh and Blood is its dominion.

~ Quote from National Geographic

I sighed heavily as I peered into the pitch black. Alex was right, as usual. I definitely needed to back off the sci-fi for a while. Intending to curl up next to my patient husband, I shifted my position but instead I fell forward, my knee hitting a hard object that shouldn't have been there. After a few moments of confusion I figured out that I was in my car, in the passenger seat, covered with one of my quilts. Something soft was rolled up under my head, acting as a pillow.

I sat up with a jolt. The last thing I could recollect was going for a walk in the state park.

An eerie feeling made me reach up quickly with both hands, feeling my neck. I sighed with relief. It was just another dream. I heard a door open with a bang and a bright light followed, temporarily blinding me. Alex began tapping furiously on the driver's window and pulling at the door handle. I reached over, one hand still covering my eyes and pulled up the lock. Alex flung the door open and slammed it shut after him.

"Where have you been, Katherine? I was very worried. How long have you been out here?"

"I... went... for a walk in the state park. I'm sorry... I was gone for ... I... I must have fallen asleep." What had happened to me?

"You went for a walk?" Alex asked, his tone doubtful. "All day? I nearly called the police. Why didn't you go to the quilt show? I went over there at one and they said you never showed up!"

"The quilt show?" Boy was my head spinning.

"Yes, the Historical Society Quilt Show." Alex turned towards the back seat and pointed. "Look, the quilts are still in the car." I didn't need to look. I knew I hadn't dropped them off.

"I don't remember anything after going for the walk." I thought over the whole lion-demon episode in my head while Alex waited. How could I tell him the truth when I didn't know what the truth was? As he stared at me in disbelief, I tried to think of something sane but came up with nothing.

The concern on Alex's face changed to impatience as he continued to reproach me. "When I returned from looking for you at the show I found a text message from you on my phone that was sent at two in the afternoon. Why didn't you call me? I must have called your cell phone fifty times. Why didn't you come into the house when you got home and why are you in the passenger seat?"

I was asking myself the exact same questions. "I'm... not... sure," I told him, choking on the words. "I guess there was more room to spread out on this side?"

Alex's look was incredulous, but I didn't care. I was home, and Alex was there and even though he was furious, I could tell he was happy to see me. I felt safe from all the demons trying to get out of my head.

"Do you know what time it is?""

I scratched my head. "No."

"It's midnight." Alex paused, letting the information sink in. When I didn't respond he continued. "Please, Katherine, where have you been? Have you been drinking?" He leaned closer. "That smells like perfume but not yours."

I ignored his questions. I looked down at my watch to confirm the time but froze when I saw the cracked glass and the hands that were stuck at ten forty.

"It's midnight?" I shrieked, my voice rising two octaves. I had been gone for almost fourteen hours.

"What happened to you?" Alex asked again. I wanted to say something soothing to him to take that worried look from his face but I was too scared. In my mind, all I could see was the recurring image of the lion with my blood dripping from its mouth. I shuddered. No, I definitely would keep that to myself. People wielding swords with mythical lions beside them only existed in the movies.

Alex continued to stare unmoving at me, still waiting for my credible explanation.

I looked out the windshield of the car, biting my bottom lip furiously. Then something he had said previously caught my attention. "I sent you a text message? What did it say?"

"It said you were with friends, that you were okay and you would be home late." When I didn't respond, Alex asked accusingly, "You don't remember sending it, do you?"

My whole body twitched suddenly as the phone in my pocket vibrated. I was tempted to remove it and check the message minder but I knew it would only frighten me further. The one detail that I was clear about was leaving the phone in the glove box. Someone else must have put it into my jacket.

No longer able to control the panic, I began to sob. Alex sighed in frustration but reached over and tenderly wiped the tears from my cheek. For some strange reason I felt the need to protect the amber-eyed people and their mascot. More importantly, if Alex heard the story that was rolling around in my head right now he would certainly send me for psychiatric care.

"Maybe we should go inside?" Alex suggested. "It's late and I'm tired."

"I am, too." Although I shouldn't have been; apparently I had been sleeping all day.

"You look tired. In fact, you look awful. Like someone beat you up or something."

"I look bad?" I began to perspire heavily, wondering if I had any blood on me.

Alex reached over and grabbed my arm. "Katherine, calm down."

"I'm all right," I said dully. "I just want to get into bed."

I opened the door. Before I could step out of the car, Alex pulled me in close enough for a kiss. "I'm glad you're home and safe. I missed you. I thought for a while there that you would end up on an episode of *Disappeared* and that I'd be standing in a police lineup."

I forced my best fake smile. "I'm glad to be home, too."

As I headed for the house, I looked around frantically, searching for the source of the honeysuckle that permeated the air. Alex didn't notice what I was doing because he was too focused on my leg.

"You're not limping. Has your knee recovered?"

"Umm, I guess it has." That was weird. After what I might have been through today, my knee should be throbbing. I sighed happily thinking that was proof that all that terror had only been a dream.

When we were inside, I went straight to our bedroom, knowing I would be out the minute my head touched the pillow. My cell phone vibrated annoyingly again. When I pulled it open, the counter showed thirty missed calls, all from Alex. I found the message that had been sent from my phone to Alex's, but not by me. The comprehension of what I had put Alex through rolled over me in a wave of despair bringing with it a fresh set of tears. He must have been crazy with worry about me. I would have to find some way to make all of this up to him.

My breath caught as I unfolded a piece of paper from the same pocket. The words "Stay safe, J" were written in a very elegant script. I angrily crumpled up the paper and tossed it into the wastebasket. In my mind I chanted the words *Just a dream*, over and over again.

I unzipped my jacket and had to put my hand up to my mouth to stifle the scream when I caught a glance of the large gaping hole on my shirt's left side in the floor length mirror. The fabric was splattered with what appeared to be dried blood. Sand colored fur was stuck in clumps in random spots around the hole. I examined myself carefully, running my hands over my neck and torso, unable to find any sign of injury. The cuts on my hands and face from the branches were gone also. The eyes that looked back from the mirror were bewildered. If I had been hurt, and from my torn shirt it certainly looked that way, how was it that I was fine now?

"The lion's bite has healing powers," the man named Joshua had said.

"No! No! No!" I whispered quietly. The stain on my shirt couldn't be blood. I must have ripped it on a branch and then fallen on a patch of mud. That was the only sane explanation that I could deal with right now.

As I heard Alex come out of the bathroom I pulled the note out of the trash and rolled it up with my shirt. I shoved them both into the laundry hamper. I would put them out with the trash tomorrow. I finished changing into my pajamas, climbed into bed and fell immediately to sleep. I didn't dream that night. I had had enough.

*

The next morning, I was startled into consciousness by a plane that I was sure was going to land on the roof. I sat straight up holding my breath. My hands flew to cover my ears against the thunderous engine noise. Alex wasn't in bed with me and I wondered if I should get up and try to find him. I waited for the impending crash, but nothing happened. I sighed in relief as the plane moved away. That was scary.

I lay back down, my mind drifting back to Saturday's events, still hoping to call to mind the missing time between the unnerving walk in the park and my mysterious appearance in the driveway. While I was pondering, I became aware of muffled voices. I couldn't tell which part of the house they were coming from. It seemed to be echoing all around me. I glanced at the alarm clock. The hands were in a straight vertical line, pointing in the opposite direction from each other. It was too early for Alex to be talking to one of the neighbors. First, I checked inside the house but couldn't find anyone, not even Alex. Then I went from window to window. I ended up in the in the kitchen, scratching my head. Alex came into the kitchen just then.

"Good morning. I was just about to put on the coffee. How are you feeling?"

"I'm fine," I said, dismissing his concern. "That plane that just flew over was unusually loud. It scared me awake. I wonder why it was flying at such a low altitude." I paused momentarily, puzzled by the confusion on Alex's face. "Did you see what kind of plane it was? It sounded like a 747."

Alex answered suspiciously, "One of those small acrobatic planes flew over a few minutes ago but it was quite a distance up."

"Umm." How could Alex not have heard that? I could still hear it even now. I wished I had stopped there but my big mouth kept moving. "I also heard voices. Were you talking to someone?"

"No, I was out in the garage alone." Alex paused, "Except for the ten cats that I had to chase away."

"Cats!" I yelled in disbelief. "What cats?"

"Yes… cats," Alex said, dragging out each word. "I counted ten sitting on the stone wall at the back of the yard looking like Egyptian sphinxes. Nutmeg was with them. They were staring at the house, like they were waiting for something." He shook his head at the thought of the disturbing event. "Well, they're gone now. I chased them all away."

I took a deep breath and relaxed. "I can still hear the voices. Can't you hear them? It sounds like they're just outside."

Alex folded his arms and stood motionless for a few seconds, cocking his head to listen. "No, I don't hear anything. Are you sure you're okay? You look better than you did last night, but there's something…something different about you."

"I'm fine, really. What's for breakfast?" I asked, hoping to direct his attention away from me.

Alex went to start the coffee but I could see by his furrowed brow that he was still worried. Alex had good reason to be worried. I was almost positive that I was losing my mind.

After we ate, Alex went to finish changing the oil in his sports cars, while I tried to catch up on the housework, but the mysterious voices were not easy to ignore. I came very close to going to the emergency room until I began to wonder what they would do for me once I admitted my problem. Probably start by recommending a good psychiatrist.

I knew I had to calm myself before Alex noticed the panic on my face. I took a book and my stitching out to the front porch ready to concentrate on something else but as the day went on, the volume of the noise increased exponentially. At first, the sounds were garbled and broken. It was similar to having a cell phone conversation where the voice on the other end fades in and out due to the weak service. Then as I listened more intently, I was stunned to realize that I must be hearing my neighbors from inside their houses.

I didn't get much sleep that first night because even though there was less people noise, the crickets and peepers, deafening under normal circumstances, were now maddening.

I was able to achieve some respite from the outside commotion by listening to one of my audio books, turning the volume up to the max. The rhythm of the narrator's voice allowed me to drift into short intervals of unsatisfying slumber. Thankfully, Alex was a heavy sleeper.

*

The lack of sleep put me in no mood to jump up for work the next day. Alex and I both worked for a medical device manufacturer, LCA Laboratories, located in Lexington. Alex was an engineer in manufacturing. I was a scientist in R&D.

"Oh," I groaned rolling myself over onto my side, covering my head with the pillow. "It can't be five already."

I heard Alex chuckle. "Time to get up, sleepyhead."

I peeked out from under the sheets. Alex was by the closet. He walked over to my side of the bed, holding a pair of brown pants, flashing one of his sexy smiles. "Let me know when you're done in the shower," he requested, leaning down to kiss the top of my head, pulling the remainder of the sheet away.

I groaned again. I wished I could be as happy and full of energy on Monday mornings as Alex usually was. As his footsteps faded towards the kitchen, I dragged myself out of bed. I could feel every muscle as I moved. The hot water from the shower unfortunately offered no relief.

After I was dressed, I found Alex having his breakfast and watching the morning news. Alex had eaten the same cereal every morning for as long as I had known him. Really, how could anyone keep up such a routine? It was a credit to his endurance. Of course, that was probably why we were still together after twenty-two years. He was the only person on this earth that got me and had the patience to put up with me. It almost seemed impossible at times, but Alex knew me better than I knew myself and he was always there for me.

While I was putting together our lunches, I become aware of Nutmeg waiting by his bowl with an irritated look. I had been selfishly involved in my own troubles all weekend and had not paid him much attention. I put his food out on the front porch in the usual spot and watched as he gobbled it down. While we were at work, he usually spent the day sleeping and keeping the garden safe from small varmints.

On the way back into the house I spied the quilts, still piled high in the back seat of the car. The site made me cringe at the thought of having to call the Historical Society with an excuse as to why I had not showed up. I was usually very dependable.

The fragrance hit me like a brick as soon as I opened the passenger door of the Honda. I rocked back on my feet. My stomach instantly filled with acid at the thought that my encounter with the lion people had evidently not been a dream. I quickly opened the rest of the car doors hoping to dilute out the unusual smell before Alex came out. I was afraid the reminder would only initiate another barrage of questions.

It would be difficult to explain that the scent was from the strange man who was holding me in his arms on Saturday, saving my life. A man whom I could not stop thinking about.

Why was I feeling guilty about that? I hadn't cheated on Alex. The analytical part of my brain reasoned that I only felt this way because I was grateful that he had saved my life. I was sure it would pass.

As I removed the quilt that I had been covered in from the front seat, I heard a dull clang. When I looked down, I found a ring. The silvery metal had been formed into the shape of an intricate flower. Automatically, without thinking, I put it on the middle finger of my right hand. It was over-sized and clunky but I liked it. I twirled it around, trying to figure out why it felt familiar. I was being absurd, I told myself. The ring must belong to one of the girls. They were always misplacing things. During their teenage years it had become epidemic. At one point, I had toyed with the idea of putting rings through their noses to attach the house keys. Just last weekend we had gone to the movies, and Josephine had forgotten her pocketbook in my car.

I put all the quilts back in the house and made myself focus on the present task of getting to work. Alex and I had a pleasant fifty-minute ride each morning along back roads, only encountering two traffic lights along the way. It was great way to catch a little extra sleep for the passenger. Unfortunately, it was my turn to drive.

It would be a long day.

As we pulled into the parking lot at work, Alex opened the glove compartment to get a piece of chewing gum but instead pulled out an unfamiliar box. Inside were ten small sealed packages, similar in appearance to the ones that held Alex's contact lenses.

"Are those yours?"

"No, I've never seen contacts like these. They're huge. I'd guess twice the diameter of mine. Plus they're dark brown which is strange because most people are trying to change their eye color from brown to blue or green, not the other way around." Alex looked at me skeptically. I suspected that he had been contemplating bringing up the weekend event during the morning drive. Thankfully he hadn't. I was trying my best to forget about it.

Alex and I both loved shows like the X-Files but neither one of us truly believed any of those stories. As a scientist, I had been taught to consider that there was always a rational explanation for everything. There were no magic wands or light sabers or cursed treasures.

I reminded myself that I hadn't done anything wrong while I showed Alex the ring that I had found. "I think the kids must have left this stuff when we went to the movies last weekend. I bet those are Steven's contacts," I said dismissively, waving my hand.

Steven was Josephine's boyfriend. "Leave them in there," I said motioning to the glove box. "I'll ask Josephine about them when we get into work." Josephine also worked at LCA. We had been fortunate enough to assist her in obtaining a position after she had graduated from UMASS.

Alex seemed to accept my explanation for now. If I were lucky, he would forget about the contacts. I wondered if I had even a shred of luck remaining or if I had used up my quota this weekend.

I wasted most of that first day at work in the ladies' room, with my hands over my ears. I could hear every conversation in the building. I knew that I had to get a handle on this quickly or I would go mad.

Without Alex knowing, I spent the every night of that first week practicing to block out the noise while I pretended to watch TV. Eventually I was able to filter out virtually all of the low-level sound. I found that it was only when I was very distracted or the sound was very loud, like a plane or a helicopter, that I had to concentrate harder.

The amplified hearing was only the beginning of the physical changes. I had many sleepless nights that followed, walking through the house like a zombie, trying to work out the ever-increasing cramps that eventually spread throughout my entire body.

I didn't complain, hoping to keep my physical problems a secret, but ever since that mysterious late night, Alex had become more observant than ever and was convinced that the Lyme disease I had developed a few years back had returned.

Deep down I knew that even modern medicine couldn't fix this, but Alex wouldn't give up and made me promise to go see my doctor.

My persistent husband hovered over me as I begrudgingly called the doctor's office and made an appointment for July tenth. I wasn't sure what I would do then. I was taking one day at a time.

Then, shortly after the July Fourth holiday, for no reason that I was aware of, I woke to no pain and no muscle cramps. My jaw still ached from time to time, but it was mild compared to what I had been going through. Maybe I had gotten sick from a virus that I had caught from the…I cringed as the memory flooded my mind. Even a human bite can be deadly. To Alex's dismay, I quickly rescheduled the doctor's appointment for later in the summer.

Although I was no longer in physical pain, I continued to see changes in my physical appearance. My body hair began to grow at an alarming rate. I was able to hide the increased grooming from Alex except when I began to look like a real-life Rapunzel.

By the end of July, my skin became more toned. The wrinkles on my face and hands smoothed out and disappeared. My freckles and age spots faded along with the cellulite in my legs. The dry spots, calluses and scars all vanished, even the one on my stomach, from the C-section when I had given birth to Lindsey.

Of course, Alex also noticed all of these changes. Over the past twenty years, we had watched each other getting older and now he was watching in disbelief as my physical growth was reversing. To my relief though, Alex took my new appearance in stride, the same way he did most of my crazy problems.

The one alteration that did have Alex worried was my apparent weight loss. I say apparent because outwardly it appeared that way. I went from wearing a size eight to a size four, which should have meant that I had lost twenty pounds. Under any other set of circumstances, having to bring down my "skinny" clothes from the attic would have thrilled me, except that the scale in the bathroom registered my weight as one sixty-five.

It was truly frightening to see how much I had changed when one morning Alex made me stand in front of the full-length mirror. I couldn't reconcile the image of the beautiful woman that stared back at me, with the perception I had of myself.

"Wow, is that really me?"

"Yes," Alex concurred. "You look incredible and your skin is as soft as a newborn. I'm not sure what you're doing to make this happen, but I like it. I feel like I'm dating a young hot chick again. If you figure it out will you let me know? I'd like to try it myself."

Alex's assessment was spot-on. If you caught sight of me next to my 28-year-old daughter, you might mistake me for her sister, not her mother. Was I really getting younger? It seemed preposterous but I couldn't dispute the evidence that was blatantly in front of me.

What I didn't realize at the time was that an even more bizarre modification was occurring and it was with the help of a tiny pest that I discovered it.

In the middle of one of our twilight dinners, Alex reached over suddenly and swatted at my exposed arm. "Oops." He grabbed a napkin. "Sorry, I didn't mean to squish them all over you." The blank look on my face made him ask, "Didn't you feel that? I counted at least five mosquitoes on your arm."

"No, I guess I was too involved in my food," I took the napkin from his hand and quickly removed the remaining insect debris. My mind was racing with the sudden awareness that I hadn't had a mosquito bite all summer. I was a magnet for the little bloodsuckers and usually had to endure at least four or five bites a week.

While Alex was inside getting the can of bug spray, I watched closely as the next few mosquitoes landed on my arm, trying unsuccessfully to take a bite. With my improved vision, I could see the mosquitoes as clearly as looking through a dissecting microscope. The proboscis from one of the mosquito actually bent as it tried in vain to puncture my skin.

Maybe there was something hard under my skin? Maybe that's why I weighed more now? I could feel my body become rigid with fear at that new revelation. Even though I was ecstatic about the younger-looking modifications, I should have known this would turn into a horror story, because that's how it had begun.

"No, no, no," I repeated over and over, covering my face with my hands. This would be yet another change that I needed to keep from Alex. Before I could compose myself, Alex came back out, interrupting my panic attack.

"Here you go," he said offering me the spray bottle. Of course, he immediately noticed me going to pieces. "Are you okay? You look like you've seen a ghost."

"I'm fine," I said, irritated, instantly regretting the next words out of my mouth. "I don't know why you keep asking me that."

Alex threw the can down on the table. It made a sharp crack as it hit the glass table and rolled off. I flinched away from the sound of his anger. "I keep asking you that because there's something wrong with you and I know you know what it is and you won't tell me." He turned and stormed back into the house.

I swallowed hard, trying to stop the tears that had begun to spill down my face. Alex was right to be upset. In all our time together I had never ever held anything back from him. Up until now there was nothing that I couldn't, or wouldn't, share with him. There was no secret that was too private. I knew this lie was putting a strain on our relationship, but honestly, what would the truth do to it?

After a few minutes, Alex came back out onto the porch and kneeled down beside me. "I'm sorry. I didn't mean to get mad. To tell you the truth, I'm a little jealous. I wish I was getting younger too."

"I know, I'm sorry," was all I could manage in between the sobs.

Alex kissed me and said, "Okay, forget about it for now. We'll talk about it whenever you're ready."

Alex picked up the bug spray from the table and handed it to me. "Here, you should put some of this on. The mosquitoes are still biting." I took the can from him, determined to look and act as normal as possible.

Later that night, after we had gone to bed, Alex tried to make up for his earlier tiff. Even though I was not in the mood, I gave into his kissing and let him seduce me.

I selfishly needed him now more than ever. We were not alone, though.

That was the first night that I made love to Joshua.

*

In addition to all of the outward changes to my appearance, there was something happening to my teeth. I was going through a toothbrush a day, shredding them into pieces. Hoping to keep Alex from finding the mangled evidence, I disposed of the brushes in the trash at work. Of course, Alex was always on the verge of finding out about everything. It was difficult to keep him from noticing when things happened, especially since I didn't know when they would happen.

One night at dinner, while I was eating furiously, I crunched down on something hard. "Ouch!" I yelled, a reflex reaction. I wasn't hurt. Nothing hurt me anymore. I pulled what I assumed was a piece of gristle out of my mouth and examined it.

"Did you bite down on a piece of bone?" That was a reasonable assumption for Alex to make since we were having steak.

When I examined the object more closely, I found that it was a piece from a filling. This in itself wasn't a surprise. In the past several years, I had had to have three caps.

"I'll be right back," I told Alex and I headed for the bathroom.

Hoping not to find a set of fangs, I pulled my lips into contorted positions in front of the mirror. It was then that I saw how brand new my teeth looked. What had happened to my fillings? Maybe I swallowed them while I was sleeping? The molars also looked different. Their edges were flattened like cutting shears and extremely pointed. There was also a slight discoloration in the middle of my tongue. It had the feel of wet sandpaper, like a cat's tongue.

I locked the bathroom door and sat on the cool tile floor, slipping into my now familiar panic mode and let the tears overflow, soaking my shirt.

Alex eventually knocked on the door. "Baby, I can hear you crying. What's wrong? Are you all right?"

I needed to pull myself together or Alex would surely be pressing for more information this time. Up until now, he had accepted my strange transformations with a surprising lack of concern.

"I'm okay. My tooth is really hurting. I'll be out in a minute. Could you get me a glass of water? I need to take some Tylenol."

While Alex was in the kitchen, I splashed my face generously with warm water. By the time he had returned, the water works had stopped. I opened the medicine cabinet and grabbed the Tylenol. I needed some distraction in order to get out of the bathroom.

"Are you sure you're okay?" Alex asked again as I opened the door. I told myself not to get irritated. Stay calm.

"Yes, I'm fine," I confirmed. "I just don't want to have to deal with going to the dentist."

"Show me your broken tooth."

I didn't know how much Alex knew about the anatomy of human teeth, but he would surely notice that I had no fillings.

"It's one of my back teeth," I admitted, at the same time stuffing the pain tablets into my mouth, chasing them down with the water. "It's difficult to see. I'll be fine." I pushed past him, heading for the kitchen.

I heard Alex exhale heavily and knew that he would let it go. There were too many things wrong these days to keep up.

The next day I called my periodontist to cancel my appointment. I wasn't able to cut my rock hard skin, but what would my teeth do to normal skin? I flinched away from the mental picture of my hygienist holding up her hands, fingers bloodied. I would also need to be careful with Alex. The biggest issue by far would be keeping his tongue out of my mouth.

Alex knew I preferred to ignore problems rather than deal with them therefore he was unrelenting in his quest to get me to the doctor.

"Katherine, it looks as though you've lost about 20 pounds over the last two months, right?"

I answered timidly, "Maybe."

He raised an eyebrow. "You should be putting on weight not losing it with the amount of food you've been eating lately."

I didn't answer. I watched as he pointed to the empty plate in front of me as evidence. I had eaten the large piece of steak in seconds without waiting for him to sit down to join me.

"Now, I know that you don't feel sick, but I really wish you would go to the doctor. It's not normal for someone our age to be taking in loads of calories and losing weight. Maybe it's a simple thyroid problem. If it is something serious, you need to have it taken care of right away. Plus I don't know if you have noticed, but at night when we cuddle, it feels like you're running a fever." I shook my head in disbelief. Alex never missed a thing.

"I feel fine. In fact, I feel great. Maybe it's my menopause kicking in to high gear."

Alex put his arms around me and began to kiss the side of my face. "I really wish you would go see the doctor. It would do a lot to alleviate my worry."

I still had the re-scheduled visit that I had been planning to cancel. While Alex was still holding me, I contemplated whether to tell him or not. I decided it wouldn't hurt to go. I was still rooting for the virus theory.

"Okay," I sighed. "I do have that appointment I made in July."

"When is it?" Alex pulled back, eyeing me skeptically. Maybe he thought I was lying just to appease him. It wouldn't have been the first time.

"It's this Tuesday at lunchtime."

I knew his curiosity was for a good reason and so it wasn't a surprise when I walked out from work on Tuesday to find Alex waiting by the car.

I frowned when I saw him. "What're you doing?"

"I thought I would drive you to your appointment, then maybe you'd let me take you to lunch?" I could see him trying to fight back the smile.

"Okay," I laughed. "Don't you trust me?"

"Well, I thought I would make sure you didn't take any detours."

Alex dropped me off at the front door of the medical building and said he had an errand to do and would wait outside for me in the parking lot. I briefly thought about making a U-turn as soon as Alex was out of sight but I knew he was worried about me and I forced myself to go in.

Even though the waiting room was full of patients, the receptionist escorted me directly to the examination room after I had checked in.

That meant Alex wouldn't have to wait too long. Then we could go to lunch. I would concentrate on that. Alex was right, again. I was starving all the time.

Once inside the exam room, the nurse took my temperature and checked my blood pressure. "Are you safe at home?"

"Yes, perfectly safe," I replied with a slight hint of hysteria in my voice that I hoped would go unnoticed. Home was fine…it was the forest that was the problem. She wrote something on my chart and left me alone to wait for the doctor.

It was only a few minutes later when there was light knocking on the door and Dr. Davis entered. She picked up my chart and began reading it closely, at the same time asking about any problems that I was having. I laughed to myself. I'm sure she didn't have time to hear about all the problems I was having. *Keep it light,* I told myself.

"I'm fine, never been better." During the time I had been sitting alone, I had made up my mind to lie to Alex no matter what the doctor found.

"Your temp and blood pressure are up."

I shrugged my shoulders indifferently. "I'm fine, really."

"Hmm, the nurse forgot to weigh you. Why don't you hop up on the scale for me real quick?"

I scowled at the reading, which should have showed one thirty-five not one sixty-five. Dr. Davis tapped the metal bar on the scale several times. When the reading didn't change she frowned and apologized for the broken scale.

I sat frozen on the exam table, realizing too late that I should have cancelled and faked the visit. No one would have noticed me sitting in the crowded waiting room pretending I was waiting to see a doctor.

Dr. Davis was still staring at my chart. I wasn't sure what she would see in my face when she looked up but it must not have been as bad as I imagined because she added, "You certainly don't look like you've put on any weight. You look amazing, actually. Have you changed your diet?"

I looked down at my feet trying to hide from her suspicious gaze as the blood rushed into my cheeks. "I've been eating lots of salads and low fat foods and exercising regularly," I mumbled.

"Oh...good." She pulled the stethoscope out from around her neck and shoved the ear buds into place. I flinched as the cold metal touched my skin.

"Wow, you have a nice strong heart beat." Then Dr. Davis grabbed my arm, sliding her hand down to my wrist. "Pulse is nice and strong also, a little fast though. Please lie back on the table. I'd like to check your internals."

I had to fight the urge to get up and run away as her fingers probed at several places on my stomach.

"Umm, you really have some muscles there in your stomach. I'm having a problem finding your organs. Nothing is swollen, though." she added quickly, trying not to alarm me.

Dr. Davis pondered for a few seconds and then said. "I'm going to order some X-rays and blood tests. If we don't find anything suspicious then we'll see you next year." I started to dismount from the exam table but the doctor reached out and stopped me. "Just one more thing before you leave. I want to recheck your temp. You feel a little warm." She put a thermometer into my mouth and waited for the device to beep.

"Hmm, still reading one-o-one." She placed her hand on my forehead. "Are you sure you feel okay?"

"I feel fine," I mumbled, my lips barely able to move. Some scientist I was. I hadn't even thought to check my body temperature.

The doctor handed me two pills. "Take these now and take two more every four to six hours for the next few days. If your temperature is not down by tomorrow morning give the office a call."

"Okay," I answered obediently. With the yellow order form in hand I made my way to the lab for the blood work. I was in a stupor, still preoccupied with the idea of my elevated temperature and I wasn't thinking about what was going to happen next.

A young woman instructed me to sit in one of the chairs at the blood drawing station. She walked away and added, "I'll be with you in a few minutes."

"Take your time," I told her glumly.

The plastic sleeve with the needle and the blood collection tubes were on the table next to me. I picked up the needle, thinking back to the mosquitoes, and carefully pushed the sharp pointed end into my arm, wincing the entire time, still uncertain of the outcome. I tried again and again, pushing harder each time until the force bent the metal tip and crushed the holder. Inside my head a voice was screaming, *Get up, stupid, get up!* I threw the unrecognizable remains of my experiment into the biohazard bucket and grabbed a few bandages along with some gauze, shoving them into my pants pocket. The young woman who had spoken to me earlier asked where I was going when she saw me running out of the room.

"I'm really sick," I told her clutching at my stomach. One glance at my face and I knew she would believe me.

I ran into the restroom and stood in front of one of the sinks, gasping at the air and splashing cold water on my face. I needed to come up with the Shakespearian act of the century before I went out to meet Alex. He was a master at seeing through my tall tales. At what point would all of my renovations eventually be too much for him to deal with? Would he leave me? Turn me into the freak police? How would I have handled this if I stood where Alex stood?

I put on some blush and placed one of the bandages along with the gauze on my arm in the spot where you would expect to see a dressing from having blood drawn and slipped out of the building.

Alex was waiting for me in the car, listening to music.

"Hi," I said smiling hugely, "ready for lunch?"

"How did it go?" I could see the worry on his face.

"It was fine." I tried to sound bored.

"Did you tell the doctor about the weight loss?"

"I didn't have to tell her, she could see that when she weighed me."

"Did you tell her you had lost the weight in just a few months? That you're also eating twice as much food?"

"Yes, they took some blood." I showed Alex my arm with the bandage in place and worked on moderating my voice. "They're going to run some tests."

"When will you know the results?"

I took a deep calming breath. I was tired of trying to make up more excuses, which like the ever-expanding ripples in a pond, were spreading fast.

"Alex, don't worry," I said in my softest voice, reaching out to touch his cheek. "The doctor will call. You know it takes a few days to get lab results back."

Alex reached his arm around to the back seat and produced a bouquet of red roses. "Don't forget you did promise me that we were going to grow old together. I love you."

Alex's strategy worked and I lost my grip on my irritation. "I love you too," I said fervently, "and we will grow old together." I leaned over and kissed him. Underneath my façade, though, I had a sickening feeling that my forever was going to be longer than Alex's forever.

Later that week, I downloaded some information from the Internet and through the magic of copy and paste printed out a perfect forgery of my supposed test results. I showed it to Alex, assuring him that everything was normal. He was skeptical about the doctor's assessment, but he didn't push me further for the moment.

Putting the physical behind me, I tried to concentrate on other important matters, such as how I was going to hide the rest of the changes that I was going through. Changes like the phenomenal improvement to my vision. My mom had taken me to get my first set of eyeglasses when I was only five years old. In addition, I had suffered from night blindness for just as long. All at once the details of life had become brighter and sharper, even on nights when the only light available was provided by the stars. The best analogy I could make to describe the change was that my previous vision had been on an outdated VHS mode and now it was on Blue-Ray mode. Of course, that upgrade also meant that I could see all the dirt that had been hiding in plain sight throughout my house. Alex watched in disbelief as I went on a cleaning spree, scrubbing areas of each room already spotless, at least to his eyes.

As my sight improved, though, my prescription lenses began to distort rather than correct but I didn't want to stop wearing my glasses. That would only be further fuel for Alex's suspicions. In order to continue my charade, I had the prescription lenses in my glasses replaced with plain glass.

The summer slipped into fall and I began to try to recover some normalcy in my life. Alex encouraged me to go back to attending Stitch Group. I was apprehensive, because I knew my friends would be astonished by the dramatic changes in my appearance.

My stitch group was a very informal gathering of ladies who all had a common interest in needlework. We took turns getting together at each other's homes for a quiet day of "stitching and bitching" as Alex teased. I had been participating in the group now for over ten years. They were the only close friends I had and I knew they were worried about me.

Alex reassured me by saying, "Just tell your friends that you're on a no-fat diet, taking vitamins and exercising regularly. You have no reason to be ashamed. You look great. Have some confidence."

Alex was right. Why was I hiding? I wasn't a criminal, although I had the sense that I had broken some law of nature and was just waiting for the punishment.

When the day came for the September meeting, I made sure I was the first one to arrive at Nancy's house. I wanted to assess her reaction to the new me before I made up my mind to stay for the day. She was flabbergasted, of course, but she didn't go running out of the house.

"Wow! You look great. I'm glad you came. We've all been worried about you. You sounded terribly depressed in your e-mails."

Karin, Madeline, Theresa, Sue and Ruth all had the same bewildered response. Donna came in last and with her quick wit asked what everyone had wanted to ask, "What the hell happened to you? Did you fall into some kind of a rabbit hole? You look like one of the Stepford wives." Even with the inquisitive looks everyone was genuinely happy to see me and after the first hour, I was able to settle back and relax. I even found myself laughing after a while.

I distracted everyone's attention from my physical appearance by pulling out the stitching projects I had completed since the last time they had seen me. I could tell they were thoroughly impressed by all the "Oh's" and "Ah's." My stitching had always been somewhat faster than most but nothing compared to what I was capable of now. I had to remind myself constantly to slow down. It would frighten them when the linen caught on fire from the friction of my needle as it did frequently when I was alone and distracted.

I wasn't bothered as much by my friend's reaction that day as I was by Nancy's dog, Csaba Roo and her cat, Pickles Pie. I loved dogs and they usually loved me. When I first arrived, Csaba growled and bared his teeth at me. Nancy was embarrassed and commented that she had never seen him react to anyone like that before, especially not to me.

Nancy's cat, which was usually only mildly interested in me, had the opposite reaction. Pickles insisted on sitting on my lap, rolling around on me as if I was a bowl of cosmic catnip. That was how my cat had been acting lately and for that matter all the other cats in my neighborhood. Alex was constantly chasing them out of our yard.

My friend's acceptance was a relief but as I had feared it would, Alex's began to wane and he became progressively distant. I noticed that when we slept he was always as far on the opposite side of the bed as he could be without falling off. I wondered if he would eventually start sleeping in one of the guest bedrooms. We hadn't shared any intimacy for a while now, especially since the night when he noticed the shine.

That night the bedroom windows were wide open to take advantage of the unusual warm October breeze. The extraordinarily full moon was a stark bright white; its light filled the room, cascading across our entwined bodies. The temperate weather had brought out many of the nocturnal animals and I could hear them scurrying around in the woods behind the house but I refused to be distracted from Alex's love-making.

I concentrated on listening to his heavy breathing. As Alex shifted our bodies, turning mine toward the streaming moonlight, I could hear his heart speed up and he quickly reached for the lamp. After a few long seconds, he composed himself and said in a somewhat shaky manner. "What the hell, Katherine. Your eyes were lit up like …like a werewolf or something supernatural."

I had no explanation as usual and after that Alex began treating me with cautious indifference.

Unfortunately, that was only the beginning of the eye problems. The change in color happened more slowly. During the summer, I noticed that my irises had begun to look slightly lighter in color but they were still brown. By the end of October though, they had changed from sepia to a bronze. That was when I began paying more attention. I had a bad feeling about what was happening and it turned out that my fears were justified. When the outside edges of my iris turned to an amber color and my pupil began to fade away, I finally understood the purpose of the brown contacts. I had known from the day that Alex found them that they didn't belong to Steven. I was glad I had saved them.

By the time the trees were bare of their leaves, my irises had completely changed and were now a mirror image to the people who I had encountered along the trail on that fateful day.

The realization that I was one of them, whatever they were, comforted me to some extent. At least I still looked human. At one point during all of this, I was afraid that Alex would wake up next to one of those... what did they call it... a Nergal?

Joshua and his siblings must have known that all of these changes were going to happen to me. What I couldn't work out was why they would have taken the time to save my life only to abandon me to figure this out on my own. I had a few thousand questions and it was maddening not to have any answers.

As unbelievable as it was, neither the reflective shine nor the color change was the most frightening alteration that I underwent. Shortly before Christmas, while Alex and I were sitting having our morning coffee, my eyes suddenly became extremely itchy. What now, I thought. Maybe I needed to change the contacts more often. I was being very conservative with the ten pairs that I had.

Alex stood up and intercepted me on the way to the bathroom. "What's wrong, Katherine?" he asked, peering intently at my face

"I don't know," I scowled as I pushed past him and closed the bathroom door behind me. I took out the contacts and put a cold compress across the bridge of my nose. That was when I noticed that every time I blinked a thin light-colored membrane trailed behind, only to disappear once my lids where fully retracted. It took me a few frozen seconds before I involuntarily let out a horrified scream.

Alex must have been getting tired of hearing me, because he didn't come to see what was wrong. I sat on the bathroom floor with my knees up to my chin.

My hands flew to my mouth, but it was a worthless gesture. I leaned over the toilet and gave in to the violent heaves.

I heard the creak as the bathroom door swung open. Damn! I had forgotten to turn the lock.

"Please, Alex, just leave me alone," I pleaded.

"That's not going to happen, Katherine. I'm not leaving until I know you're okay."

He took another face cloth out and ran it under the faucet. "If I asked you what was wrong is there even the smallest possibility that you would tell me."

I didn't answer. I stayed slumped over the toilet, still crying. Alex gently lifted my face and the shock of what he saw unbalanced him. He grabbed hold of the sink to stop from falling. I knew that this was probably the end of my marriage. What sane person would be able to deal with this?

"Your... your eyes," he stammered, "What's wrong with your eyes? They're...why are they discolored?" I heard him take a deep breath and release it as he spoke. "Katherine, I want the truth and I'm not going to let you out of this room until I get it. You're not going to blow me off like you usually do."

"I really don't know what the truth is," I told him, throwing my head back hoping to die at that very moment. I knew Alex didn't realize that he couldn't have stopped me from leaving the bathroom. My newfound strength was something else I had managed to hide from him.

"This all started that day when you came home late from the walk in the park." It wasn't a question but a statement.

I tried to give him an answer without actually lying. "I went for a walk and the next thing I knew I was sleeping in my car. Really, it's like an episode out of The Twilight Zone," I laughed grimly.

Alex took a few more deep breaths and rubbed my back soothingly. "It doesn't look like you have a pupil. How are you able to see?"

"Why aren't you running away in horror?" I asked thoughtfully. That was the only thing that was important right now.

Alex cleared his throat. "Because I love you and I want to help you."

The tears slowed. Once more, I struggled, trying to find the courage to come up with the truth. I might have many new features but courage was certainly not one of them. I was more like the cowardly lion from The Wizard of Oz than the King of the Beasts. I sucked in a ragged breath and whispered. "Maybe I am turning into a mutant but I don't want anyone to know. I feel fine and I'm afraid they'll put me into an institution and study me."

We sat silent for a few minutes, me still clinging to the toilet. "I feel fine, really," I told him in an unconvincing tone.

"You don't look fine right now. In fact you look terrified."

I decided the truth at this point was the best. "I'm sick with worry."

"When did your eyes change color and how have you been able to hide it?"

"I've been wearing brown contacts since October." I could practically hear the click in Alex's head as he remembered.

"Ohhh," he said, dragging out the word. "Those odd-looking contacts that were in the car?"

"Yes," I answered guiltily, already knowing what his next question would be.

"Where did they come from? Did someone give them to you?"

"No, they were just there that day. I don't know where they came from." That was pretty nearly the truth.

"Obviously, Katherine, whoever it was knew this was going to happen to you." I could hear the frustration in his voice.

"Yes, I know that but I really don't know where to find them or who they are," I responded, still working to keep my replies as truthful as possible.

"Maybe we should go back to the park and look?"

I grabbed at his arm. He winced under the force of my touch. "No, no, please, I'm too scared." I was never going back there ever again. *What if we ran into one of those monsters?*

"Calm down," Alex requested as he pulled my hand from his arm and kissed it gently. "We don't have to do anything that you don't want to, but please promise me that you'll tell me if anything else happens. I don't want any more surprises."

"Okay," I agreed, knowing that I had already kept the most important parts of the story from him.

"Well, except for this messy biological incident you look great." Alex paused, his blue eyes still focused on my amber ones. "You know, you and Nutmeg could be twins now." He chuckled so I guessed the worst was over for now. "Are you going to tell the kids?"

My head shot up. "No. No, please, Alex."

"Okay, it'll be our secret for now but if you start getting sick again you're going back to the doctor." He laughed nervously. "You're not going to try to eat me or anything are you?"

"No, no," I said in a small voice, just barely audible. Alex had always been very perceptive even when he didn't realize it. One other thing I didn't tell him about were the cravings.

Alex hugged me. "Don't worry, we'll figure something out. I promise."

"Thank you," I said fervently, "for still loving me even though I've turned into some kind of a freak."

"I promised you forever once and you know I always keep my promises. Besides, it's kind of cool having a freaky wife."

Alex was truly too good for me. Now, I deserved him even less than I ever had before.

Chapter 4

COURAGE
AND CONSEQUENCES

It takes courage to get through life
No one ever knows until it is too late
What the consequences of that courage might be

I've had this dream many times before and it's for that reason that I know I'm dreaming now. This dream seamlessly replaced the previous one with the tents and the stalking lion. It's always exactly the same. No matter how much I try, I can never wake myself up until it's over. Once the dream is set in motion, it must play itself out. I know that soon Alex will be shaking me awake-- trying to get me to stop screaming. The anticipation causes my breathing to accelerate. And I know I'll be screaming because no matter how many times I've had this dream, I'm always terrified, as I know beyond a doubt that the stranger wants to kill me.

I'm in high spirits at the beginning of the dream. All around me are red, yellow and green Christmas lights. It's snowing and the ground is glistening all through the Dickens village of houses that surround me. I see a man in the distance, knee deep in the snow and I'm sure it's Joshua. I get excited that maybe I've found him and I quicken my pace. I stop abruptly when the man turns to face me. The soothing blue colors of his clothing do nothing to suppress the sickening feeling welling up in my stomach. The man's features, although similar, are remarkably different from my savior. The molten amber is cold, his face cheerless, and his smile cruel and mocking. The man opens his mouth to speak but all that comes out is a high-pitched squealing.

My hands automatically move to cover my ears, trying to block the noise. The man begins to run toward me, his movement a blur. My hands fly up in front of my face protectively and I hear the sound of my own voice now..." Nooo!"

*

"Katherine, Katherine, wake up!" I felt Alex's hand on my shoulder, trying to shake me into consciousness. I squelched the next scream still trying to force its way out. Alex sighed deeply and his head made a loud thumping noise as he lay back down.

"This is getting crazy. Actually, it's beyond crazy. Did you have that same dream again?" He sounded angry.

Shuddering at the memory I manage to sputter out, "Yes."

Except for this latest horrific recurring dream, my life had for the most part gone back to the pre-lion normal. The confused looks and endless questions from my family and friends had stopped. I made sure to wear the brown lenses every day and also my glasses, which made the membrane less noticeable.

My relationship with Alex had also improved over the past winter. I think after a while even he forgot about all of the weird changes. Of course, he didn't know the half of it.

Alex's irritation with me had become increasingly worse as the dream screams had become increasingly worse. No one wants to sleep next to someone who frequently wakes you up in the middle of the night, shrieking in terror. I had offered to sleep in the guest bedroom but Alex wouldn't let me. It was depressing to think about the reason for that. It wasn't because he didn't want to sleep without me. Alex told me that my screams were deafening. At least this way he didn't have to get up out of bed in order to wake me.

This morning though, it seemed that Alex was reining in his annoyance when he returned and kissed my forehead.

"I'm going to get ready for work. It's five o'clock. At least this time it wasn't at two or three. Call me if you need me."

It was only a dream, I repeated in my head over and over. I knew that this dream, just like the previous one, was probably connected to the strange people. The man in this new dream hadn't been with the others but I knew he was one of them.

Alex came back into the bedroom, interrupting my brooding, running a towel through his wet hair. "By the way...who's Joshua?"

On certain days, and this was certainly one of them, it felt like the sword of Damocles was hanging over my head.

I froze as Alex sat down on the bed. I had never told him about Joshua, first, because of the crazy factor, and second, because I was afraid he would see the adoration I felt for the beautiful man who had saved my life. My face was an open book and Alex could read it blindfolded.

I saw Alex's Adam's apple move as he swallowed. "Are you having an affair, Katherine?"

That question shook me out of my stupor. "An affair?" I yelled. I stared back at him in utter horror. "No, of course not. Why would you even think such a thing?"

"Because you say that name in your sleep all the time, especially when you're having that nightmare. Who is he? Is there a man in your dream?" There was evident pain in his face as he spoke.

Of course I was talking in my sleep. Fate was always trying to find some way to force me into telling Alex everything. I knew I had become obsessed with the memory of Joshua. It had felt natural to be in his arms and I had spent many hours fantasizing about kissing him, fantasizing about making love to him. With all my heart, I knew that I was in love with Alex, not Joshua.

I took Alex's face in my hands. "I am not having an affair. There is someone in that stupid dream but I don't know who it is."

Alex kissed me and sighed heavily. It troubled me that Alex had spent most of the past year worrying about me and that it was probably taking years off his life.

"Okay," he said gently, "get ready for work. Promise me that if anything changes with that dream, you'll tell me. I'm beginning to think it must mean something."

That was a scary thought. If the previous dream had been any indication of the future what could this new dream possibly mean? I contemplated the horrific possibilities on the drive to work.

*

It was during our two-week vacation in July, exactly thirteen months after the meeting in the park, that I came to realize what the cravings where about. On the last day of vacation we invited Lindsey and Josephine to join us for dinner.

Josephine was bringing Steven, who she had been dating now for almost three years, to join us. Alex and I liked and admired Steven tremendously.

As soon as I heard the kids arrive I warmed up the grill and lit the citronella candles. It would be a great evening to eat out on the deck. A large school of dragonflies had already assembled to entertain us with their flying antics.

I was planning to serve fish but when I removed wrapping, it smelled rancid. Alex had just bought it that morning and thought it smelled fine. I cooked it in spite of my trepidation.

Halfway through dinner, Lindsey arrived. She told us had been late because she had just come from a job interview with a company in Boston and had great news.

"They hired me on the spot." Her face was beaming. "I can start as soon as I give Johnson Publishing my two week notice."

"Oh, that's wonderful!" we all yelled in unison. "Congratulations!"

It seemed odd to me to have a job interview on a Sunday but Lindsey was thrilled to have had one at all considering the job market these days.

"I met these people at a party on Friday night and they asked me to come right away for the interview. The Stone Foundation is an organization that raises money for charitable projects around the world. The office is located in the Financial District and I can take the subway to get to work, no more long commutes." The enthusiasm poured out of her like water.

"You must have dazzled them if they decided to hire you right away." I hated myself for being so suspicious.

"Well, it was really odd, Mom. They asked many questions about my family. I really don't think that was legal but I answered them anyway."

"Umm, what did they ask?" I struggled to keep my voice calm.

"They mostly asked about you. They wanted to know how well you and I got along and how often I saw you. Their employees sometimes see a lot of devastation in the world and need a good family support system."

That seemed reasonable. Still ….Stop it, I told myself.

"Well, that's nice." I reached over and hugged her. "I hope it works out for you, sweetheart."

When dessert was over, I stood up to start cleaning but Josephine asked me to sit for one minute. She and Steven had something to tell us. Of course, my heart started racing immediately, thinking something was wrong.

"Mom, chill out, everything is fine. Steven has asked me to marry him and I've accepted. We wanted you to be the first to know."

I was relieved that there wasn't going to be another crisis for me to deal with because I was at the breaking point with my own issues.

A million things were racing through my mind at once. I immediately started peppering Josephine with questions. "When do you want to get married and where? Have you picked out your dress? When are you going to tell Steven's family?"

"In September," Josephine laughed. "We want a very small wedding. We thought we might get married out here in the back yard. Maybe rent a tent and have a small, catered wedding."

Alex and I looked at each other. I could see he was thinking the same thing I was. This was our idea of the perfect wedding: a small gathering of family and intimate friends. We spent the rest of the night making plans.

That night signaled a momentous change for my family but it also marked another physical change for me. From that night on, foods such as vegetables and bread became increasingly unappealing to me. We purchased our beef from a local farm and it was always very fresh and as a result extremely bloody. I found myself overwhelmed by the smell each time I opened one of their sealed plastic bags. It drew me in, filling my mouth with saliva, leaving a faint metallic taste on my tongue. I began eating small portions of the raw meat before I would cook it.

Of course, eating the raw meat was disturbing but harmless. The more horrendous part of all this was that people were starting to smell like food to me also, especially Alex. Whenever I was close to him, especially when we made love, I noticed that he smelled extra good.

I don't mean good in a cologne kind of way but in a thick juicy steak kind of way. I couldn't stop myself from licking his skin any time we made love.

"Ow! What're you doing, baby?" Alex asked breathlessly during one such event. "You're getting carried away; really, I don't mind you biting but try not to draw any blood."

I was appalled at myself and couldn't apologize enough. "I'm so sorry. You know how excited I get when you're kissing me like this."

Alex took that as a compliment. The wound healed quickly but I noticed that his blood was even more delicious than the animal blood.

Coincidentally, the August issue of National Geographic had a story about the myths surrounding man-eating lions with many details about carnivore morphology. All meat eaters, but lions in particular, had a type of molar called a carnassial. I sat stunned staring at the pictures, trying to come to grips with what I was seeing on the glossy pages. The carnivore teeth and mine were identical. Maybe I was turning into a lion. I had been bitten by one. What if I started to eat people? Ugh! That would be worse than being a vampire. Why couldn't I have met one of them in the woods that day? At least Alex would have been able to easily kill me if he had to.

I bought as many books as I could find on the subject of lions. My research uncovered many similarities such as the exceptionally keen vision and the ability to see in the pitch dark and most notably the higher body temperature.

I knew that I was extra strong now, like a lion, and I wasn't as clumsy as I had been. Of course, to Alex's dismay I was still breaking things. One time I had pulled on the garden hose to unwind it and had accidently pulled the copper pipe out of the house. Alex had to spend a whole day fixing the mess.

I put the books and my fears away to keep for the future as I now had a more pressing event to concentrate on--Josephine's wedding. Except for the continuing nightmare with Mr. Creepy Crawly, it was the perfect distraction for me.

Fall slipped uneventfully into winter and before long there was snow covering the lawns. It was at Christmas that Josephine and Steven announced that they were pregnant and would be expecting a baby in June. It would be our first grandchild.

After the holidays, Alex and I went to the Maine for a three-day winter getaway. Maine was very quiet in January; no traffic or throngs of people making lots of noise and I could usually find the bargain of the century in one of the antique shops.

We returned from our Maine trip on a Sunday and although we went to sleep early, we were still late for work the next morning because Alex persuaded me to linger in bed, not that it took much convincing on my part.

"Ugh!" I complained as Alex pulled his Mazda out into the slow moving line of cars on Route 119. "The traffic will be awful this morning."

"It was worth it. I'll be smiling all day. The people in manufacturing will be wondering what's wrong with me."

"You're not going to tell them, are you?" I asked, pretending to be appalled.

Alex laughed impishly. "Don't worry, Mrs. Chambers, your virtue is safe with me."

"Good." How lucky was I to have Alex in my life.

I lay back against the headrest, planning to reminisce about our long weekend. It had snowed the night before and the temperature was still below freezing. Actually, it had snowed just about every day this winter. The piles at the end of the driveway were well above eight feet and we still had February and March to get through. The sanded roads didn't do much to alleviate the bad driving conditions. The car skidded lightly whenever Alex tapped on the brakes bringing forth a barrage of complaints about the weather and his usual threats about moving south. Soon after the first winter though, I realized that the snow acted as sort of muffler against all the extraneous noise and I loved it. While Alex dreamed of Florida, I dreamed of Alaska.

On the way, we chatted aimlessly about our trip and about Alex's upcoming retirement plans. His retirement at sixty two was just two years away. Alex longed to spend endless hours playing with his sports cars.

I was doing my best to block out all the residual noise and pay attention to Alex, but a loud high-pitched squealing kept breaking into my concentration. The noise reminded me of the sound of a cappuccino maker. Maybe the noise was coming from the Dunkin' Donuts at the intersection we were about to cross.

In that split second that it took for Alex to put on the left turn signal, I knew that the now earsplitting noise was the same noise as in my nightmare.

"Alex, Alex," I shouted, "slow down!" Alex shot me a curious glance.

"Why? The light's green. I can't stop in the middle of the intersection, Katherine."

I turned to my right, to where the sound was the loudest and saw the bright blue automobile that was heading directly for us. "Nooooo!" I screamed. My hands flew up automatically to the side window, palms out. I tucked my chin into my neck, bracing for the impact that I was sure would kill us both.

*

The two immense objects twisted and ground against each other producing the raw sound of metal against metal, followed by utter silence. Traffic in the intersection came to a dead stop. The acrid smell of burning brake pads filled the air. I could hear the beep, beep, beep of cell phones being dialed.

The oncoming car had slammed into the passenger side of the Mazda with enough force to throw us across the wide intersection and up onto the sidewalk. I gasped as I realized that the car door had molded itself around my body. Somewhere in the distance sirens wailed

I felt surprisingly unharmed and as the concern for my own safely faded, I turned to check on Alex. He wasn't moving. His head was slumped over the distorted steering wheel.

"Alex, Alex, are you okay? Please say something."

Alex didn't make a sound. Even a groan would have been comforting.

Blood dripped from his forehead. There was a police officer looking in though the broken window on Alex's side of the mangled car. The driver's side of the Mazda was up against the signpost that stood in front of the donut shop.

I had looked at that landmark every day on the trip back and forth from work for the past twenty years. The two large pieces of granite holding the advertizing boards in place didn't look damaged at all.

"Hello, miss, I'm Officer Nelson. The fire department is here and the ambulance is on the way. Try to stay calm." He stared at me for a long moment. "How badly are you injured? Are you bleeding anywhere?"

"No, not at all," and I knew that was the case. I could only smell Alex's blood. "My husband, he's unconscious. Please, he needs medical assistance!"

Officer Nelson looked at Alex with a pained grimace. "The fire department is going to remove you both from the vehicle but we're waiting for the ambulance."

I probably could have ripped the door off and gotten us both out but I was afraid of making a public spectacle of myself. I put my hands up and covered my face. What was wrong with me? How selfish could I possibly be? My husband lay critically injured not three feet from me and all I could think of was what people would think.

Alex's door had not been crushed as badly as mine had and was quickly opened by two rather large firefighters and several crowbars. I watched as they lifted him onto the gurney and placed a stabilizing device on his head, and then loaded up the sides with ice packs.

It was maddening to wait through the blizzard of grinding and cutting noises before I was free. Everyone involved in the rescue operation was amazed at how well I had fared, not even a scratch. Maybe I should have been more careful as I got out of the car with news media gathering footage for tonight's broadcast but I didn't care what the cameras might have caught. Alex was injured and my only thought was to get to him.

I waited through the longest hour of my life outside the operating room until a middle-aged doctor, who introduced himself as Dr. Henley, came to talk to me.

"Your husband hit his head and has what we refer to as an open skull fracture. The CT scan showed a lesion that we were able to remove during the surgery as well as multiple pieces of glass. He has a very high level of intracranial pressure. We've inserted a device to drain the excess fluid." The doctor paused. "Can you grasp what I'm telling you, Mrs. Chambers?"

I answered woodenly, staring past him into the abyss of my ruined life. "Of course, fluid drain. I understand."

Dr. Henley continued, his voice stoic, "We've induced a coma using a drug called pentobarbital. We don't want him thrashing around, causing more injury."

Dr. Henley paused again, waiting for me to speak but I didn't. What else was there to say? Having a Ph.D. in biology I knew that Alex's life was in grave danger

"We're doing everything that we can for your husband," Dr. Henley said, taking my hands in his.

"What are his chances of surviving?"

"The chances are not good. If there are any immediate family members…" the doctor took deep breath, "you might want to think about calling them now."

"Call… call the family?" I stuttered.

"Yes. Why don't you sit here in my office for now? We're going to transfer your husband to another area of the ER. I'll come get you in a while." I nodded, not able to budge an inch. My mind was stunned. How could this be happening?

I was shocked when the doctor led me down into a small room with dingy white walls and faded yellow blinds. If I hadn't recognized the tattoo on Alex's arm from his service in Vietnam, I would have told the hospital staff that they had the wrong person. Alex's stained yellow head was devoid of any hair. Wrapped several times around the perimeter of his skull was a wide piece of gauze. Clear tubing snaked its way out from the gauze and down along his shoulder, disappearing under his smock. His skin was a gray chalky white, the color of a corpse.

There was only one visitor's chair in the room. I stumbled into it and began pressing buttons on my cell phone. I called Lindsey and Josephine and my brother in New York. Alex had no siblings and his parents had been gone for years now.

I tried to explain to the girls what had happened, but even I wasn't sure. It wasn't Alex's fault but at this point what did it matter whose fault it was.

The nurse brought me dinner but I was too sick to eat. At around seven that night, Officer Nelson came by to check on Alex and speak to me about my version of the accident. I couldn't tell him much but I was curious about the other driver, though.

"The boy is only twenty-two years old," Officer Nelson explained. "He just graduated from college in the top of his class and has a good driving record. According to the statement he gave, he stepped on the brakes as hard as he could when the car began to accelerate but he couldn't stop it. The brakes had actually caught on fire and were still smoldering when the fire department arrived. The investigators assigned to the accident don't doubt the boy's account."

"How bad was the boy hurt?"

"He has a severe back injury. The doctors don't think he'll ever be able to walk again."

Maybe it was one of those weird problems that had been in the news lately about cars accelerating on their own. I didn't ask what make the car was and I was in no condition to feel pain for anyone else at the moment.

Officer Nelson hesitated on his next question.

"Is that all you needed?" I hoped that if I answered his questions he would leave soon. As frustrating as it was not to know the cause of the accident, it wasn't important right now.

"Well," he replied anxiously. "It was astounding that you weren't injured at all. You were very lucky. The car molded around you, protecting you."

I smiled ruefully at the officer. "It's not a crime to be lucky, is it?"

Officer Nelson shook his head. "No, not at all, but…"

I cut him off before he could go on. "Please, officer, my husband is gravely ill. Can't this wait for some other time?"

"I'm sorry. Of course." He handed me his card and promised to return tomorrow to check on Alex.

I didn't leave Alex's side the entire night as I moved in and out of sleep, waking each time to the hope that this had all been one of my nightmares. The nurse came by to clean the fluid drain and surprised me, telling me it was morning. I had barely noticed that the sky had changed to a brighter dull gray. Alex's condition had not improved. In fact, it had changed for the worse over the past several hours. His heart rate didn't sound as steady as it had been earlier in the night.

I shoved my hands in my pants pockets and slowly wandered down the hall to the restroom. I would have to make a trip to the supermarket before the end of the day. The cravings were getting difficult to suppress and I had begun to formulate an excuse to leave once the kids arrived and could stay with Alex for me.

I kept my head down the entire way to the ladies room, making sure I didn't meet anyone's gaze, hoping to avoid any small talk.

Thankfully the bathroom was empty. I pulled out one of the contacts and stared at the image in the mirror. Even in grief the reflection showed signs of a stunning beauty. I wondered who it was that was really inside this body. It certainly wasn't the same person that it had been born with. I stared back at the stranger and asked what the purpose was to all of this. Was there something I could have done to prevent this? Maybe if I had been thinking faster I could have forced Alex to stop or if I been driving. I put my hands up to the sides of my head and shook it. God-fearing people believe that everything happens for a reason. I couldn't fathom any sane reason for all the events that had happened to me. I popped the contact back in, refusing to think about this anymore. The nurse should be done by now.

I walked out into the foyer and caught sight of two men dressed in white lab coats coming out of Alex's room. They headed down the corridor in the opposite direction from me. I assumed they were doctors as they each had a stethoscope wrapped around their necks as well as masks partially over their faces. They ducked into one of the rooms further down. Something about the way they walked seemed familiar.

I shook my head. I couldn't allow my paranoia to distract me now. I hadn't had much sleep over the past twenty-four hours and I knew it was making me loopy.

The smell of honeysuckle hit me like a wrecking ball as soon as I crossed the threshold. I let out an involuntary gasp and gripped the doorjamb with enough force to leave finger marks in the wood. The nurse looked up when she heard me, but turned quickly away, back to adjusting one of the monitors positioned beside Alex's bed. "Sorry," she said apologetically, "we haven't started yet. I'm still waiting for my assistant. Did you go to the cafeteria? They're only serving breakfast until ten today. You look pale. Some food might be good for you."

I glared at her furiously. "Who were those doctors that were in here? Did they say or do anything to Alex?"

The nurse looked at me blankly. "I've been the only one here since you left." She went back to fiddling with the monitor, ignoring my glare.

My hands were shaking as I walked over to stand next to her. I grabbed her left wrist tightly. "I saw two men walk out of this room. They were dressed like doctors. What were they doing in here?"

She struggled away from me. I could see the crazed look on my face from the reflection in her eyes. "You're going to break my wrist."

I let go of her immediately. "I'm …I'm, sorry." I turned and left, probably too quickly but I was certain that I knew who the two doctors were and I needed to find them before they got away.

I followed the smell into the room where I had seen the two men go. On the floor was a white pile of clothing. I ran back into the foyer and down the narrow corridor, banging into people and objects that lined the crowded way. The scent led me to the stairwell and down all five floors into the parking garage. I could even tell the point at which they had gotten into their car and driven away.

My heart felt like it had dropped into my stomach. I fell to my knees on the cold garage floor, throwing my glasses to the ground with little care while I cried uncontrollably.

My saviors had been within my reach. They had passed within a few feet of me. Why didn't they talk to me? What had they been doing in Alex's room? A million crazy ideas ran through my head at once.

I don't know how long I'd sat like that when I felt someone touch my shoulder. I looked up, hoping beyond hope that it was Joshua, but knowing it wasn't. The honeysuckle smell had just about faded. It was Doctor Henley. His voice was full of empathy as he spoke.

"Are you okay, Mrs. Chambers? The nurse told me you were having somewhat of a …breakdown. We have counselors on call day and night if you think you'd like to speak to someone."

The doctor peered intently at my eyes. "Is there something wrong with your eyes?" I knew the brown contacts were in, concealing the unusual color, but without the glasses he could clearly see the membrane.

I put my both hands over my face and mumbled, "No. They're swollen from all the crying. I did have a small breakdown but I'm fine now. Please forgive me." I felt around on the ground for my eyeglasses, but before I could find them myself, Dr. Henley was handing them to me.

I put the glasses on and continued to face the floor, hiding from the doctor's view.

"There's nothing to forgive. It's understandable when you have a loved one that is gravely ill. Please, let's go back upstairs to my office. I need to talk to you about the results." Dr. Henley held onto my arm to steady me while he led us to the elevator. It was quiet ride up to the fifth floor.

Even though I thought I was prepared for them, the doctor's words were still a shock. Alex was going to die sooner than expected. The EEG showed the brain activity had slowed dramatically. The surgical team couldn't stop the swelling in his brain. It felt like a train had hit me. How had my completely unremarkable life come to such a tragic end?

Somehow, through all the tears, I managed to find my way back to Alex. I sat down on the bed and took his cold limp hand in mine. I couldn't endure losing him. What would I do without him? I hadn't even gotten a chance to say goodbye.

Lindsey, Josephine and Steven arrived soon after Alex's doctor had given me the devastating news, but they could do nothing to console me. I cancelled my previous idea of a trip to the supermarket. I couldn't afford to miss the last few hours of my time with Alex.

The ventilator that kept Alex breathing made a moist whooshing sound. I kept my mind occupied and calm as I counted the seconds in between each breath. It comforted me that at least Alex was asleep and not in any pain.

I listened helplessly as the stuttering of Alex's heartbeats grew more and more indistinct. Alex was pronounced dead at 1:16 that afternoon.

We were not going to get our forever after all.

Chapter 5
WHEN WE MEET AGAIN

Adam alone in Paradise did grieve,
And thought Eden a desert without Eve,
Until God pitying of his lonesome state,
Crowned all of his wishes with a loving mate.

~ *Mary Gates 1776*

I've had this dream many times before and it's for that reason that I know I'm dreaming now. As with the other dreams before, this dream seamlessly replaced the previous one-, the one with the dangerous stranger and the flashing Christmas lights. Like all the others, this one is always exactly the same.

"Dream" is really not the right word to use as it suggests something pleasant. This dream is so much more a horror movie than the others were. Except this horror movie can't be shut off when it gets to the scary parts. No matter how hard I try, I never wake up until it's over. Once set in motion it must play itself out. I hope that Alex will be shaking me awake soon-, trying to get me to stop screaming. The anticipation causes my breathing to accelerate.

The dream begins cheerfully, in a field of flowers, huge blue chrysanthemums. Hmm--I can smell the garlic mixed in with the faint odor of vinegar, olive oil and oregano. I can hear dishes clanging and a din of voices. The swirling wind is cold. Lindsey and Josephine are with me but it's from the past when they were ten or twelve. Lindsey's long brown hair is braided and tied in bows. Josephine's long red hair falls gracefully to her shoulders, its natural ringlets bouncing in rhythm to her every movement. The girls are running back and forth laughing and giggling to themselves, as children do, not a care in the world.

Then there's a sudden change in the light and I watch through squinted lids as Josephine and Lindsey disappear through a doorway on the far side of the field. Their small hands wave to me, taking the enjoyable part of the dream with them.

I'm aware of something cradled in my left arm, something soft and pink that I hold on to protectively. A thick smoky haze envelopes me, and even squinting I'm not able to see through it. The pleasant smells from earlier in the dream have now changed to an unpleasant caustic smell reminiscent of burning plastic. I begin to stumble around, desperately looking for the girls.

That's when I see it. It's exactly the same as the one I had seen in the park so very long ago. The same exact one that Nathaniel had beheaded. The monster stalks deliberately toward me and I can see the hunger to kill in its burning amber eyes. I try to find some place to stash the object I'm holding, but it's too late. The demon closes in on me.

*

My body jerked, automatically reaching out for Alex, but my search produced only bunched up sheets. I turned to look anyway. Alex wasn't there and would never be beside me again. I exhaled heavily in disgust. Why did I keep torturing myself like this?

The remaining sweat, caused by the terror of the dream, dripped down my forehead and mixed in with the streaming tears. This was the third and the latest of my strange recurring dreams. Against all of my rational beliefs, I knew the dreams were connected to the events that had occurred in my life over the past two years. The first one with the lion had come partially true. Although I hadn't been able to figure out what role Lindsey had played. That dream stopped the day after I encountered the lion. The second dream, which had begun immediately after the first, stopped right after the accident. There was no car in that dream, only Mr. Creepy Crawly, whom I didn't know but had menaced me in the dream.

My heart rate began to spike as I wondered if this latest dream meant that one of those hideous demons would be coming after my children. How would I make sure that never happened? I didn't know anything about them or the people with the lion.

As I lay in my bed, the familiar pain that had become like a drug, swept over me, and I let it willingly pull me under. I was full of guilt because I knew Alex's life could have been saved and also because even in grief, I still found myself lustful for Joshua.

Dante believed that in the afterlife there was a price to be paid for everything---whether one willing or unknowing engaged in the forbidden activity. Maybe he had been wrong and payment was due in advance.

Lindsey and Josephine took turns staying with me during and after the funeral but after a few weeks, I could see the sacrifice they were making and how I was overdosing them with Mom time. They had their own lives to live, and besides, with Alex gone there was only one thing that I wanted to do. Except how do you search for someone who could move at the speed of light and materialize through invisible doors?

I made myself go back to work and stay busy, keeping up a normal appearance for the girls. It takes more courage to stand still than to run away even though I desperately wanted to get in my car and drive as far away from my life as possible,

The worst part of the first day back at work was not being there without Alex, as I had thought. No the worst part was walking out to my car at the end of the day to the smell of honeysuckle. I knew my super-natural friends were watching me. I lingered past quitting time, eager for them to talk to me, but left alone, as I would every night. What were they afraid of? I certainly had kept their existence a secret even though they hadn't asked me.

My stitch group was happy to have me back again. At night, I tried to watch my favorite science fiction movies, but they no longer held the same interest as they had in the past. I was the science fiction story now.

April brought with it the warmer weather and Lindsey invited me to visit her in Boston. I told myself that this would be a good way to spend time with my daughter. Alex's death had made me realize how short life really was and that I needed to make the most of my time with my family.

Before leaving work for Lindsey's apartment, I changed into the outfit that Josephine had picked out for me on a previous shopping trip. I really didn't need more clothes but Josephine thought new attire would improve my outlook. I didn't have the heart to tell her that nothing of this world would do that.

I groaned and complained the whole way, reminding myself that if I had been brave enough to live through a demon attack I certainly could find the nerve to drive into Boston to see my daughter.

When Lindsey had moved away from our small town into the state capital, I had sternly objected. In addition to the safety factor, the rent was outrageous but Lindsey was good with her finances and had been able to manage.

I arrived early and waited in the car, trying to listen to one of my audio books over the brain crushing rush hour noise. By the time Lindsey pulled up, I was in the middle of my cry-athon. Not wanting to ruin the mood for our night, I tried to rearrange my expression. But I had never been good at hiding my emotions and one look at my face told it all.

Lindsey hugged me closely as we walked together arm in arm down the steps into her place, which was decorated like a page out of the Pottery Barn catalog. I was glad that she had her own style and different from mine. Ever since I was a young girl, I was a collector of old stuff. I grew up in an area populated with over fifty multi-family homes. On trash day, my brother and I would take our red wagons and comb up and down the street for treasures. My mother scowled every time she saw what we had found. She only saw the junk in it all but I saw gold.

Lindsey jolted me out of my trance. "I love that outfit on you." She paused and then added, "By the way, do we have an anti-aging gene or something?"

"I'm not sure what's going on," I told her apprehensively. "I'm sure I'll start looking my age soon enough. But please," I said making a joke, "I don't want to rush it." I wasn't sure what I was going to tell her in ten years when I still looked the same and I knew beyond a doubt that I would. Fortunately, she changed the subject. Unfortunately, she switched to an even less desirable topic.

"Mom, you really need to move on with your life. Alex wouldn't want you sitting around moping all the time and he certainly wouldn't want you to spend the rest of your life alone. You really should think about dating again."

"Dating? It's too soon for me to start dating!" I shrieked.

"Okay, okay" Lindsey said, putting her hands up to stop my melodramatic reaction. "I'm going to get dressed for dinner."

I poured two glasses of wine and settled down on the couch. Everything Lindsey had said about Alex was true. We had discussed many times what our wishes were if something were to ever happen to one of us but I couldn't imagine that I would ever find someone to love the way I loved Alex. Shame that bordered on disgust swept over me as I took into account all the fantasies I had had about Joshua, even while Alex was still alive. I poured myself a second glass of wine and gulped it down before Lindsey came back.

Lindsey joined me when she was dressed and we sat talking while she drank her wine. It was apparent that she loved working at the Stone Foundation. In addition she had found a new best friend in the owner's sister, who was about the same age. They did everything together -- shopping, going to the movies, socializing. I was glad for her new career and friendship. She seemed genuinely happy.

Even though I didn't want to ask this question, especially at the risk of directing the subject towards me again, the mother in me couldn't resist. "Have you been seeing anyone lately?"

Lindsey frowned, "No, I was thinking that I should try dating older men. The men my age are very immature. I need someone more responsible, more serious."

I laughed. "It won't be any different. Men never mature no matter how old they are." Of course I was one to talk. Lindsey's dates weren't sitting home watching re-runs of *Buffy the Vampire Slayer*.

"Actually, there is someone that I'm interested in," she hesitated for a short moment, "but it's too early yet for me to tell you about him."

I nodded and before I could comment further, Lindsey stood up and suggested that it was time to head off to the art show. I guess neither of us wanted to explore our dating prospects any further. While we were getting our jackets on Lindsey asked, "Would you mind if my new pal from work joined us for dinner? I would really like you to meet her." That was a good sign if she wanted me to meet her friend. I had been wondering if Lindsey had begun to regret inviting me after my outburst.

The art show on Newbury Street was crowded, much to my disappointment. We spent a few minutes with the artist and then the next hour appraising the paintings. I was anxious to be done with this part of the night. I didn't like being around groups of people. They always asked too many questions. It was uncomfortable for both Lindsey and me when people would comment on how much we looked like sisters.

Our next stop was the recent exhibition of artifacts from ancient Assyria at the Boston Museum of Fine Arts. My mood perked up considerably as we walked the short distance from the art gallery to the MFA. Getting lost among ancient relics would be great therapy.

The attendant at the front desk said that it would take one hour to see the entire exhibit. Lindsey suggested that we do that first. Her friend was running late and had previously seen the exhibit anyway. We would have dinner together at the museum café when she arrived.

Lindsey and I strolled through all the eye-catching displays of Assyrian masterpieces, stopping to read the information about each one and the ancient people who created them. I knew Lindsey was bored but she put on a good show for me.

One theme that was present throughout the exhibit was the amount of reverence the Assyrians had for lions, even worshipping them as gods. Nearly every carving or tapestry had some image of a lion. As we moved further along into the exhibit, I began to feel edgy. It was a coincidence, I told myself. Many ancient cultures worshipped animals. What was my problem? Everything was not always about me. Just because a lion had bitten me didn't mean that all lion-related genre was a conspiracy.

Reason as I might, paranoia at the thought of being watched began to settle in. I turned around several times, staring intently at some of the other faces in the room but the one I was looking for was nowhere to be found.

Thankfully, Lindsey didn't notice my panic attack. Half way through the exhibit, she ran into some friends and struck up a conversation. When you lived in a crowded metropolis, you automatically had many friends.

I could count my friends on one hand, and I liked it that way. Then again, who would want to be friends with me? I was such a grump. Try to look like you're having fun, I reminded myself.

While Lindsey was talking, I drifted aimlessly into the last room of the exhibit and settled down on one of the benches. The thick stone walls of the museum worked to keep out a vast amount of the noise from the city. I was drunk with the silence. I folded my hands together and bowed my head, letting my eyes follow the random patterns in the floor tiles. Even though Lindsey was not as interested in ancient civilizations as I was and wouldn't mind if I went ahead, I didn't want to rush my time with her.

Two other museum visitors joined me in the empty room. I could hear them quietly talking about the piece they were inspecting. The man remarked to his companion about how interesting it was the way the sculptor had positioned the lion. He loved the sensual way in which the animal was bending down to bite the man's neck.

I whirled around and froze in horror as I took in the carving. "Oh... My...God...!" I shrieked, dragging each word out slowly.

The man and woman stared at me, annoyed at my outburst and walked into the adjacent room. I didn't watch them leave. My attention was locked on the ancient abomination.

The carving was a perfect replica of the scene that day in the state park--the lion bending over a person, a man in this case, one paw on his neck, gently holding on and bending down to the bite the other side. The lion in the carving had an object with two crescents positioned on its forehead just like my lion. The plaque to the right of the carving showed an origination date circa eighth century BC.

"Eighth century BC?" It was over two thousand years old. I couldn't catch my breath. The room was swirling in a vortex. I gripped the marble seat with both hands, trying to steady myself without causing any damage. I was thankful that I could still hear Lindsey in the other room. She would be alarmed if she saw me going to pieces like this, especially in such a public place.

I waited for the spinning to slow and got to my feet, my plan to find the nearest ladies' room. The spinning began again when I was halfway across the room and I knew I was only seconds away from hitting the floor.

Then from out of nowhere, something touched my arm, steadying me. Sweet honeysuckle poured around me and I knew instantly that it was the same iron grip that had reached out for me so long ago in the woods.

I turned, staring wide-eyed at Joshua, my emotions on a roller coaster ride. My first reaction was joy at seeing him, followed by relief that I had finally found him. Then confusion, disbelief and finally anger set in. I opened my mouth but no sound came out.

You idiot! Focus, before he's gone again. Then I had an awful thought: what if this was a hallucination? A horrible cruel game my mind was playing on me? Maybe I was actually dreaming again. I did have a difficult time telling reality from the dreams.

Joshua's smile widened. "This isn't a dream, Katherine. I'm really here." He laughed softly as he spoke. "Wow, you look, umm, phenomenal. I love your outfit. I've never seen you so dressed up."

The tone of his voice charmed me to the point that I couldn't concentrate on what he was saying. "What? You've … you've … you've what?"

"You look really beautiful, tonight."

Before I could stammer out any more ridiculous comments, I heard another familiar voice from behind me; it was Nathaniel. "Hello, Katherine, it's nice to see you."

My answering words were like daggers. "What did you two do to me?"

Nathaniel frowned angrily. "Against all reasoning we saved your life. It would be nice if you had some appreciation for that fact."

My first instinct was to attack him and beat him silly but I reminded myself that I was in a public place with my daughter. I took a deep breath instead.

"I told you she would be remarkable." Joshua beamed.

I ignored his remark.

"Do you have any idea what I've been going through?"

"The same thing we all went through," Nathaniel replied in the same angry tone.

"Please, Nathaniel," Joshua pleaded, "you're not helping. Give me a minute here to straighten things out with Katherine. Go find Lindsey and Cassie."

Nathaniel scoffed. "It will take more than a minute to fix this mess. I told you this was a bad idea." He gave me an irritated look then turned toward the room where Lindsey was.

"Lindsey?" I tried to follow but Joshua held me. "Why is he getting Lindsey?"

"Lindsey is fine, don't worry." The smile was still plastered across Joshua's face.

"Why… why are you here and where have you been for the last two years?"

"Well, hello to you, too. I've missed you. I'm very happy to see you. For a moment it looked like you were happy to see me." He had the audacity to wink at me.

"This is not funny. I have a million questions and I want some answers," I demanded, stomping my foot and balling my hands into fists.

Joshua snickered at my tirade. "Which question would you like answered first?"

"What has happened to my …?" I couldn't finish the sentence.

Joshua quickly lost his teasing air as my tears welled up.

"I'm sorry, Katherine. Please forgive me. I've forgotten how confusing all of this must be to you." He removed a pack of tissues from his top pocket and dabbed at my cheeks.

I could hear Nathaniel's voice behind me talking and laughing. I turned toward the sound and to my alarm Cassandra, the sister, the young girl who was with them that day in the park, had one arm wrapped around Lindsey's.

"Oh… my… god," I said for the second time. This was Lindsey's new best friend: Joshua and Nathaniel's sister. What was going on? I didn't recall Lindsey telling me her friend's name.

I put my free hand up to my forehead and rubbed. My eyelids were opened so wide that I wondered how it was that my eyeballs hadn't fallen out. I was furious that Nathaniel had the nerve to be speaking to my daughter and I was anxious, not knowing if she was in any danger from him.

Lindsey came up to me happy as could be until she looked more closely. "Hi, Mom, how're you doing? You look as white as a ghost. Do you have a migraine? Should I take you home?" She fluttered around me, not sure if she should touch me or not.

"No, no," I said in a muffled voice.

Then she noticed Joshua holding my arm. "Do you know my mother, Mr. Stone?" Joshua began to release me but when he did, I swayed. He grasped my arm again. "Yes, as a matter of fact I do. Your mother gave us a tour of her laboratory one day during a business meeting." I had to admit he was a good actor.

How could I have missed this? Talk about being clueless. Lindsey's new job was working for Joshua and Nathaniel. They were the Stone Foundation owners?

"Oh," Lindsey replied. "Wow, I guess it's a small world."

Nathaniel agreed. "Yes, it really is, isn't it?" I glared at him, too upset to hide my disgust for him.

Lindsey looked bewildered and embarrassed by my reaction. At this point, there was a real possibility of my having a breakdown. Even though I had a million questions, I knew that I needed to get out of that room. I was not a very good actor. Nathaniel turned and drew Lindsey's attention from my panic attack. "Joshua, Cassie and I were planning to go to Mistral for a party. We would be honored if you and your mother would join us. Have you had dinner yet?"

"No, actually we haven't," Lindsey replied, quickly wrapping her arm around mine and leading me away from the three of them.

When we were out of what she thought was ear reach she said, "Mom, these are my bosses and Cassie is one of my best friends. They are extremely well connected. This party is at one of the nicest places in Boston. Please say we can go. I promise we won't stay too long. Besides, we need to have dinner." The longing on her face was more than I could resist.

"We would love to go," Lindsey said happily when we returned to the waiting trio. I continued to glare at the three of them.

Joshua turned to Nathaniel, giving him a disapproving look that I didn't understand. "Nathaniel maybe you could bring the car around to the front of the museum? The girls and I will meet you there."

"Sure, why not," Nathaniel grumbled and walked quickly out of the room.

Maybe it was my imagination but Nathaniel seemed to be mad at me. As far as I was concerned, I was the only one who had a reason to be mad.

Cassie grabbed Lindsey's arm once again. "Let's go. This will be a load of fun." Lindsey was beaming. She was definitely in her element.

When the girls were out of sight, Joshua took my hand in his. He held it up to his lips, gently kissing my palm. A shiver passed up my arm but I ignored it and swiftly pulled my hand away. "Please don't do that. I don't know you well enough for you to touch me in any way."

Joshua sighed. "I did save your life."

"Technically, you didn't do anything but get me injured." I snapped out loud.

I would have continued to reprimand him but several other museum visitors had begun to wander into the room.

"Maybe we should move along," he suggested taking hold of my hand again in spite of my previous request.

This time I didn't protest as our hands locked effortlessly into place. Joshua's skin temperature matched mine perfectly. The cool touch of my family and friends was always uncomfortable and I struggled constantly not to pull away whenever I touched them. This felt natural.

While we were walking, I replied to his earlier comment, keeping my voice low. I knew he could still hear me. "I am grateful to be alive but I'm not sure you did me a favor. What has happened to me?"

Joshua gently rubbed the inside of my hand with his thumb in a soothing manner. "I know you have many questions. We can talk after we get to the restaurant."

My voice was heavy with despair as I explained to him, "I thought I was going crazy. Why did you save my life only to walk away and leave me all alone? I've been hoping every day that you would come back to find me. I saw you at the hospital when Alex was...and I know you were outside my work. I could...smell you." I was embarrassed at admitting such a silly thing.

"Yes, Nathaniel and I were there at the hospital. We had seen the coverage of the accident on the news. It was awful. I'm sorry we couldn't save Alex for you. I know how much you loved him. I hated leaving you in the dark but I had made a promise not to interfere with the human part of your life until it was over."

His confession that I was no longer human gave me the strength to pull away from his hold. Irrational anger overtook me, causing me to lash out. "Oh, really, you just about get me killed by some monster, then you have your lion friend bite me and turn me into a ..." I spluttered ... "a whatever and then, you hire my daughter to work for you! What exactly is your definition of not interfering in someone's life?"

"I'm sorry about everything. The events in the forest happened before we had time to think through the ramifications," Joshua admitted. "Hiring your daughter was Nathaniel's idea. He thought we would be able to keep an eye on you, through her. You know she talks a lot about you. She has a lot of respect and admiration for you."

This declaration stopped me for a moment. My relationship with Lindsey was comparable to the poles of a magnet--she the positive, me the negative. We had a strong bond but opposite properties which had made for a rocky childhood. It had just recently started to improve. As soon as I recovered, I realized that Joshua was probably trying to distract me, and that made me even madder. I shouted at him, not concerned any more about being overheard. "I want you to fire her tomorrow. I don't need any one keeping an eye on me and I don't want either of you anywhere near her."

Joshua looked puzzled. "Why would we do that, Katherine? We like Lindsey. She's a hard worker. This is a great job for her and she's very happy working for us. You don't have to worry. We aren't dangerous. No harm will come to her."

One of the museum associates began to walk towards us, probably to see what all the commotion was about but Joshua towed me swiftly out the front entrance.

I froze when I stepped through the revolving door. Seriously, for someone that supposedly had above average intelligence there was so much that I had missed. Sitting in front of the museum was a Mustang--the same Mustang that I had parked beside two years ago.

"Cool, I love this car," Lindsey said as she bounded down the stairs.

Joshua wrapped his arm around my waist. "Everything will be okay, Katherine. Take some deep breaths. Try to keep it together for a while."

The girls sat with me in the back seat babbling away, discussing the unimportant details about their outfits-, where they had bought them and the shoes they had chosen to wear.

I stared out the window trying to keep the tears from overflowing. The despair felt like a one-ton block sitting on my chest. I concentrated on not throwing up. I chuckled darkly to myself that it would serve Nathaniel and Joshua right if I did make a mess of their nice shiny car.

Nathaniel turned and scowled at me. Joshua hit his brother's arm and he reluctantly turned back toward the front of the car.

I had yearned painfully for some answers these last two years. Now I was scared to death to get them. Ignorance is bliss, as the saying goes. Did I really want to know what had happened to me? Would the truth make things worse? Probably. In my experience that was usually the way life worked.

We had a short walk to the club from the parking garage. Joshua and I trailed behind while the girls went ahead with Nathaniel, one on each side, their arms looped around his. It worried me to see her that close to him.

I pulled my eyes away from Lindsey as I felt Joshua's intense stare. I wished he would stop; it made me very uncomfortable.

"I'm sorry," Joshua said, gushing, "I'm worried that if I take my eyes off you, you'll disappear."

I didn't answer him because I was afraid to admit that that was exactly how I felt. I made myself rein in my apprehension and concentrate on the obvious. For example, the eyeglasses and the same brown contacts that they were obviously wearing. Joshua answered my question before I could ask it. "Yes, we're all wearing the same contacts as you. Our eye color raises too many questions with the humans."

"Humans?" I replied. Panic leaking through my voice. "I'm really not human anymore?"

"Calm down, Katherine, I promise I will explain everything. Take some more deep breaths."

"Okay, okay." Even with the extra breathing it was difficult to remain calm.

Halfway to the club we crossed to the other side of the road coincidently just before we came face to face with a man walking two very large Rottweilers.

"Are you afraid of the dogs?"

Joshua laughed. "Definitely not. We try to avoid confrontations with other animals. I'm quite certain that man would be upset if I injured his pets."

"Oh," I said bearing in mind the reaction of Nancy's dog.

"Other animals don't like us," I confirmed, gritting my teeth, wishing I had thought more carefully before using the word "us." I refused to accept that I was part of his merry little band of freaks.

"That's correct. Other species have much more heightened senses than humans and most perceive us as predators. Felines, on the other hand, are strongly attracted to us, drawn by our scent."

I nodded. Maybe that was why I found myself attracted to him. I felt Joshua squeeze my hand and I flushed deeply, embarrassed at the thought that somehow he knew what I was thinking.

I was actually relieved when I saw the long line of people outside of the club. Maybe we wouldn't get in. Then I could go home and back to pretending that everything that happened to me since I first met Joshua had really been a dream.

Nathaniel led us to the front of the line. He shook hands with the door man who immediately opened the rope. I sighed. Nothing was going my way tonight.

The inside of the restaurant was like something out of a movie set. Expensive-looking white linen covered each table. Most of the lighting came from the hundreds of candles spread around the room. I had the strongest urge to turn and run out. The only thing keeping me in place was Joshua's arm. This was a place for the very rich and pretentious. The only club I fit into was the Redneck Yacht Club.

Joshua squeezed my hand again. "I won't let go of you. I promise." He didn't seem to realize that at this point his promises meant nothing to me.

The headwaiter escorted us through a side door into a smaller adjoining room with French-style doors that opened onto a patio crowded with bodies, all seeming to be moving in unison to a song I recognized from the radio.

Our host and his wife came immediately to greet us. The woman peered at me with overstated curiously while Joshua made the introductions. I stood in silence, pretending to look around at the décor while they talked. Joshua let go of my hand and wrapped his arm around my waist. The gesture only embarrassed me more.

After the introductions, the husband invited us to make a visit to the buffet tables, which were filled to the brim with a pageantry of colorful foods. These people obviously had an overblown sense of their importance. Joshua looked down at me, his lips pursed into a tight frown.

The girls found us a table. Joshua held out a seat for me and then for Cassie. Nathaniel did the same for Lindsey and then offered to get some wine for the table but I asked for a gin and tonic, ignoring Lindsey's pleading look.

Now that I didn't have any demons chasing me down, I was able to more closely examine my saviors. The term exceptionally attractive was an understatement. They looked like Greek gods. For all I knew, that's what they were.

Joshua was about six feet tall, slightly taller than Nathaniel, and a bit older-looking with the features of a man in his early thirties. Both of them were the perfect weight for their height and fit and trim. Their suits were obviously tailored, probably Armani or Versace.

The last time I'd seen them, the day of the fight with that hideous beast, they had beards; now they were clean-shaven, their hair cut short. If their hair grew as fast as mine did they would have to cut it every day to maintain that length.

Cassie was indisputably as beautiful as her brothers, but younger, barely old enough to have a driver's license. The blue dress she wore fit her to perfection. Her long blond hair hung loosely down her back, not braided, like the first time I had seen her. I froze slightly as I realized the startling similarity in our features. I hoped Lindsey didn't notice.

I swallowed hard and forced myself to talk about the unimportant with Lindsey as we headed back from the buffet. Before I could take a sip of my second drink, Nathaniel and Joshua stood up to greet a woman who had stopped at our table. Her abnormally taunt skin showed evidence of having had an excess of plastic surgery. Lindsey leaned over and told me that the woman was carrying a Birkin bag. My only response was a shrug.

With a disbelieving look Lindsey asked, "Haven't you ever heard of them, Mom?"

"No, should I have?" My favorite clothing stores were Old Navy and The Gap; what would I know about expensive pocketbooks?

"There's a waiting list for that bag. It costs over ten thousand dollars." I could hear the weight she placed on such a purchase. Lindsey shook her head and gave up trying to impress me. It was beyond me why anyone would spend that much money for a pocketbook when there where people starving all over the world.

My attention was drawn away from Lindsey when I heard the same woman ask, "Joshua, would you mind if I spoke to you about Monday's meeting?" The woman slipped her arm around Joshua's and led him away from us.

Although I wasn't sure why, I was irritated by this. The music from the sound system was blaring but because of my now heightened senses, I could hear their discussion clearly. After the business talk, the woman turned and gave me a quick disparaging look. She turned back to Joshua and said, "When you're done with your, umm, charity work tonight, perhaps you'd like to stop by my place for a visit?"

Joshua's voice stayed calm as he answered her. "Mrs. Ramsey, that beautiful woman will be my wife some day. I expect you to show her the same respect you show me."

Mrs. Ramsey stuttered out an apology. "I'm...I'm very sorry. I didn't know, Joshua. Please, accept my apology."

"Yes," Joshua replied, still calm. "I'll see you on Monday." He turned his back on the woman who stood locked in place, too shocked to move.

I stared at Joshua skeptically as he walked back. Why would he say such a ridiculous thing to that woman just because she insulted us? I could feel the despair trying to overwhelm me again and all I wanted to do at that moment was crawl back into my own hellhole and die.

Joshua sat down beside me. He leaned over close enough to touch my ear with his lips. I felt a shiver shoot down my spine.

"That is not going to happen."

"What is not going to happen?" I spit.

"You're not going to crawl into a hole and die. I won't let you."

"I don't understand how you're doing that but would you please stop? It's very annoying."

He sighed. "I'm upsetting you again. I don't want to do that."

"Yes, you really are." I replied sourly, my lips curling into a grimace, but then added, "Thank you for being a gentleman but that woman is right. We don't fit in with this crowd. You didn't have to make up a story."

"I'm not making up any stories and don't let that woman upset you," he growled emphasizing the word woman. "I know that you can't understand but trust me, in fifty years all of this will be inconsequential."

I shook my head, staring down at the table. I could feel the tears beginning to well up. "You're right. You talk in riddles. I thought you were going to explain everything, not confuse me even more." I dotted the water away before anyone noticed.

Joshua turned away from me and then quickly looked back. "Come dance with me, please?"

"I can't dance," I protested, but he ignored me and pulled at my hand until I stood up.

"I won't let you fall."

"Okay, fine, but you'll just embarrass yourself."

When we reached the edge of the crowded floor, Joshua placed our entwined hands on his chest up against the lapel of his jacket. His other hand moved slowly down my free arm pausing at my hand, which he placed on his shoulder.

I shivered again, uncontrollably and embarrassingly, not because I was cold. Certainly not, I was just the opposite.

Joshua gently touched my waist and pulled us closer together.

I was too befuddled to gripe. Did he have some magical powers like vampires or warlocks? It felt like he was hypnotizing me.

The DJ had put on a new song. It was slow and sexy. I was enjoying this closeness to Joshua much more than I had a right too. Joshua's heart thundered in my ear when I laid my head down against his shoulder. I knew mine was doing the same. It had been a long time since I felt like this, since someone had held me like this. Even though Alex and I were still in love, the passion between us had settled into a comfortable smoldering.

The thought of Alex brought back the guilt. What was I doing? Alex had been gone only three months and here I was dancing intimately with a man I hardly knew, but I didn't pull away. I heard Joshua sigh and felt his lips on my ear. He lingered there for a long moment before he spoke. "I've dreamed of this moment for longer than you can even imagine."

Joshua's declaration brought back something he had said the day of my first encounter with them. About me being the woman in his dreams. "Why would you be dreaming about me?"

He stared at me for a long moment, seeming frozen in thought. "It's a long story and I will explain it all to you. You must try and be patient."

That was easy for him to say. His whole life was not a confused jumbled mess. Joshua and his sibling were obviously used to being freaks and had found a way to fit in. I had never felt normal even when I was normal.

"Can I ask just one more question?" I begged. Maybe this one would be answered.

"Yes," he agreed.

"What does the stone carving in the Museum of Fine Arts have to do with you? Are you Assyrian?"

Joshua had a pained look as he answered. "Yes we are. The carving in the MFA is of our friend Issy. Well... you've already met her." He swallowed hard. "Katherine, our tale is as old as time itself."

Joshua's answer shocked me into silence. Two thousand years? I couldn't wrap my mind around such a number.

I stopped moving as soon as the song was over. "I do have a million questions but we really can't talk in front of Lindsey."

Joshua nodded in agreement. "Tomorrow is Saturday. Are you free? Maybe I could come by for a visit?"

I started to panic at the thought of him leaving me. He reached up and touched my cheek. "Don't worry. I will be at your house tomorrow. For tonight you need to keep up the pretense for your daughter." He chuckled. "What would she think if you left her and went off with me for the night?"

"Very funny." I hated to admit it but he was right.

"You promise?"

"Yes. We're going to need a considerable block of time."

I was instantly excited at the thought of time with him. "I'm free all weekend," I blurted out much too quickly." Then I added, "Will you be bringing the, uh, lion?" My voice broke at the end. Joshua smiled warmly at my trepidation. "Issy would never hurt you, but no, she won't be coming with me. I'll be alone."

"Okay," I sighed. Even with his reassurance about the safety of the lion, I was overly relieved that she would not be coming along. "Do know where I live?"

Joshua's happy expression changed to chagrin, "Yes, I do." Of course he knew. I had figured out long ago that they must have driven me home that night.

I extracted myself from his arms, intending to get Lindsey, but Nathaniel was there blocking my way. He asked Joshua if he could cut in. Joshua eyebrows narrowed. "It's all right," I acquiesced. "I want to talk to him anyway."

"Please, behave yourself, Nathaniel," Joshua pleaded as he surrendered me.

We swayed for a few minutes to the next song before either of us spoke.

"So was there something you wanted to say to me?" I thought I would be polite and let him begin.

"You don't like me very much," Nathaniel stated.

"No and I can tell the feeling is mutual." I replied curtly.

"I was wondering why."

"Why ask? Can't you just read it for yourself?"

"Answers are easier to find if the person is thinking it consciously, therefore I have to ask the question in order to get you to think the answer."

I pulled away, stunned.

Nathaniel pulled me back in. "Are you going to answer my question?"

"The bottom line is that I don't want you near my daughter. She's normal and you aren't."

"Might I remind you that you aren't normal either?" Nathaniel chuckled. "Would it smooth out things between us if I told you that I'm very fond of Lindsey?"

Nathaniel's face was as mesmerizing as Joshua's. I scowled at him, trying not to let him soften my mood. "Not even if you meant it."

He chuckled. "You and Lindsey are quite different aren't you?"

"You must have an enormous number of dating choices that are more appropriate considering your lifestyle." I was certain he would eventually break her heart.

"I like Lindsey very much. She's unpretentious and has no agenda. It's refreshing …and I have no intention of breaking her heart, either."

I stopped dancing. "Look, I don't care what your intentions might be. I want you to stay away from her."

I tried to pull away again but he held me tight. "You don't realize this yet but you're the only woman of our kind that's not related to us."

"Are you trying to be annoying or is this a natural talent?"

Nathaniel shrugged. "It's natural. Tell me, what do you think Joshua will do if I kiss you?"

I could feel the heat from my anger spreading across my neck. "He won't have to do anything because I'm going to punch you in the mouth and break your jaw."

"I doubt you're strong enough yet to cause any damage," he smirked, releasing me. "Go ahead and give it a try if you want."

I felt Joshua at my side in that same instant, pulling me into his arms. "Okay, you two have had enough fun for the night. I think we should take the ladies home." Joshua glared at his obstinate brother.

"Chill out Joshua. I was just having some fun."

Lindsey stood up at the same time we approached the table, her attention focused completely on Nathaniel's face. I touched her arm and she unwillingly turned in my direction.

"I'm beat." I told her in my sternest motherly voice. "Would you mind if we went home?"

Joshua agreed. "Yes, it's getting late. We'll drive you home."

Normally I would have objected but my irritation with Nathaniel had completely overwhelmed my stubbornness.

Joshua walked us to the door of Lindsey's apartment. While Lindsey was fiddling with the key, he reached for my hand, lifting it to his lips. The movement was blindingly fast, not giving me any time to pull away before Lindsey saw his gesture and giggled. I scowled a curt, "Goodnight."

After we were inside Lindsey started immediately with the third degree. "Wow, Mom, Joshua was infatuated with you. Do you like him? How long ago was it that you met him?"

"Oh, I don't really remember," I said going along with Joshua's charade. "His foundation was looking to buy some of our medical instruments."

"It's kind of funny that you didn't say anything when I told you I was working for them. Had you forgotten?" Lindsey was too observant sometimes.

"We meet so many customers over the course of a year and we don't know the names of the individuals."

She must have bought my lame explanation because she changed the subject. "Mom, I had fun tonight and I really like Nathaniel. This was the first time I had been out on a date with him. Did you like him?"

A date, I thought to myself. I didn't know it had been a date. "I think he is too old for you," noting darkly to myself that was probably the biggest understatement ever.

Lindsey frowned at my disapproval, "Not really. Nathaniel is only thirty-two. That's only four years older than me."

I shrugged, "Well, that's fine but I think he'll break your heart." I could see how my words stung her. I shuffled quickly trying to make up. The last thing I wanted was to take out my frustration on Lindsey. "Well, I think Nathaniel likes you a lot. He was goo-goo eyed all night whenever he looked at you."

It worked and her expression brightened. "That's what I thought too, although it might be sort of strange anyway, you and I dating brothers."

"What makes you think I would be dating Joshua?"

"Well, it looked to me like you two were getting cozy."

It had felt that way to me also. I stared back at Lindsey seeing the hope and worry for me mixed together in her expression. When had our roles become reversed?

"I think it was fate that you met Joshua tonight." Lindsey declared, sounding smug about her role in coordinating the meeting.

"Why is that?"

"It's just a feeling, but you seem made for each other. You look like them, you know."

I didn't answer her as I struggled to keep my eyeballs from bulging.

"Come on, Mom, you must have noticed. Cassie looks more like your daughter than I do."

"Well, we both have blonde hair but lots of people do," I offered as an explanation.

"That's true, but it goes deeper than that," she mused. "It's the way you walk, the color of your skin and the way you smell. I hadn't realized it until I saw you together tonight."

I sighed. I was running out of ways to rationalize this. "I'm not sure about anything anymore except that I'm very tired."

I closed the bedroom door, instantly relieved to be alone. Seeing Joshua tonight had brought back all the fear and anxiety that I had tried to overcome these last two years. My thoughts went scurrying in a million directions while I stared at the patterns in the tin ceiling, thinking about what Lindsey had said about fate.

At any given moment, you could find yourself in the wrong place at the wrong time. I could attest first hand to that. It grated against my inner being to think that something had orchestrated my course and put me in the forest that day with the Stones. I wanted to be in control of my own life. My life's experience, although limited, had taught me that what we want and what we get aren't always the same. What we want doesn't always matter. Then again, what we want can be all that matters.

KAREN ANN

Chapter 6
THE HYBRIDS

The number of breaths we take should not measure life;
instead, life should be measured by the moments
that take our breath away.

Lindsey said she was disappointed when I woke her at six to tell her that I was going home, but I had a feeling she was happy to see her crazy mother leave.

The first thing I did after walking through my front door was to take a shower. I needed the hot water to help calm me down. It did at first but its effect wore off quickly as I whirled around the house like a tornado on steroids, straightening up anything that seemed out of place in the already spotless rooms. After waiting through hours and hours of time, there was still no sign of Joshua.

I slipped in a DVD and began stitching to distract myself but I fell asleep before the movie was over. Depression washed over me as I awoke and glanced at the clock on the bedside table. Joshua must have changed his mind. I turned onto my back, planning to continue with my nap. What else was there to do? Abruptly, the smell of something sweet engulfed me and in place of the dejection there was relief. My protector was sitting beside me. I jumped at the sight of him. The corners of my mouth stretched to their limits. "You're here. I didn't think you were coming."

"I was here at one but you were fast asleep. You looked very peaceful. I didn't want to wake you."

"Oh…I wish you had." The disappointment was obvious in my voice.

"Well, I thought you might need the sleep. You looked stressed out last night."

I frowned. Joshua was right and I was more relaxed now, especially since we were alone to talk. I got up off the bed, nervous about being this close to him in such an intimate setting. I self-consciously began to straighten my hair and shirt.

Joshua laughed quietly. "You look great."

"Yeah, right!" I could only imagine how I looked, although I wasn't sure why I was worried about it in the first place. "I need a minute. Promise me you won't disappear?"

Joshua frowned apologetically. "I promise I will never disappear on you again. If you don't mind, I'm going to pour myself some of your wine. Would you like a glass?"

"Sure," I replied hesitantly. How did he know I had wine? Maybe he'd been snooping around while I was sleeping.

My hands were shaking as I pulled the towel off the bathroom mirror. I looked sick, excited and scared all at the same time. I had to remind myself that this was what I wanted. It was finally time to see what fate had planned for me. I took a few deep breaths, and opened the door to the beginning of my new life.

Joshua was standing in the dining room looking at the needlework that covered every available bit of wall space, not to mention the quilts, hooked rugs and punch needle that decorated every other nook and cranny in the house. I was embarrassed.

"Umm, I've kind of overdone it."

"They're all exceptionally beautiful, very impressive."

"Thank you," I said, blushing more heavily. I quickly looked down at my feet. Joshua put his hand under my chin, lifting my face up to his. As I stared back unable to pull away from his gaze, I found myself wanting to reach out and touch his scruffy beard. Instead, I balled my hands into fists, trying to control myself.

Joshua rubbed his hand across his chin. "Sorry, it's nice once in a while to take a break from the constant grooming. Nathaniel and I have to shave two or three times a day and cut our hair every morning, otherwise it would be as long as yours, which is not very presentable for two CEOs."

He laughed at his own thought, then without pausing asked, "Katherine, you have a lot of antiques. Why do you collect them?"

"I like old things," I admitted sheepishly. "Do you collect antiques also?"

"Well, actually, I'm sort of an antique myself."

"Ummm…" I muttered. The image of the BC-dated lion swirled in my head. I decided I was going to need that drink after all. "Where's that wine you promised me?"

Joshua handed me a full glass.

"You had no problem finding everything?" I asked stupidly.

"I was snooping." He smiled guiltily. I stared at him with my mouth open. The mind reading was obviously true and it was unquestionably going to be a problem. I didn't have much control over my emotions or thoughts and I definitely didn't want anyone knowing what I was thinking.

"I have a very long story to tell you." Joshua reminded me, taking hold of my hand and leading me to the couch. I felt my heart flutter involuntarily. He tapped his glass lightly on the side of mine and spoke the words, "To all the great moments of our past lives and the ones yet to come."

I was blushing ridiculously. "Okay, where do you want to start?" I asked, hoping to pull his focus away from me.

"Umm, give me a minute." While he thought, he stroked the inside of my palm with his finger. I squirmed. This felt too sexual. Was he going to try to seduce me? I choked on the sip of wine as I realized that he would have heard that thought also.

Joshua laughed softly and touched my check. "No, but there'll be plenty of time for that later if you want."

I stood up quickly, my face on fire now. "This is infuriating. You need to stop reading my mind or whatever it is that you're doing or you're going to have to leave."

He grimaced at my mini tirade. "I'll stop. I know it will be difficult for you to understand this but I'm... I'm infatuated with you. Please don't be self-conscious. I have the same thoughts about you."

I fought against the knowledge that his confession also applied to me but my embarrassment made me lash out again. "You're infatuated with me? How could you? You've only known me for one day. We've only spoken twice in two years. You don't know anything about me."

"You're wrong," he said tenderly. "I know you nearly as well as I know my brother and sister."

I glared at him.

"I know that you love country music, that you'd rather own an old dry sink than a Picasso painting, that on chilly mornings you sneak out to your garden to pet the bumblebees. You have a passion for science fiction movies and you cry yourself to sleep every night because you miss your husband."

I let out a gasp. "I knew it. You have been watching me. Why...why haven't you contacted me before now, to explain all of this, tried to warn me?" I could feel the tears running down my cheeks. I didn't bother to wipe them away.

"It's true. I have been keeping watch. It was very selfish of me, I know. I told myself it was to make sure you were safe when in actuality I wanted to find out who you were. It killed me not to be with you but I promised Issy." His voice was distraught. "Katherine, you have been in my dreams for a thousand years and I am overwhelmed with happiness to have finally found you."

Joshua reached over and wiped some of the tears away. "Calm down, Katherine. I will explain it all to you. It's going to be all right."

I desperately wanted to embrace his assurances, to finally look in the mirror and see the peace on my face that was so evident on his. I glanced up at the container holding Alex's remains, wishing more than ever that he were here. "Why were you at the hospital the day Alex died?" I demanded.

"Nathaniel and I came to see if we could save his life for you." Joshua looked down lost in thought for a moment.

"What would you have done? Have your lion friend bite him?" I paused, thinking about that for a few seconds. "Why didn't you do that?" The tears continued to stream down soaking the collar of my shirt.

"Nathaniel and I are trained physicians. We tried to find something his doctor overlooked." He paused and took a deep breath, "We couldn't and as far as Issy biting him, she wouldn't have done that."

"Why not? She did it to me.... and ruined my life," I mumbled.

Joshua frowned apologetically. "Katherine, I need to start my story, and then you'll understand."

I nodded and concentrated on not crying.

"I'll give you the short edition for now," he said with evident pleading. "You must be patient though. Even the short version is long."

I nodded again.

"I was born in 740 BC in a city named Calah in the Kingdom of Assyria. The land of my birth now includes the countries of Syria, Iraq, Jordan, Israeli, and sections of Turkey, Iran and Saudi Arabia. Even Egypt was part of my kingdom. I was one of the many children of King Sargon II."

I was doing the mental math while he was still talking but before I could finish he replied, "Yes, it's mind boggling but we're all very ancient. I'm two thousand seven hundred and fifty two years old, to be exact."

My mouth twisted into a sharp smile. "You couldn't possibly be that old. Only rocks and fossilized bone can survive that long."

"Do you really want to hear this story?"

I made a gesture of locking my lips.

"I have two surviving brothers and one sister. You've met my brother Nathaniel and our sister Cassandra. I'll tell you about our brother, Regulus, or Reggie, as he calls himself nowadays, some other time. That's another long story and not very pleasant." Joshua said in a stern tone.

"Not pleasant, uh?" I couldn't imagine anything less pleasant than the story of being bitten by a lion.

Joshua frowned at my consternation before continuing. "The Assyrian Empire was at the peak of its eminence at that time. Few empires have ever rivaled it. The capital at Nineveh was the grandest of all cities, with tall stone dwellings that appeared to reach for the heavens and colossal stone figures, some thirty feet tall. Fifteen monumental gates guarded the entrances to the city. Marble stairs led down from each building to the lush banks of the river that flowed past the city. It was said that the river sang in happiness, so honored was it to be a part of the splendor." Joshua paused briefly, his gaze distant.

"The Assyrians believed that the king was a direct descendant of the gods, a divine being and we, his children, were also. Nothing was beyond our reach. Heavily lined in gold and studded with every jewel imaginable, the walls of our palace glinted in the noontime sunlight. Even the fabric for our clothing was made from gold and silver thread. We had a multitude of slaves at our disposal. It was a life most people, even the super rich of today, couldn't imagine." He paused again, taking a deep breath before continuing.

"In the mist of all the beauty there was a shadow over our land. War was endemic in the age that I grew up in. Our armies reduced the greatest of opponents to vassalage. The militia's standing orders were to take no quarter and as a result, millions of innocent people were murdered. Those that did survive were either tortured, or if they were lucky, sold into slavery." Joshua sighed heavily. "But that was the way of the world back then."

I scoffed, "It's still the way of the world. Just in the last hundred years alone there have been two world wars not to mention the numerous other smaller wars."

Joshua shook his head, "It was much worse back in the time of which I am speaking. People long ago defined themselves and their countries by conquering others. Assyria, the Greeks, the Romans, every ancient civilization was infected with the disease of war. For most, it was a national hobby similar to what football or soccer is today. Learning to kill was a rite of manhood. In these modern times there are many people that want peace and work towards achieving that goal."

I shook my head in disagreement but didn't interrupt. "Nathaniel, Cassie and I were forced to go to battle with our father, forced to kill his enemies. It was kill or be killed. Every life I took haunted my dreams." He shook his head in disgust.

"In 705 BC there was a great battle between my people and a horde known as the Cimmerians. A hundred thousand soldiers from each side spread out around the plains of a city known as Tushpa. Even though it was one of the hottest summers in decades, neither side was discouraged from going to battle

"During the first day of the fighting, an enemy regiment broke through a section of our barricade and attacked Sargon's tent. We went to his defense when we realized what was happening."

Joshua stopped and stared at me.

"What's wrong? Is it too difficult for you to go on?" I hoped he wouldn't stop his story. I was enthralled.

"The battle I'm speaking of is the same one that was in your dream, the one with the tents and the stalking lion."

"I haven't had that dream ever since the day in the park. How did you know about that?" I glared.

"You were recalling the dream while you were on the ground injured. Wondering how the lion had gotten out of your dream and into the park. We all saw what you were thinking, even Issy."

"Why was I even dreaming about the lion in the first place, and this battle?"

"I'll tell you what we think after I finish this part of my story. When we arrived at our father's tent, the enemy soldiers attacked and wounded us also."

"Reggie, Nathaniel, Cassie and I laid for days in agony, praying for death to come swiftly. Without antibiotics and the surgical skills of the doctors that exist today death could be excruciating."

"On the third night following the battle, I was awoken by the sound of a breath panting heavily. I didn't even call for the guards when I spied her. They were gods to us and I assumed that the lion had come as our escort to the next world."

"To my horror, though, the lion did to us what she did to you."

The clear memory of the bite and the resulting pain made me warm and uncomfortably clammy.

Joshua paused in his storytelling, to give me a moment. When I relaxed, he continued.

"My siblings were unconscious and not able to utter a sound, but I did. My screams awoke the whole camp. The guards did not see Issy, even though she walked right past them in her retreat. Everyone assumed that the fever had made me delusional. What I didn't know at the time was that Issy is able to bend light in such as way that makes her invisible to humans, not to us of course. We refer to it as shimmering. To a human it merely looks like the waves of heat rising from a hot surface. You witnessed it with Nathaniel and Cassie the day we met in the park."

"Is that something I can do?" For the first time, I felt enthusiastic about my new capabilities.

Joshua smiled hugely at my expression. "Yes, eventually you'll be able to do all sorts of incredible things once you're up to full capacity. The lion's serum is constantly working inside you, making you stronger physically and mentally. It takes about four to six years for the complete transformation to take place. Any other questions for right now?" he asked softly.

I rolled my eyes. "I have a million, but you should finish your story. Then I'll be able to organize my thoughts. I'm pretty overwhelmed at the moment."

Joshua nodded. "After that night, my siblings and I all regained our health. Our wounds healed very rapidly and we became aware of some remarkable physical *changes*," he held his hands and made quotation marks with two fingers.

"Because we didn't have the benefit of contact lenses to disguise the changes that our eyes went through, the people in my kingdom became wary and accused us of consorting with witches. Eventually, afraid for our lives, we four had to flee our father's house and even our homeland not realizing at the time how strong and indestructible we had become. It was very difficult on all of us, but especially on Reggie." Joshua sighed. "For centuries after, we became nomads, staying away from large populations of people, only going into cities when we needed supplies.

"Issy found us again years later. When she came wandering into our campsite, we picked up our weapons, planning to attack her until we realized we could see into her mind and vice versa. Through Issy's thoughts, we saw a future in which we were to become great friends and companions and also how she came to be bound into an animal form."

I could hear his profound admiration as he spoke of the lion.

"Will I be able to read minds?" I asked warily. I wasn't sure that I really wanted *that* ability. It was busy enough as it was in my head.

Joshua nodded. "We can only read the minds of the ones that have been given the lion's serum. It takes a little getting used to but it helps us co-ordinate our moves and keep each other safe when we were hunting and fighting the Nergal but we need to be close, within twenty miles or so of each other."

I nodded without comment this time mentally adding two more questions to my list. Joshua continued.

"Have you ever read any of the tales about the life of an ancient king known as Gilgamesh?"

"Gila who?" I whispered.

"It's pronounced Gil_ga_mish. He was a great Babylonian king who lived around 2700 BC in Assyria. Many stories were written about Gilgamesh's adventures, especially the ones about his escapades with the many deities that lived in those days."

I had to stop him now. "When you say deities, do you mean gods, like Zeus and Apollo?"

Joshua laughed at my analogy. "I'm not completely sure of what they were because most of them had perished by the time I was born. They were not the same type of god that modern people pray to, the one true God that most Christians, Muslins, and Jews call upon. By human standards though, they were immortal."

"We refer to those super-humans as 'originals' and to ourselves as 'hybrids.' From what Issy has told us, they were born with their abilities, not changed as we have been. Their powers of telepathy dwarfed ours and some even had telekinetic capabilities."

"They could move objects with their minds?"

Joshua nodded. "Only the very strongest among them had that power. None of us have it, probably because our blood is blended."

"Issy, or Ishtar, as was her given name, lived with her family and her husband, Adid, all of them originals. Still in a human form at that time and worshipped by humans as the God of Love, she was very powerful and could turn humans into hybrids even then. Gilgamesh was one such human that Ishtar had turned.

"Issy had a confrontation with Gilgamesh. A very bad confrontation that resulted in the death of Adid's son, Humbaba.

"Adid was devastated. He left Ishtar and persuaded the others that his son's death was due to her recklessness.

"Some thought that Ishtar should be put to death, but the majority of the originals were worried that without her influence the world would not have love and they came up with a form of punishment other than death."

Joshua's tone was laden with sadness as he spoke the next words. "Issy has wandered the earth for thousands of years in this strange form, devastated by what she did to her husband and the loss of his love for her.

"That was not the end of the horror for Ishtar, though. As if being bound was not enough punishment, Humbaba's mother, Ramâmu, a formidable witch, was enraged that Ishtar had not been put to death.

"A witch!" I gasped. "Oh, come on. You don't really expect me to believe that." I don't know why this part of his story seemed so unbelievable to me. The whole thing was unbelievable.

Joshua smiled warmly and asked, "Should I go on?"

I sucked in a deep breath. "Yes, sorry for the outburst. Please go on." Although, I was beginning to imagine how the sultan must have felt listening to Scheherazade's stories.

"Ramâmu did not possess the strength to kill Issy herself hence she used her powers of necromancy to conjure up the spell that brings forth the demons. The Nergal are savage and uncontrolled and depending on how populated the area is where they show up, they wreak havoc, causing the death of many, while trying to find Issy."

"Why do you call them Nergal? That's quite a mouthful." Joshua smiled patiently. "The Nergal were the hunters in the Assyrian underworld."

I opened my mouth to ask the next question but Joshua put his fingers to my lips.

"In due time. I need to get through this first."

I frowned but nodded an okay.

"After the all the originals were gone, Issy was alone and it was during this time that she began dreaming about my siblings and me, but she didn't know where to find us until one day, when she came across a great battle among the humans. When she found us wounded and dying, she knew how to save us but there was no way to communicate with us so she kept her distance, watching over us for the next few years. The answer came the day she become conscious of our thoughts. Issy entered our camp, introduced herself and our journey through time began."

I yawed and glanced involuntarily at the clock on the mantel. It was after nine.

Joshua noticed my distraction. "This is a lot to take in at one time. Do you want to call it a day? We can always....."

"No, please, I have so many questions."

Joshua grasped a loose strand of my hair and secured it behind my ear. "I know it will take time before you feel safe and understand what is happening to you, but I promise you I will be around for a long, long time."

I frowned. "You have your own life to attend to. I'm sure you're not going to want to be babysitting me all the time, especially Nathaniel. He doesn't seem to like me much."

Joshua frowned disapprovingly. "Katherine, most of my life has been about finding you. It's true that I've driven Nathaniel and Cassie crazy but they understand and are happy for me. Nathaniel will come around."

"Hmm..." I mused. I wasn't sure how I felt about being the object of someone's obsession. How could someone be this stubbornly fixated on finding a person they knew only from a dream?

"So what exactly am I doing in this dream of yours?"

Joshua didn't answer. He looked...guilty?

"You've been dreaming about me for a thousand years and now you've found me and you won't tell me about the dream?"

His eyes were cautious. "I'm concerned that you'll think me too presumptuous."

Since this was the main reason for him saving my life that day in the park, I decided that I wanted to know.

"Tell me, please?" I asked in a soft persuasive voice.

His voice a whisper, his eyes soulful, told me the last thing I thought I would hear. "We're getting married."

*

It took a long moment for the shock of what Joshua said to register. "I can guarantee that is not going to happen." I laughed almost on the point of hysteria. "So I guess when you told that to Mrs. Ramsey in the restaurant last night you weren't joking." Joshua looked down and folded his hands.

The heavy silence made me immediately aware of how hurt he was by my dismissal and I didn't want to hurt him. I tried to explain my viewpoint.

"You obviously don't know anything about my previous relationships. I've been married three times and except for Alex, the others ended in disaster. I don't have much of a track record."

"It will be different with us. No one in your whole human life has ever loved you the way that I will love you," Joshua stated indisputably.

"How do you know you'll even like me after you get to know me?"

"I just know." Joshua turned to look out the window, deep in thought.

I decided that this was a preposterous subject to discuss right now. There were too many other important things that I needed to understand. "You know," I said, offering a compromise, "I think we have to take it slow here. Spend some time getting to know each other. Evidently, we have that?"

Joshua grinned happily. "Yes, that sounds wonderful. We should take a break. We haven't had dinner yet." He stood up and started for the door.

"Where're you going?" I could hear the hysteria building in my voice.

"I brought dinner. It's out in the car. I will be right back, I promise."

I waited patiently for him to return. When he did, he was holding a small cooler.

"I must explain another important aspect concerning our... umm... condition." His voice hesitated on the last word, "It's about our diet. Obviously Issy is a lion and I know that you're aware of what a mortal lions eat."

"Yes, they hunt other animals, mostly herbivores."

"They eat red raw meat, and we, being part lion, or more appropriately having the essence of the lion's serum in us, need to do the same."

"I've been eating other foods, and I don't seem to be having any problems." I was worried now.

"That's fine; you can eat regular human food. The human part of you still needs the vitamins that come from a balanced diet. The lion part of you, however, needs red meat. You must make sure that twice a week you have some. It keeps us strong and diminishes the craving. Otherwise, humans will begin to smell like food to you. You might take a bite out of one of them."

We both shuddered at the same time; me because of the night I bit Alex. I wondered who Joshua must have taken a bite out of.

The metallic smell of the blood hit me instantly as the lid on the cooler came up. My mouth watered uncontrollably. Joshua laughed as he saw the change in my expression and I was instantly embarrassed. Up until now, I had been eating in secret, like a drug addict trying to hide an addiction.

"Don't feel embarrassed, you'll get used to this and you need to do this in order to stay healthy and to keep the humans around you from turning into prey."

I frowned. "Fine, but I'm still human." I picked up the knife and fork and started eating.

After a few minutes of chewing in silence I laughed.

"Will you let me in on the joke?"

"I was just wondering. I haven't been out on a date for twenty years now. Is this something they serve on first dates?" I asked, pointing to the bloody entrée in front of me.

Joshua's eyes widened. "Is this our first date?"

"I guess." I shrugged, turning red.

"I haven't been on a date in a millennium." He looked uncomfortable at having to confess this.

A small laugh of disbelief escaped. "Why not? Have you ever been married or had a girlfriend? Not that it's any of my business," I confessed, at the same burning with curiosity.

"I don't mind telling you. I was married when I was human. It was an arranged marriage like most in those days. Neither of us was very happy though. I've had some brief encounters with other human women through the years but it was nothing more than lust, mostly due to Nathaniel's insistence that I act like a normal man. When I started dreaming about you, I knew that you were the one for whom I was destined." He laughed. "I know it sounds corny."

"Very!" I began twisting my wedding ring nervously. "You know, that's an awful lot of pressure for one person to live up to. I hope you're ready for some significant disappointment. I'm just an ordinary boring person. You and I don't even come from the same class of people."

Joshua looked at me, annoyed. "Do you seriously think that after dealing with humans for such a long time that wealth or status impresses me? Frankly, I am insulted that you would think that about me."

"What else would I think? In this world, the rich look down on the poor and you obviously are extremely wealthy." My tone reproached him.

"Katherine, it wouldn't matter to me if you were washing floors or cleaning toilets. A person's monetary wealth doesn't determine a person's worth. Nathaniel, Cassie and I use our money and status to fund our charities. Our main goal is to convince the more fortunate to work for the good of humanity."

"Sure," I replied sarcastically.

"Please, Katherine, I don't want to hear that you feel that way. As far as I'm concerned we are equal in all respects. You should get some sleep now. I've talked enough for one night."

"Won't you stay, please?" I could feel the blood rushing up through my neck, flooding my cheeks.

Joshua raised one eyebrow. "You would be comfortable with me staying here?"

"Well, I think the fact that you did save my life means you're trustworthy, plus the fact that you think we'll be getting married someday." I raised my eyebrows.

"That is one thing I am pleased to hear. Okay, off to bed with you then. I'll make us some tea." He hesitated. "Oh, do you like tea?"

I laughed. "You can drop the pretense. I know you know that I like tea."

Joshua smiled mischievously as he turned towards the kitchen.

I searched manically for my good pajamas instead of what I usually wore--sweat pants and old cotton shirts. I shook my head. Why did I care?

When I opened the bedroom door, Joshua was standing there, holding a tray with a pot of tea, two cups and a plate of cookies. How did he get the water heated up that quickly? I wondered if the hybrids had X-ray vision like Superman.

"Why don't you get under the covers and we can have the tea in here. It will make it easier for you to sleep," he suggested. Joshua saw my hesitation and asked, "Do you still think I'm trustworthy?"

"Yes, of course."

Joshua poured us each a cup of tea, and then sat down in Alex's chair. It made me sad to see another man in Alex's place.

Joshua noticed that also. "I'm very sorry that you lost Alex so soon. I know you miss him very much."

"Yes, he took good care of me and loved me unconditionally. His support kept me focused through all this craziness--helped me keep the essential part of myself that I thought I was losing." That was a life that seemed very distant now, ironically very nearly a dream.

"I'm glad that you had him, then."

"May I ask you something else?"

"You can ask me anything."

"If one of you had met someone that you loved," I paused, struggling with my question, "why is it that Issy wouldn't change that person?"

"Issy only changes humans that she has seen in her dreams. She has a very strict rule about this, or at least she did up until we met you."

"What difference would it make if she had been dreaming about someone or not?"

Joshua looked sick as he explained this next part to me. "Issy changed someone once who was not in her dreams. It ended badly."

"Oh, and who was that?" Even as I asked, I knew he wasn't going to tell me.

"That's another long story and I wish you would let me tell you about it some other time," he beseeched.

I nodded. "I'll add it to the bottom of my list."

"Our Assyrian ancestors believed that dreams were a window into the future and in our case they were exactly right. Your dream about the tents and Issy was a premonition." He laughed darkly to himself. "Or you might think of it as a warning, that you would meet us. Once you found us you stopped having the dream, didn't you?"

Joshua posed the last sentence as a question but what was the point---he knew the answer.

The dream played over again in my head. "Do you think that was why Lindsey was in that dream? Because she was the means by which I would meet you again?"

Joshua nodded pensively. "Sometimes the dreams are difficult even for us to figure out."

I thought about that and the argument Joshua and Nathaniel had over me the day we met in the park.

"So was Issy dreaming about me also?"

"No, only I had been dreaming of you."

"Well, if I understand what you've told me so far, and if I hadn't been in Issy's dreams …then why did she save me?" In my mind, the jury was still out on whether or not she had done me a favor or not.

Joshua knelt down beside the bed, reaching across to take my hands in his. "Because of me. Otherwise you would have been another unknown casualty of our demon war." Joshua shook his head and the tone of his voice changed to disgust. "I couldn't believe the appalling circumstances. I could touch you and hold you, but you were dying. I still don't know how I allowed that to happen. I should have been paying more attention to the Nergal but I was stunned that I had found you."

I interrupted before he could continue. "Even though you had a bad experience once, think of the lives that could be saved. You could virtually wipe out disease, pain and suffering." Something that I didn't want to think about was warring in my head. Would I want them to change my daughters when the time came for them to die?

Joshua's laugh was sad. "The thought horrifies me. We might end up creating a completely new race of monsters. Can you imagine if someone with Hitler or Stalin's personality had been changed?"

Joshua paused only for a second, not letting me ask the next question. "Nathaniel didn't want me to change you because he knew that I wouldn't be able to stay with you while went through your transformation. He was worried about what you would become without guidance."

"I still don't understand why you wouldn't stay in touch with me and why have you come forward now?" I was still trying to pinpoint the details of this long involved story.

"You were still married and Issy didn't want any of us interfering with your life," he said adamantly.

"How did you know I was married? You didn't even know where I was until that day and since I was still," I choked on the word, "human, you couldn't read my mind."

"I am impressed. Your comprehension of all this is astounding."

"It's from watching hundreds of science fiction movies." I replied darkly.

"Well, you see, that was the strange thing."

I raised an eyebrow.

"Sorry, I know everything is strange right now. We were stunned because we could read your mind. That had never happened with a mortal before. While you were lying on the ground injured, you were thinking about Alex, grateful that he was not with you. All of us, including Issy, could see into your mind.

The reason Issy was persuaded into breaking that strictest rule was that she had seen you in my dream and could see herself in the dream you were recalling. We all realized that a latent connection to us must have existed even in your human form."

Joshua took my teacup away.

I slumped further under the covers, stretching out on my side.

"Try to get some sleep. It's been an eventful day and I've given you a lot to think about. I'm sure you will have a new list of questions tomorrow." He chuckled at the thought.

"I still wish you had gotten in touch with me, if only to let me know that I wasn't turning into a flesh-eating zombie? I was really worried about that possibility." My eyelids were heavy but I fought to keep them open.

Joshua frowned. "What you were becoming…we didn't want that to have any influence on your decisions about your life. You knew that you were changing but didn't know that you would live for a long time. I could see what you were going through and it broke my heart."

I sat up. "How often did you come by to spy on me?"

Joshua looked down guiltily. "I came by quite often, at least twice a week. I had to make sure you were safe. I watched you having dinner at night with Alex and your family, watched you at your daughter's wedding. It comforted me to see how very happy you were."

"Really, Joshua, what harm could one phone call have done?" I thought about all the suffering I had endured while he was joyfully watching me from a distance. "How closely were you watching me?"

Joshua shook his head in disgust while I turned red at the idea of how much of my private life and thoughts he had seen.

"Katherine, please take a breath," he requested, reaching across to touch my arm, rubbing his hand up and down its length. "Your heart is beating very quickly. I'm not going on if you don't calm down. I don't want you upset."

I lay on my back taking deep ragged breaths, trying to compose myself. I needed to keep him talking. My eyelids were wide open now, sleep all but forgotten in my panic.

"If I live a million years I will never forgive myself for leaving you in the dark. It killed me not to be with you. I wanted you more than I ever wanted anything but I couldn't jeopardize your relationship with Alex. I wanted you to continue living exactly as you had been living. I owed you that much.

"After Alex was gone I convinced Issy to come here one night. She knows what it feels like to lose the love of your life, to be alone, and she didn't want that for you any more than I did.

"I'm sure you've figured out that the night at the MFA was not a coincidence. Lindsey had told us your plans and I couldn't wait any longer. I convinced Issy that it was the right time to introduce ourselves. Nathaniel agreed to go along with my plan to meet you as long as I promised to come back to work and stop acting like a crazy person."

My head was still spinning. I was having trouble breathing again. I was not someone that anyone would be obsessed with, never mind being in someone's endless dream.

"Okay," Joshua said adamantly. "That's really enough. Please, Katherine, close your eyes."

"Okay," I whispered as I forced my eyelids to close. "Promise you're not going to leave."

"I'm not going anywhere." His voice was fervent.

"Joshua?"

"Yes?"

"What would you have done if Alex had lived to be a hundred?"

"I would have waited another thousand years if that's what fate demanded." His voice held no hint of any doubt.

"You can use any one of the beds in guest rooms," I offered.

"If you don't mind, I'll stay right here. I don't want to miss a moment of my time with you."

"I'm even more boring when I'm asleep."

"Nothing you do will ever bore me," he replied passionately.

"Hmm, just wait." I felt something touch my head as I drifted off to sleep.

KAREN ANN

Chapter 7
THE OPEN HEART

It must be noted, that nature has a plan,
Although, at first it may not be apparent,
That when one life ends another will begin

I awoke the next morning to bright sunlight and the smell of bacon and coffee, the well-known smells reminding me of Alex. I went immediately to the bathroom, brushing my teeth and hair. I threw the towel back over the mirror, refusing to look at myself any further. Inside I was distressed with my lingering thoughts of Alex, but on the outside I looked ridiculously excited.

I walked into the dining room, my attention wandering out through the French doors to the porch. The table on the porch looked like a romantic setting at a sidewalk café with vases of flowers and lit candles. Joshua came out of the kitchen, holding two cups of coffee, one of which he offered to me.

"Good morning. I thought we might have breakfast out; it's such a nice day."

"That would be great," I agreed, taking the coffee cup from his hand.

Joshua opened the screen door and gestured for me to go first.

I hesitated, the familiar scene, only a scene that had included Alex, continued to haunt me.

"What's wrong?"

I sighed. "Nothing. This is very nice." I gulped down the hot coffee.

"Would you like some more?"

"Yes, please."

Joshua returned, balancing two plates with one arm and the coffee pot in the other hand. Each plate was filled full of breakfast fixings. My hand blurred as I shoved the food into my mouth, not pausing until I realized that I was making a spectacle of myself. I stopped abruptly my mouth half full of un-chewed food.

"I'm sorry; I have no manners." I flushed red. I knew he was used to dealing with people who had more refined behavior.

He shook his head. "It's fine, and I'm pleased you enjoyed the food."

"You're quite a cook. I'm surprised."

"Why's that?" he asked, a little piqued.

"I would imagine that you have maids and butlers to do all of your cooking."

"Katherine, we do not have servants anymore. We do our own cooking and cleaning. I've lived in many different places and can cook any type of food... Greek, Italian, Middle Eastern, English, French, American."

"Hmm," I nodded in reply, still chewing.

"When you have thousands of years to practice, you can become an expert at anything."

Infinite time was something I couldn't imagine right now. I shook my head.

"What?" Joshua asked inquisitively.

"I guess when Cassie told Lindsey that she had already seen the exhibit at the Boston Museum of Fine Arts, she wasn't lying."

Joshua chuckled. "Nathaniel and I had that piece commissioned. The carver was a Phoenician friend that we stayed with from time to time during our wandering."

My mouth flew open and I gawked at him in disbelief but he ignored my reaction.

"You have a beautiful home."

"Thank you. Now that I've been," I cleared my throat, "umm, renovated, I can do everything myself. My strength is incredible."

Joshua nodded. "You'll continue to get stronger. Eventually you'll be able to lift the couch with one hand."

"I wonder what the neighbors will think about that," I mused.

"Probably not a good idea to advertise," he suggested, laughing heartily.

It was bizarre to be talking this casually about ourselves as if we were Marvel Comic characters.

"So," I asked hesitatingly, "exactly how old where you when Issy found you?" I had figured he was 35 from the dates he had told me last night.

"Katherine we have slipped in and out of every era in human history for the last two millennia. Age means nothing to us."

"You know I prefer older men," I stated teasingly.

Joshua smiled warmly. "Good, because you now know that I'm one of the oldest men on this planet."

He quickly changed the subject. "What do you want to do today?" His tone was bright, expectant.

"I'm not sure," I hedged, feigning indifference. I didn't care if we sat on the porch all day, as long as he didn't leave. "What do you usually do on Sundays?"

"I work."

"That doesn't sound like much fun." That meant he would have to leave.

"What do you usually do on Sundays?" he asked back.

"Not much, but I don't work. I told you I have a very boring life. Especially with Alex--" I stopped short at that thought. I needed to concentrate on other things today.

"May I make a suggestion?"

"Sure, as long as we stay together," I demanded.

"Would you be up for a ride?"

"Okay."

"Do you have a favorite place to drive to?" Like all men, he seemed excited about the idea of being in a car.

That was easy. Shelburne Falls was a place where Alex and I went. I wasn't sure I wanted to share that with Joshua though. I could feel the sadness as it crept across my face again.

Joshua quickly backtracked, "Or we could stay here if the thought doesn't appeal to you." He scrutinized my expression. "Katherine, not to minimize the tragedy of Alex's death, but moving on with your life doesn't mean that you will forget about Alex or stop loving him. Even a thousand years from now your memory of him will be crystal clear."

"A thousand years," I answered cynically. In retrospect, my life with Alex had gone by at a high rate of speed. I automatically looked down at the hand that still wore his wedding ring. I sighed. Lindsey was right, Alex would want me to move on, or at least figure out the direction I was going in. I raised my face to Joshua and met his somber gaze. "A drive sounds like fun. Have you ever been to a place called Shelburne Falls?"

"Not into town, only in the woods on hunting trips."

I looked at him questioningly and he grimaced. "Something else to save for later."

"Okay," I agreed. I had enough unsettling information for the moment. I stood up, picking up my plate and coffee cup, but he put his hand out. "Leave the dishes. I'll clean up while you're getting ready."

"I don't need to be waited on."

"You're going to have to get used to this." Joshua bent over and kissed the top of my head.

I proceed to the bathroom, mumbling ridiculous under my breath.

When I was ready, I found Joshua in the now spotless kitchen speaking into his phone in an unfamiliar language. I could hear the woman on the other end of the conversation speaking the same.

"What language was that?" I asked as soon as he hung up.

"It is old dialect of Aramaic, or some refer to it as Akkadian. It was the language of my people when we lived in Assyria. I'm sorry, that was rude of me. We unthinkingly slip into it sometimes."

"It's fine," I assured him. "It must be nice to know another language. I can barely speak English."

"We'll work on that." He stated without elaborating on what he meant. "That was Cassie. She was trying to persuade me to bring you back to Boston and have dinner with her tonight. She is very eager to spend some time with you."

"Why?"

"I haven't been the only one dreaming about you."

"Don't tell me she's been dreaming about marrying me also?"

"No," Joshua chuckled, "but she has longed for a friend, a female friend. She is really tired of hanging around with Nathaniel and me."

"She must have many friends. Why would she need me? I'm kind of old for her..." I paused and we both chuckled.

"It's difficult to spend a lot of time with humans." I winced when he said the word human. "We have to constantly be on guard. We have had to assume fictitious identities and fictitious lives in order to fit in. It's nice to be with someone who knows us. Besides Issy, Cassie is the only female of our kind and it would be difficult for Cassie to have a shopping day or girl's night out with a lion."

"Yes," I said, irritated, "Nathaniel explained that to me last night. Well, I'm afraid Cassie will be disappointed. I don't go out much or do much shopping, either." However, I was also beginning to appreciate having someone to hang out with that you didn't have to keep secrets from all the time.

"After we're done in Shelburne Falls, maybe you'd like to see our place in Boston?"

"Won't it be late by the time we get back? I have work tomorrow. I'm sure you do also."

"It will be late, but you're a big girl now," he countered in a teasing manner.

"It will be a lot of driving," I rebutted, trying to think of other reasons to get out of going.

"I like driving. I could drive for days if I had to." I sighed and he seemed to hear the surrender in it.

"I'll drive you to work in the morning. Cassie and I both have extra bedrooms."

"Okay." I frowned.

"Excellent," he beamed.

I took a few deep breaths, trying to calm my racing heart. I could feel that imaginary cord tugging at me again, slowly pulling me into the arms of my protector. Seriously though what woman wouldn't? Joshua was charming and debonair but it was beyond me why he would like me, even if he had been dreaming about me.

I felt guilty as I put Nutmeg out on the porch with his food and water. I didn't like leaving him alone. He pinned away for Alex as much as I did.

Joshua was waiting out in driveway leaning up against a shiny new model Audi. It made my Honda look like a rusty old tool and was a good analogy of the way I was beginning to feel about the differences between us.

"Where's the Mustang?" At least that was more my style.

"The Mustang belongs to Nathaniel. This is my car. We could take your Honda if that makes you feel better." I could see him straining to keep from smiling.

"We should probably take yours." I would be mortified if the Honda broke down on the drive.

"Why don't you drive your Camaro?" Joshua motioned to the car sitting in the driveway under the cover.

"It needs some work. I just…" I paused. "Alex used to do all that. I need to take it to my mechanic for some repairs."

"What does it need?" Joshua asked.

I didn't understand why he would even care. What did he know about cars anyway? His new cars probably never broke down and if they did, I was sure he had some service to take care of them.

"The air conditioning is not working, not that I would use it. The heat doesn't bother me anymore, or the cold, no matter what the outside temperature is." I looked at Joshua and he nodded in agreement.

"That's correct. Our bodies are capable of generating an enormous amount of heat when we need it and also the ability to keep us cool." Joshua stared at me waiting for me to finish answering his question.

I sighed. "It also needs a tune up, plugs, wires etc... and the alternator is starting to go."

"I can do the repairs if you'd like. We'll pick up the parts next week."

"You don't strike me as someone who likes to get his hands dirty."

"Really, Katherine, it's insulting the way that you assume I'm some spoiled rich kid."

"What else would I think? Look at you." My hand trailed along the length of his torso.

Joshua sighed. "Nathaniel, Cassie and I have owned many automobiles," he explained while he opened the Audi's passenger door for me, "since the time when they were first invented. We're expert mechanics, even Cassie. In fact, your Honda looks like one of the first cars we bought. What year is it, 1901?"

I made a clucking sound with my mouth and slapped his arm. "Don't be disrespectful. The Honda and have been together for a long time and besides it's difficult to find a car with standard transmission these days." I grabbed the door handle and slammed the door shut.

Joshua walked around slowly to the driver's side of the Audi and climbed in. He had a puzzled look.

"Seriously, why don't you buy a new car?" he asked not letting go of the subject.

I shrugged. "This one still works fine." I turned my head, facing out the passenger window, away from his sharp gaze as the tears began.

Joshua reached over, putting his hand under my chin, gently tugging until I turned back. "I promised you I would not invade your privacy but would you please explain why this has upset you?"

"You wouldn't understand. It involves death."

He grimaced heavily. "You'd be surprised at what I understand about death."

"I don't want to talk about this, please."

"All right," he agreed and but then added, "I would love to buy you a new car."

"No," I stated, my voice rising to a higher pitch. Then hoping to change the subject I asked, "Do you know how to get to Shelburne Falls?"

Joshua grinned happily, and pointed to his head. "Built in GPS, one more benefit to being us. We have the maps of the world memorized. It saves time when we're tracking the Nergal."

"The maps of the world." I was impressed. "Well, that will be a nice change. My geography was never very good and my sense of direction was even worse when I was…"

Joshua finished the sentence for me. "Human? Don't worry. You're still you. You're just an industrial strength version now."

"Whatever," I said dismissively. He chuckled at my irritation. "How much information does your brain hold?"

Joshua answered as he pulled out of the driveway. "Everything I've ever seen or done or read. We have photographic memories. You've noticed this, haven't you?"

"I have." Although in my case, there were things I wished I could forget, like bad dreams and car accidents, which brought up another of the most important questions on my list.

"Shortly after the dream with the tents came to an end, another began. In that second dream there was a man that I didn't recognize, but he was definitely one of us." I cringed as the "us" slipped out.

Joshua's knuckles protruded sharply as his grip on the steering wheel tightened. "That was our brother, Reggie."

"Why was he in my dream? Did he have something to do with Alex's death?" My voice sounded frantic.

"No, no. We studied all the news footage very carefully and he wasn't anywhere near the accident scene. We haven't had any communication with him in four centuries." I heard Joshua sigh. "We do think it means that you were going to meet him. Something must have caused that course to change."

I took a deep breath and settled back against the headrest. This new life had too many ifs, ands and buts.

Joshua drove very fast but smoothly, weaving in and out of the traffic like an Olympic skier. I glanced over a few times and saw the speedometer permanently stuck at one hundred. The speed limit on the two-lane highway out to our destination was only fifty-five. Driving this fast didn't bother me as it did when I was ...Besides, if we did get into an accident, we obviously wouldn't be injured. I had already had that experience. Focus on the present I chanted to myself.

"What's special about Shelburne Falls?" Joshua asked, interrupting my daydreaming.

"Alex and I used to come here frequently on our motorcycle." I thought this might bother him--me taking him somewhere that was special to Alex and me but he replied eagerly.

"I have a few motorcycles. Maybe you'll go for a ride with me sometime. We could race each other to the next time zone."

I shook my head while I recalled where the next time zone began. "Let me guess. I bet you own an Indian Motorcycle."

"Yes," he confirmed, "and also a Harley Davidson. How did you know?"

I shrugged. "It's what rich people buy for motorcycles."

"You know they're made in America and supports our economy," he offered.

"Our economy?" I asked dubiously.

"Yes, our economy." He turned toward me, obviously insulted again by my remarks, "Do you not consider me to be an American?"

"You told me you came from Assyria; I just assumed you thought of yourself as such."

"I was born there, yes, and although we still consider ourselves to be of Assyrian descent, we have been on this continent since the seventeenth century, before most present day Americans' ancestors had arrived. We have fought in many of America's wars, the Revolution, the Civil War, WWI and WWII. In Vietnam, we served as doctors. We didn't join the Gulf War or the War in Iraq. We couldn't bring ourselves to fight in that region."

I could hear his voice change at this point from indignant to poignant. "It's our birthplace and even though all our families are gone, it didn't seem right to fight against our descendants."

I sat quiet, realizing that I had insulted him for no reason except that I wanted to lash out at someone. I was a really a mean person.

After a moment he continued, "So yes, we do consider ourselves to be Americans."

"Okay, I'm glad we got that settled." I laughed hoping to ease the tension.

Joshua nodded still lost in his own thoughts. I went back to staring out the window, thinking about his speech. Trying to figure out how I was ever going to be able to understand all of this. How would I ever be able to wrap my head around thousands of years in just a few days?

The silence stretched on for some time until Joshua asked, "Did you bring along your list of questions?"

"Yes and it's a long one," I warned him.

"That's okay. We've got loads of time." He winked. "I have a question for you first if you don't mind me asking."

"Shoot." Although there was probably little he didn't already know about me if he had really been spying as much as he claimed.

"Why are all the mirrors in your house covered up?"

Uh-oh! I knew I shouldn't have let him ask. I swallowed hard. "I don't like looking at myself."

Joshua shot me a perplexed glance. "Why? You're absolutely beautiful. I imagine that most men, as with me, can't keep their eyes off of you."

"Please, Joshua, I thought I was supposed to be asking the questions."

"You're right, forgive me. Go on."

I sifted through the questions that I had mentally compartmentalized into sections with titles such as demons, physical abilities, and what the hell have you been doing for two thousand years? I decided to begin with demon questions. "I'd like to know more about these …Nergal? Where do they come from? How do you know they're here? Do they ring your doorbell like the Avon lady? Ding Dong, Demon calling."

In spite of my attempt at joking, Joshua's voice became tense. "Issy sees many things in her dreams, even the Nergal. They show up in a different part of the world each time but fortunately, the setting in Issy's dreams usually helps to pinpoint the location." He stopped, waiting for my next question.

"How often do they come?"

"Always a few hundred years between each visit." That was a relief; at least I had some time to think about where I could hide from the next one.

"Ramâmu was a skilled necromonger and we're fairly certain that the Nergal are grown from dead human bodies buried in cemeteries. Their skin has that leathery appearance because the original human skin has dried like a prune. We've analyzed the yellow substance that's left after they melt and found it to be a type of plant-based protoplasm."

"How gruesome!" I said sourly. "Why do they melt?"

"You're familiar with the stories about vampires and werewolves? That the only way to kill a vampire is with a wooden stake and werewolves with silver."

"Of course, but those creatures aren't real …are they?" I was ready to believe anything at this point.

Joshua chuckled. "We've never run into any, but we haven't discounted them either. My experience has been that most human legends are based on some truth but in either case, a similar principle also applies to our demons. Our sword blades are forged from substance known as magnetite. It is the only metal that will penetrate their skin and," he turned to look at me, holding my gaze with his piercing eyes, "it's the only substance that can penetrate ours."

I gasped. "Do we melt?"

"No, but we can be wounded and killed by it."

"Why not use guns with bullets to kill the monsters? Those swords are sort of conspicuous."

"We tried bullets but they only slow the Nergal down. They heal very quickly, as do we. They must be decapitated. Once the head is severed from the rest of the body its biological structure degenerates." He grinned. "Too bad, wooden stakes and silver bullets would be much easier to carry around."

"Go ahead and laugh," I said, "I've got news for you. You and your merry little band of lion people are just as mythical as the vampires and werewolves."

Joshua reached out and touched my cheek. "We are just as mythical."

"Umm…" I just nodded. We could argue about that point some other time.

"What was the weapon that injured me?"

Joshua opened his mouth but no sound came out. I waited patiently during the deep silence for him to collect his thoughts.

"We don't know. That was the first time we had ever seen that. We're still trying to figure out how the Nergal was smart enough to construct a weapon at all. We had assumed that their thoughts were on a primitive level and that the spell was unchangeable. Obviously we've missed something." He paused and his brow wrinkled. "We'll figure it out eventually."

"You're not worried about this change?"

"No, there are enough of us around to take care of anything the spell sends for us."

"Three of 'your' kind doesn't seem like much of a force against those things." I shuddered at the thought of what would have happened if there had been more than one monster in the park that day.

"Actually there are sixteen others of 'our' kind, two on each continent."

"There are others." This information stunned me into silence for a few seconds. "Issy has been a busy little lion, hasn't she?"

"Yes. They've all been in Issy's dreams and we have successfully transitioned them into be of assistance in controlling the Nergal."

I decided to change to a less scary subject. "How've you managed to stay hidden all these years? I would have thought someone would have noticed you. Contacts were only invented in the last fifty years."

"That you know of," he said taking his eyes off the road to smile at me.

"What does that mean?"

"We've had contacts since the fourteenth century," he remarked smugly.

"Fourteenth century," I scoffed.

"Nathaniel can be very ingenious. He came up with the idea one night after having too much to drink and woke to find himself staring through a colored glass of ale. We hired a Vienna glassmaker to create them."

"Oh," That did explain a lot.

"Even with the contacts, most of us are all about keeping a low profile. The charity organization is the most public endeavor that we three have attempted and I'm afraid we're getting too contented with this life style. Someday we may have to slide off the map and disappear again to some remote area. That's assuming we can find a remote area. Nowadays this tiny sphere holds seven billion humans. Up until this last century we could roam the forests for decades and never run into anyone." His mouth twisted unhappily. "Cassandra won't be thrilled if we have to return that life. Of course solitude might be best course for Nathaniel. I have all I can do to keep him reined in, to keep him from becoming a public spectacle."

"What does he do to make a spectacle of himself?"

"Driving around in a McLaren with a celebrity woman tends to put you on paparazzi radar and we have to be careful that we aren't recognized from being around a hundred years earlier. It wasn't a problem until photography was invented."

"Speaking of Nathaniel," I said apprehensively, "what's his interest in Lindsey?"

Joshua sighed in disapproval at my question. "You've spent the last two years transforming into a mythical being and one of your most important questions concerns my brother dating your daughter?"

I was peeved. "My daughter's well-being is of utmost concern to me. I really don't want Nathaniel near Lindsey. You need to tell him to stay away from her."

"Katherine, Nathaniel is pretty serious about Lindsey. She's good for him. Cassie and I are hoping she will get him to settle down."

"Really, Joshua, do I look as stupid as you think I am?" I saw him cringe but it didn't stop me from speaking my mind. "Tell me... what will happen when she continues to get older and Nathaniel doesn't? He will have to leave her eventually." Of course I didn't know what I was going to do about that situation either.

"Katherine, please, for now just let them work it out. You and I have more essential things to discuss."

I folded my arms across my chest and tried to slow my breathing. "Fine, but we're not done talking about this," I warned him.

"Oh, I'm sure we're not. Next question please."

"So your swords are made out of this magnetite? I know avian brains contain small quantities that help them navigate but you would need a huge amount to make a sword. Where do you get it from?"

Joshua took his eyes off the road again to answer me and I noted how the car never swayed one inch from its path even at the high speed. "You're correct and we do have a supplier. Magnetite is a naturally occurring mineral, known in ancient times as lodestone. We could use any design for a cutting blade, but the swords are easier to explain."

"Easier to explain than what?" I laughed incredulously. "This is the twenty-first century, Joshua. People don't go around wielding swords."

Joshua shrugged, unperturbed. "We belong to a club that teaches archery and fencing. It's a legal sport. Having had thousands of years of practice, we're all very skilled at sword fighting. Besides, where would be the fun in hunting with guns?"

"Right," I said, frowning. "Where would the fun be in that?"

Then Joshua said something that I was very much unprepared for. "Speaking of swords, you'll need to learn how to fence also. I'll teach you."

"Fencing? I'm not going to be going anywhere near those things."

Joshua pursed his lips, holding back a smile. "You don't need to go fight them--" he raised his eyebrow innocently "--unless you want to."

I scowled back. Why did he think this was funny?

"Nathaniel and I will be taking care of the monsters but you need to learn how to defend yourself, just in case." He had lost the humor in his voice.

"Just in case of what? What is it that you're not telling me?"

"Calm down, Katherine." He reached out to touch my cheek with the back of his hand, instantly drawing me out of my panicked state. "We just killed the Nergal that injured you two years ago so there won't another one for a very long time."

I took a deep breath. "Okay, then I won't have to take any lessons for a very long time."

"It would help me to sleep at night if you knew how to defend yourself," he implored. "We'll start your training next week."

"All right," I said, unhappy but resigned. My head was now full of the dream image of the stalking demon. It was probably a good idea to know something about fighting.

"We're here," Joshua said.

"Already?" Time passed quickly when you were driving at twice the legal limit..

Joshua shut the engine off and reached over, taking my hand in his, trying to soothe me further. "I will make sure you're safe. The demons never come out at the same place. The next one will most likely show up in Asia. We won't even have to deal with it."

"Okay." That information would satisfy me for now. I picked up my bag, reaching for the door handle but Joshua would not release me. "I really wish you would wait for me to get the door for you." His face was within inches of mine. I pulled back as far as I could, while I attempted to collect my thoughts. "I can do it myself, I really don't mind."

"I mind," he stated adamantly.

"I told you I don't want you waiting on me. It's just the way modern women are."

Joshua sighed heavily. "All right, we'll have to work on that."

"There's nothing to work on," I snapped, stepping out of the car and closing the door behind me.

"You can be stubborn, can't you?" Joshua commented as he walked over to stand by my side. He took my hand again. I shrugged my shoulders not bothering to assure him that he couldn't even imagine the extent of my stubbornness.

We spent the next two hours visiting the small town of Shelburne Falls. It was Saturday and the stores along Main Street were busy. We enjoyed a stroll over the Bridge of Flowers and peered eagerly over the black rod iron fence that separated onlookers from the edge of the waterfall that the town was named after. One couldn't resist the mesmerizing effect of the cascading water. Joshua wrapped his arm around my waist. My insides were at war. Part of me knew it was wrong to feel so comfortable in his arms and the other half was taking an immeasurable pleasure in it.

"Are you having fun?" he asked shyly.

"Yes," I replied honestly. "Very much, this has been nice. I have to admit it's a relief to be out of the closet."

Joshua chuckled. "Does that mean you'll go out with me again?"

"Maybe," I told him enthusiastically, "if you take me for lunch." My stomach was rumbling. I was sure he could hear it also.

"I'm hungry too. Where should we eat?"

"On the other side of the bridge is a restaurant with a porch that overlooks the water."

"Lead the way." Joshua kept his arm wrapped around my waist as we walked to the Copper Angel. After we were seated in the perfect spot for viewing the waterfall, the waitress came to take our order. She stared at Joshua the whole time.

Joshua ignored her attention and ordered a beer and a burger, cooked rare of course. His choice sounded delicious but before I do the same, Joshua spoke up and ordered for me. I stared out at the water trying to hide my irritation at him for reading my thoughts again. Eventually, to my embarrassment I couldn't resist looking at him. The pull was too strong.

"Tell me what you're thinking about, please?"

"Don't you know?" I asked accusingly.

"Sorry, I'm really trying to give you some privacy. My siblings and I are so accustomed to not having any secrets from each other that we don't even notice most of the time. I hope you will forgive me if I slip?"

"It doesn't matter, does it? I wouldn't know if you where listening to me or not unless you slip up."

"I'm truly not purposefully listening to your thoughts."

I looked at him carefully---a picture of perfect sincerity. "Okay, I believe you."

Once we had our drinks, Joshua lifted his glass and motioned for me to do the same. "To fate," he offered.

"I really don't like fate too much these days."

"Fate is all we have sometimes to guide us. We all have a destiny to fulfill."

I laughed. "You're getting corny again. This is not some ancient Greek adventure."

Joshua raised his eyebrows. "It could be."

"Joshua, if what you say is true then I'm going to do everything I can to change my destiny. I didn't ask for any of this."

He didn't look happy about my admission and changed the subject.

"Did you know that the Assyrians were the first to brew beer?"

"Finally," I said teasingly, "a worthwhile contribution to modern society."

Joshua smiled. "This really is a beautiful place. Thank you for suggesting it and for agreeing to spend the day with me."

The server came with our food and I ate mine quickly, embarrassingly, of course. After the waitress cleared our plates, I went on with my questions asking the next in a whisper. "Am I going to live for a long time, like you?"

"Yes, you will," Joshua confirmed leaning across the table and answering in the same low tone.

"How long?"

"As long as the planet Earth exists."

"What will I do with that much time?"

"The same thing we've been doing, getting the most out of life."

"We don't ever get sick?"

"No, none of us have had any illness since the day Issy bit us."

"That will be nice. I guess I can sell my stock in Kleenex. So are we like Super Man? Faster than a speeding bullet—able to leap tall buildings?"

Joshua chuckled loudly at my analogy. "Something like that."

"What happens if you get shot with a regular bullet? Does it hurt?"

"It stings, but can't penetrate our skin."

Joshua pulled a few bills out of his wallet and I automatically did the same but he gave me a questioning look. "I think even in these modern time the man usually pays for the meal when on a date, is that correct?"

"Yes," I laughed, "smart-aleck."

When we were back in the privacy of Joshua's car, I got up the nerve to ask about one of the scariest aspects of my new features.

"What's up with the eyes?"

"Issy's serum contains a mixture of magnetite and corundum which is a crystalline form of aluminum oxide. You would know it as sapphire. After a human has been bitten the serum reacts with their blood, replacing the normal divalent iron compound in the hemoglobin with the ferrous-ferric oxide or magnetite. Corundum, in the presence of iron, turns amber. The cells in the eye and blood seem to absorb the color the most." Joshua looked at me curiously.

"I hope I'm not being too technical. I know you're a schooled biochemist."

It really bothered me that he actually knew so many things about me. Stay focused, we're talking about blood now. "My blood is that same amber color?"

Joshua nodded and chuckled at the same time. "Imagine what the doctor would have said if she had seen that."

I stared at him crossly. Most likely he had been watching me the day I went to the doctor.

Joshua shifted uneasily in his seat. "Of course, all the metal in our blood has created an issue for us getting around in these modern times. It sets off metal detectors before we even get within twenty feet of them. We can't fly any more...at least on commercial airlines. We've had to make do with chartering a private plane if we are not in the mood to run."

"Oh! That's why the metal detectors keep going off whenever I go in and out of stores, and the access panel at work."

"Yes."

"Well, at least you don't have to deal with us commoners when you fly."

He frowned at me. "Next question."

"Why has my pupil disappeared?"

"The serum changes the entire structure of the eye. Our hybrid eye processes light in a much more efficient manner than a human eye does."

"Does the serum change our DNA? Are we a different species?"

"We have a few extra chromosomes and several of the human genes are replaced with Issy's genes but we are still a type of hominid."

Joshua waited quietly, letting me absorb this new information.

After a few minutes I shook my head. "I love science fiction but I never thought I would be part of the fiction." The thought depressed me.

"Maybe you've had enough for today?" His voice sounded hopeful.

"No, not nearly," I said, launching into my next question. "Why is our skin impenetrable to everything but this magnetite?"

"Sapphire is a very hard mineral...a nine on the hardness scale, only diamond is harder. Every cell in our body including our skin cells are imbedded with nanoparticles of the sapphire compound. The reason we're faster than humans is due to the way the magnetite is bound to our hemoglobin. It has its own super-sized oxygen molecule giving us a constant supply to fuel our energy demands."

"How did you figure all this out ...about the magnetite and hemoglobin and the sapphire?"

"The originals, back in ancient times knew that magnetite was the only substance that could injure them. That's how they managed to kill each other. We took a chance from the information that Issy had given us that it would work against the Nergal. We only recently discovered the DNA and hemoglobin information from when we owned a biomedical research company back in the 1970s. We performed blood tests on ourselves using magnetite syringes. Similar to the effect on the demons, we think that the magnetite causes a molecular breakdown in our skin allowing it to slip between the nanoparticles of the sapphire compound." He paused, looking hesitant.

"What?" I asked.

"Well, we were hoping that maybe we could continue our research with your assistance, especially since there have been huge amount of breakthroughs in genetics lately. We could go back to school together."

"Sure, why not?" I replied cautiously. "What else is there to do with all this time?" I didn't mention that this only made me feel even more like a high school science experiment.

"Why don't we age?"

"Our skin is analogous to a stone, smooth and hard and it doesn't wear easily. We do age but the subtle changes to our appearance are not easily detectable even by us." Joshua continued onto other aspects of our physiology that he probably knew I would be asking about. "The lion serum has anti-microbial properties similar to honey which keeps away any infections. Our hearing is accelerated, we think, due to the exchange of genes. Then there is the mind reading...and the dreams. Where do they come from?" He laughed at himself, incredulous. "I also have a long list of questions about this life that I would like answered."

"Issy doesn't know?" After all, I thought, at one time she was considered by many to be a god.

"No," Joshua sighed. "She only knows what we can do--she doesn't know the why's or how's."

"Oh, that's too bad." The scientist in me was disappointed also.

"Do you understand everything I've told you up to now?"

I nodded, staring vacantly out over the dashboard. "I think so. It's not really a matter of understanding, is it? It's only a matter of acceptance. I can't change anything even if I wanted to." My words came out with a hiss. Maybe it was just the frustration at being bombarded with so much information. Or maybe it was a natural reaction to not having been given the choice to make for myself. I knew it was illogical to be mad about this. Joshua and his family had saved my life.

"Do you wish that we had let you die?" I could hear the pain in Joshua's voice.

"Before I answer, tell me, how do all the others feel about this life, the other sixteen?"

"They're happy and well adjusted but everything was explained to them before they were changed. Issy would never have forced them."

"But she forced me," I stated.

"Please don't blame her. It was my fault...all mine."

I touched his arm and moderated my voice. "I'm not blaming anyone." I let my head fall back and closed my eyes. "It's just been a lot to adjust to."

"You didn't answer my question," he pressed.

"No, I don't wish that you had let me die. What I wish for the most is that I hadn't gone into the park that day." I looked over at Joshua's strained expression. I knew that was not what he wished for. "This might sound crazy to you, but I feel that I've been robbed of something." I could see the disbelief in his expression. I sighed and gave up trying to explain how I felt.

The uneasy feeling that I had been so much a part of my life for the last two years had returned, having been chased away only for the few hours spent in Shelburne Falls. I had no more questions for the remainder of the trip into the city.

KAREN ANN

Chapter 8

THE MOMENTS
OF YOUR LIFE

You will find, as you look back upon your life,
that the moments when you've really lived
are the moments when you've really loved.

Joshua wound his way through the narrow Back Bay streets, taking random lefts and rights. When we arrived at the underground garage for his apartment building, I shook my head. The sign on the outside of the building read, "Avalon at the Prudential Center." How much must these places cost, I wondered?

When we pulled up to the front gate, the guard handed Joshua a clipboard. He signed on the next open line, all the while watching my reaction as he wrote.

I raised my eyebrows and smiled. "Impressive." It came out sounding a little sarcastic.

"How's your daughter, Paul? Has she started school yet?" Joshua asked the man in the booth as he returned the clipboard.

"Yes, she's great Mr. Stone. She wanted me to thank you again for the scholarship."

"You're welcome. Let me know when Jessica graduates. If she needs a recommendation I'll be happy to write one."

"Thank you," the man answered back fervently.

Joshua pulled to the back end of the garage complex and parked next to several sports cars wrapped with the same cloth covers that Alex used for his. He turned off the ignition but didn't make a move to get out of the car. He stared motionless out the driver's side window.

After an uncomfortable moment of silence I asked, "Is there something wrong? Did you change your mind about having dinner with Cassie?"

Joshua shifted his position to look directly at me. "Do you have an issue with me being rich? Is it going to interfere with us dating?"

"I thought we were getting married," I asked joking lightly.

"Do you not like money? I find that most people do."

I didn't answer. Why did he care what I thought? Don't start crying, I told myself over and over but the chanting didn't work.

"What are you doing?' he asked incredulously as he wiped a tear from my cheek.

"Crying… apparently."

"Please tell me why." Joshua's voice was gentler now, more soothing.

"Why don't you just find the answer for yourself?" I sputtered. "Then I won't have to tell you. You'll be mad."

"I can't imagine that." He sighed. "This is very confusing. Now you want me to read your mind? Why won't you answer my question?"

"All right, but I guarantee you won't like it." I took a deep breath and sighed. "It's not that I don't like the fact that you're rich. I'm just waiting for you to realize that I'm not. I don't feel comfortable in this world."

"Katherine, in my long life on this planet I have never seen or found anything more important than love."

He leaned in towards me, coming within inches of my face. His warm, sweet breath mussed the loose strands of my hair. "It may take some time but I will prove it to you. Will you please give me a chance?"

"Yes," I replied in a small voice, too stunned to say anything more. I still didn't understand why he was able to befuddle me like that.

"Katherine, please close your eyes and count to five."

"Will you be performing a magic trick?"

"I hope you'll think it's magic."

I closed my eyes and began counting, one, two, and... Before I could say three Joshua was opening the passenger door.

I stared at him astonished, "Well, that was quite a trick. How did you get over here that fast?" I looked over and saw that the driver's door was shut tight. I hadn't heard it close.

"I can move quite fast when I want to but that wasn't the magic I was referring to."

Joshua pulled me out of the car and into the circle of his arms. I wondered if my ribs were strong enough to keep my throbbing heart from breaking through my chest.

"You smell wonderful." His voice was uneven, with a nervous edge to it. "May I kiss you?"

The question stunned me and instinctively I pulled back. I was scared--scared because in the blink of an eye, he and his world could disappear again. Joshua had been a distant fire whose heat I had longed to feel. I had been having an illicit affair with him from the moment I'd met him--secretly and disgracefully--while Alex slept quietly by my side. Guilt overwhelmed me in that same instant but it was not enough to pull me out of his arms. I doubted there was a force on earth that could have done that. I wanted this. This was mine.

My breath stuttered and I found myself nodding.

Joshua paused for a fraction of second. Then with the slightest touch took hold of my neck, under my hair, and pulled me in until our lips touched.

I can quite honestly say that I wouldn't have a clue as to what it would feel like to be struck by lightning, but I imagined that it would have been comparable to kissing Joshua. First, there was shock as I tried to wrestle with the overwhelming feeling of pleasure, followed by numbness. My legs buckled as they turned to the consistency of rubber. All that kept me from falling was Joshua's arm around my waist. His kiss was just the right mixture of fury and delight. Our lips fit together like two pieces of a puzzle. It was like magic.

Joshua pulled back slowly and I stood frozen with anticipation, like a child waiting for another piece of candy. "That was the magic."

"Hmm," I said, nodding, trying to slow my breathing.

"We should go up. Cassie is very anxious to see you. Any more kissing and I don't think we'll make dinner."

"Oh, of course, let's go." I had just about forgotten the whole world for those few moments.

The control panel of the elevator took up the entire left wall. Joshua pressed one of the large buttons marked P.

"What does P stand for?"

"Uh, Penthouse." He looked down, embarrassed.

I had upset him enough with my jaded views about the rich for one night. "Wow, you must have a great view of the city."

It worked. "It's extraordinary," he beamed with enthusiasm.

We stepped off the elevator into a foyer the size of my living room. It was decorated with two hotel-style tables each flanked by comfy-looking chairs. Generic-looking paintings hung on the walls, separating the three doors in the hallway.

"Cassie's apartment is to the right. The middle door is Nathaniel's and this is mine." When we were a within a few feet of the door I heard a metallic click and it swung open on its own.

"Magnetic locks." Joshua explained. "It was a novelty when we first moved in. Now it's just annoying."

"Aren't you worried about burglars? Isn't Cassie worried?"

Joshua chuckled loudly. "Any burglar would be in for the shock of his life when he encountered Cassie."

"Right …demon hunter."

Joshua gave me a quick tour. For what I was sure was one of the most exclusive places in Boston his apartment was unexpectedly modest in size and sparsely furnished. Two bedrooms, two bathrooms, a small open kitchen area, and an office populated the floor plan. The outside walls of all the rooms were exposed with floor to ceiling windows to take advantage of the breathtaking city scene.

The front door popped open again and Joshua sighed heavily. "That will be Cassie. Come in," he said loudly, I guessed mostly for my benefit.

Cassie swept into the room with the grace of a ballerina, coming up to me so quickly that it was difficult to follow her movements. She wrapped her arms around me and gave me a long hug

"I'm ecstatic that you came!" she gushed. "It will be wonderful to have a girl to hang around with." She shot a disapproving look in Joshua's direction. "Men can be so annoying. I'm positive they're a different species that somehow mistakenly ended up here with us women and now we're forced to share this world with them."

I laughed loudly at her comic rhetoric. My mouth hurt from the unexpected force of it. I hadn't laughed like this since... *Stop it* I told myself, don't start. "I'm glad to see you also and I agree, men can be very annoying at times." My eyes flashed to Joshua.

"Okay, you two, enough with the humor at my expense." He complained, but I could see his delight over the instant bonding between Cassie and me.

"I have dinner prepared. Please don't be too long. We have lots to talk about." Cassie declared gushing again with excitement.

"All right, run along now, Cassie. We'll be over in a minute." Joshua's words rebuked her but in an adoring way.

"See what a mean brother he is?" Cassie stuck her tongue out at Joshua as she left.

All of a sudden the anxiety of the day began to wear me down. Joshua came to my side and steadied me. "We can skip dinner if you prefer."

"No, no, I'll be fine," I assured him. "Everything is happening very quickly. I just need a minute."

Joshua led me over to the couch and I willingly let the plushy cushion envelope my head. "I thought I was ready for all this. You dreaming about me, Issy and her issues, the kissing." I sighed heavily. It felt like there was a weight on my chest again.

Joshua took my hand. "Nothing will happen until you're ready for it. You can have all the time you need and if you decide in the end that you don't want it at all, that will be fine also."

"Joshua," I assured him, "I just need some time. Oh and one more thing. I'm not going to run into Lindsey, am I?"

Joshua winced. "No, I asked Nathaniel to keep her away while you were here. I figured you didn't want her to know too much yet."

"I don't want her to know anything ever," I told him in a clipped tone. The thought of Lindsey snapped me out of my fainting spell and I was able to get back to my feet.

Cassie's apartment was very similar to Joshua's but had more of a woman's touch with the décor. One corner of the living room held the most beautiful variety of musical instruments I had ever seen. Some hung on the wall, others sat on the floor in their own stands. I asked Joshua about the strange-looking double-headed drum.

"It's called a dola, spelled d-h-o-l. Our ancestors used it. This one is very old."

"Does Cassie play all these instruments?"

"Actually we're all very talented musicians."

"Really? That's amazing."

Joshua shrugged modestly. "We've had a lot of time to practice. I'll teach you to play if you'd like."

"Even though you may have a lot of time, you'd be wasting it trying to teach me music."

"You'll be able to learn quickly now. I guarantee it."

"Maybe."

Joshua sensed my trepidation. "Just think of all the things in this world that you would have tried if you had no boundaries-- things such as skydiving or bungee jumping, or swimming the English Channel. You can do anything you want now without fear. I know it's difficult at the moment to forget your human frailties but you will in time."

I heard Cassie clear her throat behind us. Joshua took my hand and led me to the table. At first I thought that maybe the Queen of England was coming to dinner. Each of us had three wine glasses of various sizes all neatly arranged at the top of each place setting, which was surrounded by a horde of silverware. I hoped I wouldn't break any of it. Seriously, a paper cup would have been fine with me.

Cassie shot me a disparaging look, obviously seeing my mental assessment of her table setting. I would have to talk to her also about this mind reading thing.

Joshua opened a bottle of red wine. Before we began to eat, he raised his glass and spoke the word "Saa..ha."

I looked at him perplexed.

"It's Aramaic which means, essentially, to your health."

They must toast to this out of habit, as they certainly didn't need to wish for good health.

"We do." Cassie said. I frowned at her.

"How many languages do you speak?" I asked quickly before she could pry again.

"Over one hundred--and Nathaniel even more." Cassie replied matter-of-factly.

"One hundred! Nobody can speak that many languages."

They both stopped eating and stared at me.

"We've lived in nearly every region around the globe at one time or another. In order to blend in, of course, it required that we learn the language and since we never forget anything--" Joshua stopped and shrugged his shoulders, leaving it up to me to figure out the rest of the point he was trying to make.

"You can remember them all?" I asked, still doubtful.

"Yes, and so will you if you desire so."

I thought about that. "I'd like to learn this Aramaic." It seemed that if they were going to be speaking to each other in this language I should learn it also.

Joshua smiled hugely. "Great! We'll work on it a little every day."

Steak was for dinner. Joshua had his raw; Cassie and I had ours slightly cooked. I still didn't like to eat raw meat even though I craved it and to my relief neither did she.

"It was the happiest day of my life," Cassie told me, "when I realized that I could buy meat in a store. I only do raw when I'm out hunting with the boys. They love to hunt of course."

I didn't understand what she was saying to me about hunting and she could see this in my mind.

"Katherine doesn't know about the hunting? I thought you told her everything."

Joshua looked at her incredulously. "I've told Katherine as much as I thought she needed to know in two days." Joshua turned in my direction to explain. "Sometimes when we're out hunting the Nergal and we need to eat, we may take down a deer. It's clearly not something you need to concern yourself with now."

As far as I was concerned, it would never be something I needed to be concerned with. They both frowned at me.

The three of us talked for a long time after dinner. Actually, Cassie did most of the talking. Even though I kept reminding myself that she terrifyingly old, she acted like a young girl. Her interests were closer to my daughter's than to mine. I could tell she was disappointed with my lack of socializing and my disinterest in clothes shopping also.

At midnight I began to yawn. Joshua took the hint and we said our goodnights.

"Thank you," Joshua said when we were back at his place.

"For what?"

"For being patient with Cassie. It's nice for her to have a female friend that's one of us. She's been without one for too long now and without a mother figure."

"I like Cassie. I think we'll be great friends."

Joshua smiled contently as handed me a set of headphones. "You'll be able to sleep more soundly with these. They cancel out most of the clatter."

"Thanks. I usually don't stay over in the city because of the noise."

"Good, then maybe now you'll stay over more often." His eyes were optimistic.

"Maybe." I felt a sharp pain at the thought of leaving him even to sleep, but I forced myself to say, "See you in the morning."

I could feel the lines in my life trying to shift yet again, and I struggled against the certainty that I would not be able to stop it this time either.

KAREN ANN

Chapter 9

ISHTAR

*You are not wrong, who deem
That my days have been a dream
Yet if hope has flown away
In a night, or in a day
In a vision, or in none
Is it therefore the less gone?
All that we see or seem
Is but a dream within a dream*

~ Edgar Allen Poe

"Katherine, are you up?"

I glanced over at the clock and saw that it was five a.m. For once, the sense of dread that usually accompanied waking was gone. The comfort that came with finally understanding was refreshing.

"Come in," I said groggily.

Joshua opened the door, beaming. "Did you sleep well?"

"Yes, it's very comfortable here. Those headphones worked great."

"Once your mind is stronger you won't need them. I've made some coffee. What would you like for breakfast?"

"Coffee sounds great, no food though. I'll eat at work."

Joshua turned and left with a disappointed look. I came out with my bag in hand ready to leave and noticed the table. Of course Joshua had ignored me. He was holding out a chair for me. I sighed.

"I think you should eat before we leave. I can hear your stomach growling."

"Fine." I reached for the coffee and put some of the food on my plate. It did smell good.

I noticed Joshua staring at my ring, not my wedding ring, the one on my right hand, the one I had found in the car.

"This was from you, wasn't it?"

"Yes." Joshua sighed. "I stole it from Cassie. It was a silly thing to do but it comforted me knowing that you had some small token of me."

"The ring is made out of magnetite, I assume."

Joshua nodded. "I told myself that it was necessary for you to have it for protection. Just one touch of this ring on a demon's skin will injure it and slow it down. Of course you didn't know that. Issy was upset with me because ..." He trailed off.

"I'm glad you gave it to me. Just the feel of the ring on my finger kept my hope up that I would find you." I glanced up and noticed the time. "Oh, I need to get to work."

"Yes, I should go also. Nathaniel will be pacing the floor waiting for me."

When we got to the garage I couldn't resist asking about the cars under the covers. Alex had loved sports cars and some of his enthusiasm had rubbed off on me.

Joshua eyed me warily.

"No more spoiled rich kid comments," I assured him.

"They belong to Nathaniel." Joshua proceeded to uncover the front of each one. I easily recognized the Dodge Viper, as well as the second one--a reproduction Ford GT40. The side emblem gave away the maker of the third one--a Ferrari.

I had to laugh when I saw the tags on the Viper: "Once Bitten?"

Joshua winked. "It's an inside joke. Let's go or you'll be late for work."

I could feel my face fall as we pulled up to the back door of LCA.

"What time will you get out today?"

"Usually at four but I can get a ride home from a co-worker who lives in Townsend." I hoped Joshua didn't notice my disappointment. It was embarrassing for a woman my age to be acting like a goo-eyed teenager.

"Why don't you let me pick you up after work, then we can talk some more?"

I took a breath. The truth was I wasn't sure what I wanted. On the one hand I was afraid to spend too much time with Joshua, it would hurt even more when he left and I knew that was inevitable. There was a sharp pain in my chest however at the thought of us being separated. Joshua had truly become my protector.

While I was still contemplating my dilemma, Joshua handed me a business card. "My cell phone number as well as Nathaniel's and Cassie's are on this. You should memorize them." Then he leaned over and kissed me. Joshua had to end the kiss also, as I found myself clinging tightly to him. "Have a nice day. Call me if you change your mind about tonight."

I stepped out of the car in a daze. My footsteps were weightless as I made my way through the back entrance of the building that led directly into the company cafeteria. The usually brightly lit room was dull in comparison to my weekend in fantasyland. It was difficult to step away from the rabbit hole. I snickered to myself as I walked to my cube. My friend Donna didn't know how dead on her assessment had been.

I had lunch with Josephine who launched into a barrage of questions the moment we sat down. "You seem to have lost your usual aura of doom and gloom, Mom. Did something happen over the weekend?" she asked, scrutinizing my face.

I tried to keep it simple when I went over the story about going out with Lindsey and meeting her boss but nothing about spending the weekend with Joshua. It was bad enough that Lindsey had become unknowingly mixed up in this freaky world.

"Do you like this Joshua?" Josephine asked, trying to act casual. Obviously, her sister had dished about everything.

I shrugged, also trying to act casual. "He's nice."

Josephine seemed aggravated at my apparent lack of interest in this subject. "Mom, you can't sit around for the rest of your life alone." It had only been three months but I guess when you're twenty-three that can seem like a lifetime.

Josephine waited for me to respond and when I didn't she tried again. "So are you going to see Joshua again?" I could tell she wasn't going to give up until I told her something.

It was too much trouble trying to lie and I knew I wasn't very good at it anyway. "We might go out for dinner tonight."

Josephine gushed, "That's wonderful. Where are you going?"

"I'm not sure. Now can we please change the subject?"

Josephine nodded happily, her curiosity satisfied.

At around two o'clock my attention span reached its limit. I agonized over what to do and what I wanted. In the end it came down to will power, of which I had none, and I found myself reaching for the phone, not able to fight the urge anymore. Joshua's hello was high-spirited, making me instantly suspicious. My work was certainly within the range of his ability to see my mind. I wondered if he could hear the thumping of my heart also.

"I've decided that I'd like to talk some more. I thought you might want to come for dinner tonight?"

"Great, I'll pick you up after work."

At four on the dot, Joshua was waiting, leaning against the passenger door of his car, still looking like a Greek god. Even when he pushed himself off the side of the car to open the door, it was with such with grace I wanted to cry. Would I … could I ever be that graceful?

"What took you so long?" I teased lightly as he climbed at a normal human speed into the driver's seat.

"We don't want to scare your fellow employees, now, do we?" Joshua leaned over to kiss me but I pulled back seeing several of my fellow employees walk past the car.

"No one can see us through the tinted glass."

"I don't want people to go running to Josephine about us."

"That's fine, but eventually you'll have to tell them."

"But not now," I pleaded.

Joshua pursed his lips and nodded.

We stopped at the market in Bedford for dinner supplies. Joshua was right about his cooking skills. The steak was fabulous and we talked in between bites about work. Well, it was mostly me talking. I was stalling. Even though my curiosity had not be quelled in the least bit, the more I knew the scarier it got.

I took a deep breath and prepared myself for the next barrage of information. "I was wondering... why do you live here in America? You could live anywhere you wanted without all the pretenses."

"That's true, but America is a very diverse country and we blend in quite well."

"Why are you living here in Boston when you could live anywhere?"

"I told you we move around." He raised his eyebrows. "Next." Some inkling told he was holding back. "How is it that you happened to be living here in New England at the same time as the person that you've been dreaming about for a thousand years?"

Joshua stared at me for a long moment before answering. "I suspected that you were here."

"How?"

"In my dream..." he hesitated.

"The dream?" I prompted.

Joshua spoke so quickly that I had to concentrate to catch each word. "The dream was very foggy for a long time. It was maddening. I couldn't get a clear vision of your features. Then about fifty years ago, I now know that it coincided with your birth, the woman's face began to clarify as well as the place."

I shook my head in frustration. Marriage and love should not be arranged even by something as nebulous as fate. "Do your dreams always come true? Are you positive that we'll get married?"

Joshua pursed his lips then said, "This one I'm sure of. Next?"

I sighed in frustration but went on. "Well, I was wondering...why do you have so much money? Where did it all come from? Is it left over from when you lived in the palace?"

"No, that wealth is long gone. We've been in the stock market since it began back in the early 1900s. Nathaniel has quite a talent for making money."

I wished I hadn't brought this subject up. It made me uncomfortable. I began fidgeting with my wedding ring.

"Katherine, for a long, long time we lived like nomads, with nothing more than the clothing that we wore and the weapons we carried. When the world began to get more crowded, it became increasingly difficult to avoid humans. I admit we overdid it at first; it was a new sensation to have money and so much money, but it didn't bring the happiness that we thought it would. There was still something missing in our lives. It was in the early sixties when we started our foundation, trying to ease some of the pain that exists in the world. The pain caused by war and disease." He paused for a moment, lost in thought. "It was actually President Kennedy who gave us the idea. We went to his inauguration and after listening to his speech we knew we had the answer to how we wanted to spend our time."

"What was it that he said?" I could only recall the "Ask not" part of the speech.

Joshua proceeded to recite word for word President Kennedy's lines. "With a good conscience our only sure reward, with history the final judge of our deeds, let us go forth to lead the land we love, asking His blessing and His help, but knowing that here on earth God's work must truly be our own."

"Oh," I said, still perplexed.

"What he was saying was that our deeds will be the judge of how well we've lived our lives. That it's not enough to say that we believe in God, that we must do the work that we believe God would do while we're here on Earth." Joshua shook his head. "If only more humans practiced what they preached. Americans alone could feed billions just on the scraps of food we throw away."

"Do you believe in God?" I couldn't imagine that since he was very nearly a god himself.

Joshua sighed. "Faith is not something I've ever been able to understand or embrace. Even after I found Issy, whom many have worshipped, I couldn't think of her as one. I have found spirituality in giving, though, and the moral lesson that faith teaches I do believe in. I'm pleased that humans have a god that gives them hope and comfort." He shifted closer to me as he continued. "I truly hope that there is a place for the good to go when they leave this earth and also a place for the bad but this is something we'll have to wait a long time to find out about." He paused as we both contemplated his words. Then in a witty tone he said, "Next?"

I was glad for the subject change also. Religion was something I didn't like to discuss either. I was certainly in the minority when it came to my non-beliefs. Being a scientist I was a card carrying skeptic when it came to the supernatural. I had trouble believing in anything that I couldn't see and touch. I sighed as I realized that that aspect of me was also beginning to change.

"Doesn't the government think it's weird that a person named Joshua Stone has been around for the last three hundred years?"

"Since the beginning of our existence there have been people that forge documents. I've been born and died many times. You're right to question this, though. As humans have advanced it's become an increasing challenge to hide our true identity."

"Do you always go by the name Joshua Stone?"

"We used other names until the American Revolution. At the time we become close friends with the families of two brothers, Joshua and Nathaniel Stone who lived in Hancock, NH. We knew they suspected something but they welcomed us into their homes regardless of their fear. During one of the battles outside of New York the both brothers were killed. With Joshua's dying breath he asked me to take care of his family and not let his name die out..." Joshua's voice drifted for a moment. "We decided the best way to memorialize them was to immortalize their names." He winked. "Besides, the name Stone describes us more appropriately than anyone knows."

Then for no reason that I could perceive Joshua stood up.

"Is everything all right?" I stood up also looking for whatever it was that had startled him.

"Issy has come to visit." He turned to see my reaction.

"The lion!" The hysteria slipped out even though I was trying not to be hysterical.

"Issy wants to meet you formally. You'll be perfectly safe."

"Okay," I said, wincing. "As long as she doesn't bite me again."

Joshua leaned over and kissed the top of my head. "You're silly."

I watched wide-eyed as the mystical mascot strode casually across my back yard. I looked up at Joshua, even more anxious. What would the neighbors say if they saw this?

Joshua squeezed my hand. "We're the only ones that can see her."

Issy came springing up the stairs onto the porch. I was aghast at how enormous she was. My memory from that day in the forest had not done her justice. The crest of her back was higher than Joshua's hip. Issy greeted Joshua the same way a domestic cat would by bumping him with her colossal head and twisting along his side. Joshua patted her adoringly. No sound was made in greeting as their form of communication was within their minds.

"Maybe we should go inside?" I whispered. It was difficult to accept that we were the only ones that could see her.

Issy followed us inside, her footfalls made no sound. I watched perplexed as she walked in and out of each room. Joshua explained that she was taking in the scents of the house. He said it was a lion thing. We all settled into the living room after Issy finished smelling the house. Joshua and I sat on the couch together. Issy curled up beside Joshua on the floor. She reminded me of an Egyptian Sphinx-- very proud and majestic.

"Are you communicating with her through your mind?"

Joshua nodded. "Issy likes you."

I laughed. "That's because she doesn't know me yet."

"She can read your mind. She's a pretty good judge of character."

"Except for that Gilgamesh character." I reminded him.

Issy's head whipped around, a growling sound came up out of her throat. I flinched and moved closer to Joshua.

"Umm, Katherine, it's best not to bring that up. As you can see she's still sensitive about that subject."

"Okay," I agreed. "No bringing up the past."

Issy was definitely lion-like but you would never mistake her for a mortal lion. In spite of my fear, I had this overwhelming urge to pet her.

"You can sit with her if you want," Joshua said encouragingly.

"Okay, I guess I need to get over this."

Joshua put his hand under my chin. "You are a part of Issy now. She would never harm you."

I stood up, trying to control my shaky knees, and moved to sit on the floor beside the huge animal. Issy's beauty mesmerized me. I rubbed behind her ears the way I did with my cat and her responsive purring had the same soothing quality. Issy's tail, sporting the familiar firecracker-like splash of fur, swished sporadically. I took that as another sign of her contentment. I reached out slowly to touch the dark colored disc on her forehead, gently tracing the lines of the two incised crescents. The object was smooth and cool to the touch. I wondered why she would have such a strange thing stuck to her head.

I looked up and realized that Joshua was watching me, gauging my reaction. Maybe he was afraid that I would run away screaming. I wasn't so sure that I wouldn't.

Before I could ask about the head ornamentation, Joshua volunteered the answer. "No, it doesn't come off. The ancients concentrated and embedded her powers into the magnetite disc. It enables her to kill the demons."

I sat staring at the exquisite animal in front of me, trying to bear in mind that she was once a person or at least in a person form. It was difficult to imagine how Issy must have felt about her transformation. I had gone through some extraordinary changes but still had the same outward human appearance. My life for all essential purposes had gone on as it was before. I felt a huge amount of remorse for all the disparaging thoughts I had about her after being bitten. I could appreciate more clearly now why Issy had changed the Stones and even me. It would be dreadful to have to spend eternity completely alone.

"How has she gotten through all the centuries in this form?"

"It's been an arduous journey but she's learned to accept this life and is at peace with herself."

"Hasn't she been punished for long enough? How long a sentence was this supposed to be?"

"The knowledge to break the binding spell died with the ancients. Early on we searched the entire globe hoping to find the witches spell book but we were unsuccessful. Witchcraft is a long-lost art. Of course, being bound in this form is most likely the reason that Issy is still alive. She was absent for the war that resulted in the death of the other originals."

Just then, Nutmeg came walking across the back of the couch. I reached for him, fearful of his reaction. Joshua stopped me. "Wait, it will be fine."

My cat and Joshua's cat greeted each other affectionately. Nutmeg settled in between the lion's enormous outstretched legs. He was braver than me.

"Issy is friends with all cat species," Joshua explained. "She spends most of her time socializing with lions and tigers and even hunting with them. They accept her as one of their own and she finds companionship with them. She can't stay with us in the human world."

"Hunting with other lions? Like in Africa?"

"Yes, and the tigers in India and Asia."

"How does she get there? What about the oceans? Does she hitch a ride on a cargo plane?" I imagined her slipping by some unaware guard on a military transport.

"Issy swims, actually."

"Swims? She swims the ocean?"

Joshua laughed. "We're exceptional swimmers. Nathaniel and I have swum the Atlantic and the Pacific many times. Not Cassie though. She doesn't like getting wet. We could go together if you ever want to try it."

I looked at the ceiling. That was the most preposterous idea I ever heard. "No, thanks. I'm with Cassie. No swimming the planet's oceans." Conquering new boundaries and feats of strength were definitely a guy thing. Apparently even with superhuman men.

"Okay, but you don't know what you're missing out on."

"I don't want to know," I said with a stubborn tone. Joshua looked disappointed.

We sat quietly listening to the rhythm of the purring cats. I chuckled uncontrollably at a random thought.

"What's so funny?" Joshua asked.

"You know, when I was young I always wanted a lion for a pet, especially after I went to Lion Country Safari and had my photo taken with one of their cubs."

Joshua pursed his lips then said. "She's not our pet."

"Sorry, I warned you that I had no control over my thoughts."

At that, Issy stood up. I looked at Joshua for a translation. "Issy is going now."

"Why?" I was worried that I had accidentally insulted her with the pet comment.

"She just prefers the outdoors as most cats do," Joshua said in a soothing voice, calming my fears. "Issy likes you. Your thoughts are soothing to her."

"My thoughts are soothing to her?" That was funny. My mind was usually in utter chaos. I found it doubtful that anyone found my thoughts soothing--even a giant mind-reading lion.

Then as quickly as Issy had appeared, the colossal lion bounded out the door and was gone but not before she had jumped up on my shoulders and gave me a wet good-bye lick across my cheek with her sandpaper tongue.

Nutmeg followed her out, eventually stopping at the end of the yard to join the rest of the cats that had gathered there.

"Well, I guess there's no problem with the cats getting along. Mine's obviously crazy about yours."

Joshua nestled me in his arms. "Yes, that's one less thing for you to worry about. You know, if you frown enough your features may become permanently set like that."

I blanched. "Could that happen?"

Joshua's smile widened. "Of course not."

"Not funny, Joshua." The kissing began before I could scold him further and I did forget about all my worries for the moment.

Chapter 10
THE FOIL

*First, he cleared the grove of Zeus of a lion,
and put its skin upon his back, hiding his yellow
hair in its fearful tawny gaping jaws.*

Euripides, Hercules, 359, the killing of the Nemean Lion

"Hi, beautiful," Joshua cooed on the other end of the phone. "Are you blushing yet?" I could hear him stifling a laugh.

I shook my head. "You know I am." It was frustrating that he could read my face even when he wasn't looking at me.

"What time I should collect you from work? It's Friday and I thought we might celebrate by going to dinner after we're done with your lesson."

For the past two weeks, Joshua had coerced me into fencing lessons. He knew how much I disliked the tedious training. Each lesson consisted primarily of drill after drill to practice my stance, with Joshua constantly correcting me.

"Katherine, your feet are too far apart--your feet are too close— try to keep your right foot pointing straight out." Then there were the drills to practice my attempts at lunging. That brought on a new round of critiques such as, "Katherine, you need to lunge with your back knee which should end up perfectly straight when you've completed the move." I told Joshua repeatedly that I had no athletic skill but his answer was always the same--that issue only applied to my previous human life.

Of course, the training would have been more enjoyable if I knew it wasn't in preparation for fighting ugly demons. "Fine," I said, exasperated. "Maybe tonight you could actually put a sword in my hand. Then at least I can feel like this is leading to something." I knew I was whining but I didn't care.

"It's called a foil," he corrected me.

"Ugh, I know what it's called, Joshua."

I took a deep breath. I didn't want to squabble with Joshua about this. The Nergal were not my problem. This was not my war. I was an innocent bystander who happened to be in the wrong place at the wrong time.

"We need only practice for one hour tonight," Joshua promised.

"Okay," I grumbled, "I'll see you at four." I couldn't stay mad at Joshua so I added, "I miss you."

"I miss you too. See you later."

After we were on our way to the sports club Joshua asked, "It looked like you were deep in thought when you came walking out from work. What're you thinking about?"

I eyed him suspiciously.

"What?" Joshua asked, feigning innocence. I had been thinking that if I had to spend eternity with someone, spending it with Joshua wouldn't be so bad but I wasn't ready to admit that to him.

"I don't trust you sometimes."

"I'm very trustworthy." His teeth glinted as he spoke in spite of the dark window tint.

"You know, when my mind reading does begin, you won't be able to get away with this anymore."

"Oh, I know. That's why I'm taking advantage while I still can," he declared shamelessly.

"Unbelievable," I grumbled. I folded my arms across my chest. "Are you familiar with the saying payback can be a bitch?"

This time there was an unfamiliar dark edge to his answering laugh. "I certainly am."

I was thrilled when we pulled into the empty parking lot. "Do we have to gear up?" I asked. "We're the only ones here tonight." We didn't need to wear any protective equipment but the club had rules and the Stones were all about keeping up the impression of being normal.

"Katherine, you know we do."

"Yeah, I know." I trudged off to the dressing room, my shoes scuffing purposely.

Joshua had purchased a beginner foil with a French grip for me. He preferred to use a foil that had an Italian style grip, which was a more classical style. Of course it was classical because his was over 400 years old.

The practice room was about the size of a high school gym with hardwood floors and high ceilings. The chips of sapphire glistened under the fluorescent lights giving an iridescent glow to our skin.

Joshua refused to begin the lesson until I put on the bulky head covering. Even with my super-duper vision, I had trouble seeing out of it.

I listened patiently, for me anyway, while Joshua droned on about the importance of foot position again. After two minutes, I put up my hand to stop him.

"Why do I need to know all of this? The only thing you need to teach me is how to behead these things."

"There are other reasons for learning defense above and beyond the Nergal."

I took off my helmet and placed it under my arm. "Other reasons? What other reasons?"

Joshua removed the glove from his right hand and placed his palm across my cheek. "It's nothing that you have to worry about right now."

I knew there was more to that statement than he was divulging but I also knew that he was trying not to overwhelm me or scare me with too much information at once. "Okay, let's continue."

During the first thirty minutes of the practice session Joshua killed me at least ten times, or would have, if we had been using magnetite. I wasn't able get one valid hit on him.

When the hour was nearly over, Joshua managed to orchestrate a move that brought our foils together and we fell into each other's arms, giggling like children. We removed our headgear and I was expecting and looking forward to his automatic kiss when suddenly I felt him stiffen.

I shook him, trying to free him from the trance. Then in a much too familiar motion, he whirled around, putting me behind him in a protective position. It was a gesture that meant there was danger nearby, just like the day in the park. I held my breath as I stood up on my toes, peering over his shoulder to see what was coming for us. I gasped loudly as I caught sight of the mysterious man that had been in one of my previous dreams.

Even if I hadn't known his face, it was immediately apparent that this man was one of us--his amber eyes shone like beacons. At first glance, he appeared to be identical in age and appearance to Joshua and Nathaniel. His transformation had left him with the same stunning good looks. His long blonde hair, tied into a ponytail, hung loosely over his right shoulder.

Except there was something different about this man. This man's eyes where full of unfathomable bitterness and his expression lacked the compassion that I had become so accustomed to seeing in Joshua's face.

I blinked and in that same instant the man had moved half the distance to us from where he had been. He was twirling a swashbuckler style sword in each hand.

Joshua didn't move from his protective stance as he greeted the man in a determinedly unpleasant voice.

"Hello, Reggie. What are you doing here?"

"Marodeen," Reggie replied tonelessly, calling Joshua by his given Assyrian name. "Is that any way to greet your big brother?"

I guessed they were speaking out loud for my benefit, but I could only imagine what was passing back and forth in their thoughts. Joshua hadn't gotten around to telling me the story of his estranged brother but from the comments that Cassie had dropped during some of our conversations I got the idea that he was the black sheep of the family.

Reggie peered at me over Joshua's shoulder. He placed his right hand, still holding on to the sword, across his heart. "I'm hurt, Katherine. Marodeen didn't want us to meet. Why would that be, brother? Especially since I know that Katherine has been dreaming about me. Isn't that charming! I hope it was a pleasant dream?"

Reggie's voice was diabolically sweet with the slightest hint that he knew the dream hadn't been. It scared me to think that he might have been outside my bedroom window listening when I had been having the dream or maybe, he had gotten it from Joshua's thoughts. Stupid mind readers! All this invasion of my privacy was really beginning to annoy me. Reggie laughed.

"Get used to it. You'll never have any solitude ever again," he said in a scornful tone.

Joshua interrupted him. "Speaking of thoughts, I'm having some problem reading yours. Your mind is ...fuzzy. Are you sick?"

"I'm in perfect health."

"Then why are you here?"

"I heard through the grapevine that you had finally found your dream girl and I've come to meet the new Mrs. Stone. I didn't get an invitation to the blessed nuptials. I'm sure that was just an oversight."

Of course, my thoughts told Reggie what he wanted to know. "What? Why not? Don't you find my brother as charming and debonair as everyone else does?" I was momentarily distracted by the fact that he used the same adjectives to mock Joshua as I had been using to complement him.

I moved out from behind Joshua to stand at his side, taking his hand in mine. It upset me to have Reggie ridiculing him.

"Our relationship is none of your business. Now if you're done aggravating us we have things to do." I pulled on Joshua's hand to get him to move but he stood as still as a statue.

Reggie began twirling the swords in the air at an incredible speed. They nearly disappeared from sight. Show off, I thought to myself. Clearly swordsmanship ran in the family.

Joshua re-positioned himself, forcing me to stand behind him again. "I'm not going to fight you, Reggie." Joshua's voice was calm but adamant.

Reggie laid one of the swords on the ground and with his right foot thrust it towards Joshua who intercepted the travelling weapon with his foot. He didn't bend down to pick it up though.

"Well, then, perhaps Katherine would like to spar with me for a while?"

Joshua clenched his teeth and the sound caused a tightening in the pit of my stomach. "Leave now, Reggie, before I regret all the times that I could have killed you and didn't." My hand hurt as Joshua's grip tightened.

Reggie shifted his stance and began stabbing the tip of his sword into the gym floor, spinning it idly. It carved a noticeable divot in the wood.

"I'm not leaving yet, not until I'm done with my visit …and by the way, how is my real brother doing?"

Real brother? Reggie's comment confused me.

"Nasir is fine. I'm sure he'll be upset that he missed you." I could tell by Joshua's tone that the truth was the complete opposite from what he had stated.

Reggie chuckled darkly. "Yes, I imagine he will," His eyebrows furrowed. "Have you been keeping secrets from your betrothed?"

Joshua took a calming breath and I felt his hold on my hand loosen somewhat. "I haven't gone into much detail about our parents yet. While we all have the same father, Reggie and Nathaniel were born of a different mother than Cassie and I."

"Oh," I replied, shrugging my shoulders. I couldn't understand why this would be an issue in the first place. Blood was blood no matter how diluted it might be.

"Our family has many dark secrets, Katherine, and I'll bet they haven't told you any of them. Especially the secrets about our dietary peculiarities."

Reggie had his answer simply from reading the bewilderment on my face, in addition to whatever else was going through my mind.

Reggie glared at Joshua. "Are you worried she won't want you once she knows the truth? That you're as much of a monster as I am?"

Joshua picked up the sword at his feet and led me towards the front entrance but Reggie moved in a flash to block our escape.

"Katherine, I can see that you're about to be a grandmother. Congratulations." Reggie broke out in a fit of laughter so great that he had to hold his free arm at his waist. How did he know about Josephine and why would he find her pregnancy comical?

Joshua let go of my hand and pointed toward the emergency exit. "Katherine, go outside, please. I'll meet you at the car." I had never seen Joshua this angry and I knew this confrontation was probably going to end in a fight but I did as he asked.

When I had reached the safety of the door, I looked back and could see Reggie, his sword now raised, moving to attack his brother. At the same time that I reached for the door handle, their swords clashed. Like a roll of thunder, the sound had a force of its own pushing me against the wall. I squeezed my hands tightly over my ears. The brawl was intense--as intense as wild lions fighting-- with each participant growling and snarling at the other. I was afraid for Joshua because I knew Reggie was strong enough to hurt him or worse, maybe even kill him. I wondered what could have happened to make them hate each other this intently. They were more than just brothers. Except for the few others of their kind, they were alone in the world.

I stayed crouched, while the combatants moved fluidly around the room in perfect choreography, recreating a scene from a pirate movie--except this re-creation moved at warp speed. Neither brother appeared to be gaining position until Reggie's sword streaked across Joshua's right arm, drawing a line of sparkling amber across his stark white jacket.

I gasped in alarm as I realized that the swords, which at first I had assumed were regular steel, were unmistakably magnetite. The only material that Joshua said could kill the demons--the only material that could kill one of us.

Instinctively, protectively, I bolted away from the wall towards Joshua screaming, "Nooo!"

Joshua turned towards me, his arm out to hold me back and protect me but in doing so lost his focus on his brother. Reggie continued his attack. His sword locked around Joshua's pulling it from his hand. It flew across the room and hit the wall with a loud thud, cracking the blade in two.

Reggie held the tip of his sword against Joshua's neck, drawing out more amber-colored blood. It flowed down Joshua's neck in crooked patterns. "You will never defeat me, Joshua, because you're too softhearted. You've never had it in you to be a killer."

"Don't misconstrue my tolerance of your lifestyle as a sign of weakness. I will kill you if I have to."

"Stop this!" I hissed. "You're brothers! What's wrong with you?"

Reggie turned toward me and winked. Then he lowered his sword. "You're right. It's just some friendly playing between siblings." Reggie reached out with his free hand and patted Joshua's shoulder. Joshua flinched but didn't move away.

"No harm done," Reggie continued, ignoring Joshua's angry stare. "Marodeen...excuse me Joshua, will be as good as new in an hour or so."

Reggie threw his sword to the ground. "You really should do something about the shoddy quality of these new swords. They don't seem to be holding up very well." He chuckled, adding, "Life is going to be a lot more entertaining with Katherine around. I've been so bored over the last few centuries."

I felt Joshua relax somewhat the second Reggie was out of sight. "I'm sorry you had to see that. I shouldn't have let him provoke me. Reggie is despicable. We all loathe him. It's times like this when I wish one of Issy's demons had killed him."

While I wiped the blood off Joshua's neck, I had a chance to get a closer look at the shiny substance. I swirled it around between my fingers. It was as thick as honey and had a gritty feel like pumice. I resisted the urge to taste it only because Joshua was watching me warily.

Surprisingly Nathaniel was outside waiting for us by Joshua's car. I looked around but there was no other car in the lot. How did he get here so fast? The apartment was at least ten miles away. Joshua answered Nathaniel's unspoken question. "I think he's gone. I can't see him anymore. Can you?"

"No, nothing, but I didn't see him at all until you did," Nathaniel stated, sounding confused.

They didn't continue the conversation vocally although I knew they were still silently conversing. Joshua threw the weapons from his fight with Reggie along with the fencing equipment into the open trunk of his car but the lid wouldn't close when he tried to shut it.

"What happened to the car?" It was fine earlier when Joshua had picked me up from work.

"Reggie broke into it and stole my swords. He knows we always have them with us." Joshua explained in a tense voice.

Once the trunk had been secured and we were in motion, Joshua said without question, "You're either going to stay at my place tonight or I'm going to stay at yours."

I reached over and touched his hand. "Okay. I would prefer to go to my house. I didn't leave Nutmeg with any food."

Something was up with Reggie and it confused me to see Joshua this visibly unnerved. After all, for the last two thousand years he had been facing down things that from my perspective appeared to be far more dangerous than his brother. A strange twinge rippled through me. It was beginning to feel like more than a coincidence that Reggie had been in my dream and that it had stopped immediately after Alex's death. I had written off any suspicion that it had been but a mere tragic accident, mostly because the police hadn't been able to find anything wrong.

Cassie was waiting for us when we stepped off the elevator having seen the whole event through Joshua's thoughts. "Thank goodness you're okay. What a nerve Reggie had coming here to bother us! Don't worry, Katherine, we'll make sure he doesn't hurt anyone."

I stared at her. "Why would he do that?"

Joshua shot Cassie a warning glance and she wouldn't answer me. "I need to get changed and pack a few things." He took my hand and led me into his apartment with Cassie and Nathaniel following.

While Nathaniel attended to Joshua's cuts, which were merely weeping now, I went and sat on the couch, staring blindly at the skyline. I wondered about all the people going about their normal lives not even vaguely aware of what was going on in my freaky abnormal life.

I could tell the siblings were silently communicating, moving their heads back and forth like normal people would when carrying on a three-way conversation.

"You know I hate it when you talk to each other like this. If I'm going to be part of this life and this family you can't keep secrets from me. Now I have a whole new set of questions." I could feel the tears welling up. "The first one being why was I dreaming of Reggie and could he have had anything to do with Alex's accident?"

Cassie came to my side. "You're right. You need to know so you'll be safe. We've all seen your memory of the accident and there is no indication from your recollection that Reggie was involved in any way." I unwillingly dredged up memory of the accident and watched as her expression became fixed and glazed, shuffling through each fraction of a second along with me.

"No Reggie, but," Cassie paused as I waited anxiously for her to continue. "There's something...strange...about the driver of the other car. It's too bad you closed your eyes at that moment."

"I thought I was about to be killed," I huffed accusingly.

Unperturbed by my accusation of them leaving me in the dark from the beginning of my life change, Cassie continued, "Rules are rules. We've survived all of these years by following Issy's rules."

"Fine, but that still doesn't explain why Reggie was in one of my dreams and none of you had ever been."

"You must understand that our dreams are only snapshot of a probable future. One dream may take the place of the next without the previous dream ever being satisfied. Umm... let me see if I can explain it this way. Think of life as a Rubik's Cube with each square a different path. There are hundreds or thousands of combinations to choose from. We think the dreams are fuzzy at times because the future is wavering--waiting for the right combination of colors to fall into place. Periodically the matching colors come together while the mixed up colors continue to be twisted and turned in anticipation of finding the correct arrangement. The dream you had about Issy and the tents was a color combination that had already been acquired. Of course we still have our free will. At the last minute you could have unknowingly turned the dial on the cube and we might never have met. Although that's unlikely since Joshua was still dreaming about you."

While Cassie was still going on about the dream possibilities, I was staring fixedly at Joshua. I knew he didn't want me to be thinking what I was thinking. Joshua had told me that his dream of me was still foggy in parts. I wondered if that meant there was still a possibility of that future changing course. I wrenched my eyes from his poignant face and turned back to the city view. That future wasn't important right now. However, it was comforting to know that I was still in charge of my own destiny, whatever that might be.

Joshua came to sit beside me on the couch, taking my hands in his and kissing me on the cheek. I ran my hand over the spot on his arm where Reggie's sword had cut him. All that remained was a faint yellow line that was fast disappearing.

Cassie sat opposite us. Nathaniel excused himself. "I'll let you two fill Katherine in on our loving brother. Don't wait up for me."

Joshua gave him a funny look and shook his head. Nathaniel stopped when he was half way through the door, "Don't forget to tell her about Tsavo. Katherine needs to know just how dangerous Reggie is if we are to protect her and her family."

Why would Nathaniel tell Joshua, who hadn't forgotten anything in two thousand years, not to forget something? Probably because Nathaniel knew it would be something that Joshua didn't want me to know. I had a feeling that this was going to be another epic story.

"Regulus is the oldest of us," Joshua began. "He, along with his twin brother, Sennacherib, was next in line for the throne. Our father spent years grooming them for this position, even sending them to a special school for training. We had much fun teasing them about it." He paused to laugh warmly at the memory. "None of us had any jealousy or animosity towards either of them. It was just the order of things. They were the first-born sons of our father and would be the next kings. We all loved Reggie. We protected him and would have died for him. Even now, after all we've been though, I question whether any of us would really be able to kill him."

Cassie interrupted. "Well, Nathaniel might."

Joshua ignored her comment. "You remember the first time I told you of our story, how after we had changed we were forced to flee our home?"

"Yes. You said it was difficult for all of you."

"Reggie took it the hardest. He had to give up becoming king-- king of the known world. He was this close to having it all." Joshua made a gesture using his thumb and forefinger showing a half-inch space. "After we left Assyria, Reggie's twin Sennacherib had his name struck from all carvings. It was against the law, even punishable by death to speak of him. To this day there is no record of our lives in the Sargonid Era of Assyria. Our families were either killed or forced to flee also. Reggie's wife became Sennacherib's consort. What Reggie didn't realize and refused to accept was that Sennacherib had already begun plotting to kill him, and the rest of us for that matter, before our father had even died. Sennacherib was extremely jealous and paranoid. We tried to talk to Reggie about it many times but he wouldn't listen. If we had stayed in the palace and had not been injured and saved by Issy, we most likely would have all been dead. Reggie was very bitter about losing his heritage, his family and his throne. He hates Issy and has blamed her for what he considers his misfortune." Joshua paused to take a calming breath.

I did understand how Reggie felt but now that I had had time to adjust, I was beginning to feel differently. No one ever wants to die if there is a chance. Of course in my case, Alex was the only person in my family who knew about my transformation. I hadn't been forced to flee my home...but what if I had? What if Alex hadn't been able to handle the new me? What if I had lost touch with my children?

"Reggie has convinced himself that he might have recovered. He couldn't appreciate how badly wounded he was. I was probably the only one that would have lived. By the time Issy found us, Nathaniel, Reggie and Cassie had lain for days in a coma. We were fortunate Sennacherib hadn't assassinated us as we lay dying."

"Reggie never lost hope that he would be able to return to Assyria to take his rightful place as its king. When our home was invaded and destroyed in 612 and the Assyrian Empire fell into ruin we knew there would be no going back and Reggie grew even more resentful, twisting the story in his mind until he perceived Issy as a villain that had robbed him of his destiny.

"In time Reggie left us. He refused to participate in the hunting down and killing of the Nergal, no matter how much destruction they caused. We don't have much interaction with him except when he shows up unexpectedly, like today." The remorse on Joshua face was so heavy it distorted his features.

"How awful! It must have been heartbreaking for you to watch him go through that and then to be estranged for so many years."

"Yes, it has been." Joshua was staring down at his folded hands, wringing them tightly. I reached out to touch him, hoping to offer some comfort, but he pulled his head up quickly, his gaze set on Cassie. I looked back and forth, waiting for one of them to speak.

"Tell her the rest of the story, Joshua, or I will," Cassie demanded.

Joshua nodded to her begrudgingly. "When we lived as nomads we hunted animals for food. The difference from when we were human was that we ate the animal flesh raw, as wild lions do. At first we hunted with weapons but in due course we realized that we were strong enough to hunt like lions, in packs, bringing down animals with our bare hands."

As he spoke, I tried to picture this. I reasoned that this form of hunting was not any different from the way tribes of spear-wielding humans would hunt. Still the image made me shudder.

"Cassie hated hunting like this. We all did to some degree but we had to eat, the cravings can be overwhelming."

Joshua took a depth breath collecting his thoughts. "You know that wild lions and tigers will sometimes become renegades?"

I could feel my features form into a grimace. "By renegades you mean man-eaters?"

"The first time it happened we were out hunting for gazelle. During the chase we became separated from Reggie. We couldn't find him for about an hour. We were frantic--searching everywhere up and down the plain. Then Nathaniel and I heard Cassie screaming. We found her, lying on the ground, crying. Reggie had come across a local tribesman and had drained the entire body of its blood and was consuming its flesh. Cassie had tried to stop Reggie but he thought she was trying to steal the man's body from him and had actually attacked her."

I gasped and stood up. "Reggie was eating the man--like a cannibal?"

Joshua pulled gently on my arm, forcing me to sit back down.

"Why? Why would he do that?" I wasn't able to comprehend the horror of what he had just told me.

"We think that Reggie was probably so focused on the hunt that when he came across the man he merely acted out of instinct. The smell of the blood and fresh meat overwhelmed him." Joshua shook his head in disgust. "Reggie didn't have much self-control even when he was human."

"But I still don't understand. Did he continue to hunt humans after that?"

"At first he was remorseful about what he had done. Then he began stealing off alone. It became more and more frequent. We became suspicious because he would go far away, out of our ability to hear him. Once, when we were able to follow, we found him s o intently consumed with what he was eating that he didn't even hear us…"

I put my hand up to stop him from going into further detail. I got the picture.

I sat silent while I thought about this new horror story. I could see why they didn't want anything to do with Reggie. "Is there more?" I asked, hoping that the answer would be "No", but knowing it wasn't.

"Once Reggie had a taste of human flesh he became addicted. He craved it the way a drug addict craves a drug. We all tried to intervene but in the end none of us could deal with it and we went our separate ways." He paused for a few seconds then cleared his throat. I waited, watching as he wrenched his hands back and forth. Obviously there would be more gore.

"In the fifteenth century, in Russia, Reggie had come back, trying to reconcile with us. We became friends with a local innkeeper and his family, especially his young daughter, Zhanna. Nathaniel and Reggie vied for her attention until one day Zhanna told Reggie that she was in love with Nathaniel and had accepted his marriage proposal. Reggie didn't take the rejection very well." Joshua stopped. I could see a pained look on his face as if it was physically hurting him to go with the story.

"What happened?" Deep down inside I knew the answer but was too horrified to think it.

Joshua dropped his head into his open palms and mumbled, "We found her dead. Reggie had killed her and feasted on her flesh."

I stood up again, "How could he do that to his own brother? That is just sick. It's beyond sick." I couldn't think of a bad enough word.

"I'm so sorry. I was hoping not to have to tell you this. We hadn't seen Reggie in so long now, we..."

Cassie chimed in, finishing Joshua's sentence. "We had hoped that maybe Reggie had been sucked into a black hole never to be seen again." I could tell by the tone of Cassie's voice that there was no love lost between her and her half-brother. "That's why

Nathaniel acts the way he does. He's been afraid to get close to anyone since then."

All three of us sat in silence for a while--me just trying to clutch at some sanity after hearing such an insane story. We had all read the stories of people lost in plane crashes eating human flesh to stay alive, but those people had died in the crash or by an act of nature. They weren't hunted down and killed as if they were a piece of filet mignon.

I looked at my watch; it was seven. "I need to go home. Nutmeg is waiting for me." That was the truth but I also had an overwhelming urge to get out of Joshua's apartment, to breathe some fresh air and clear my mind. Joshua was right not to have told me all of this. It was too much for one person, superhuman or not, to take in all at once.

On the drive back to my house I put on an obnoxious rock CD and closed my eyes. I knew Joshua probably thought that I was angry with him and I was angry. It was upsetting to think that there was a person in the world going around killing and feasting on humans. It was bad enough that humans killed each other. They certainly didn't need any help.

After we pulled into the driveway, I put my arms around Joshua. He looked humiliated. His brother's conduct had no bearing on the way I felt about him and to prove that to him I gave him a long slow kiss.

"I am so sorry..." he began when I was through but I put my fingers on his lips and pinched them together. "Stop apologizing. It's not your fault. Reggie is an adult, a very old adult and he clearly knows the difference between right and wrong."

"Thank you for being so understanding but I have more to tell you and you're not going to like it."

I sighed. "You can tell me later." I didn't mention the fact that that I hadn't liked most of what he had told me in the last four weeks.

The smell of fresh blood hit us immediately when we stepped out of the car. Joshua looked at me with a pained expression. "Did you leave your cat out this morning?"

"Joshua....noooo." He grabbed my hand as we followed the smell around to the back of the house. There was something lying on the outdoor table. Different shades of tan and red were jumbled together in a mass with no form. Nutmeg's blood had formed a pool on the wooden flooring. Beside him was a piece of cloth with words in bright red. The script was elegant and graceful, in sharp contrast to the horror.

Just a little wedding gift. Hope you like it! R

What kind of a monster would do something like this? I began to sob. Words that usually never came out of my mouth flowed like water. Joshua caught me as I began to collapse. My mind swirled, fighting for control.

"Joshua, why, why? I'm not responsible for anything that has happened in Reggie's life. I'm as innocent a victim as he is."

Joshua pulled out his phone and dialed Cassie's number. He spoke to her for a few minutes in Aramaic. Then he dialed Nathaniel's. I was glad that I couldn't understand what he was saying.

"Cassie is going to stop by Josephine's. Make up some excuse as to why she's in Concord and stay overnight with her and Steven."

"What?" I screamed, grabbing his shirt collar. Reggie wouldn't hurt one of the kids, would he?" I was in a full panic now, hitting Joshua's chest, my arms flailing uncontrollably.

Joshua held both my hands in one of his and used his free hand to hold me down. "It's just a precaution." I could hear the hesitation in his voice. "What else haven't you told me, Joshua?"

"Before Reggie killed Zhanna he also killed her entire family."

I tried to get up but Joshua wouldn't release me. "What about Lindsey? We need to get to Boston, Joshua. If anything ever happens to her because of this..." I didn't finish because I couldn't bear the thought of that maniac hurting one of my children.

"Lindsey is fine."

"How do you know?" In the back of my mind I was still wondering how Cassie knew Josephine and Steven well enough that she could stay overnight at their place. I would deal with that issue later. Keeping the girls safe was all that was important now.

"Lindsey is with Nathaniel."

I slumped into Joshua's arms, my whole body going numb. I didn't know what to do to stop this.

"You are part of us now and your family is our family. We will protect the girls. Reggie knows we will hunt him down and kill him if he harms any of your family. He saw that in my mind tonight. Nathaniel and I are going to call upon the others of our kind. Reggie will be punished for this."

"Okay," I said my voice so low I wasn't sure I had actually spoken aloud. I was mentally exhausted. Joshua picked me up and carried me to bed. I slipped off to sleep as soon as my head hit the pillow but I did not sleep peacefully. I woke up several times during the night and Joshua was there each time trying to soothe me, but his face was only a reminder of the horror story that was now my life.

*

My eyelids were dried stuck and at first I didn't try to clear them off. I had always been more of an ostrich than a lion and I wished there was a hole somewhere for me to stick my head into now.

When I unwillingly opened my eyes, Joshua was still by my side. I realized that I was under the blanket clothed only in my underwear. Joshua answered my unspoken question.

"You undressed yourself in the middle of the night saying something about needing to breathe."

I put my head back down on the pillow, pulling it tight against me. Joshua rubbed the back of my neck, trying to loosen up the knots. He bent down and kissed my exposed shoulder. My heart began racing. I was about to have another panic attack--this time for a much different reason.

"Joshua, I'm ...I'm..."

He pulled back, appalled. "I'm sorry. I didn't mean to give you the wrong impression. I was merely trying to be comforting." He stood up quickly and left the room while I was asking myself why I was thinking about love in the middle of all this horror?

After I joined Joshua in the kitchen I got up the courage to ask, "Where's my kitty?"

"I buried him on the side of the house beside your other cat."

"I hope the neighbors didn't think you were burying me?"

Joshua flinched, not amused at my humor. "I'll start the coffee."

I went to the back porch but could find no evidence of the previous night's carnage. Even though I loved Nutmeg terribly, the thought of Joshua or Cassie getting into a fight with Reggie was more upsetting. "I don't know what you'll decide to do about Reggie but I don't want you going off and getting hurt, any of you, over this."

"Some of our kin will be here tomorrow and we can discuss the problem together." Joshua's tone brightened. "They're looking forward to meeting you."

The thought of having more people around probing into my head was disheartening. I changed the subject. "I think I should stay at your place for the next few nights and then we can come back and check on the house. That way I'll be closer to the girls. Will that be okay?"

"Of course," Joshua agreed, surprised at my suggestion. Just then his phone rang. When he hung up Joshua said that Reggie was back in Mexico. "Ki and Ko are with Issy and they'll be watching him much more closely from now on."

"Ki and Ko?"

"Our Blackfoot Indian brothers."

I nodded. "Reggie lives in Mexico? Why does he live there?"

Joshua shrugged. "I guess he likes it there."

I sighed. "Joshua, please explain to me why he lives Mexico."

"Many of his victims are overlooked by the police, assumed to be fatalities of drug related crimes."

I gave him a disapproving look. "And?"

Joshua sighed. "Reggie also has a house in Tanzania. He likes to live there because of the frequency of real lion attacks. He knows there won't be any investigations. We have the same tooth structure as the carnivores." I nodded. This was something I already knew about from my previous research.

"Reggie also likes to go to places where there are plagues or wars....."

I put my hand up to stop him. "Okay, that's enough detail on that subject. I get the picture." It was similar to the stories in many of my favorite vampire movies. I wondered if Reggie had gotten the idea from them.

Joshua poured me a cup of coffee. The heat from the hot fluid was soothing.

"I need to tell you the story of Tsavo." This was the story that Nathaniel had mentioned. I had forgotten all about it, distracted by the chaos with my cat.

"Okay." Might as well get all the horror stories over with at once, I thought. ...and I knew it would be

"Have you ever watched a movie called The Ghost and the Darkness?"

"Yes." I had seen that movie several times actually. "That's a great movie. It's about two man-eating lions in Africa and the two men who hunt them down." Joshua frowned as he watched my expression change.

"That was Reggie?" I whispered.

Joshua nodded. "The British were building a bridge over the river Tsavo. Mortal lions were involved in several of the attacks but most of them were Reggie's doing. Since we have Issy serum in us and we smell like her, lions recognize us as one of them. Reggie took advantage of this and trained two lions to kill humans. By the time we intervened there were over one hundred dead." Joshua shook his head and said, "Reggie is Issy's biggest regret. It makes me shudder to think what kind of king he would have been."

"Why did he train the lions, though? Why didn't he just kill the people himself?"

"Playing a sick game. Reggie knew Issy would be horribly upset when his pawns had to be destroyed. He has no respect for life of any kind. In truth Reggie probably would have killed Nathaniel and me by now if he didn't enjoy torturing us so much."

"If I remember correctly the movie showed the incident taking place over a long period of time, nine months. Why did you wait so long to intervene?"

"The railroad company tried to keep the incident quiet. It used to take months not minutes as it does these days for information to circle the globe. Reggie will never be able to get away with that again. I've noticed that lately his killings have become more clandestine making me think that for some reason he doesn't want us involved."

"Why doesn't Issy just kill Reggie if he's such a terrible person? She kills the demons. He doesn't seem any different than them, really."

Joshua sighed. "It's because of me. I thought for a long time that we could get him to change. That future doesn't seem possible anymore."

After a few minutes of silence something I didn't want to ask occurred to me.

"Joshua, did you ever eat a human?"

Joshua groaned. "I was hoping you wouldn't ask this."

I recoiled from him in shock. Were they all monsters? Would I turn into a monster someday? It took me a moment to collect myself. "Tell me about it, please."

Joshua wouldn't look at me.

"Joshua, I need to know everything about you, good or bad. No secrets."

"It was in Europe in 545 AD. We had been away from humans for a while living in the thickly wooded forests. Cassie begged Nathaniel and me to take her into town for a few days, to sleep in a real bed and clean up. We came across a fairly large town in Rumania and found an inn with a vacancy and an innkeeper that didn't ask too many questions."

"Cassie was going to spend the entire night immersed in a tub of warm water while Nathaniel and I made a trip to the local pub. Nathaniel was planning to find some female companionship and I was planning on drinking the pub dry."

"Why do you drink so much alcohol? It doesn't seem to affect you very much."

"Alcohol numbs the craving. Especially when we're around large numbers of humans. They do smell good." He sighed. "Plus the only way to escape from your memories when you can never forget anything that you've done is to cloud up your mind."

I frowned. I could certainly relate to Joshua's pain. I was only a newcomer to this life, an infant really, and I already had things that I wished I could forget. I couldn't imagine two thousand years of things to forget.

"Nathaniel and I had been at the pub for a while when two ladies of the night came and joined us. Nathaniel was thrilled and went back to his room with one. I stayed and drank some with the other lady. It had been a long time, hundreds of years since I had been with a woman but I had no desire to be intimate with this one. I wanted more than lust. I left her and went out wandering the streets. When I had sulked enough for the night, I turned and headed back to the inn but as I turned down one of the alleyways, I could hear a woman crying. I followed the pleading voice and found the same prostitute that had been with me earlier. Two men, religious zealots were holding her down, beating her and cutting her with knifes. They tried to convince me that they were performing the Lord's work." Joshua began to shout at this point in the story. "I was outraged that they would harm such a defenseless woman. I don't know what happened, something snapped. Maybe it was because I had seen so much violence in my long life and I needed some outlet myself. I sent the woman away and proceeded to kill them--breaking their necks."

I shuddered. The tears began to spill over in a torrent while the despair overwhelmed me. Joshua was my savior. I didn't want to know that he was also a killer.

"Should I continue? I understand if it's too much for you." I could hear the hope in his voice that I would say no but I took a breath and held on to my resolve.

"It doesn't matter if it's too much for me. I need to hear this," I demanded.

"After I killed them I decided that the ultimate punishment would be to defile their flesh. Of course, I couldn't keep what I had done from Nathaniel and Cassie. We left quickly the next morning."

Joshua covered his face again. I tried to pull his hands away but he wouldn't let me.

"Joshua," I said in a soft voice, "it's all right, that was a long time ago and I am guessing you've never done it again?"

We both sat frozen for a long moment, me from the realization that this was not the end of his story.

"I liked being able to punish those men. Whenever I would come across a criminal in the act, or some type of injustice, I would punish those involved. I had the audacity to convince myself that I was a kind of superhero--defending the weak." Joshua paused and laughed manically, sending another shiver down my spine.

"Nathaniel and Cassie finally made me realize that I was just as guilty as the priests that I had first killed. Of course they were worried that I would become like Reggie--addicted to human flesh.

I stopped and except during the times of war when I was a soldier I have never killed anyone. I will leave justice to the just." Joshua wiped his hand swiftly across his cheek, wiping away a tear he didn't want me to see.

"Okay, then." I gently placed my hand across his cheek.

"Aren't you upset about this? Please--tell me why aren't you running away in horror from me?"

My jaw fell open. This was the same question I had asked Alex when he first realized the extent of my renovations. Alex hadn't run away because he loved me. Of course I hadn't admitted to murdering and eating people. What if I had? Would Alex have left even then? This was something they had never taught me to deal with in Sunday school. What do you do when someone you cared deeply about admits to doing wrong? I knew I should be horrified, but I couldn't find it in me to want to and I couldn't imagine my life without Joshua now. I wondered what my reaction would have been if I didn't know about Joshua's dream, didn't know the most likely outcome of our relationship? That thought stunned me even further. Had I already been brainwashed like him into thinking that his dream was our future, no matter what the past?

"Well, there's certainly something to be said about having some mystery in a relationship. Besides those people you killed probably would have been caught and punished anyway." I knew I was rationalizing. "You've done so much good since then."

"That only makes me feel better. Reggie is right. In the end, I'm not any less of a monster than he is. That's why I can't allow Issy to kill him."

"It was a long time ago." I leaned over and kissed him. He didn't kiss me back, though.

I wondered if my next question would upset him. "I have something else to ask you and after you answer it I don't want to talk about this ever again. Okay?"

He nodded woodenly.

"What does human meat taste like?"

Joshua raised his eyebrows. "You're not thinking of trying it, are you?"

"No, of course not! I am curious."

"There are no words in any language that I know to describe the irresistible pull. The war that ensues within you nearly tears you apart. Your conscious mind tells you "no" while the stronger primitive side says "yes"." He swallowed hard. "I would never have been able to stop if it wasn't for Nathaniel and Cassie, always in my head, always leading me down the right path."

"You were able to stop though. Why didn't Reggie?"

"Reggie could if he wanted to. We have very powerful minds and can exert much self-control when we apply ourselves."

Joshua looked at me longingly and I could tell he wasn't just talking about Reggie anymore.

"When Reggie was human, he was treated as a god and now with all his extra abilities, he thinks he is one. It's his way to fulfill the destiny he feels was stolen from him."

"What about Nathaniel and Cassie? Did they ever...?"

Joshua shook his head adamantly. "Never! Cassie doesn't even like eating animal meat."

"Okay," I said taking a deep breath, "enough horror stories for one day."

Joshua grimaced at my remark, but I didn't apologize for it. I stood up and went to get ready to leave for the city.

A few tears escaped while I was packing but I wiped them away. Another chapter, the innocent chapter, of my second life had ended.

Chapter 11
IN THE COMPANY OF FRIENDS

Tell me ye knowing and discerning few
Where I may find a friend that's firm and true
Who dares stand by me when in deep distress?
And then his love and friendship most express

~ 1829 Sampler Verse by Harriot Farr

The latest unfamiliar language coming from the living room of Joshua's apartment signaled to me that the Mongolians had arrived. I saw the two strangers shaking hands with Nathaniel and Joshua when I emerged from the guest bedroom. The newcomer's eyes pierced mine. I was glad for Cassie's exuberance, drawing their attention away from me as she came running in through the front door.

"I'm overjoyed to see you. It's been too long," she gushed in English, giving both men a welcoming hug.

"Yes, Cassie," the taller of the two men replied, "it's been much too long since we've seen our American friends. I only wish we were here for a different reason." He kissed the top of her head.

Cassie sighed. "Reggie will be our burden to bear forever and ever."

"We'll take care of him. Don't worry." The English flowed smoothly from the stranger's lips with no hint of an accent, which was surprising considering his appearance. The bulked up man was unmistakably one of us but with the distinctive epicanthic fold that confers on East Asian eyes the appearance of being narrower. His entire head was perfectly round and smooth shaven except for the thin blond mustache whose sides hung down loosely over his lips. The second man, who was shorter than the first, was identical in his appearance and grooming details. They were both dressed in rugged looking clothing as if they were about to set out on the Appalachian trail for a month.

Joshua came to my side holding my waist. "Come, meet our friends."

"Joshua, I need to get changed."

"You look beautiful." I scowled at him. My displeasure did nothing to deter him from pulling me along.

"Katherine, this is Tomor and Khun," Joshua said indicating each person as he spoke their name. "Tomor and Khun, this is Katherine."

Joshua pronounced my name with such reverence it made me blush.

Both men laughed slightly at my reaction and before I knew what was happening Tomor was hugging me. "It's wonderful to finally meet you, Katherine. We have all waited a long time for Joshua to find you." Khun reiterated that sentiment in the same perfect English.

Obviously, they had also been privy to Joshua's dream. I flushed even deeper with embarrassment.

"Thank you for coming," I said fervently.

"It's our pleasure," Tomor began but Khun finished the thought. "We're happy to be able to be of some service." Tomor paused for a moment before continuing. "Joshua, you haven't told us exactly what the problem is and I can see that you're not going to let us know from your thoughts, therefore I can only assume that you were waiting for your fiancée to join us to be included in the discussion."

I grimaced at the word "fiancée" but I knew it was pointless to protest. They wouldn't understand how I felt about all this dreams are the future crap. All five of them gave me a disparaging look.

"Joshua, please!" I begged.

"Katherine has asked that we give her some privacy for the time being, including you, Cassie."

"Of course," Tomor said. "We'll do our best but you have to understand that it's counterintuitive for us." Cassie huffed and folded her arms across her chest. Joshua raised his eyebrows at her.

"Fine," she told him.

"Of course we'll all speak in English until Katherine has a chance to catch up, which I know won't be very long. She's already moving along quite speedily with her Aramaic lessons."

I looked at Joshua, hoping he would see my consternation at being the center of all this attention and move on.

"Please, gentlemen, let's sit down." Joshua filled the new comers in on what had happened when we met Reggie at the fencing club and the resulting carnage with my cat. The Mongolians listened silently, no hint of what they were thinking evident in their features. When Joshua finished, the two men shot one another a disbelieving glance before Tomor spoke.

"Joshua, I hope you and your fiancée won't be offended, but we're having trouble understanding why you have called upon us from halfway around the world to avenge a dead cat." I winced as his words stung me. "This is a man who kills humans and eats them just for the sick pleasure of it and you're upset about a house cat."

Cassie interrupted him. "Tomor, please keep in mind that our mentor is a cat."

"Yes, but she's not a real cat." Before Cassie could continue the dispute the Mongolians both turned to gawk at me, both speaking at once. "Children? You have human children and a brother?" I wondered if they were rummaging around in my head or Joshua's. I sighed and told myself that I needed to concentrate on the essentials right now.

"Yes," Joshua confirmed, "and it's their safety that we're concerned with. We don't want a repeat of the Zhanna incident." I turned in time to watch Nathaniel recoil at the name of his murdered love.

Tomor, his eyes squinted in confusion, asked me, "What will you do when ..." He didn't have to finish his sentence. What would happen when my children began to age and I didn't?

"We haven't figured that out quite yet," Joshua told him in a clipped tone, obviously aggravated with his question. "We'll either have to find a way to tell them or find a way to leave."

I stared at him in disbelief. "I'm not leaving." And it was for certain that I wasn't going to let the cat out of the bag about our little company of freaks.

"Well, in either case the important matter right now is the safety of your family and yourself," Joshua countered, ending our never ending argument before it began.

Khun asked the next question. "What makes you think that Reggie is planning anything? You know how he likes to screw with you and Nathaniel. Except for that one time, which was five centuries ago, he hasn't done anything to harm any of the humans that we've been involved with." Nathaniel didn't offer any comment through the entire conversation. He just sat with his hands folded together, staring at the ground.

Joshua continued to explain the urgent call that had brought the Mongolians from so far away. "Gentleman, you weren't with us when I met Reggie in the club. His mind is a cesspool of dark thoughts, full of hate. I had trouble reading him clearly. Reggie knows he won't be able to cause much trouble as long as we have a strong showing of force. We feel confident he'll be put off by your presence. He's really a coward underneath all his bravado." Joshua took a deep breath and in a sincere tone added, "We're very grateful that you came but if you feel that you can't stay or that this is not a matter that concerns you we'll understand."

"Joshua, for sure we have no intention of leaving if you need us. I still fail to see how our presence would deter him any more than yours would. You out number him three to one."

Nathaniel finally spoke up. "Reggie knows that you will not hesitate to kill him. Even though I have dreamed of it many times I don't trust myself to be able to do it. When we lived in Sargon's palace we would have given our lives for our brother and future king. Our feelings run deep---so deep that even after all this time they are difficult to ignore."

At that moment Tomor and Khun laughed in unison. My eyes widened in shock. They turned toward me but obviously they meant the question for Nathaniel. "You're dating Katherine's daughter?" They both saw the annoyance on my face and stopped laughing immediately. "Sorry," they murmured in unison.

Tomor quickly changed the subject, "Well, I suppose we have some surveillance to do. Let's have breakfast first. I'm starved. Then we can work out our plan."

Khun grinned widely at the mention of food but quickly lost it as he warned, "Understand that neither Tomor nor I will hesitate to kill Reggie if we find him and judge him to be a danger." The three siblings nodded grimly.

While Cassie fed the visitors I excused myself and went to change. I could smell the meat the moment she opened the refrigerator. Even though part of me craved the smell, part of me was sickened by it.

Joshua followed me. "You should eat something."

"I'm not hungry. My stomach is upset. I'll make some eggs when you guys are done."

When I rejoined everyone in the kitchen, Cassie was grumbling at full volume about our visitors manners. She had tried to make the Mongolians use silverware but half way through the meal they had reverted to using their hands. The whole table was a bloody mess.

While Cassie cleaned, the Mongolians and Nathaniel sat by the oversized picture window talking in hushed murmurs, planning the day of surveillance. Except for when they needed to tell me something I wondered why they spoke audibly at all.

Tomor responded to my unarticulated question, not complying with Joshua's request. "During certain periods in our history we didn't have any human contact for ten or even twenty years and we were concerned that we would lose our ability to speak if we stopped." I frowned at him. "Sorry, I'll keep working on the privacy issue buts it takes more effort to not read your mind than to read it."

I would have thought just the opposite. I couldn't imagine how they were able to keep the conversations that were going on in each other's heads from being mixed up with what they were saying vocally.

"Do you mind if I ask how Issy came to find you, Tomor?" I was genuinely curious to see if it had been similar to my story.

"I would be honored. It was the year 1239 during the invasion of Veliky Novgorod in Russia by Genghis Khan. Being part of his army made for a very disturbing life. Each soldier had a quota of killings. I hated the slaughter, especially of the women and children. They only allowed me to see my family every few years and during one of times when I was away they were all killed. I was never able to forgive myself. I became horribly depressed and deserted the army. Joshua, Nathaniel and Cassie found me half dead wandering the forests. They explained the story of Issy to me and asked me to join them. For me the deciding factor wasn't the immortality, I couldn't imagine it anyway, still being human. What made me choose this life was the idea of being free from war's terrible toll. I was happy at the thought of finding peace and having fellow companions who felt the same. Killing a Nergal every four or five centuries was a welcome alternative to combat. So I allowed Issy to give me her gift."

"You think of this as a gift?" I asked indignantly.

"You don't?" Tomor paused for a moment, pulling at his moustache. "All of us hybrids were soldiers and desperately wanted a way out of our lives. I can understand why Nathaniel was concerned. How interesting." Tomor's tone was clinical.

"Nathaniel didn't even know me, though, so why was he worried?" Maybe I could get the answer from them. Joshua was always avoiding the subject.

Tomor shot Joshua an apprehensive glance. When Joshua nodded the okay, Tomor continued. "The reason for Issy's rule, about who to change and who not to change, was because she had saved Reggie's life at the same time she saved Nathaniel, Cassie and Joshua's, but Reggie had never been in any of her dreams. Issy didn't realize the significance of it at the time."

"I don't think Issy should blame herself for the way Reggie turned out. She thought she was doing him a favor. Besides who would hold onto a grudge for two thousand years?"

They all stared at me with an incredulous look. "What?" I asked confused about their reaction.

Khun answered for them all. "Katherine, humans have been retaliating against each other now for just as long. Revenge is a stronger emotion than love. Whole civilizations have based their existence on getting back at others for crimes that most had only been told about—handed down in stories that may or may not be true."

"Reggie is different," I countered. "He has everything and every opportunity to do anything that he wants with his life with no fear. Why would he choose this path?"

Khun shrugged, "Is Reggie so different? Even as a human, Osama Bin Laden for example had every opportunity to use his skills and money to benefit the world but he decided on the same dark path as Reggie. It's amazing really that the human race has survived this long with all the vengeance that takes place." He sighed long and heavy as if trying to remove the dark thoughts. "Humans aside, we all would have fewer problems if Reggie had been left to die. One of our gifts is being able to see the future through our dreams. It's upsetting to think we might not be interpreting them correctly."

Joshua turned to stare at me. Even without the ability to read minds, I knew that Joshua was wondering about my reaction to Khun's last remark. I ignored his stare. I was finally getting some worthwhile information from our visitors and I wanted to keep them talking.

"How did you come to be a part of this merry little band, Khun?"

"My story is similar to Tomor's. My full name is Khünbish, which ironically translates to not a human being." He giggled a little at his joke. "For me it was just providence that I would end up being a part of Issy's family. Like the rest of our kind, I was a soldier forced into a life that I hated. Joshua and Nathaniel found me fighting in Kublai Khan's army in the Battle of Dali in southern China in 1253. I was more than happy to join them and find peace also."

"What do you do with all the time?" Maybe they could help me figure out what I was going to do.

"Tomor and I have raised horses and sheep for centuries now."

"Aren't people suspicious about you?"

"The Mongolian people are a tough breed of humans carving out a living on the barren steppes of Asia. They have no regard for rules and are more willing to accept the unusual as they frequently see the unusual in their wanderings. Horses are an important part of Mongolian life. No one could survive without one. We give most of our horses away. A man without a horse is like a bird without a wing, as the saying goes in my country."

"Do you all run charities?"

"Yes," Joshua confirmed. "Tomor and Khun were the first. The charities are all very diverse but the main theme is to be of assistance to the human and animal species and allow them to continue."

I turned back to Khun. "Have you ever met any of the others?"

"Yes, many times. We have a reunion periodically, usually in some remote place. It's most enjoyable being among our own kind. Life can be boring without any challenges and the human world doesn't offer much of that for us. Now that we have a new sister, we should make plans to get everyone together to meet you."

Great, then there'll be a whole horde of mind readers ransacking my thoughts. That sounded like a lot of fun. Khun laughed again and then apologized, "Katherine, I'm sorry but your thoughts are quite comical."

"That's me, a barrel of laughs. I could be the entertainment for the reunion party." As soon as Khun was able to stop laughing, I asked him to tell me about some of the others.

"Avinash and Pravit are in India. They were found in 321 BC during the siege of the city of Pataliputra. The Egyptians, Gamba and Salim, were found during the Roman Battle of Actium in 30 BC. They're charged with watching Africa.

"The Vikings, Valfrid and Bjorn, were found during the Viking raids of Lindisfarrne Island in 793 AD. They watch Europe.

"Tupac and Itzcali, the Aztecs, were found in the 14th century. They watch the southern Americas and the Pacific islands. The Irish, Shamus and Nevan are our backups for both the European and American continents.

"The eighteen hundreds were a busy century for Issy. That was when Ki and Ko who watch North America, were found. Issy also found the Australians, Anaru and Coorain, in that same century, during the Black War. It was a terrible massacre of the native Aborigines." Khun paused and shook his head. "I've seen their memory of that time and it's obvious why they wanted to leave that life. Including you, Katherine, that brings our numbers to twenty now."

I grimaced and stole a look at Joshua. He mouthed the word sorry.

Khun stroked his moustache again. "Hmm…we're extremely curious to see what role Katherine will play in our little group. She obviously has no fighting skills and won't be of assistance with the Nergal."

I frowned at his spot-on assessment of my abilities. Although I didn't want to be fighting demons, I didn't want to become a burden to them either.

Before I could make any snide remarks about demon-hunting the noise from the news program that Cassie had been watching caught our attention.

Nathaniel looked up from the map of Boston and said to Khun, "What will you and Tomor decided if the war in the Middle East gets any worse?"

I interrupted before Khun or Tomor could answer. "I thought you had a no interference clause like in Star Trek."

They all chuckled at my analogy.

"Although we try to not interfere with anything humans do, there have been times where we've felt it was necessary in order to keep world peace. This planet is our home also," Khun explained.

"What were you all doing during WWI and WWII, taking a nap?" My voice can out sharper than I had intended it to.

Khun stood up and paced back and forth, both hands tucked into his pants pockets. "We fought in those wars and made sure that the balance of power was tipped towards the side that was able to end the war and keep a permanent peace, but that's the extent of our interference."

"You could have killed Hitler and ended that war early." I still had trouble understanding this policy of theirs. Here they were all running charities to alleviate human suffering yet they stood by and let them die in senseless wars.

Tomor stood up and joined in. "Humans need to find their own way. They can't be forced into peace. People must want it and be able to make it work for them. If we forced our peace on them we would just be taking the place of another of their dictators."

"War is a terrible price to pay for peace," I voiced sorely.

"It's the only price that can be paid in this world," Tomor added grimly.

I turned toward Joshua. "Doesn't the fighting in the Middle East upset you? It's your homeland."

"Yes, it upsets us deeply…."

Tomor interrupted him. "The rest of us have speculated for quite some time now that one of the originals must have placed a curse on that region and its people--a curse that would never allow them or their descendents to find peace."

"It does seem that way," Joshua agreed. "Our people have been corrupted and allowed themselves to be persuaded by others who claim justice through God. Those same people use hatred as a weapon. Make no mistake, the Assyrians were brutal, but we gave our enemies fair warning. When I killed a man, I made sure to look him in the eye. That's the way a man should fight and die. We didn't slink around in dark corners and strap bombs on ourselves. That's a coward's death."

"No matter how you kill someone it's still kill…." I stopped before I finished my sentence recognizing that our visitors were here to most likely kill Reggie.

Joshua nodded. "It's a dilemma, isn't it—judging others and trying to find the path of right through the crooked path of wrong. The day we fled the palace was the day we left our heritage behind us. We won't get involved in their wars unless we think it will affect the natural balance of our planet."

Cassie, who had been silent throughout this whole discussion chimed in with her usual perkiness. "Okay, I've had enough of this. Could we please talk about something pleasant?"

"You're right," Joshua added. He turned toward our guests. "We want to make your visit as enjoyable as possible."

"Great," Tomor replied eagerly. "We haven't had a good ball game in decades and it's going to be a new moon tomorrow night. Are you up for a beating?" There was a twinkle in his eyes as he directed his question toward Cassie.

Cassie huffed. "If my memory serves me right... and I know it does...we beat the heck out of you last time so it's you that will be getting the beating."

Tomor and Khun laughed heartily. "Shamus and Nevan, and Ki and Ko will be here by then and we'll have enough for a few teams if Katherine will join in."

I looked at him incredulously. "You're going to play a ball game in the dark?"

"Of course," Tomor replied matter of factly. "It's not much of a challenge in the light."

I took a deep breath. "I'll just watch." Life was challenging enough for me right now. I couldn't imagine looking for more.

Chapter 12
CHARITY

To laugh often and love much; to appreciate beauty; to find the best in others; to give of one's self; to leave the world a bit better, to know even one life has breathed easier because you have lived—this is to have succeeded.
Bessie Anderson Stanley, 1904

The Irish and Blackfoot arrived on Monday and in the short amount of time spent with them I was impressed by how genuinely happy they were with their immortal lives. They all seemed as well adjusted as the Stones and just as committed to their causes.

Kí and Ko were striking specimens. Their long lean bodies were ballet dancer graceful. Due to the effect of the imbedded sapphire, their skin, typically a reddish tan had a pink tinge, similar to the soft texture of sandstone. Intricately braided blonde colored ponytails hung down their backs--their native jet black color having been replaced during their transformation. Their eyes, although familiar, appeared to be more depthless and full of wisdom. Except for the greeting when they had first arrived--Oki Ni-kso-ko-wa-- which I was told meant Hello, greetings to my relatives in their native language-- they also spoke in the same perfect English as the others.

Similar to the Mongolians, the Native Americans and Irish were more than eager to tell me their story. Kí, whose full name was Kísomm, meaning sun, and Ko, whose full name was KoKo, meaning night, were the perfect complement for each other, as their names suggested. The Stones found them one night in 1837, on deaths door, after a raid on a neighboring tribe. The other warriors in their party had died of what was to be one of the worst epidemics to hit their tribe in hundreds of years—smallpox. Of course Issy's serum healed them quickly. Ever since then, both had dedicated their long lives to helping all indigenous peoples around the globe.

The two Irishmen were so identical in appearance that I was sure they must be twins. I could only tell them apart by the style of their hair. Like the other hybrids, they had also been forced into a war when all they wanted was peace. It turns out that Shamus was Nevan's great-grandfather, which explained the similarity in their features.

The surveillance of my family would be the number one priority for all the visiting hybrids. Ki and Ko would go to New York to watch my brother, Kevyn. I couldn't imagine how bad the noise would be in the Big Apple but the Native Americans were overjoyed to have the opportunity to see some city lights.

The Irish would stay in Boston for an undetermined time while the Mongolians would go to Mexico in a few weeks to meet up again with Issy. Khun was determined to confront Reggie. Because the debate was silent for the most part I didn't hear the arguments for or against, but afterwards the Asians promised Joshua to simply observe and report back.

In order to keep Lindsey and Josephine closer, I gave in, against my better judgment to keep my other life a secret, and announced that I was dating Joshua. It would have been only a matter of time before I ran into Lindsey anyway and I know it made Joshua tremendously happy that he could legitimately refer to me as his girlfriend. Joshua would have liked it even more if he could have used the word fiancée instead, but even he had to agree begrudgingly that at this point in our relationship it would be socially awkward to explain our sudden engagement.

"It's all right," he said after having this discussion for the hundredth time. "I've waited an epoch amount of time to find you and make you my wife. I guess a few more months won't matter."

"A few more months?"

"Okay then, years if you'd rather."

I shook my head in disbelief. "You're incorrigible."

"I know." Joshua's smile, as always, made it difficult to keep up my side of any argument for too long. At times though I was really beginning to think he was delusional. It was hard to imagine that anyone would want to spend eternity with me.

Tuesday night was the ballgame under the twinkling stars. I went along mostly out of curiosity but ended up enjoying myself more than I could have imagined. At one point I thought about joining in, but my still lingering human frailties, as Joshua referred to my lack of self confidence, kept me on the side lines.

On Wednesday night there was a Stone Foundation event that Joshua asked me to attend with him but it was a business meeting and I didn't want to be in the way.

"I really don't have to go," Joshua confessed.

"No, no, you all work very hard and I don't want you to miss the fun, especially Cassie." What I really felt bad about was being babysat.

Joshua gave his much-loved sister a stern look. "Cassie has been to two thousand years of parties. She can miss one." Of course, even a psycho killer brother did nothing to curb Cassie's enthusiasm. With unbridled optimism she stuck her tongue out at Joshua and suggested taking me to New York to do some clothes shopping instead.

"No thanks, I'd rather stay here and watch re-runs of Lawrence Welk." I sighed, "Maybe I'll go home." I really missed the quiet of my small town.

"Cassie will stay with you until we get back." Joshua's tone was firm.

"Fine," she agreed sitting down on the couch beside me. "You're awfully grouchy tonight, Katherine."

"Gee I wonder why-- horrendous demons and sadistic brothers?"

Cassie picked up the remote and began flipping through the TV channels at lightning speed.

"Cassie, you're going to burn out the remote," I complained.

"Katherine, you need to practice so you'll be able to keep up with us."

I grabbed the remote from her hand at a speed that had me laughing at her shocked expression. "Well, you wanted me to keep up."

Cassie clapped her hands. "Good job. You're getting faster."

Joshua was behind me, out of sight, when I heard him walk out from his bedroom. I could tell he was fiddling with something metallic. I turned around and froze. Joshua was even more impossibly beautiful dressed in black. When he looked up, he asked in a concerned voice, "Are you all right? Katherine, you're not breathing."

Cassie giggled, "She thinks you're drop dead gorgeous."

I glared at her. How many times had I asked her to keep of my head?

"Take it down a notch, Katherine. I've never met anyone whose face gives away their thoughts as much as yours does."

Joshua knelt down in front of me. "Are you sure you won't come with me?" I stared quietly at him while my fear of crowds fought a small battle in the pit of my stomach with my need for Joshua.

"I have nothing to wear," I mumbled, looking down at my jeans.

"You and Cassie are about the same size. I'm sure she could find something suitable."

Cassie perked up immediately. "Yes, we won't stay for the whole night. You'll be tucked back into bed before midnight."

That didn't sound too awful and I would get to be with Joshua. "All right," I agreed grudgingly.

Before I could blink, Cassie had grabbed hold of my hand and was towing me into her apartment. I was truly frightened when she opened the door to the room where she kept her clothes. It looked more like a library than a closet, with its dark mahogany woodwork and sliding ladders to reach the upper storage units. "This should fit perfectly," she announced, handing me a dress plus a pair of brand new nylons and a satin slip. "While you're getting changed, I'll find the shoes that match."

I trudged reluctantly into the bathroom. Cassie was right about the dress size; it fit perfectly. My intuition told me that this had all been a conspiracy on both their parts.

"Stop it," I said out loud. I needed to save my paranoia for more important things than going to a party.

The double wide full-length mirror made it difficult to avoid looking at my reflection. I stared back motionless, trying to reconcile the image I saw with my perception of myself. The flowing satin dress was a deep blue and clung sensually. Thin spaghetti straps trailed down over my shoulders meeting the low V-neck that revealed more of my skin than I was usually comfortable with showing. I wanted so badly to jump back into my blue jeans.

Cassie knocked on the door. When I opened it she was holding a pair of shoes in one hand but her other hand stayed hidden behind her back.

"What other torture are you planning to put me through?"

"I need you to trust me on this, Katherine. Close your eyes and take a deep breath."

In spite of my misgivings, I complied with her request. My lids snapped shut and I felt her hands on my hair followed by the sound of metal on metal. Startled, I reflexively opened my eyes to find that my hair now hung in a flawlessly straight line just above my shoulders.

"Much better." Cassie said and reached for the curling iron that was heating up on the bathroom counter. Where had that come from?

"Why did you do that?" I protested as Cassie blatantly continued.

"Katherine, you're Joshua's fiancée."

I scowled at her. Her brother and I were not engaged. Joshua hadn't asked me to marry him. Just because he had some silly dream about us didn't mean we were getting married. Cassie went on, still fiddling with my makeover. "You need to get used to proper etiquette when you're out in public... blah, blah, blah." I tuned her out as best I could.

Cassie moved to my face next. The different colors of the makeup made me look like a Cherokee in war paint. "Please, Cassie, that's enough already. No one is going to be looking at me tonight."

"Oh, everyone is going to be looking at you tonight."

"Thanks. Now I feel much better."

Cassie tried to hand the pair of shoes to me next. "I'm not wearing those. They're too high. I'll probably fall and break my ankle."

"Katherine, you can walk in these, trust me. Your ankle is as strong as a steel girder."

I grabbed the torturous looking footwear out of her hand and stomped into my bedroom.

"Don't forget to put in your contacts."

"Yah, yah."

Of course, the shoes fit perfectly and in spite of my apprehension, I was able to walk easily in them. Cassie motioned to me with her right hand as I walked back into Joshua's living room. "There. She's very nearly perfect, if I do say so myself. I'm a fashion genius—don't you agree, brother?"

Joshua looked up from his computer. My makeover had an eye-popping effect on him. I blushed, embarrassed at his reaction and Cassie laughed. "Now you're perfect."

Without talking his eyes off me Joshua said, "Thank you, Cassie." I heard him swallow hard.

"Katherine, you look absolutely ... amazing." Joshua walked to my side holding a small velvet covered box. "I have something for you." The box opened with creaking sound. Inside attached to a bright silver chain was a beautiful blue stone.

"Oh! Joshua, it's beautiful."

"The stone is an amethyst, a rare type known as a Deep Russian."

"Hey, that's my birthstone!"

Joshua kissed my shoulder after he had secured the necklace. "I know." Of course he knew.

"You'll be the most sensational woman there tonight. It will be very difficult for me to concentrate on my work."

"Maybe I shouldn't go then." My tone reflected the hope that I could still get out of this.

Joshua and Cassie each grabbed one of my arms and in unison said, "No way, you're going."

The Boston Harbor Hotel was crowded as Joshua pulled up to the main entrance. He turned to me apprehensively. "I have something to tell you, Katherine. Please don't overreact about this as you've already promised to go."

I pursed my lips. I already knew what he was going to tell me. "Lindsey is here with Nathaniel."

At least I could take comfort in the fact that he was keeping her safe, from Reggie anyway. I sucked in a deep breath and said, "Okay, I guess there's really nothing I can do about that. There is something I would like you to do for me in return."

"Okay," he agreed looking wary of my request

"Please don't refer to me as your fiancée. Especially since Lindsey will be here. Just say we're close friends. "

Joshua winked. "You know how I hate to lie."

I pursed my lips again and shot him a warning glance.

"Fine, it will be our secret."

I held up my hand, palm side out. "Whatever, Joshua."

He chuckled. "I'll park the car and meet you girls inside."

I skidded to an abrupt halt upon entering the dazzling lobby. It reminded me of a special I had seen on PBS about Buckingham Palace. The floors were a combination of elegant rugs and warm brown marble. An outrageously decadent chandelier hung from the middle of the vaulted ceiling. Hidden lights ran along the entire perimeter, giving the room a muted effect. Cassie had to pull on my arm several times before I would let her tow me along to the conference room.

Lindsey spotted us immediately when we entered the Wharf Room. I watched as she skipped happily towards us, snaking her way around the multitude of linen-covered tables. She was still so very much a child--still my little girl. "Mom, I'm so happy to see you. Isn't this place great? I love your haircut." I shot Cassie a stern look. She ignored me.

Lindsey noticed me scowling at Nathaniel who had tagged along behind her. Before I had a chance to embarrass her Lindsey linked our arms together and walked me to the windows that overlooked the harbor. Joshua was wrong about one thing. Lindsey was the most sensational woman here tonight. "I love your dress, sweetheart. Is it new?"

Lindsey cringed as she confessed, "Nathaniel bought it for me. I didn't have anything elegant enough."

Well, at least Lindsey would get something out of this relationship besides a broken heart. I hoped Nathaniel was listening to that.

"It looks great on you," I admitted and heard Lindsey sigh in relief, obviously happy that I wasn't going to overreact.

"What's really beautiful is this view," Lindsey commented, cleverly drawing my attention from her. I turned my gaze out the window. The brightly illuminated harbor made it difficult to tell that it was actually night time. The lights, which stretched up and down the ships' riggings and along the railings, outlined them in perfect silhouettes, bestowing a dreamy feel to the scene below.

Lindsey gushed as she explained about the presentation for tonight and the enormous amount of assistance the foundation provided around the world. I found myself caught up in her enthusiasm. Maybe this experience would be good for her. I was beginning to see more humility and compassion in her whole being--even a sense of contentment.

While we were talking, three women, all dressed impeccably, approached and stopped at the next window. One woman wore a stunning red outfit that accented her curvy body and large breasts.

I was not purposely listening to our neighbors, but of course I could still hear their banter over my conversation with Lindsey.

My head turned involuntarily toward the woman in red as she spoke the only word that could have drawn my interest from my beautiful daughter. "Oh, look, there's Joshua. I hope he's alone tonight. My god," she murmured, "he is gorgeous, isn't he?" Her companions nodded in obvious agreement, as they followed him through the crowd.

"I think you're out of luck, Jessica, Charlotte Ramsey told me that he's engaged."

I involuntarily clenched my teeth and hoped Lindsey hadn't heard that.

The third woman in the group spoke up next, speaking louder than the others, trying to be heard over the music that had begun filtering over the sound system. "Well, I hope the girl realizes how lucky she is. I would sell my soul for just one night with Joshua."

Lindsey heard that comment and asked in an anxious tone, "Mom, are you okay?" I nodded, too dazed to speak at the moment. I leaned back against the railing of the window, putting my hands behind me on either side to steady myself as I looked for Joshua. As our eyes met, a weird sense of euphoria overtook me.

My whole body was tingling with some strange sensation that I had never felt before. I let out a small squeak.

"What's so funny, Mom?"

I shrugged my shoulders, still silent, too absorbed in watching Joshua work the room.

Lindsey touched my arm, drawing me out of my stupor. "Nathaniel's waving to us to come and sit down."

"You go, sweetheart, I'll be along in a minute. Don't worry," I assured her, "I won't make a scene." Lindsey nodded and headed across the room.

Joshua met his siblings at the bar. He put his hand on Nathaniel's shoulder as he greeted him. I heard Joshua ask Lindsey if she thought her mother would like some wine. Lindsey replied, "Yes, definitely." Lindsey paused for a short moment before warning Joshua, "Uh, you might want to get my mom before she says anything to those ladies." She knew me too well.

"I'll retrieve her in a minute," Joshua told her reassuringly. He picked up two of the wine glasses from the bar and left them on our table before heading in my direction.

"Joshua is coming this way. How do I look?" The woman in red asked, fussing with her outfit.

"Beautiful," answered one of the other women.

It amused me to some extent to know they had no chance with him. I wanted to turn and give them a smug smile but I knew it was petty. Joshua was a gift that fate had handed to me on a platter. I only needed to reach out and he would be mine. I was instantly mortified with myself. Nothing came this easy in life. Good things had to be earned and I had done nothing to earn this love. Even though I had no spiritual beliefs, I did believe that there was a price to be paid for everything. I shuddered as I wondered what price I would pay for Joshua. Would I be selling my soul also?

Joshua's fervent gaze told me he wanted me and I flushed at the thought. I could smell the honeysuckle from his breath as it carried on the air ahead of him.

"Good evening, ladies," was the extent of Joshua's greeting to my three neighbors They all replied with a low salutation but before they could start up a conversation, Joshua quickly turned his back to them.

Even though I wasn't looking directly at them, I could hear the heavy disappointment in their sighs.

Joshua wrapped his arm around my waist and spun me towards the window. "Hello," he whispered dreamily in my ear.

My heart fluttered. "You're going to have to stop doing that if you expect me to be able to walk across this room."

Joshua beamed. "Not a chance. I'll carry you if need be."

I heard three women huff and walk away, leaving us alone.

"Are you having fun?"

"I am now. Thanks for inviting me tonight."

"They're about to start the program. We should take our seats. Wait until you see what an over-the-top job Lindsey did putting this together."

I could feel the boring glares from the other women in the room as we took our seats. Joshua gave me a reassuringly look and handed me the glass of wine, which I emptied in three gulps. I quickly asked the waiter to bring me two more. Cassie rolled her eyes at me. Lindsey shot me another please don't embarrass me look. I ignored them both.

An older gentleman stood up at the podium and lightly tapped the microphone, immediately drawing the room into silence. He welcomed and thanked everyone for attending before launching into a colorful showing of the foundations accomplishments during the past year. I gawked at the images as they came into view on the two panoramic screens positioned behind the podium. Images of schools built for children of every color, environmentally friendly dams and projects designed to bring clean water to poor areas of the world flashed before us in a mesmerizing choreography. The foundation's work stretched from Africa to Australia and from Alaska to Antarctica. Forests, rivers, islands, and coral reefs-- nothing was untouched by the foundation's philanthropy. One of their greatest projects was the worldwide conservation effort to save the big cats. That was not surprising seeing that one of their best friends was a lion.

I glanced over a few times to see Lindsey beaming. When the hour-long slide show ended, the same man asked for Joshua and Nathaniel to say a few inspiring words.

Joshua turned to me, smiling hugely, putting my hand to his lips. I frowned as I watched Nathaniel do the same with Lindsey. The entire room went dead quiet as the two brothers walked side by side to the podium, so confident it made me jealous. Joshua's speech was short, expressing his and Nathaniel's personal gratitude for all the hard work and effort that had gone into making the foundation's projects successful. Nathaniel stood with his hands in his pockets looking humbly down at his shoes. When Joshua finished Nathaniel leaned in to the microphone and said, "Thank you everyone. Enjoy your dinner."

The room burst into a round of applause and simultaneously the two doors in the back of the room opened and a line of waiters strode out among the tables, leaving plates of food in their passing.

After dinner Nathaniel and Joshua made another sweep around the room thanking everyone once more. This time Lindsey, intermittently bouncing with joy, tagged along with Nathaniel. He introduced her to everyone as his girlfriend. I, on the other hand sat quietly with my arms folded.

If I was being honest with myself, which didn't happen too often, I was feeling better about Nathaniel. He couldn't be as spoiled rich as I had first assumed if he was willing to spend his life, a life in which he could choose any path imaginable, to help others.

Joshua's voice pulled me from my contemplation. "Are you ready to go?"

"Yes definitely." I had some plans of my own for the remainder of the night. Joshua laughed at my eagerness and I flushed red wondering if he had been peeking again.

Nathaniel and Lindsey had plans to stop at another party.

Lindsey gave me a warm hug before she left. "I'm so glad you decided to come out with us tonight, Mom. It was great having you here."

"I'm glad I came." I admitted. I turned to Nathaniel and with as much sincerity as I could muster told him, "Thank you for bringing Lindsey with you tonight."

Nathaniel nodded, pulling their entwined hands up to his lips. "I'm delighted that Lindsey agreed to accompany me. It made the night so much more enjoyable for me."

Lindsey smiled tenderly at him and then turned back toward me to wink. "Okay, Mom, I'll call you tomorrow."

On the way back to the Prudential we dropped Cassie at a friend's. I was glad when she was gone. I didn't want her around eavesdropping. Of course, I knew she would be listening no matter where she went. I had previously figured out that if Cassie was reading my mind and Joshua was reading hers then it was no different from him reading my mind directly.

As we drove through the city, I reached over and touched Joshua arm lightly. "Hey." My voice was shaky.

"Yes?"

"Why don't we go dancing?"

Joshua shook his head, "No, not tonight."

"Why not? I thought you liked dancing?"

"I thought you didn't like dancing?" he countered.

"Well, maybe I'm changing my mind about it."

"Not tonight. We need to talk when we get back to my place."

My heart began to speed up. "I'm really not in the mood for any more of your horror stories."

He frowned and I wished I had left off the horror adjective. "That's not it. I want to talk ..." he hesitated... "about us."

"Oh." A lump formed in my throat. As we had spent more and more time together the electricity between us had become stronger. Even though I was torn between what my heart was feeling and my stubbornness to make up my own mind about this relationship, I was anxious to know the outcome.

After we were back at his apartment, I took Joshua's hand and led him to the couch. "Joshua, tonight, well--" I was having trouble finding the right words. "It was incredible. The work your foundation does is extraordinary--especially the big cat conservation. Issy must really like that."

"Yes, over the past fifty years the lion population in Africa has declined by a record 90%. Issy lets us know where the problem areas are and assists in hunting down the poachers, but she can't be everywhere at once and we're losing ground rapidly. We're troubled by the idea that a hundred years from now our mythical companion might be the only wild lion left." Joshua shook his head. "For a species that believes their one true god created this planet and all its life, humans aren't doing a good job taking care of his creation."

I nodded in agreement. Animal conservation had been something I was adamant about when I was human but the little that I could do didn't really feel like it was making much of a difference. I realized now that in this new life I would have a second chance to make that difference.

"I hate to admit it but I was even impressed with Nathaniel. I'd ask you not to repeat that but I know it won't do any good."

Joshua chuckled. He put his hand under my chin and with the lightest of touches let his lips brush mine, lingering there for a few seconds. I instantly went numb. Before I could respond, he leaned away. "I'm glad you enjoyed the evening but I need to get out of this suit," he complained pulling at his tie. "I hate wearing these things."

Before Joshua could get up I grabbed his arm and repositioned myself. "Here, let me do that," I offered.

My hands were shaking as I loosened his tie and I was sure Joshua would not miss that. I had known that this relationship would be more difficult than others I had had in my human life. The force of that realization unnerved me but didn't stop me from moving on to the buttons of his shirt. It might have been a relief to put this off being as nervous as I was, but I couldn't overcome the rejection that began coursing through me as I felt Joshua's hands wrap around my wrists and push me back.

"You've changed your mind about us, haven't you?"

"Absolutely not." He sounded insulted. "Katherine, my need for you is causing me great physical pain."

I looked at him, perplexed. "Then what's wrong?"

Joshua pulled me toward him and whispered. "I don't want to do this here. Each time a plane takes off from Logan it's like being launched out of a cannon barrel. The only sound I want to hear when I make love to you is the sound of your beating heart."

It took a few seconds before I could speak again. "I thought you had some kind of supernatural brain power. Even I'm able to block out the din of the city," I bragged.

"That's true, while we're awake and fully alert. Think about what it's like when you relax and try to sleep. Don't you still wear your headphones when you're here?"

I nodded. Having to wear the accessory didn't seem very romantic.

"There are people and noise everywhere." It was embarrassing how whiney my voice sounded.

Joshua smiled playfully. "What would you think about Nantucket for a week?"

I didn't have to think about that at all. "I love Nantucket."

"If we go in September it will be practically deserted and we would be out of the hearing range of Nathaniel and Cassie and the others."

That was certainly a plus for me. Then it dawned on me--it was May and Joshua wanted to wait until September.

"There must be somewhere else we can go before September." My face was so hot you could have fried an egg on it.

"It's very romantic on the island and I have a friend who owns a house in a fairly remote area. That should be quiet enough even for us." Joshua reached out playing with a strand of my hair.

"Besides, I figured you'd probably want to wait until after Josephine has the baby and gets settled back at home, before you took off for a week."

I shook my head in disgust. Some mother I was. "Oh, right. In September then," I agreed, my words coming out in a drone.

Joshua chuckled and kissed me again. This time I held on tightly.

"Please," he said breaking away breathlessly, "let's not test my self-control--I'm sure it's not as strong as we think it is."

"Yeah, right," I griped as I unhappily released him.

"I promise you we will be together. It's late now." He stared at me with eyes as soft as butter while his hands gently cupped my face. "Please don't look so dejected. I've waited a millennium to have you wrapped in my arms, Katherine Ann. I want everything to be perfect."

I nodded but my heart had not found a steady rhythm yet. "I'm going to put on a movie. Will you stay up with me?"

"I will but first I need to get changed and take a shower. A cold shower."

"All right," I acquiesced. "I'll work on practicing my self control also."

"Whatever movie you decide on, make sure it's something with lots of blood and guts, please, no romance."

I flipped on the giant blue screen and began searching for an action movie. In spite of the fact that the night hadn't ended as I had originally planned I was somewhat relieved. It was difficult enough in a normal relationship to swallow all your fears and give yourself unconditionally to another person. Never mind a person who had been waiting an extraordinarily long time to find you and had expectations that I was sure I couldn't live up to.

Chapter 13
THE RACE

I will fall upon them like a bear robbed of her cubs.
I will tear open their breast, and there I will devour them like a
lion, as a wild beast would rip them open.

~ Hosea 13:8 ESV

The Mongolians sat for hours plotting their route home across the Pacific and they weren't planning to use a plane or boat to get there. With no more visits from Reggie, we had all begun to relax, and Joshua and Nathaniel felt it was safe enough for the Asians to return to their beloved homeland. They would make a detour through Mexico and meet up with Issy to get her report and as Khun had promised Joshua, they would not confront Reggie in any way.

Shamus and Nevan were the complete opposite of the Mongolians. They loved visiting America and were in no hurry to leave.

Being around the others of our kind was comforting, but one thing that had not changed with my transformation was that I was still a tree hugger. I felt instant relief the moment I crossed the "Entering Townsend" sign on route 119 on the few nights a week that Joshua let me go home alone.

"How was your evening?" the silky voice that caused my heart to flutter asked when I answered my work phone one Thursday morning. "Were you able to get some rest?"

"Too much," I complained. "I missed you."

"I missed you also. That's the reason I'm calling. Do you think you could arrange to get the rest of the week off from work?"

"Umm... It's tempting." I only had one report to finish and my new project wouldn't begin until next week. "Why, what's up?"

"I'll explain when I see you."

"Okay, pick me up at noon." I wasn't a good employee these days. I would use any excuse to leave if it meant seeing Joshua.

Joshua's mood was completely the opposite of what it had been earlier during our phone conversation as he greeted me in the parking lot.

"What's wrong?" I demanded as soon as we were both in the Audi.

"I have to go away for the weekend."

I swallowed quietly past the lump. I wanted to scold him. Why had he asked me to leave work if he was planning to go away anyway?

Joshua reached out and gently touched my cheek. "Everything is fine, Katherine. We're not in any danger."

Joshua had misread my alarm. The demons and now Reggie were always something to be considered but they were lower on my list than the thought of being without Joshua.

"Nathaniel and I promised to help a friend. I was hoping you would want to join us."

"Where're you going?" I would have followed Joshua to the ends of the earth but with Josephine due in just four weeks, I didn't want to be too far away.

"Lime Rock, Connecticut. Our friend is short a driver for the auto race this weekend. He asked Nathaniel and me to fill in."

"Lime Rock," I sputtered. That was only a few hours away. "You can drive a racecar? Are we staying overnight?"

"Yes, to both your questions. I've made us a reservation at a local bed and breakfast. Lindsey and Cassie are going with us." Joshua paused, waiting for my usual overreaction to his brother's relationship with my daughter but I let it go. I was more interested in the upcoming weekend.

"What type of car will you be racing?"

"A brand new Chevy Camaro. Nathaniel and I have raced there before and we know it well." He pointed to his head and laughed. Joshua's eyes were bright with anticipation. "You know, I met Paul Newman once at Lime Rock."

"Of course you did but it would be more impressive if you had said Julius Caesar."

Joshua's smile widened.

"Don't tell me. You met him once also?"

"I did ... at a chariot race in Rome."

"Really and what did he think about that shine in your eyes?"

"He was intrigued, of course."

I laughed loudly. Joshua was always making me laugh. That was an important quality in a boyfriend. My laugh changed to a smile as I realized that was the first time I had ever had that thought and I liked the sound of it.

Joshua touched my check, trying to refocus my thoughts. "Okay, Mr. Wonderful, time to drive me home so I can pack." On the way, I called Josephine to let her know about our weekend away. I could hear the road noise on the other end of our conversation and my mother gene kicked in. "Are you sure you're okay?"

"I'm fine, Mom," she sighed, aggravated by my constant fretting. Soon enough Josephine would understand.

"That was a strange conversation," I told Joshua after I had hung up."Do you think she's all right? Maybe I shouldn't go?"

Joshua put his hand on my leg. He meant the gesture to be reassuring but it gave me palpitations.

"Josephine is fine. You need to calm down and try to relax. I promise you she will be under constant watch the whole time we're away."

Joshua thought I was worried about Reggie, and I was, but my immediate concern was childbirth. In my experience bearing children is one of the most dangerous undertakings for a human woman, even in this modern age.

Joshua looked perplexed as I handed him my small suitcase. "Where are your other bags?"

I shrugged. "That's it."

"You know Cassie will just buy you clothes if she thinks you're not dressed to her standards."

"We're going to have to do something about that, Joshua. I'm an adult. I can dress myself."

"Good luck convincing her of that."

Our next stop was Boston to switch cars. Joshua wanted to drive Nathaniel's Viper to the track. Lindsey and Nathaniel were taking the Ford GT and Cassie was taking Joshua's Audi with the suitcases. Neither the Viper nor the GT had room for anything more than the racing gear. Not that a helmet or fire protection was necessary for my hybrids. According to Joshua we couldn't be burned or injured by anything man-made. However, the racing association regulations specified mandatory safety equipment and the Stones were all about following rules.

Nathaniel was in the garage working under the hood of the Viper when we arrived. The girls were upstairs still packing.

"You'll really enjoy riding in this," Nathaniel bragged about the Viper. "It will go over a buck eighty without breaking a sweat." Great and Lindsey would be in his other rocket on the way out to the track.

When they were done with their auto checklist, I asked Joshua if he could give me a moment alone with Nathaniel. They both laughed.

"What?" I demanded.

"You know that I can hear you even on the top floor of this building and then in Nathaniel's mind."

I scowled. "Then stay if you want."

"No, I'll go let the girls know we're all set." Joshua turned and went to the elevator.

Nathaniel shut the hood and crossed his arms. "I know what you're going to say, Katherine. I would never do anything to endanger Lindsey. I'm insulted that you would even feel the need to say anything to me, as if I was one of your children, which thank goodness I'm not."

"I'm going to say it anyway."

"Of course you are," Nathaniel said shaking his head.

"I just wanted to remind you that Lindsey is human. If you get into an accident in that hundred-fifty-thousand-dollar gem of yours, you'll walk away but she won't."

Nathaniel stood motionless, glaring at me. "Are you done?" Then without waiting for my reply he went to finish packing up.

As I stomped toward the elevator, the door opened and Joshua was there, a small knapsack in his hand.

"If you're done scolding Nathaniel we can be on our way." I didn't know why he thought this was funny. Joshua had never had the experience of losing someone he loved in a car accident. Joshua opened the passenger door of the Viper for me and as I went to get in he caught my arm. He looked appalled.

"I'm sorry. You're right, I've never had that experience and I can see how painful it is for you. Nathaniel will be careful with Lindsey."

Nathaniel was standing beside me now also. "Joshua's right," he said, sounding contrite, "I will be extra careful."

"Thank you," I nodded, for once not upset that they had been scanning my thoughts.

Boston to Lime Rock was a two-hour ride and Joshua was having a grand time. Then again, what guy wouldn't? The Viper was a dream car for most men, superhuman or human.

"What has you worried, Katherine."

"What makes you think I'm worried? Are you spying on me again?"

"You're trying to chew your bottom lip off and your teeth are strong enough that you will if you keep this up."

"I was just trying to figure out what I had done to piss off Nathaniel. He didn't like me from the start."

Joshua frowned. "Cassie and I are not very happy with his behavior. He's a little jealous of you."

"Jealous?" I asked incredulously. "In what universe would Nathaniel have any reason to be jealous of me? He has everything. Including my daughter," I mumbled.

"All of us have accepted Issy's rules all of these very long years, without question. We are tightly bound to each other as friends, but none of us has a mate, a hybrid mate, and any human mate will eventually perish. Nathaniel struggles with this more than the rest of us. He's afraid of losing Cassie and me, although he would never admit that. I've spent the past two years obsessing over you and hopefully this weekend will give us some bonding time."

"I didn't purposefully push my way into becoming part of his family."

"You haven't done anything wrong, Katherine. Nathaniel will come around."

"Okay," I said, placating him but he was wrong about his assertions, especially the first one. I still felt like I had done something wrong.

I looked out the passenger window at the scenery that was streaking past me at blinding speed again.

"Aren't you worried about hitting a deer? I know your reactions are lightning fast but you can't change the laws of physics. The car can only decelerate at a certain rate." I didn't have to be an auto aficionado to know that.

"Katherine, I've never been in an accident and I've been driving since cars were first invented. I can hear the deer coming from miles away, long before they step out in front of the car."

"Of course you can."

We changed direction and began heading north on Route 91. I stared at Joshua, waiting for an explanation. I knew the way to the track and this was not it.

"I thought that maybe we could take a side trip, stop in Northampton. We have plenty of time." His voice was pleading making me instantly suspicious.

"You're up to something?"

"Katherine, it's simply me taking you to dinner. Humor me, please? You won't let me buy you anything. At least I can make sure you eat well." I didn't believe Joshua's weak explanation but I couldn't argue with that intoxicating smile.

North Hampton was a bustling community with a downtown that was reminiscent of the late 70's. I did love visiting there and I found myself relaxing while we did some window-shopping. When we had made our way back to the car Joshua opened the driver's side door and said, "Why don't you drive for a while? I'm tired."

I shot him a disparaging look while I scrambled around in my head trying to come up with as many excuses as I could think of. "I'm not driving this. Its dark out and I don't know the roads. Plus Nathaniel would be upset if anything happened to his car."

"Your night vision is far superior than it ever was. Get in, Katherine. I guarantee you will love it. The speed is exhilarating. I won't take no for an answer." Joshua reached out and pulled me in to his arms. He began kissing my neck--too seductively. "It's time for you to stop worrying about everything and start enjoying your new life. What's the point of living forever if you can't have some fun once in a while?"

I pushed him away and had to lean against the car to keep from falling. He wasn't playing fair.

"Fine," I said, breathing heavily. "You'll be sorry when you have to explain to Nathaniel what happened to his car."

"I'll teach you how to listen for the deer."

I got in behind the wheel of the Viper and immediately began to whine. "I'm not sure about this, Joshua. I can't see the end of the hood."

"Pull the seat up further. Go ahead, start the engine." I turned the key. The engine roared to life, seeming to taunt me with its vibrations. I started to whine again but Joshua ignored me.

"Katherine, we need to get to the B&B before sunrise," he joked.

Without waiting for me to gripe any further Joshua released the emergency brake. The car began to roll and I lifted the clutch pedal and gently pushed down on the accelerator. The Viper snarled and lurched forward. The Viper's gears shifted smooth and true and once I settled down, I did begin to enjoy the drive.

Joshua gave me directions to the turnpike, all the while playing with my hair, twisting it round his fingers. I hadn't had a haircut since the night of the Stone Foundation meeting. It had grown back within three days and was in "Rapunzel mode" again.

"You're distracting me. This will end badly if you don't stop."

Joshua dropped his hold on my hair. "Do you have any more questions for me while we're alone?"

"Does the word eternity give you a hint as to the amount of time you'll need to answer all my questions?"

"All right then, what's next?"

"I want to know more about this shimmering. Can you do it at will or do you have to drink some magic potion?"

"Katherine, you have quite an imagination," Joshua laughed. "Our bodies generate a magnetic infrared wave that bends the visible light surrounding us. Humans aren't able to see at that frequency, hence we seem to disappear.

"Umm," I pondered. "I'll be able to sneak out of work without anyone seeing me. Maybe even pull off a few bank heists. The possibilities are endless."

"Katherine Ann Chambers, I think maybe you have a devious side that I haven't seen yet."

"I have many sides that you haven't seen yet," I mumbled.

"And I'm sure I'll like them all."

"We'll see," I warned darkly.

Joshua had me get off the highway onto Route 7. It was narrow and winding with a speed limit of forty and I stayed well below it.

"A herd of deer is approaching. It will cross our path in about two minutes." Joshua warned me as the Viper glided easily around a sharp turn.

"What?" I slowed down below twenty, looking back and forth from one side of the road to the other.

"Keep driving. Open your mind and let all the sounds flood in." I let the car inch forward, slowly, moving the gears from first to second and remaining there. I could feel the engine beseeching me to shift up.

"When I do that it's a huge pandemonium. It's like being in a room with five televisions, all of them set to different channels. The sounds mash together."

"Try to block out any words. Listen to the forest around us--the breeze—concentrate on any sounds that have a pattern to them."

"Okay," I replied irritated that he was making me do this.

"The deer are coming at us from our left." I listened more intently in that direction. A faint clump, clump, clump, clump that corresponded with the crinkling of dried leaves, keep rising above the other sounds. Then it was upon us. I slammed the brake and clutch to the floor. The back end of the Viper fishtailed, leaving the car at an odd angle in the middle of the road. Three deer ran quickly across the road missing the front bumper by only a few inches.

Joshua laughed heartily. "Excellent, Katherine."

"Excellent? I just barely stopped in time." My heart was pounding.

"Next time it won't be as close. Eventually it won't be any different than stopping for a changing traffic light."

I didn't answer him. If only I had known...... If Joshua had been around and had taught me, maybe... maybe things would have been different in the accident. I put my hands up and grabbed the sides of my temples. The memory burned red hot and felt like would split me in two.

Joshua misconstrued my reaction. "This takes practice, Katherine. Don't be discouraged. Our abilities get stronger with time."

I put the car in neutral and pulled up the emergency brake.

"What're you doing?"

"I really wish you would drive now." I opened the door and climbed out.

Joshua did the same and without any argument. After we were moving again, I realized that there were tears welling up under my lids and I knew Joshua wouldn't miss that. "Are you thinking about Alex and the accident?"

"I should have been able to prevent it, Joshua. I heard the other car coming but didn't know what it was."

"I am so very sorry, Katherine. We didn't know," he whispered, his voice thick with remorse. "It's upsetting to all of us, considering all the things that we can do, to realize how many things we can't do."

"I know you did what you thought was appropriate considering how Reggie turned out, but this huge amount of guilt that I have over Alex's death feels like it's crushing me sometimes. I... I'm scared."

"Of what in particular?"

"I'm afraid that over time, that one day, I will lose my memory of him and our wonderful life together."

"You won't." It was quiet for a few seconds before Joshua spoke again. "I can still bring to mind the way my mother's golden hair sparkled among the sea of black at palace functions." Joshua reached his hand out reflexively in front of him to touch something that only he could see. "Her given name was Ella. Every night before bed she would tell us stories of her childhood and of a magical land where the evening sun would shine on the summer snow..." he trailed off deep in thought.

"You miss your parents?" The longing in his tone was unmistakable.

"My father was very stern and distant. No one could get close to him, not even Reggie and Sennacherib, his heirs. I do miss my mother though. Ella was a strong woman who deeply loved and defended all of us."

Joshua spent the remainder of the drive telling me stories of his childhood. They were happy stories.

I was surprised and elated when Joshua pulled the Viper into the driveway of the 1802 House. Alex and I had loved to stay here. It felt like home to me.

Nathaniel and Lindsey were waiting for us on the front porch, holding on tightly to each other. Lindsey let go of Nathaniel's hand when she saw us and ran to greet me, wrapping her arms around me. "I'm so glad to see you, Mom. We're going to have so much fun."

Lindsey was glowing. Her look of contentment made realize that she maybe had finally found the right direction for her life in this strange supernatural family. It grated against my natural aversion to Nathaniel, but the more time I spent with him, the more I could see many of the same qualities in him that I admired in Joshua. Nathaniel treated people with respect and more importantly he treated Lindsey with respect.

I had suspected that Joshua was hiding something from me all day and that something was evident as I walked through the front door and saw my pregnant daughter and her husband, Steven, sitting on the couch.

After I fretted for a few minutes about Josephine being away from her doctor, she reminded me that women all over the world delivered babies in less elegant surroundings and were fine. I took a few deep breaths and tried to let it go.

Friday's forecast was for sunny weather in the seventies-- perfect for racing. Nathaniel and Joshua were expected at the racetrack by seven. Steven, Lindsey, and I were planning to go along to watch the race preparations. Cassie was staying behind with Josephine which made me feel less guilty about leaving her until Cassie reminded me, during a brief moment when we were alone, that she had been a nurse in Vietnam and was perfectly capable of delivering the baby if she had to.

"Not helping, Cassandra. Please promise me you'll call an ambulance if it comes to that."

"You worry way too much," she declared, dismissing my concern. What I didn't say out loud was that she had it backwards. Cassie never worried enough.

Lime Rock was not your typical racetrack. Rolling hills and expanses of lawns dotted with ample trees surrounded the track. Watching an auto event at this venue was similar to having an old fashioned picnic in the 1920s except with different style clothing.

Joshua's friend, Paul, was thrilled. He must have thanked Joshua and Nathaniel ten times for saving his career. The boys didn't waste any time getting to work. I watched in awe as they concentrated their efforts at aligning the Camaro's front end using a piece of equipment that looked like a three-legged spider. If they didn't like the reading on the digital display of the camber gauge they would make some adjustments and retake the measurements. Joshua explained that when the measurements matched up, the alignment would be perfect. I had no doubt about that.

Practice sprints, which allowed the drivers some time to familiarize themselves with the lay of the track, were on the schedule for the first day. That wasn't necessary for my supermen—and their reputation preceded them. A few men from another team wandered into our area during the afternoon break. When they saw Nathaniel and Joshua, one of them commented with disappointment, "Oh, great, the Stones are here." Frowning he turned to the other two men accompanying him and said, "Well, gents, I guess we can all just go home."

Nathaniel stood up to greet the man, shaking his hand. "Oh stop fretting, Harry, I promise to keep the car in third gear. That way you'll be able to keep up."

Joshua gave Nathaniel a disapproving look and went to talk to the men, trying to smooth things over. Even though Nathaniel had an unnatural edge over all the other men racing in this event he still had a competitive edge about him. The Y chromosome syndrome.

Toward the end of the day one of the racecars leaked fluid onto the track, forcing the officials to cancel the remaining stints, which made me extremely happy. Even with the earplugs that Cassie had brought for me, the constant screeching of tires was excruciating.

The seven of us headed to 20 Railroad Street for dinner. We sat at the front of the restaurant near the wall of windows that looked out onto the main street. Joshua held my seat out for me but before he could get around the table to sit across from me, Nathaniel had taken that spot.

"Be good," Joshua warned and he went to sit by Steven.

"Don't you want to sit next to Lindsey?" I was having a good time and I didn't want to start arguing with him and ruin the evening.

"I'm not going to argue with you. I wanted to ask you about driving my car. Did you enjoy it?"

Mentally I told him that if he didn't want to argue with me he could start by staying the hell out of my head but verbally I told him, "Yes, I did… very much."

He chuckled. "Oh, good! You'll have to ask Joshua to take you out in the Ford GT sometime. That car is even more over the top."

I stared at him skeptically and I asked, "Why are you being nice to me?"

"Well, it appears that you and my brother are going to be together for some time." He winked playfully. "Apparently we've gotten off on the wrong foot. Maybe we should try to be friends or at the least friendly."

"Okay," I agreed quietly. I was willing to try if he was. The rest of our dinner conversation was mostly about Nathaniel's work at the Stone Foundation and then my work at LCA. I had to say I was even more impressed with the enthusiasm and commitment he had for his job. Nathaniel was easy to get along with when he wanted to behave.

The boys left early again for the track on Saturday. On the docket today were qualifying races to determine where each car and driver would line up at the start of the actual race on Monday. At Cassie's insistence, I was staying behind with the girls who had planned a day at the outlets in Lenox. Even living forever couldn't do much to bolster my enthusiasm for shopping.

The bright spot of the morning was the delicious breakfast we had out in the gazebo of the 1802 House. The chipmunks entertained us with their antics as they scurried from one hole to the next. I was pleased at how well Cassie melded into our family, as if she had been a real sister to my daughters. Of course that was mostly due to Lindsey and Josephine's unquestionable acceptance of her obvious peculiarities.

When we were done with breakfast, Cassie went with Josephine to pack a few things for our shopping spree, leaving Lindsey and me alone to finish our coffee. When they were out of sight, Lindsey turned to me and asked, "Mom, have you noticed how strange the Stones' eyes are?"

Lindsey was a smart girl and having spent as much as time as she had with the hybrids it was surprising that she hadn't said something sooner.

"I have," I admitted shakily, deciding that it was more prudent to go with the truth even if only partially. I wondered for a split second if she had noticed my eyes.

"Joshua told me it was a genetic mutation in their family."

Lindsey shrugged. "I guess. There are other weird things. Nathaniel is incredibly strong and he knows everything and I mean everything. I swear they know what each other is thinking--like they can read each other's minds and, for that matter, mine too. Sometimes Nathaniel answers my questions before I ask them."

I quickly put my hand over my forehead and feigned a headache.

"Are you okay, Mom? You look sick all of a sudden."

"I'll be fine in a minute," I mumbled, taking a deep breath. I had a long day ahead of me and it was unlikely that I would be able to get Cassie alone. Besides, this was between Joshua and me.

The race team was taking a break when we arrived at two. Joshua's welcoming kiss made me forget my irritation over the earlier surmise that somehow Nathaniel could read Lindsey's thoughts. I put it out of my thoughts for the moment because honestly it frightened me to wonder about the implications.

After the hellos, we girls headed off with the chairs and coolers to the lawn by Big Bend.

Steven stayed with the boys. You could hear the reverence in his tone whenever he spoke of Nathaniel and Joshua. Steven was as awed by them as the rest of us. He had been without a father figure for most of his life and I could see how easily Nathaniel and Joshua could fill that void for him.

That night we attended a special showing of Gone with the Wind at the Mahawie Theater. Joshua whispered in my ear during the entire four hours, correcting the historical facts that the producers got wrong. Not that I minded the whispering in my ear, but all the facts took the fun out of watching the movie.

Due to an agreement with the neighbors, there was no racing on Sundays. For something different we attended the morning concert at Tanglewood and then spent the afternoon in town. The kids had many questions about the civil war after seeing the movie and Joshua and Nathaniel, having actually participated in the hostilities, entertained us that night with stories about the war that couldn't be found in any books. Of course the kids thought the Stones knew as much as they did merely because they were history buffs.

As I sat in the gazebo listening to the laughs and oh's and ah's, I considered the peculiar set of coincidences that had pulled us together, superhuman and human. What was I going to tell the kids fifty years from now? I was counting on Joshua to figure out something. The hybrids had never had to deal with this situation before. When humans started getting curious they simply disappeared. That was not going to happen this time.

On Monday, the day of the race, the men headed to the paddock area while the girls and I went straight to the spectator area. Advertisers' logos melded into a kaleidoscope of color each time the cars screeched around the track. The sea of spectators would stand in unison, similar to a massive wave, in response to the occasional spinouts, none of which resulted in any injury.

The smell of burning brakes began to unnerve me and I decided to take a time out from the constant screeching by browsing through a few of the vendor's tents on the far hill. I forced myself to get absorbed in the stacks of books that I found on gardening, crafts and home design. After about a half hour, I heard the click as the book merchant locked his register and walked up behind me.

"Excuse me, Miss, I need to go next door to get some change. Since you're the only one here I thought I would sneak out for a few minutes. If anyone does come in will you let them know I'll be right back?"

I was confused because just two tables down was another person absorbedly reading one of his books. "Sure, no problem," I told him politely. After he left, I looked more carefully at the other customer. In a flash, the man whirled and was beside me.

"Well, hello, Katherine," Reggie exclaimed wearing a huge grin. He had the brazenness to speak to me as if we were old friends. "Funny seeing you here."

Reggie reached his hand out as if to touch my face but I slapped it away. "Stay away from me."

"Now, is that anyway to greet your future brother-in-law?"

I instinctively, stupidly, raised my closed fist to strike him. Of course, Reggie knew exactly what I was planning and with lightning speed blocked my attack. I winced as I struggled uselessly to free my hand from his crushing grip.

"You need to be more careful, Katherine. You see, my diet," he paused and cleared his throat, "makes me much stronger than you hoofers. Something I'm sure Joshua neglected to tell you."

Although I knew about his diet I wasn't sure what he was taking about and I didn't care. All I could see were chaotic images of my dead cat. "You son of a bitch," I screamed. "Why did you kill my cat? I've never done anything to you." The tears had begun to cascade down my cheeks. Why oh why couldn't I hold my emotions in just this one time?

"Sorry. That may have been too theatrical but how else was I going to get my siblings' attention?" He sighed. "They don't write or call. I haven't heard from them in centuries. Plus I wanted to be sure my shining star of a brother told you everything. I know he's trying to protect you."

"What does it matter to you?"

"Because my brother is not as much of a saint as he pretends to be. Why should Joshua be allowed to find happiness when the rest of us can't?"

Reggie moved closer staring deeply into my eyes. Underneath the hard lines of his face was an indisputable beauty that was difficult to look away from. I shook my head, refusing to let him distract me from my rage. "It's your own fault that you haven't found happiness, not Joshua's and certainly not mine." I looked down at my hand.

"Take your paws off of me."

"I can hear the fear in your voice," Reggie disclosed as he released me. It stung as the blood rushed in. Before I could move away he grabbed my forearm and pulled me in until our bodies touched. I shivered involuntarily to the repulsive touch when his free hand stroked my face.

"You certainly are beautiful," he cooed, "and you don't even realize it do you. I can see why Joshua wants you so desperately. It must be refreshing to make love to someone that's not so fragile, and I do like my sex rough. When your partner dies before you're done it takes the fun out the activity." He shrugged unapologetically. "Of course most of my tiffs end in meal time anyway. You know the young ones are the tastiest."

My mouth twisted in disgust. "Let go of me," I demanded, at the same time trying not to think of anything private but I knew I had.

"What's this? Joshua hasn't made a move on you yet?" Reggie laughed again and shook his head. "Well, if you want a real man you can always look me up when you're ready."

"Awh," I said, swallowing back the awful thought. "You'd have to kill me first."

Reggie raised his left eyebrow. "That could be arranged."

"You obnoxious swine! Do you have any sense of right or wrong at all?"

"Apparently not." He twisted my arm and watched gleefully as I winced again.

"Wait until Joshua finds out you're bothering me again," I said, trying to threaten him, but my voice sounded weak.

"Speaking of which, here come my loving brothers. Good." Reggie seemed pleased that he had been able to orchestrate this meeting.

"Good is right. I hope you brought along a shovel, Reggie, because you're in deep shit now."

Reggie chuckled. "You're adorable. A kitten acting like a lion."

In the next second, Joshua and Nathaniel were there, both their faces masks of fury.

Joshua pulled me away from Reggie and positioned me behind him and Nathaniel. I rubbed at my now aching limb.

"Are you all right?" Joshua asked his voice laden with concern.

"My arm is fine," I said crossly glaring at Reggie from in between Joshua and Nathaniel.

"How are you doing that?" Nathaniel asked Reggie.

"I've discovered several new tricks, brothers." Reggie leaned back against one of the tables of books, his arms crossed, not a care in the world.

Nathaniel and Joshua exchanged a quick glance. I couldn't follow along with their thoughts and that made it difficult for me to keep up with the conversation.

"What are you doing here, Reggie?" Nathaniel growled.

"The same thing you are. Racing, of course."

Joshua was appalled. "We're not getting onto the track with you."

"Too bad. I haven't had a good laugh in a while now."

"Let's go," Joshua said. He reached out for Nathaniel's arm but Nathaniel shook him away.

"Nathaniel," Joshua's stern voice bellowed.

Reggie headed towards one of the tent's entrances pausing before stepping out of view. "By the way, Nasir, I am so hoping you'll introduce me to your latest girlfriend." Before Reggie was done with his sentence, Nathaniel and Joshua both strained their necks and looked at me. Reggie grabbed his waist-- beside himself with laughter. "Oh, isn't this wonderful. Nasir is dating Katherine's daughter? Talk about kinky. You two kids."

Nathaniel tried to lunge at Reggie, but Joshua grabbed him. "This is not the place, Nathaniel."

Reggie chortled loudly at his angry brother, "Don't forget to buckle up," and he disappeared quickly. With one arm wrapped around my waist, the other around Nathaniel's forearm, Joshua led us outside, heading in the direction of the parking lot. Nathaniel was steaming mad. The fierce rumble coming from his throat was frightening.

"Where are we going, Joshua?"

"To get the girls and leave. I'll let Paul know we can't drive today," Joshua explained, frowning. I knew he didn't want to let his friend down but I was glad. Reggie was obviously here to cause more problems.

Nathaniel stopped walking and in a calm, assertive voice declared, "I'm not leaving."

Joshua stared at him as if he were deranged. "You're not going to race with him. He's doing this to piss us off. Katherine's girls are here. We can pick a fight with him some other time when we have backup."

"Oh, I'm pissed all right and I'm not doing this your way this time, Joshua. If that degenerate of a brother thinks that I'm going to stick my tail between my legs and run away as usual he's in for a surprise. I'm going to teach Reggie a lesson."

"You can't teach Reggie anything and he can't be reasoned with," Joshua hissed. "I only agreed to this because I knew you and I would be careful, but he doesn't care about the humans. Someone will be killed. I don't know how Reggie was able to keep us out of his head but without being able to read his thoughts you'll be blind out there."

Oh so they couldn't read his mind. I was instantly jealous of Reggie's talent and for a split second wondered if he would share his secret with me. It would be nice to have my privacy back again.

Joshua stood within a foot of Nathaniel, both of them glowering at the other. I had to give Reggie credit. In only a few minutes he had been able to instigate a fight between Joshua and Nathaniel, pitting them against each other. I was sure wherever he was he was smiling hugely to himself. A small crowd of onlookers was beginning to assemble, watching the argument. Joshua must have been pretty shaken, as he usually never let his carefully choreographed façade slip like this. I touched his forearm hoping to remind him of where he was. He instantly relaxed, taking a deep breath at the same time.

Nathaniel took advantage of the pause and moving at a faster than human speed walked away.

Joshua sighed. "I'll walk you back to where Cassie is and you must promise me to stay with her no matter what happens on the racetrack."

"I don't understand. What's going on, Joshua? Why is Reggie here?"

"Reggie never passes up an opportunity to screw with us, especially Nathaniel. He really knows how to push his buttons. Right now I have to stop Nathaniel." Joshua kissed me fiercely and said, "I'm so sorry."

"This is not your fault. I can get back by myself. You go and get Nathaniel. He could be my son-in-law someday and I don't want anything to happen to him."

Joshua looked pleasantly surprised. "Okay." We turned and walked in opposite directions from each other. Cassie intercepted me on the way back. "Joshua and Nathaniel are getting ready to go out on the track."

My eyes widened. "What? I thought we were leaving!"

She put her arm around me. "Nathaniel and Joshua will be fine. Joshua is worried about the other drivers, the human ones. He's going to race in hopes that he can keep Reggie from purposely causing a crash. Try to stay calm. We don't want to upset the girls."

I took a deep breath. "Okay, you're right, stay calm."

While I was waiting for the race to begin, I splashed water on my cheek, trying to wash away the feel of Reggie's tainted touch. I was lost in thought when the PA system screamed out the names of the drivers. Joshua Stone, Nathaniel Stone and Reggie Nemcan, were among the ten names on the list. I don't know why I was surprised that Reggie didn't have the same last name as his siblings.

I glanced at Cassie who just frowned. "You'll explain it to me later?" I asked in my head.

She nodded. I had to admit mind reading did have some advantages. Cassie snickered.

Joshua was out first. He and Reggie jockeyed around the track for the lead. At times the bumpers of their cars were mere inches apart but I knew Joshua wouldn't lose his temper and cause an accident.

Nathaniel was out next and I was sure Lime Rock had never seen a duel quite like this. Most of the drivers here were in million dollar autos and didn't take many risks. Nathaniel and Reggie's cars tore around the track at record speeds, far ahead of the others.

On the fifth lap, the Camaros were side by side as they came into the wide curve at Big Bend. The engines screamed in protest as the men punched the throttles to full speed on the straightaway. Both cars wobbled slightly and began to fishtail as the boundaries of control were reached. I watched in utter horror as the back end of Reggie's Camaro hit the back end of Nathaniel's. The crowd stood up, many of them putting their hands up to their faces in alarm as the speeding missiles spun wildly off the track in opposite directions. Reggie's came to rest on the wide grassy area to the right; Nathaniel's rolled repeatedly before being stopped by the guardrail to the left. Gasoline sprayed out in all directions, dotting the landscape with small fires. Both cars burst into flames, further intensifying the show. The fire trucks were dispatched immediately.

Lindsey was in tears. "Mom, what happened? Do you think Nathaniel is okay?"

"Yes," I assured her. "They have on plenty of fire gear." It would be a different story when I got hold of him though.

Cassie was standing with her arms on her waist. "Well, this is just great. Now we'll have to go home early." Josephine, Lindsey and Steven looked at her with incredulity at her unconcerned attitude for her brother's safety.

The firefighters were able to rescue both Reggie and Nathaniel quickly. The announcer told the crowd that both drivers were unharmed and it was surely a miracle. I could only imagine the look on the EMTs faces when they saw Nathaniel and Reggie jump out of the burning cars without a scratch on them.

We were still in the spectator area, watching the crews clean up the track, when Joshua came to get us. He assured Lindsey that Nathaniel was fine and would be waiting for us in the parking lot. Lindsey was still crying as she rushed to Nathaniel who opened his arms wide to receive her, lifting her off the ground, kissing her fiercely. "It's okay, baby. Don't cry. I'm fine. I told you I'm like Superman."

Nathaniel's words sent chills through me. This stunt wiped out any admiration I might have begun to have for him. "More like super idiot," I said aloud. "Put Lindsey in the car."

Nathaniel grinned and opened the GT40 passenger door. Lindsey turned towards me before getting in. "Mom, don't you say anything to Nathaniel. He could have been killed today."

I nodded to her in appeasement. What I really wanted to tell her was that if I could I would kill him myself right here and now.

Joshua glared at his brother. "That was the stupidest thing you have done in centuries. You made a mess out of the track and ruined Paul's car."

Nathaniel's response was unapologetic. "Leave me alone, Joshua. I gave the track and Paul my credit card to pay for the cleanup. I'm not going to let Reggie push me around and threaten us."

Joshua continued to scold Nathaniel vocally in a civil manner but I imagined that mentally he was screaming at him in a not so polite a tone.

"We were fortunate that none of the other drivers or any of the spectators were killed. You could be going to jail right now or be up on manslaughter charges."

Nathaniel huffed, "Yeah, like that would happen."

Cassie joined in. "Joshua's right, Nathaniel--that was stupid and selfish. You need to start thinking with your brain and not your pride. We have other people to be concerned with now, not just us three."

I didn't want Lindsey driving back to Boston with Nathaniel in the state that he was in. What if he ran into Reggie on the way home? Lindsey would be the one on fire if the car crashed.

Nathaniel stared at me, obviously listening to me fret about Lindsey's safety. He took a deep breath. "You're right, of course. I shouldn't have let him provoke me. With every bone in my body I truly hate him. The thought that he might harm Lindsey made me even madder."

Joshua put his arm on Nathaniel's shoulder. "We need to get out of here. Shamus and Nevan will be waiting for us at home." Joshua grabbed hold of my hand, "Katherine, I need you to come with me."

On the ride back to the B&B, Joshua made a sudden turn onto an unmarked dirt road.

"We're meeting Issy," he explained in an anxious voice. "She was going to keep an eye on Reggie and warn us...." There was a short pause and then an, "Oh no!" The car sped up leaving a cloud of dust behind.

In a small clearing adjacent to the road I could see the huge lion and Reggie facing each other down. A young woman stood to Reggie's left holding his hand.

"Please stay in the car." Joshua pleaded.

I gave him an dubious look. "No way."

"Of course not, but promise me you'll stay behind me."

"All right," I agreed, not sure I would keep that promise either. The hatred I felt for their mentally disturbed brother was on the rise.

Joshua reached behind his seat and grabbed his sword. As we approached, Reggie held up his hands in surrender. "Please, Joshua, do you really think there will be any need for that?"

"You know I'm going to kill you, Reggie."

"You wouldn't do anything to harm me in front of my fiancée now would you?"

"Fiancée?" Joshua muttered, stunned into stillness by this information.

That was when I took a closer look at the woman. She was young and I could tell by the color of her skin that she was human. My gaze wandered across her face and froze when I reached her eyes. Joshua had told me that only Issy had the power to create the hybrids and that Cassie and I were the only females.

"What've you done, Reggie?" Joshua asked in a disgusted tone.

"Rules, rules, rules. You're so hung up on all your rules, Joshua." Reggie shook his head. Really, and where have they gotten you? You've spent your life in remorse for everything that you've done."

"Those rules are there to protect others, not for our benefit. How is it that this woman has our eyes?"

"By doing something you would have never done. Melissa has been getting regular transfusions from me."

"Transfusions?" I gasped.

"You have no idea the potency of our blood. Of course my blood is more potent." He paused to chuckle at himself. "The effect of the transfusion on humans only lasts for a few months but look how young and beautiful she is."

We both glared at him. His science experiment smiled at him lovingly. Ugh! It gave me the creeps. Was she aware of what his regular diet consisted of?

"Melissa is a witch," Reggie continued, "coincidentally descended from one of the original Salem witches." I doubted there was any coincidence in that. "With her natural talent boosted by my blood, we will be unstoppable."

"What are you up to? Spell it out," Joshua demanded.

"Oh, you'll know soon enough and don't bother trying to guess, it's worse than you can imagine."

"It usually is when you're involved. How is it that you're able to block your thoughts from us?" I wanted to know that also.

Issy scratched at the dirt nervously with her front paw, making a large hole.

"Joshua, I'm shocked that you haven't figured it out yet. When you were indulging on humans," he paused to look at me. "Oh, good, Joshua told you and I can see that it doesn't matter to you. It's good to know that even the most righteous of us will pick and choose our own rules."

I flushed, embarrassed at his conclusion about my lack of morality.

Reggie turned back to Joshua. "You didn't stay on that diet long enough for the full effects to take hold. It's the reason I was able to sneak up on you at the club and at the racetrack." Reggie turned toward the great lion and bowed. "I guess you're not as powerful as you thought your highness. Like a one-way mirror, I can read your mind but you can't see mine." He paused for a few short seconds listening to Issy's mental reply. "You don't like the way I'm behaving? Bite me. Oh, you've already done that. It didn't turn out very well, did it?"

Issy must have been threatening Reggie because the next thing he said to her was, "I now have a huge advantage. If you try to kill me it will only make things worse. You know how unforgiving I can be." There was a second moment of silence while Reggie listened again.

"Really? Well, I had no problem with those two geeks from Mongolia that you sent." Then Reggie closed his eyes. "Look, now you can see what I see."

I felt Joshua release my hand and with a loud shriek leap at Reggie, his sword held high ready to strike. Seeing the direction of Joshua's every move before he made it Reggie moved quickly out of the way, jabbing a small blade into Joshua's chest as he passed. Issy pushed off her back legs propelling herself into the air. Even though Reggie could see her every move as well, her mass was so much greater than his and she used all of it against him as she exposed her gleaming sharp teeth and bit into him. Issy pulled the combatants apart and I cringed as a chunk of amber colored flesh landed close to my feet. Reggie recovered quickly, though, grabbing his shoulder with one hand and Melissa with the other. Their retreat was lighting fast.

I ran to Joshua. He pulled the knife from his side, wincing as the pain ripped through him. I flittered around putting pressure on his wound hoping to slow the loss of blood. Joshua stroked my cheek. Why was he trying to comfort me? "I'm fine, Joshua. You're the one that's hurt."

"I'm sorry. I didn't want this for you. I wanted you to enjoy our life and…"

"Stop," I commanded and put my hand up to his mouth before he could continue with his unnecessary apology. "I don't ever want to hear you say that again. We will deal with Reggie together." I turned toward Issy. "Are you able to follow Reggie and stay with him no matter where he goes?" The lion's huge head bobbed frantically and she spun around, taking off after the culprit. Of course, once Issy was out of hearing range, I didn't know how she would be able to warn us if Reggie did return. I was almost certain she couldn't use a cell phone.

When we arrived back at the B&B, after stopping for dressings for Joshua's wound, everyone was packed and ready to leave. Lindsey looked upset. In my head I warned Nathaniel to make something up and that I would never forgive him if he told her the whole truth. He nodded to me before getting into his car.

It was a quiet and somber ride back to the city. Joshua held my hand the entire time kissing it at random intervals, only letting go to change gears. I had many concerns fretfully rolling around in my head, especially my suspicions about Lindsey, but I decided they would wait for another time. I would give Joshua a chance to work on the more important issues at hand.

"I'm sorry about your friends. I really liked them."

Joshua nodded. "We haven't lost anyone in a long time now and that was to one of the Nergal. To lose someone to our own kind..." he shook his head. I didn't ask him to elaborate on what I assumed was another horror story. I was sure he would get to it over the next thousand years

"We think of ourselves as a higher being--to the point of being smug about it. We've watched humans prey and kill each other with a disgusted attitude for a very long time now. We stayed out of their business because we felt that they had to come to a consciousness on their own."

"We made so many mistakes with Reggie." Joshua looked at me for a long moment. "Issy thought she was giving him the greatest of gifts. When he started killing humans we ignored it, deluding ourselves into thinking the people Reggie killed didn't matter because many people died anyway at the hands of others and of disease."

I was beginning to grasp how it was that the Stones had lived for over two thousand years and hadn't changed anyone else. Why they had spent an eternity alone and why it was important to follow the rules and what the consequences could be if one didn't. Nathaniel was right. They had taken a huge chance with me. I shuddered at the possibility of becoming a monster like Reggie. It was not something I intended to have happen. I wondered if Reggie had had the same intention once long ago.

Chapter 14
GRANDCHILDREN

Parents seek thy children dear
Now await thy coming here
Long to hail thee in the sky
When thou dost from earth arise

~ Sara Cook Sampler
Pilgrim Monument Museum

Steven had to go on a last minute work conference the week following our return from the track. He was reluctant, as Josephine was fast approaching her due date, but the trip was equally important. It had the possibility of a promotion if he was able to finalize the details.

Joshua convinced Steven to go explaining that statistically the first birth was eight days late on average. I had to admit it was nice having a walking encyclopedia at my disposal, and more convenient than a computer.

The Stones were devastated over the loss of the Mongolians. Reggie had never gone this far before. In addition, there were many discussions about the fact that he had been able to give his fiancée a transfusion. Reggie had been right about one thing, the Stones would have never experimented with a human.

For the two nights while Steven was away, Joshua and I would stay with Josephine in Concord. It was poignant that Josephine would be having her baby, giving life to a new person, in the same place where I had spent my last days with Alex. The cycle of life, Joshua reminded me. Something I would have to get used to dealing with in my new life.

I hadn't seen Josephine in over a week and to say I was shocked when she greeted us at the front door was an understatement. It looked like she was carrying a baby elephant. How had she gotten this enormous in just a week?

After dinner the three of us watched the DVD that Joshua had brought along. Josephine laughed through the very girly film about dresses and weddings. It was nice that Joshua understood the girls so well.

After Josephine had gone to bed, Joshua tried to get me to do the same. "Don't worry, I'll listen for her. I can hear her heartbeat and the baby's. They sound fine."

"Her heartbeat sounded awfully fast to me," I mumbled.

Joshua gave me a funny look.

"What?" I asked trying not to sound irritated but not succeeding. Sometimes I think he forgot I couldn't read his thoughts.

"Katherine, I do have a few medical degrees. One from Harvard and another from Berkley and I was a surgeon in Vietnam. I could deliver the baby if you want, save Steven and Josephine the medical expense," he chuckled.

"Right, I'll ask Josephine in the morning if she wants her mother's boyfriend to deliver her baby."

Joshua raised his eyebrows curiously. "Am I your boyfriend?"

"That's what I'm telling people. You can continue to tell them whatever you want, even if it's a lie."

"I think you're right, boyfriend is appropriate for now."

I sighed in relief. "Thank you." I leaned over and gave him a kiss.

Before I turned in for the night I decided that now would be as good a time as any to ask about Lindsey.

I cleared my throat nervously. "Now I know that you know that I know that you can see Lindsey's mind, so let's not beat around the bush, okay?"

Joshua laughed at my convoluted statement. "Okay, let's talk about it."

His easy admittance left me speechless.

"Cat got your tongue?" he asked playfully.

"How long have you been able to read her mind?"

Joshua didn't answer.

"I want the truth, the whole truth, Joshua." I demanded.

"Shortly after the umm …incident in the state park Nathaniel began having a dream about us attending a colleague's engagement party. It seemed insignificant at the time, but Nathaniel was curious. You can imagine our surprise when we arrived at the party and found Lindsey…mind wide open to us. Except for you, we had never met another human whose mind we could see. That she was your daughter was even more astounding. Lindsey must have inherited the ability from you. I wonder if one of your parents…."

I sat silent while Joshua went on contemplating the genetic probabilities. Was my whole family going to become one of them? One of us?

"Can you see Josephine's mind?"

Joshua folded his hands and looked at the floor, "No."

"What does that mean?" I could feel myself beginning to cry.

Joshua deflected my question and muttered something in such low voice that I could barely hear him,

"Nathaniel is thinking of telling Lindsey about you and us."

"Is that allowed? I thought Issy had rules. I thought we weren't supposed to tell anyone."

Joshua pursed his lips holding back a smile. "Katherine, this isn't some secret vampire clan. We won't have to kill her if she finds out about us."

"Are you sure?" I shot back sardonically.

He ignored my sarcasm. "Lindsey suspects something about Nathaniel and she knows that something strange is going on with you. She's constantly asking questions."

"Well, let her ask."

"Nathaniel doesn't want to keep any secrets from her."

"Why? After they break up it won't matter anyway."

"What makes you think they'll be breaking up?"

"I just assumed Nathaniel would become bored and move on."

"Just assumed or were hoping?"

"Both." Our conversation paused for a few seconds.

"Please promise me that Nathaniel won't say anything to Lindsey. If you were still human and someone offered you a chance to stay young and live forever without really knowing all the consequences, what would you have said?"

Joshua shook his head. "What consequences?"

This time I remained silent.

Joshua lifted my chin. In a much softer voice, he asked, "Please tell me what you're thinking. It's very frustrating for me when you look like this and you won't answer my questions. I am truly interested in your feelings even if you think I won't like it."

"Well there's the sick masochistic brother for one and the demons..." I took a deep breath and let it out slowly. "When I was human, I always felt like I didn't belong. Now I feel even more alienated. I'm not sure I would have made this choice for myself. Can you understand that?"

"It's difficult to understand that. Most mortals would jump at the chance for immortality. However, I'm glad you told me. I want to know how you feel always. You're wrong about one thing. You do belong. You belong with me and my family and you always will."

I frowned. "Furthermore I don't like the idea that maybe my fate has been predetermined ...and for what reason? To kill the Nergal? You've been doing that just fine up until now. What will I be doing for the next thousand years?" I babbled on until I was hyperventilating and Joshua made me go to bed.

Although I had no dreams while I slept some unexpected noise woke me. "Katherine, you need to get up. Josephine has gone into labor. She's having some difficulties. I've already called an ambulance."

I sat up in all of an instant. "Are she and the baby all right?"

"Their fine right now but we need to get them to the hospital as soon as possible."

The smell of fresh blood drew me down the hallway into the back bedroom.

"Oh my god," I screamed when I saw Josephine's ghost-white complexion. She was panting and holding her stomach. Her clothes were stained with large spots of sweat---the bed sheets with blood.

Joshua came to my side. "I think the cord is wrapped around one of the babies' heads, tearing at the placenta. They'll need to perform an emergency C-section as soon as she gets to the hospital."

"The babies," I shrieked, "as in more than one baby?"

Joshua didn't answer me. He cocked his head to one side and asked himself. "Where is that ambulance?" The next thing I heard was the front door opening and Joshua was not by my side anymore.

I shivered as I took Josephine's cold hand in mine. "The ambulance is on the way." I tried to sound reassuring, but failed miserably.

"Mom, I'm scared." Josephine's eyeballs were stuck out like an exaggerated cartoon character, highlighting her frantic features.

"The ambulance just pulled up," Joshua announced as he picked Josephine up in one quick swoop with little effort. I followed them down the steps to the waiting ambulance. White lights buried in the truck's doors flashed manically, piercing the utter blackness of the night.

As Joshua placed Josephine on the gurney, she grabbed her stomach and her whole body began to shake. A fountain of blood gushed out from between her legs. Joshua shot a quick look at the lone EMT. "Do you know how to administer an epidural?"

The man's expression was blank. "I've only performed it a few times and only under strict supervision, sir. We're short drivers tonight and we didn't expect to have any problems with this call."

Joshua pushed Josephine over on her side and ripped her shirt open. I grabbed his hand. "What're you doing?"

"We have to get the babies out. They're suffocating. The placenta has ripped." His voice was surprisingly calm.

I grabbed Joshua's arm more firmly, forcing him to look at me. "We need to get her to the hospital. It's just five minutes away."

"There's no time. All three will be dead by the time we get there." Joshua's voice was still calm and untroubled as he continued.

"Josephine, your placenta has ripped. Your babies' lives are in danger. Do you want me to deliver them for you?"

Josephine looked at him stunned for one long second. Before she could answer she grabbed hold of her stomach again, trying unsuccessfully to hold in the next spasm. Then a blood-curdling scream emerged. "Yes, please do something. I can feel them kicking."

Joshua features were still unruffled as he stared at me, "I'm going to perform a C-section and I need you to assist me. Do you think you can do that?"

"Yes," I said, in between the gulps of air that were now coming way to fast.

"What is your name, son?" Joshua asked the EMT.

"Neil." The young man looked as shocked as I was.

"My name is Joshua, Neil. I was a surgeon in Iraq. I'm going to deliver these babies." Joshua declaration was said with such authority, such absolute confidence, that anyone who heard it would not doubt his ability.

"Babies? She's carrying twins?" Neil asked.

"Yes."

Joshua snapped his fingers in front of EMT's nose. "Find me a Tuchy needle and some lidocaine." Neil began looking for the items while Joshua continued barking out commands. "I need gloves, a scalpel and a suture kit."

Then Joshua did something shocking. He stuck his left finger into one of the small puddles of Josephine's blood that had formed on the gurney and raised the bloody finger to his lips. Neil still had his back to us, frantically searching through the doors lining the ambulance wall for the supplies.

"Josephine is O positive. Do you carry that blood type, Neil?"

"Yes, we do."

"Good. Her fibrinogen is critically low. She'll need the blood immediately."

Joshua inserted the Tuchy needle in Josephine's back and administered the anesthetic. After a short moment he asked, "Josephine, can you feel the epidural starting to work?"

"Yes." I watched as her eyes turned up into their sockets.

"Katherine, keep Josephine alert. We don't want her to pass out." I went to stand by her head while Neil inserted the IV into Josephine's left arm and started the blood stream.

"Neil, go now. Get us to the hospital."

"You can't operate while the ambulance is moving."

Joshua put his arm on Neil's shoulder. "All you need to worry about right now is getting us to the hospital."

Neil turned, closing the doors behind him. He hopped into the driver's seat and tried to start the engine but it wouldn't turn over. Neil turned back to Joshua who said, "Keep trying."

While Neil continued to work on starting the engine, Joshua donned a pair of surgical gloves and painted Josephine's stomach with a reddish brown solution. The monitor for Josephine's heart sounded out a long sharp beep that ripped through me. Joshua began immediately pumping Josephine's chest.

"Joshua, what's happening?"

"Josephine has lost a lot of blood. We might lose her."

My arms splayed out as I fell back against the wall of the ambulance. It felt like I had been hit by a train again—a hundred trains—worse than when I had been told this about Alex.

All the sci-fi movies that I had watched for years and years flitted through my mind. Without thinking I lifted my arm to my mouth and tried to bite down as hard as I could. Nothing happened. My teeth didn't make more than a faint pink mark. Joshua looked at me for less than a fraction of a second and I knew he knew what I was thinking.

"Quickly, give me your ring." When I didn't move, he grabbed my hand and removed the magnetite ring from my finger. He handed me a large syringe and ordered me to open the packaging. Joshua made a large slice along his arm using my ring. The sparking amber fluid began flowing. He filled the syringe and inserted it into Josephine's IV. Then he went back to pumping Josephine's chest. After a short minute I could see that the transfusion was working. The blue line that had been dancing erratically, slowed to a more normal beat.

The ambulance's engine roared to life, but the swaying vehicle did nothing to encumber Joshua's steadiness as he made a wide incision transversely across Josephine's stomach. I grimaced and turned my head away from the gushing blood---the red now mixed in with the amber.

Joshua handed me a suction cup. "Katherine, suction out this blood while I remove the first baby." His voice was cold, clinical. I moved closer and the smell of the raw flesh stunned my mind and drew me in, like Eve to the proverbial apple. I could fully appreciate what Joshua had gone on about and why Reggie was so addicted. The urge to feed was more powerful than any drug I had ever had.

Joshua touched my face, instantly pulling me from the trance. "Katherine, get a hold of yourself!" he demanded. "Try holding your breath."

"I'm fine. Keep going," I grunted through clenched teeth. I picked up the suction and cleared away the blood.

I watched in amazement as Joshua's skilled and careful hands reached in through the incision and pulled out the first baby's head, my first grandchild.

"Katherine, please, apply a small amount of pressure here on Josephine's stomach." Joshua pointed to the spot.

The baby's tiny head bobbed like a rag doll as Joshua removed the umbilical cord from around its tiny neck. Joshua cleaned out the baby's nostrils and mouth, and started CPR. I began to cry, amazed and frightened at the same time. The baby sputtered out a breath. Joshua wrapped it in a silver blanket that made a funny crinkling noise.

"Congratulations, grandma. Your first granddaughter."

I reached out for the swaddled bundle, still in awe. "Granddaughter?"

The baby stared back at me, quietly content--the bright amber eyes in sharp contrast to the bluish gray skin. A few seconds later the second baby was cradled in my other arm.

I had to concentrate to keep up with what Joshua was doing next. He placed his hand back inside Josephine and pulled out something slimy and disgusting looking. The placenta, he explained. My mouth began to water again but I forced myself to ignore the sensation. Joshua then proceeded to sew along the inside of Josephine's stomach, inserting surgical staples on the outside of the original incision.

Josephine was still alert as I held the babies near for her to see that everything was fine. Just then the ambulance doors flew open and a flurry of activity ensued as Josephine was removed. I tried to follow but froze in place when I reached the automatic sliding doors of the ER. The smell of the disinfectants couldn't mask the smell of death. The place reeked of it. How much more loss could I take before it pulled me under? How would I be able to get through hundreds, maybe thousands of years of seeing death like this? Past the bright blue walls of the emergency room a line of ominous purple clouds was building against the horizon.

A nurse came to me, arms outstretched. "Hi, my name is Cindy. I'm part of the neonatal resuscitative team. I need to take the babies to check their vitals."

I pulled the twins closer, not wanting to let go of my tiny packages. What would the doctors think when they saw the shiny orbs that couldn't be missed? Joshua wrapped his arm around my waist. When I turned, an automatic response to his touch, he nodded. I put the babies grudgingly into the nurse's waiting arms. She disappeared quickly down the long hallway. A second nurse led Joshua and me to a small room, cluttered with unmatched chairs and worn reading material.

"Don't be worried. Everything went very well," Joshua told me confidently. I couldn't speak yet.

Joshua and I stood up when the attending physician reached out to shake my hand.

"Hello, I'm Doctor Henley." My heart fell into my stomach as I recognized the name. It was the same doctor who was here with Alex. I just nodded to him.

"Oh," he said somewhat taken aback, recognizing me immediately. "Mrs. Chambers, how are you? I didn't realize this was your daughter." Dr Henley paused for a moment. "Your daughter and granddaughters are doing fine, thanks to the person who delivered them...." He turned to Joshua expectantly. "Neil explained to us that you performed the surgery right there in the moving ambulance?" His voice was incredulous and impressed at the same time.

"Yes," Joshua answered matter-of-factly. "It was fortunate that I happened to be visiting tonight." How did he do it? I was a nervous wreck. It took all my self-control to stop from shaking.

The doctor seemed dazed for a moment, peering intently at Joshua. After a long moment he shook his head. "Well, you did a fantastic job with the delivery. I'm very impressed. You told Neil you were a surgeon in Iraq?"

"I was stationed in the Karbala province in 2001, working with a forward medical team." Joshua's voice was smooth, calm and confident. No one would question his story.

"Well, I must say you're a very skilled surgeon. How did you know where to make the incision? It was exactly right. Most military surgeons aren't too familiar with C-section procedures."

Joshua shrugged deprecatingly. "I read several medical journals to stay up on current techniques."

This doctor was smarter than the average person and I could tell he didn't buy Joshua's explanation. No one could learn surgery from a medical journal—no human that is. However, what could he say? The evidence was right down the hall. "We've administered pitocin and antibiotics. It's a good thing your ..." he trailed off waiting for me to clarify the relationship between Joshua and me.

Joshua answered quickly. "I'm Katherine's fiancé."

I could feel the corners of my mouth fall and even though I wasn't looking at him I could tell Joshua was beaming. The doctor nodded. "Just one more question. We found a thick sticky yellow fluid in the IV line. Do you know what that was?" I stiffened but Joshua answered smoothly again, unperturbed. "I'm not sure. I didn't set up the IV. You'll have to talk to Neil about it."

"I did. He didn't know either. Also the babies' irises were quite yellow when they first came in. The yellow is more or less gone now, changing to a more normal blue. Are you sure you didn't add something to the IV?"

Joshua, still calm, said, "No, nothing. What could have been added?"

The doctor didn't look happy. "I can't imagine."

I zoned out now, not able to keep up the pretenses any longer, while Joshua launched into an explanation about bilirubin in newborns.

Obviously insulted by Joshua's nebulous explanation Dr. Henley stated adamantly, "We'll run some tests and figure it out."

"Good. Please let me know what you find," Joshua replied genuinely. It wasn't a rouse. He was always anxious to learn new information, especially about our kind.

Then in a somewhat apologetic tone the doctor asked, "Are you the same Joshua Stone that runs the Stone Foundation?"

"Yes, I am."

The doctor's manner changed immediately from suspicious to grateful. "Oh, it's so nice to meet you, Mr. Stone. Your foundation offsets medical cost for our less fortunate patients. Actually I met your....father years ago." He paused for a long moment scrutinizing Joshua more closely again. "It's amazing. You're the spitting image of him. How is your father?"

I could feel the acid creeping up my throat and I hoped Joshua could also before I threw up. "Please, call me Joshua and unfortunately Dad is no longer with us but I'm glad our efforts are going to such a worthwhile cause." Without giving Dr. Henley the opportunity to ask more questions Joshua looked at me and said. "I think we need some rest. It's been an eventful few hours. When will we be able to see Josephine?"

Joshua was an expert at distracting unwanted attention. "We're going to keep her in the emergency room for two hours and monitor her vitals. You can visit when we move her."

My strength was gone and the sounds of the emergency room began flooding my ears.

After the doctor had gone Joshua tried reassuring me again. "Josephine is fine."

"The babies?"

"Also fine. They didn't go more than thirty seconds without oxygen. Their APT test was quite high thanks to your quick thinking."

"My quick thinking?"

"Yes. I might have performed the surgery but it was your idea about the blood. That's what saved them. We make a great team, don't you agree?"

I pulled back to look at him more fully. "I'm not going to take any credit for this, Joshua. I'm sorry I doubted you. Thank you."

"You're welcome. Now let's get you some rest."

"Okay, but I'm not going to sleep. I just realized I haven't had a chance to call Steven and the rest of the family."

It also dawned on me when we walked out to the parking lot that we had no car. Joshua laughed at my dismay. "We can run very fast. Come on, I'll race you." He grabbed my hand but I didn't move.

"The highway?" I inquired, looking across the lot at the speeding traffic.

"Are you afraid? I'll carry you if you want."

"No," I replied indignantly and I felt my feet jolt forward before the word was completely out of my mouth.

The term warp speed was the only analogy I could make to the velocity at which we moved. As I ran everything around me blurred into a wall of mixed colors. The resulting wind lashed at my exposed skin, stinging my eyes and pushing my hair behind me. We didn't slow one bit as Joshua deftly maneuvered us between the moving cars. I waited to hear the protesting horns, but there were none. We stopped a few seconds later when we had reached the edge of Josephine and Steven's back yard.

"That was, was…" I bent over, empting the contents of my stomach. Joshua took the house keys out of my bag and returned a few seconds later with a cold cloth for my forehead. "Sorry about that. The first few times can throw off your equilibrium."

"I'm fine," I told him. After several minutes my stomach settled and I was able to walk into the house on my own. When I was done spreading the good news Joshua tried to get me to lie down, but I was having none of that.

"All right," he sighed, "go ahead."

"How did you know about Josephine's blood type?"

"All human blood types have their own smell and taste. Sugars and fats add to the particular flavor of each person's blood. When we were in medical school, Nathaniel and I experimented."

Yuk, I would take his word for this.

"Why did you tell Dr. Henley that you were in Iraq? You told me it was Vietnam."

"It was Vietnam. The three of us were assigned to a MASH unit, like the TV show." He stopped and stared at me, waiting for me to understand what he was saying.

"Remember Joshua I can't read your mind."

"I was in Vietnam at the same time that Alex was there. You were so close." Joshua paused and took a deep breath. "The reason I told them I had been in Iraq was because I don't look old enough to have been in Vietnam. That war was over forty years ago."

"Oh, that's right. Keeping up the pretenses." I could feel my eyelids beginning to close involuntarily, giving away the extent of my exhaustion.

"Okay, time for bed."

I ignored him. "How could you be a surgeon and resist?"

"It was difficult. Of course I had Nathaniel and Cassie in my head for encouragement. After a while I became desensitized to the smell. Now it repulses me like the smell of smoke does to an ex-smoker."

"As much as I don't want to be, I'm grateful to Reggie," I said watching as Joshua twisted nervously in his seat. "I know he's a terrible person, but if it wasn't for him, Josephine might be dead right now."

"I'm sure Reggie will be upset to learn that something he did actually worked for some good. It would have been devastating to all of us if there had been a different outcome to tonight's events.

That aside, Reggie needs to be stopped." He took my hands in his. "We will find a way to make you and your family safe."

I nodded and I knew Joshua knew I was not completely reassured. He was serious but so was Reggie.

KAREN ANN

Chapter 15
PASSION

Passion--it lies in all of us, sleeping, waiting,
and though unwanted, unbidden, it stirs,
opens it jaws and howls.
It speaks to us, guides us. Passion rules us all and we obey.
What other choice do we have?
Passion is the source of our finest moments: the joy of love,
the clarity of hatred, and the ecstasy of grief.
It hurts sometimes. More than we can bear.
If we could live without passion,
maybe we'd know some kind of peace.
But we'd be hollow, empty rooms, shuttered and dank
Without passion we'd be truly dead.

~ Angelus, Buffy the Vampire Slayer

We left for Nantucket on a breezy, warm September morning. From my seat at the front of the ferry I marveled at the perfect coloring of sky and ocean, the latter only a shade darker than the former. I spent most of the two-hour trip stitching while Joshua read on his Kindle. Although I was impressed at how fast he could scan through each book I had to eventually remind him to slow down. It was unusual for him not to be mindful of his actions in public. I wondered if he was as nervous as I was.

Because he seemed totally engrossed in this one particular book, I was curious as to the subject. To my surprise he said, "Finances."

"You're a genius at making money. What else do you need to know?" Joshua could probably author several books himself if not for the fact that it would draw unwanted attention to the details of his life.

"There's always something new to learn. You should read it also."

"No, thanks, I haven't figured out how to balance my check book."

"You seem to do all right. No bankruptcy filing yet," he chuckled.

"True but financial stuff bores me. Alex had always taken care of all the bills and investments."

"When you're ready, Nathaniel and I will advise you. I could make you a millionaire, if you'd like," he offered smugly.

I shook my head. "I wouldn't know what to do with the money anyway."

Joshua put the Kindle down. "It would be prudent for you to have some investments. You're going to live a long time and you can't work at LCA forever."

I looked at him perplexed, shrugging my shoulders. "I have a pension and Social Security."

Joshua raised his eyebrows. "You really haven't thought much about this, have you?"

I flushed at my awkwardness of being financially inept. "What do you mean?"

"When you're still collecting your pension and social security at one fifty, someone is going to start wondering what's going on."

"Oh, I hadn't thought of that."

"I'll have Nathaniel set up the same type of fund for you that I use. Then you'll always have some cash to draw on."

"That really brings new meaning to saving for the future," I stated keeping my features smooth as I laughed at my own wit. I hoped Joshua wouldn't see what was really in my thoughts, but he did.

"Don't worry; I'll take care of you for as long as you want me."

"As long as I want you?" Hadn't I made my feeling towards him clear enough over the past two months? "This is supposed to be a romantic weekend, Joshua, what sort of a thing is that to say?"

"Just letting you know that you always have a choice, always."

"What about your dream?"

I watched as Joshua's face fell. "Like Cassie told you, it's only a snapshot of what might happen--a possibility."

I shook my head and went back to stitching. Joshua was the only comfort in all of this craziness. Besides, I was sure that it would be him that would leave me. For the remainder of the trip I contemplated my future, a scary future that now stretched out endlessly in front of me.

After we had retrieved our luggage, Joshua asked me to wait for him at the dock.

"Sure," I sighed wondering what he was up to now. I entertained myself by watching the other visitors scurrying like ants in all directions--some heading for the next ferry, some heading for their accommodations. It was comical as they tried to navigate their suitcases over the cobblestoned lined streets.

Joshua returned with a woman he introduced as Molly Leblanc, a local realtor. "I'm so happy to meet Joshua's fiancée. The Historical Society is so grateful to his foundation for all the support. We're thrilled for both of you."

I replied calmly in spite of my aggravation. "Yes, Joshua is very generous."

Molly winked as she handed Joshua a set of keys. "Now you two have fun."

As soon as Molly was out of hearing range, I turned to Joshua, letting my irritation spill out.

"Really Joshua, we've discussed this more times than I can keep track of. I thought we had agreed that boyfriend and girlfriend were the appropriate terms for our relationship. I wish you would stop telling people that I'm your fiancée and if you insist on telling them..." I trailed off exasperated. What was the point?

"I'm sorry," he said, not looking the least bit, "It's easier than any other story."

"Are you delirious? Easier than what? That we're just dating? I thought you said I had a choice? Well, I haven't made up my mind yet and besides you know you haven't actually asked me to marry you." I ground my teeth wishing I had stopped before that last sentence had come out.

Joshua's smile stretched from ear to ear. "You're correct, I haven't asked you yet."

"Does that mean you're planning to?"

"Are you planning to say yes if I do?"

I couldn't answer him with either a yes or a no, but I quickly came up with a logical retort. "You know you don't ask before you ask."

Joshua pulled me in close and said, "That's what I thought."

I held up my hand to him, the palm facing outward. "Whatever." It was useless to talk to him about this. He had a one-track mind.

Joshua laughed, paying no heed to my frustration. "I'll go find the car."

I folded my arms in defeat. "Fine."

Joshua pulled up next to me in a white Honda Civic that was similar to mine except newer. I knew it wasn't a rental because it had regular license tags.

"Where did this come from? I don't want to be seen in this," I teased. "Don't they have an Audi dealer?"

"Funny," he replied, opening the passenger door for me. I didn't move and he shot me an annoyed looked. Good, it was his turn.

"Please get in, Katherine."

"All right, but I hope I don't see anyone I know."

"Ha! Ha! One good thing about spending eternity with you, Katherine, is that I know I won't stop laughing." Joshua paused and his tone became more serious. "Put on your seat belt. It will be a rough ride."

I rolled my eyes at him. Like I needed a seat belt.

As we made our way through town, my hands stayed locked around the seat cushion while the Honda did a good imitation of a jackhammer. I wished I had put on my seat belt. When we finally turned onto a paved road and my hands were free I reached for the lever to the glove box, intending to check the registration. Joshua's hand was on mine in a flash. "It belongs to a friend."

I stared at him, instantly suspicious.

"No, you promised me that while we were here you wouldn't worry about anything--no children, no work, no scary monsters."

"It's not a light switch. I can't just turn it off whenever I want. I'm genetically programmed this way."

It had been five weeks since the birth of Josephine's twin girls, my granddaughters--Halee and Hanna. They were the most adorable, the most precious children I had ever seen. Of course I was a little prejudiced, I admit. Both Josephine and the girls had recovered fantastically from the unexpected C-section that Joshua had performed. The procedure had saved their lives and I was eternally grateful to Joshua for it. I had vacillated back and forth for weeks about going or not going on this trip, torn between my concern for my family's safety and my desire for Joshua. Although not completely gone, my fears were somewhat calmed, knowing that the other hybrids were closely watching my family back home.

Joshua touched my cheek, pulling me from my musing. "Just this week, please."

I leaned into his silken hand. "Okay, I'll try. By the way where're we going?"

"Madaket Beach, near Sheep Pond. The house there sits on twenty acres of land. It will be very quiet."

I quickly turned to look out the window. The heat radiating from my face told me that it was probably two shades of red. Why was I so nervous again? Hadn't I already made up my mind to go through with this? I made myself concentrate on the breathtaking scenery.

If the Grand Canyon was the art form of the land then Nantucket was the art form of the sea. Millions of years of relentless wind and wave action had shaped it into a radiant beauty.

We spotted snowy egrets, American oystercatchers, several species of ducks and gulls, orange-crowned warblers, a pied-billed grebe, a peregrine falcon, horned larks and my favorite--several ospreys. I didn't need my Audubon bird guide because Joshua knew each species upon sight.

Except for the few paved roads, Nantucket looked the same now as it had in the eighteen hundreds when the island was the center of the whaling industry. Picture-perfect Cape Cod style houses, sheathed in weathered gray clapboards, were nestled between the open expanses of shrubby low-lying marshes.

We took a right turn onto a gravel-lined road that was more of a path than a road and drove for two miles before the outline of a house came into view. I only gave the structure at the journeys end a momentary look because I couldn't wrench my gaze from the amazing view that framed the residence.

The Atlantic Ocean was boundless to the horizon and the water in it was the perfect mixture of the bluest blues and greenest greens. Sunlight reflected off the dynamic surface in a kaleidoscope of sparkling whites. Wave after wave rushed hastily up the wide sandy shore, racing to meet a deadline. The deafening noise was surprisingly soothing.

So bleached white was the color of the sand that lined the foot path leading down to the beach that at first glance it appeared to be snow covered. Low growing shrubs splattered the rolling dunes, many of them smothered by wild vines. The vista was broken sporadically by outcrops of dwarf pine trees bent at poetic angles in response to the never-ending wind.

"Do you approve?"

"Wow!" I said my jaw involuntarily hanging wide open.

I reluctantly pulled myself from the ocean view as Joshua towed me towards the house. When I finally focused on the half cape residence, I stood in awe again as I took in the size of the huge center chimney that dominated the roofline. The placard over the front door read "1774". The original house was flanked on either side by several additions that had been added over the long years with a blooming grandiflora rose that climbed up the shingles on the shorter side, its stalks thickly snarled and ancient.

"The house is small," Joshua said apologetically, "but I thought you'd like this."

"It's just perfect, Joshua, thank you."

Joshua unlocked the thick wooden door and waved me in. As was normal for a house of this era the massive fireplace jutted out into the middle of the room, the opening large enough to walk into. The back of the house had a modern open floor plan and a wall of floor to ceiling windows with the kitchen flowing tastefully into the dining and living areas.

"I thought we might have lunch outside." Joshua offered opening the French doors onto the patio.

"How did the food get here?"

"Molly went shopping for us."

"That was really nice of her. You must be a great patron to get service like this."

"I do a few things for them from time to time," Joshua explained, not bothering to elaborate. "If you're up for it, there are bicycles in one of the rooms upstairs. Jetties Beach is hosting a sandcastle contest. The sculptures should be amazing."

"That sounds like fun." It felt like I could actually begin to relax as Joshua had requested.

We biked from Madaket Beach to Sconset to Wauwinet, always keeping the ocean within our view. We ended the tour on our own private beach, watching the remains of the day disappear. I laid my head against the back of the bright blue Adirondack chairs that had been conveniently placed at the end of the path for just that purpose and sipped wine…totally contented.

The sun hung on the horizon like a huge untethered ball. Miles and miles of long striated bands of clouds stretched along the wide-open sky. The color morphed from red to pink then finally amber as the lower clouds kissed the horizon.

"I have a strange question to ask you."

Joshua smirked out a "Yes?" most likely hearing the shakiness in my voice.

"Well," I began but stopped. My curiosity on this matter now seemed silly.

Joshua laughed, "I wish you could see your face right now. I've never seen you so red. Are you all right?"

"I'm fine. Just forget it."

Joshua got up from his chair and knelt beside mine. He slipped his hand around my neck. I couldn't think straight when he was this close.

"Now what was it you wanted to ask me?"

"Ah …well…I wanted to know if you were, well, anatomically similar to a male lion."

Joshua pulled back. "I'm not sure I understand your question."

"Really, I've changed my mind. I don't want to know." I could feel more blood rushing up my neck.

After a few seconds Joshua roared with laughter. "In two thousand years I've never had anyone ask me that before."

"Well, why would they?" I placed my hands on his chest and struggled to push away from his gaze. "No one but me has known about all this."

"I guarantee everything about me is anatomically normal, that is human normal not lion normal." He was still chuckling. "Only a biologist would wonder about that."

I shrugged. "It's a little known fact about male lions, mortal lions that is. I always felt bad for the lioness. They have a difficult enough life as it is. Mating should be pleasurable, or at the very least not painful."

"I promise the last thing you will feel is pain," Joshua said all trace of humor gone.

"I don't suppose you can keep this from Nathaniel."

Joshua winked. "I'll try, but as you know I can't make any promises." He touched his finger to his head.

"I have one more question, since we're on the subject."

"I'm truly looking forward to it. Please continue."

Joshua hadn't lost his impish grin. I took a deep breath. Why was this so difficult?

"Will I, we, need to use protection? I love my children very much but I'm done having children, no matter how long I'm going to live, and since I have de-aged or whatever it is that's happened I want to make sure that I won't … I won't get pregnant." What I was really worried about was giving birth to a Minotaur like lion child.

Joshua looked stunned. After a long minute he sighed. "The originals were able to sire offspring with humans and with themselves, but none of the hybrids have ever had any children. We suspect that we're comparable to mules---sterile because our chromosome count is uneven. As much as I wish it were possible…no, you don't have to worry about that."

"You wish you could have children? Why?" That seemed preposterous to me. They would outlive them--just like I was going to.

"I never had any children when I was human. I would have liked to."

I put my hand on his arm. "Tell me about your wife. How long were you married?"

"Ten years, but Sienna and I had no relations. In those days, all royal marriages were arranged for political purposes and if you wanted to stay in the good graces of your family there was no alternative. " He stared at me with soulful eyes. "Every road I've gone down has led me to you, Katherine, and I don't regret anything that happened in the past."

I frowned. I hated when he put me on pedestal like this. I didn't deserve this categorical admiration. Joshua went back to sit in his own chair, still deep in thought. I climbed out of mine and into his.

"I'm cold," I lied, answering his questioning look.

I leaned back against his chest and his arms enveloped me. The sun in the process of sinking had turned the entire sky into a fire red color.

"I'm sorry I didn't mean to bring up sad memories."

Joshua squeezed me tightly. "Oh, I'm not sad. Melancholy is the more correct term."

Joshua pulled my face up to meet his. "Katherine, I'm happier here with you than I have ever been in my whole long life. Please don't feel bad about asking me anything."

I kissed him gently. "Okay, and by the way I'm happy, too."

It was the most perfect of all perfect moments. When the light from the sun had been replaced with a dark blue bowl of stars Joshua suggested that we go up to the house and put on a movie.

Without reading the titles, I slipped one of the movie discs into the player. My stomach had now started to do flips at the thought of what was coming next.

Joshua poured more wine and we sat on one of couches, further apart then seemed natural for two people who were more than just friends. I hadn't brought up the subject of romance since I had tried to take his shirt off the night of the fund raising event and he hadn't either. Maybe he had changed his mind. Don't be ridiculous, I told myself. Why else would we be here?

Half way through the movie, Joshua moved closer, brushed my hair out of the way and began kissing the back of my neck. I stiffened uncontrollably. I wondered if he was reading my mind. Trying to figure out what I wanted. Good luck with that.

Of course, I cried, as I always did at the end of this movie. Joshua smiled as he wiped the tears away, "You need to sleep."

"I'm fine. I want to stay up."

"Do you mind if I put on one of the auto racing DVDs?"

"Sure," I said relived and dejected all at the same time.

That was the end of our first night.

*

The sound of manically squawking gulls woke me early. I realized why as soon as I looked out the window. Roaming around in the bushes that ringed the cottage was a small herd of cats. They began to meow loudly when they saw me.

Still dressed in the shorts and tank top from the previous day, I wandered out to find Joshua sitting by the outdoor table, playing with several of the strays.

"I don't think you should encourage them," I told him as I poured myself some coffee. "They may not go home."

"I don't have the heart to send them away. They'll go home when they're hungry."

"I guess." I did love cats but this was getting crazy. Joshua set down the cat that was on his lap and stood up. "After breakfast I thought we might visit the Whaling Museum."

I smiled hugely. Even though it was a heartbreaking reminder of the destruction that humans can wreak on the environment, it was one of my favorite places. I comforted myself every time I visited the museum with the fact that the whales were still here and the whalers were gone.

Once inside the museum I dragged Joshua past the enormous skeleton of the sperm whale that hung in the main lobby to the upstairs gallery to see the museum's collection of antique samplers stitched not only by the women who spent many long hours waiting for their husbands to return but also by the whalers themselves. We spent a lot of time admiring the museums phenomenal collection of scrimshaw also. At 10:50 I took Joshua's hand again, intending to lead him to the auditorium to the talk about the Essex. The story of the crew's ordeal had been the inspiration for Herman Melville's Moby-Dick.

"I'll meet you outside. I've heard the story before." Before I could stop him, Joshua turned quickly and disappeared down the back staircase.

Afterwards I found him outside on one of the benches. "Sorry, I didn't know."

"Don't apologize. It hurts to have reminders of my weakness and the harm I've caused."

The Essex crew, as it turned out, had to resort to cannibalism in order to survive.

Later in the day, we joined the rest of the tourists, shopping through the myriad of stores nestled up and down the cobblestone streets of the town. We stopped for chocolate frappes and roast beef sandwiches at the Pharmacy on Main Street.

The next four nights we spent as we had the first, with me falling asleep in Joshua's arms, only to find myself tucked into my bed in the morning, alone. Joshua was truly a gentleman and I appreciated that. What man, human or otherwise, would bring a woman he had been waiting to find for over two thousand years, to a place like Nantucket and not make a move on her? I knew the answer to that question--a man like Joshua--a man who had spent an unbelievable amount of time practicing his self-control. We would be going home soon and if anything were going to happen, it would have to be tonight.

"What movie do you want to watch?"

"Watching movies with you is no fun," I complained. "You always ruin them with facts."

"What do you want to do then?"

"I think…I'd like to go dancing."

"Dancing?"

"Yes, dancing."

Joshua smiled hugely. "Great. I know the perfect place."

I laughed. "Of course you do."

The nightclub was jumping by the time we arrived. The atmosphere inside was warm and sultry. Joshua held me close, resting his head against mine. His body temperature and mine were perfectly matched--warmth against warmth. I felt Joshua move his lips to my ear. "Are you wearing underwear?"

I pulled back and smiled playfully. "You know that's not something a gentleman would ever ask."

"Umm," he murmured, "I never claimed to be a gentleman."

"Well, you put on a good act."

"I am a good actor, I'll admit, but you didn't answer my question."

"Yes, of course I am."

"Too bad that's not the way I was imagining it." I blushed scarlet as Joshua's hand moved slowly up the front of my shirt caressing my skin ever so softly.

"Well, at least you're not wearing a brassiere."

"Okay, it's time for us to leave before you do something that will get us arrested."

Joshua drove back to the cottage at an unusually slow speed. It was a quiet drive that matched the quiet night. All I could hear as we walked into the house was the rhythmic wailing of the distant foghorn.

Joshua poured more wine and we sat on the couch. This time close and touching. Every nerve, every muscle in my body was tingling as I stared into Joshua's blazing amber eyes--each one their own separate suns. I started to unbutton his shirt but he stopped me, for a second time.

"Joshua, are you having second thoughts, again?"

"Katherine, I've never had second thoughts. I want you more than I've ever wanted anything in my very long life." He paused for a few seconds playing with a strand of my hair. "Are you sure this is what you want?"

"You know, you're not a very good mind reader."

He chuckled, gently touching my cheek. "What I do know is that all of this has happened very quickly. I want you to be sure because...I... I'll never be able to let you go after tonight."

If it were possible for a body to spontaneously combust, it would have happened to mine at that moment. "I'm ready," I whispered softly.

Joshua nodded. "By the way, I'm not reading your mind but since you brought it up, maybe you would allow me into your head tonight."

"Why?"

"Would you understand if I told you I was nervous?"

I laughed incredulous. "I haven't been able to find one thing that you don't excel at and I doubt this will be any different. However, if reading my mind will get you to stop talking then fine, go ahead."

Joshua lifted me in one quick motion onto his lap, my legs straddling his. He slipped one arm around my waist, reaching up to pull my hair into a loose ponytail.

I could tell the exact moment when Joshua gave in to his own needs, abandoning his self-control. Every kiss was ravenous. I went back to his shirt but he didn't wait for me to finish. Buttons went flying everywhere as he pulled the shredded fabric up over his head.

I imagined this was how the ancient women of Greek mythology felt when they had affairs with Zeus and Apollo. My hand automatically reached out for his bare chest, memorizing the contour.

"This will be like nothing you've ever felt."

Then something I had never felt flooded my consciousness, sending me into a tailspin. A sensation of numbness and pleasure filled me from head to toe. My lips parted slightly, a small puff of air escaped from my lungs and my entire body slump dreamily. "What's happening, Joshua?"

"Don't fight it; it's just me in your head. Relax." I did as Joshua requested and allowed the overwhelming desire that I had for him to engulf me--- certain that it would crush me if I didn't give in to it.

It had begun to downpour outside, the steady pounding encircling us in a cone of silence. From that point on the only sound I heard was Joshua's heartbeat, keeping a steady rhythm with my own.

*

Still entwined in each other's arms on the living room's enormous white fur rug, the light from the rising sun began to brighten the small room, reminding me of the existence of the outside world.

"Wow."

"I agree," Joshua said, kissing the back of my head, burying his face in my now tousled hair.

"What was that? It was amazing. Talk about being on cloud 9." My whole body felt frozen and sluggish in a good way.

"Did you enjoy it as much as I did?"

I wrestled around to face him. "I enjoyed it immensely... but you already know that."

"It seemed that way, but I like hearing you say it out loud." Joshua's smile was blinding.

"Why was it so, so--I can't even think of an adjective to explain it."

"My mind is very powerful. Up until now I've only gleaned thoughts from the upper part of your consciousness. I have the ability to become deeply immersed in your subconscious. It tends to have a numbing effect on the recipient."

I tried to move but Joshua held me tightly.

"Where do you think you're going?"

"Well, unfortunately, being super human doesn't release you from some basic human functions. You know, vampires and werewolves don't have this issue. I think maybe you should talk to Issy about it."

Joshua laughed but didn't let go of me. "I'll let her know."

"So are you going to let me up?"

"Do you promise to come back?" I could tell he wanted to continue.

My stomach growled loudly. "Umm, ...I think I need some nourishment if you expect any more... umm ...exercise from me."

"We're not through." Joshua stated adamantly

"Joshua, I seriously need to get up."

He released me reluctantly. I stood and stretched my legs. They felt like Play Doh.

As Joshua walked into the kitchen area he said, "I'll start the coffee. Oh and don't put on too many clothes. It will just take me that much longer to get them off." Of course, I turned red.

When I was done with my mundane human functions, I sat on one of the kitchens stools, unable to keep myself from staring at his half naked beauty. As my eyes inadvertently wandered up along his perfectly formed upper body, I gasped. Several discernible semi-circular shaped marks blotted the skin on his neck.

"Did I do this?" I reached out and gently touched the reddened area.

Joshua ran his hand through his hair casually. "Yes, you got a bit carried away. It's a natural instinct for us as it is for all felines."

"I'm... so... sorry."

"I really didn't notice. They'll be gone in a few hours."

"Still, they must hurt? Why did you let me do this to you?"

"At the time you and I were... umm… preoccupied."

I grimaced apologetically.

"Katherine, there wasn't a moment last night when I didn't think that I had died and gone to heaven. I am deliriously happy. You can bite me any time you want." While he was kissing me I promised myself to never let that happen again. It was time for me to work harder on *my* self control.

Joshua as usual made a ton of food and we ate every morsel, apparently starved from all the activity of the previous night.

Out on the deck, watching the blue green ocean glimmer before us, I noticed something odd breaking the surface.

I stood up craning my neck to see. "What's going on down there?"

"They're jelly fish," mister-know-it-all explained. "Would you like to walk down and see them?"

"Yes, could we?"

"Okay, but it's only because I know you're a biologist that I'll let you distract me this time."

When we arrived at the water's edge the ocean was inundated with brightly colored blobs. Many of the jellyfish had already washed up on the shore. Their gelatinous white bells flattened out unnaturally, resembling plate size pancakes, gasping out the remainder of their life onto the sand.

Joshua stood with his lips pursed and I could tell he was dying to say something. Finally, he asked, "Do you happen to know the name of this particular species of jellies?"

"No," I chuckled. "I have no doubt that you do."

"They're known as Lion's Mane."

My jaw fell open. "Are you making that up?"

"It's a remarkable coincidence," Joshua said beaming.

I wanted to pick up the dying ones and return them to the ocean, but my old human instinct stopped me. Joshua saw my hesitation. "Go ahead, Katherine. Their nematocysts can't sting us."

I shrugged. "I keep forgetting."

Joshua watched as I gently picked up a few of the slimy invertebrates and placed them back into the surf. "Aren't you going to help?"

"No, you're wasting your effort. They'll just wash back up. It's all part of their cycle of life and death," he said nonchalantly.

"How can you just stand there and watch them die?" I was irritated at his indifference towards such a remarkable creature.

"As far as I know, and I do know a lot"--he winked--"every living creature on this planet eventually dies, except for our kind. I don't mean to sound callous but it's true. Life is very fragile, especially human life. It can take a force with less power than a whisper to end it. Nathaniel, Cassie, and I have come to realize that death is as important as life for all species. Without death there would be no life on this planet. All the natural resources would be quickly used up if any one species, including humans, were not kept in check."

"How can you believe that? Your foundation works to save lives all over the world."

"Our goal is to improve the quality of lives. We know the lives we help will eventually end. Species live forever by passing on their genes. That's why it is important not to allow them to go extinct.

"So I shouldn't try to save the jellyfish?"

"Well, you can if you want but they're numbers are not in danger." Then a mischievous look broke across his face. "How would you like to go swimming with them?"

"Swimming with them?" I couldn't imagine that.

Joshua took something out of his pants pocket and quickly wound my hair into a bun. I was still clueless as to what we were about to do as we started toward the surf.

"I need to get my suit on if we're going swimming. Cassie gave me these shorts. I don't want to ruin them."

"Umm...that's probably a better idea anyway." Joshua quickly removed his shirt and tried to take mine off as well.

"What're you doing?" I pulled my top back down, holding on to it firmly.

"We don't need our suits."

"But...but..."

"Katherine, trust me, there's no one around for miles." With me still protesting, Joshua removed the rest of our clothes and walked our naked bodies into the salty water. When we were up to our necks Joshua said, "Take a lungful of air and close your mouth."

"All right, but I can't hold my breath for very long."

Joshua smiled meaningfully as he pulled us under.

At the point where the light from above began to fade, Joshua directed me to look up. The hundreds of brightly colored petticoats attached to long bundles of purple confetti floated effortlessly in the water above us. I was sure that no human had ever viewed this scene quite like this, unimpeded by human frailties.

While we were in the water, Joshua entertained me with his swimming abilities. His technique reminded me of a seal as he glided with little effort through the water. I kept waiting for my lungs to scream at me with the stress of oxygen depletion but after what felt like hours later, our heads broke the surface.

"That was awesome. Can we do that again tomorrow?"

"I'm glad you enjoyed it. This is just the beginning of the amazing things you'll be able to do."

A flood of happiness overcame me. This life wasn't going to be that bad after all, especially with Joshua as my teacher. Half way back to the house Joshua stopped.

"Umm," he mused, "I was just thinking how great you look in that wet tee shirt." Before the blush had a chance to fully color my cheeks the kissing began and that was another time that we didn't make it into the bedroom.

Chapter 16
INEVITABILITY

Remember that great love and great achievements
involve great risk.

~ Dalai Lama

I know I'm dreaming because I've had this same dream before... many times before. Of all the dreams this is the longest running and as always, it's almost exactly the same every time. I say almost because although the sequence of events is consistent, the details of the dream are getting clearer--the lines around the monster becoming sharper. Furious eyes bore into mine, craving my death. I can see the ripples of its muscles flexing as it moves towards me. I wait, terrified, for Joshua to wake me--to stop me from screaming. Aha...there's the flash of light and I know it's over.

*

"Katherine, Katherine, it's all right. I'm here." Joshua's voice was thick with worry. "Shh, shh. It's over."

The last thing I remembered after swimming with the jellies was being on the enormous fur rug in the living room. We had spent most of the day and night there, again. Now I was upset because the thought of stalking demons usually ruined my mood for an entire day and this was the last day of our vacation. The whole week had been more relaxing than I could have hoped.

"I'm really tired of watching that monster come after me. You would think I would be getting used to it by now. Why am I still so scared?"

"Because it's like the Nergal is here with us."

I sat up and stared at him, "You've been watching the dream?"

Joshua nodded guiltily.

"These days there are more important things to be upset about than my privacy but I wish you'd wake me up before I get to the screaming part next time." There was no doubt that there would be a next time.

"I want the dream to play out. Maybe I'll get a clue as to where it's taking place."

"Well, I hope I'm not going to be having this dream for the next four hundred years."

"Four hundred years?"

"Yes, didn't you say it was hundreds of years before the next demon would grow?"

Joshua stood up, his voice somewhat stifled with panic as he spoke. "Maybe we shouldn't wait until tomorrow to go home."

Before I could answer him, to tell him I didn't want to leave, his phone rang, sending a bone-chilling shudder down my spine. Before we left for Nantucket, Joshua had given instructions to both Nathaniel and Cassie not to call him for any reason unless Reggie or one of the Nergal was coming. The fact that Joshua's phone was ringing at this moment meant that one of those two possibilities was occurring.

Joshua gazed vacantly out the back door as he listened to Cassie's shrill voice. Their conversation was all in Aramaic. Even without a translation I could tell that it was bad news.

When Joshua hung up he said, "We need to pack."

I nodded, not able to speak yet, my imagination running wild. Had Reggie hurt someone in my family or Joshua's? I walked slowly into the bedroom and pulled my suitcase out of the closet. I heard Joshua dial his cell phone and arrange for a taxi. Why was he calling a taxi? We had a car. Take a deep breath I told myself over and over.

My clothes and toiletries fell quickly into a jumbled pile. When I was finished packing I went to sit on the couch dragging my suitcase carelessly behind me.

Joshua joined me and began removing the contents of a manila envelope. In as soft a voice as I could manage, considering the panic that was brewing inside me, I said, "You need to tell me what the problem is."

Joshua ran his hand through his silken blonde hair. "A Nergal is coming. Nathaniel and I have to go after it."

I sighed in relief. Of the two possibilities for trouble, the demon was actually the least worrisome. I knew from my previous firsthand experience that Joshua and Nathaniel would be able to deal with this threat quickly and easily.

Joshua continued his instructions to me, his voice frantic. "Nathaniel will meet us when we get to Boston. You need to go to our apartment and stay with Cassie and the girls until we get back. Do you understand?"

"I understand what you've told me," I said trying to force some saliva into my painfully parched mouth. "What I don't understand is why I have to go with Cassie."

"Because I need to know that you're safe while I'm gone."

"Why wouldn't I be safe?" Even after all Joshua had told me over the past four months I still didn't understand what he was upset.

"If the Nergal found you before we found it..." Joshua trailed off and I saw him shudder.

"How exactly could the demon find me?"

"I didn't want to frighten you." He paused to rub his forehead. "I didn't think I would need to tell you this for a long time."

"Well, Joshua, now it's time to finish telling me. I can handle it, I promise you."

Joshua stared at me for a long contemplating moment. "The Nergal find Issy by smelling for her and because we have her serum in us, they can find us also."

"Of course," I said softly. My head spun as a scene other than the one in front of me replayed itself. Seeing a monster sniffing at the air and then turn away from me. "That's why it didn't attack me that day in the park."

"Yes," he confirmed, "and any place that you've been, your scent will linger. The demon can follow your trail... just like at the hospital, when you were able to follow Nathaniel and me down to the parking area."

"What?" I shrieked. I stood up, not sure of what I was going to do or where I was going. "You mean it can find me at my house? At Josephine's? At Lindsey's? At work?"

"Cassie has Josephine and the twins. They're en route to Boston as we speak. Steven is away on a business trip and won't be back for a few days. Lindsey will be coming over after work. They're staying for one of Cassie's slumber parties."

"Okay, good," I said, relieved. "What would stop the Nergal from coming into the city?"

"Humans in great numbers dilute out our scent. The beasts get confused. Plus we're fairly certain that they haven't figured out how to use an elevator yet."

"Oh," I smiled disingenuously. The image of the stalking demon in the park from long ago was still crystal clear in my mind and I had no intention of putting my human children or myself in its path.

The sound of a car pulling onto crushed shells snapped me to attention. "Katherine, it's time to go. There's a plane at the airport waiting to take us to Boston. Nathaniel will pick us up when we land."

"A plane," I sputtered. "Why are we taking a plane? Your car is still in the ferry parking lot."

"We'll get the car some other time. We need to get off this island and I need to get my weapons. If the Nergal were to catch us here …" There was no need to finish the sentence.

Joshua picked up all four suitcases and headed to the front door. "I'll tell you the rest on the way."

The rest? My stomach instantly filled with wasps, each one stinging me relentlessly. I chanted to myself over and over to hang on.

As soon as the plane left the runway, Joshua pulled out the manila envelope again. "This is the deed to the house on Nantucket. Put it away somewhere safe when you do eventually get home. It's yours and please don't argue with me."

"What are you talking about?" I snapped. Joshua must know me well enough by now to know that there would most certainly be arguing.

"The deed? What deed? Why would you give it to me?"

"It's in your name. I bought it for you." He spoke each word slowly and carefully.

I wanted to scream at him for this. Didn't I have enough to deal with as it was? I could feel the tears beginning to stream. Couldn't this have waited until the crisis was over and the monster that was coming for us had been killed?

"Why would you do that? When did you do that? Are you crazy? I have a house. I don't need another one."

Joshua laughed quietly at my blizzard of questions. I glared back frostily.

"I want you to have it." He shrugged. "Something for you to remember me by."

"Are you going away again?"

"No, not intentionally. In case something should happen to me one of these times."

"Is there a chance that something would happen to you?" I couldn't even think of that possibility.

"I told you that there had been casualties."

I swallowed hard, concentrating on my breathing, taking one slow breath after another before I spoke again. "This was really nice of you but I really, really wish you hadn't." I could see his disappointment at my rejection of his gift.

"Well, it's yours," Joshua said adamantly. "If you don't want the house you can sell it and give the money to charity."

"Don't think I won't consider that," I said, not able to keep the sarcasm out of my voice.

Before I could continue with the argument, I felt the planes wheels drop out. Nathaniel was waiting for us, leaning against yet another expensive new car.

Nathaniel answered before I could ask. "It's one of Cassie's." I frowned disapprovingly at him but he continued undiscouraged. "Did you have a good time on Nantucket?"

"What?" I sputtered. Why was he asking me about vacation? Who cared right now?

Nathaniel didn't give up. "Your vacation--how was it?"

"I had a great time," I answered quickly, not wanting to talk about it but uncontrollably thinking of it anyway, Joshua and me in each other's arms, rolling around on the beach. The memory inundated my mind to the point that I could feel the sand stuck between my toes. I frowned knowing that Nathaniel was now seeing those thoughts also.

Nathaniel laughed and I blushed. He turned to Joshua. "One would think that you would be in a happier mood after finally getting what you've been waiting a thousand years for."

Joshua was not amused. He folded his arms across his chest. "Just drive and mind your own business." Nathaniel shook his head mumbling something about Joshua's sense of humor.

Nathaniel didn't seem upset at all about this latest demon. Why was Joshua? Hadn't they been through this situation many times before? When I had seen them in the park, Cassie and Nathaniel had made it seem like it was about as serious as playing a video game.

Nathaniel and Joshua exchanged glances back and forth during the drive, silently talking but I was too troubled to ask about what.

The news about the latest fiend didn't seem to have Cassie the least bit ruffled either. When we arrived at the apartment, she had already fabricated a story for Lindsey and Josephine that Joshua and Nathaniel were to give a fencing demonstration in Connecticut and would be gone for night. They appeared to accept it easily.

In the middle of the talk about the night's plans, Joshua excused himself and headed for his apartment. He tried to stop me from following him but I told him silently that I would make a scene if he didn't let me go with him.

While Joshua was putting on the contraption that held his sword I got up the nerve to ask, "Do you think you'll have a problem this time?"

"Not likely," he admitted sheepishly.

"Please tell me what has you so upset."

"I would if I knew. Something doesn't feel right. We haven't been able to find Issy. She disappeared this morning after giving Cassie the news. Usually she stays around to make sure the monster has been disposed of. "

"Maybe Cassie should go with you."

"I'll be less worried if Cassie's here with you. We've taken care of it without her and Issy before. It's just me. I'm on edge... maybe because I have someone to think about besides me now."

Joshua pulled me close. I heard the front door pop open while we were still kissing.

"Are you ready?" Nathaniel asked his sword and bow in hand.

I couldn't release Joshua. "Please be careful and call me as soon as you have a chance." The tears began spilling out and down my cheeks.

"I will," he promised. Then Joshua said that last thing I would have expected him to say--or more, wanted him to say.

"I love you."

I heard my breath catch and I was speechless. After all that had occurred between us, why couldn't I be sure about my feeling? Joshua smiled at my chagrin. "Katherine, you don't have to say anything. I know how you feel even if you don't." He gave me another long, dizzying kiss, proving his point.

Nathaniel sighed. "All right, lover boy, time to go. I told Lindsey I would be back before breakfast." By the time I had opened my lids they were gone.

Grief overtook me instantly. What if something happened to Joshua and I never saw him again? I ran to the bathroom and fell onto the floor, sobbing uncontrollably. How could I have let him go like that? Joshua was the best person in the world and I was the worst.

I wasn't aware of how long I had sat there before Cassie came to find me. She frowned when she saw me surrounded in a sea of white.

"Do you want to talk about it? I'm a good listener, you know."

I gave her a disparaging look. Of course she was good listener because she was always listening.

"I'm very confused right now."

"I know none of this has been easy for you. You have to believe that in this life there's a purpose for everything," she said reassuringly. "The stars, or in our case dreams, are lined up in your favor."

I laughed weakly at her zany remark. "Joshua told me he knew how I felt about him, but how could he when I'm not sure?"

"When you read someone's mind, you see their thoughts from a different viewpoint. You see feelings that they've tried to bury."

"Umm," I mused.

"Well, for now I see that your future is to entertain your daughters and keep them safe. Are you up for that?" Cassie asked with her usual enthusiasm.

I nodded.

"Good. The sushi will be here shortly and we're all waiting for you to put on the movie. Living a life that's all about keeping up appearances is difficult at times but it's the best way to keep your family safe."

"Don't you worry about them?"

"Of course not. Joshua and Nathaniel are extremely capable and they never have any problems." I knew she was just pacifying me because Joshua had told me that there had been an accident once.

I tossed most of that night. For the short period of time when I did fall asleep, I had the demon dream again. Thankfully, I felt Cassie shaking me awake before the end.

"Cassie," I said, sobbing into her shoulder, "I'm afraid to go to sleep."

"The dream has gotten clearer and that usually means that the event is getter closer to happening."

"Cassie, if you have any inkling as to what this means you must tell me."

"Joshua will be mad."

"Forget about what Joshua wants. It's my dream."

Cassie took a deep breath. "I'm sure it means that the demon will be coming after you and your children. There won't be another one for a long, long time once this latest creature is gone. Then we'll see if you're still having the dream. Really, there's nothing for you to worry about."

I was tired of them all trying to pacify me and I began to scream at Cassie. "Why, why, why is the demon here again and so soon?" Cassie put her finger to her mouth cautioning me into silence as we heard Lindsey's repeating footsteps.

"Mom, is Cassie in there with you? Are we still going for brunch?" Lindsey's voice was wary. With any luck, she hadn't heard me yelling.

"She didn't," Cassie assured me. I frowned angrily with the new realization that Lindsey's privacy was being invaded without her knowledge.

"We'll be right out, sweetheart," I yelled hoping to stall her while I rearranged the set of my jaw. Cassie's disposition had changed from serious to playful in an instant of course. "Yes, we're still going." Cassie told Lindsey as she opened the bathroom door. "I'm starved. Is your sister up? Do you need something to wear? You can raid my closet if you want." Out they went, arms locked together, to play dress up.

Cassie had promised the girls brunch at a new place that was all the rage in Boston. She had assured me that we would be safe in the city among the smelly humans.

"The Nergal are only attracted to us. That's why it's easy to lead them out into the countryside and avoid human casualties."

"You purposely lead them out?"

"Sure, they follow us like a pet dog."

"Great," I said sarcastically. "I'll remember that if I ever want to put one on a leash."

My phone rang as we were piling into Cassie's car. The caller ID told me it was Joshua. I was relieved to hear that Issy was with them. Fresh terror over took me when I learned where they were-- in the park where we had first met. The demons were no longer following their regular pattern. Maybe my existence had been the catalyst for that change.

I wanted to grab my family and run as far away from this place as I could. Frozen by my fear I stood motionless staring into the car window. Cassie had to get out and shake me vigorously.

"Your mom is always so freaked out whenever we go anywhere in public," Cassie said dismissing my panic attack to the girls, who were squashed into the back of the Audi between the baby seats.

"Mom, try to relax," Lindsey requested. "My friend Christine told me the food at this restaurant is to die for." I hoped not.

Cassie and I smiled at each other as we passed by the tall stone lion statues guarding the front entrance of the 75 Chestnut Street restaurant --maybe a good omen for a change. As we had anticipated the new venue was crowded and we had to take a booth near the busy kitchen. The soft leather-covered seats were comfortable though and we settled down for some girl time. Josephine and Lindsey filled me in on the whereabouts and adventures of their mutual friends while we sipped on Mimosas.

Halee began to fuss and I picked her up so Josephine could eat in peace. Hanna was the opposite of her sister; not even the noise in the restaurant could keep her awake. After our meal Lindsey went to powder her nose. Cassie stood waiting for Josephine, intending to do the same.

"That vent is blowing out too much cold air." Josephine said reaching under the table and pulling out a bright pink blanket. "Mom, please put this on Halee. I don't want her to catch cold."

It felt like I turned to stone.

Josephine touched my shoulder, "Mom, what's wrong?"

I listened to Josephine's panicked voice as I walked into my dream. Cassie's focus changed as she watched with me.

While Cassie was still listening to my thoughts, I said to her, "Quick, take Josephine and go find Lindsey."

Cassie grabbed Josephine's hand and towed her toward the restroom, saying, "Let's go, Josey, we need to find your sister. Your mom looks sick. We need to take her home."

It was then as I watched Cassie and Josephine weave their way around the irregular arrangement of tables, that I saw the blue chrysanthemums that the waiter was arranging in vases on the tables. I shook my head, trying to clear the old nightmare away and focus on the real one. I heard the all too familiar bloodcurdling noise, intensifying as I listened over the din of the crowed restaurant.

I wrapped Halee in the blanket and bent down to pick up the still sleeping Hanna, intending to follow Cassie. We could run more easily without the bulky stroller. Before Hanna was securely in my arms there was a bright flash of light followed by a loud crack and in that instant everything around me was in motion, flying into the air as if caught in a vortex. I fell onto the stroller still cradling Halee--using my body as a shield--waiting for the monster that I knew beyond a doubt I would inevitably have to confront.

*

As soon as the floor stopped shaking, I was on my feet. Halee was crying, but she didn't appear to be hurt. The stroller with the now wide-awake Hanna was remarkably still intact. Sunlight streamed in, unhindered, cutting through the pall of smoke and dust that hung in the air. The kitchen had been completely obliterated, the scene reminiscent of newsreels from a war zone. Electrical wiring and copper pipes hung exposed, water poured out from several places. The tables had been reduced to nothing more than piles of large match sticks. An eerie quiet prevailed for an unendurable moment as the humans around me tried to come to grips with the carnage before them. Then the screaming and moaning began. People clutched at bloody limbs.

Through the thick haze, I could see a bright white sparkler coming in my direction and I knew that the same monster I had seen in the park when my new life had begun would at the other end of it. Except this time the beast sniffed the air and headed straight for me. I imagined myself moving but I wasn't a fighter. It was one thing to practice combat. It was another to have skill at it.

Then I saw Cassie. She was holding something shiny. Cassie's presence distracted the monster from me and it threw the sparkling rod in her direction. She easily deflected the projectiles with one of the still intact chairs. Then Cassie lunged and her knife sank deep. The beast swiped angrily. The force flung Cassie into the last remaining wall, cracking the plasterboard in two. Cassie rebounded quickly and came to my side, trying to get me to stand. "The boys will be here in thirty seconds we need to hold it off for that long."

"With what?" I screamed all the while my eyes fixated on the monster as it pulled the knife from its torso and continued toward its unrelenting goal. Instinctively I put my hand up to my forehead and my ring scraped against it.

"Here, try this. Joshua said it would slow them down."

"I was wondering when you were going to give this back to me?" Even on the verge of death she was still joking. She put the ring on her finger, running towards the monster and jabbing her fist into its stomach. Another howl was released as the Nergal stumbled backwards, hitting the ground with a loud thump, dust and debris engulfing it. Undiscouraged for the second time, the monster got to its feet. It was at that moment that I saw the two shadows moving at lightning speed. Joshua and Nathaniel ground to a stop, swords raised.

My feeble human memory could not reconcile the differences between the monster in the park and the one that now stood before us. It seemed to tower over my protectors more than the first one had and its facial features were not as distorted.

Both Joshua and Nathaniel attacked full on, but the monster threw them across the room with little effort. Then certain it had taken care of the threat from behind, it turned again towards Cassie and me. I wasn't terrified for myself. It was for Halee and Hanna. I knew the Nergal would kill them while it was killing me. I handed the twins to Cassie.

"Run, Cassie, get them out of here!" I turned my back on her fully intending to meet the grim reaper, hoping that the beast would be satisfied with my death, or at least preoccupied with it long enough to allow their escape. Out of the corner of my eye, I saw Nathaniel but his way to us was blocked by the rubble from the explosion.

"Katherine, take this," Nathaniel said calmly, tossing me his sword. I caught the glinting steel in midair as the monster closed the distance. With my eyes closed shut and with as much force as I could muster, I plunged the heavy blade out in front. The deafening scream told me the sword had met its mark.

Joshua appeared to my left. "Katherine, move back." I leaped out of the way. Joshua raised his sword and in one quick motion the monster was dead. Its head dropped haphazardly onto the floor next to me; its body fell limply to the floor. In its place stood my savior. I rushed into Joshua's arms, kissing him, crying and laughing at the same time.

"Thank you Joshua, thank you." He hugged me tightly.

I looked around for Cassie, making sure she and the twins were safe, and for Nathaniel, to thank him, but they were gone.

Joshua grabbed hold of my hand. "Come with me quickly."

"Where are Josephine and Lindsey?" Joshua didn't answer.

When we entered the area where the restroom had been, human body parts painted the walls and floors. My search found Josephine and Lindsey both on the floor, red from head to toe. Lindsey was moving from side to side crying in pain. Josephine was still. I stood with absolute dread, looking from one to the other, trying to decide which to go to first. Nathaniel was standing by Lindsey. I watched as he bent down and cradled her in his arms. Then he spoke thunderously to Issy--the words hauntingly familiar.

"You have to save her. Bite her quickly, before it is too late. You did it for Joshua. Please, Issy, don't let her die."

Issy turned to look at Joshua who simply nodded.

"No," I screamed moving toward Lindsey. Joshua held me. "Katherine, Lindsey will die without Issy's serum. What do you want us to do?"

"Just give her some from your arm."

"It might not be enough, she's barely clinging to life, and her injuries are too extensive."

Nathaniel scowled at me as Lindsey began calling for me, her voice faint. I could hear the beat of her heart slowing. They must have read the resolve in my mind as Nathaniel turned back towards Issy, positioning Lindsey closer to her. The next few moments were an eerie re-run of a horror movie. I knew exactly what would happen but I was still scared to death. The lion held Lindsey's head with her paw and bent down, biting into her neck. I saw the last of Lindsey's red blood mix in with the sparkling amber blood. Lindsey screamed, as I had done, trying to break free from the lion's grip. She slumped effortlessly into Nathaniel's arms as I imagined I had done in Joshua's.

Knowing Lindsey was safe my attention turned towards Josephine. Cassie and Joshua had begun CPR on her but I could see that their efforts were ineffective. A disfigured piece of copper pipe was sticking out from her side, where most of Josephine's blood had spilled. I grabbed Joshua's arm.

"Please, before it's too late." I had finally decided that saving her life was the only important thing right now.

Issy came to stand beside me. She shook her head manically. I grabbed a handful of fur. She howled a loud snarl and I fell to my knees, my face only inches from her huge fangs. "How can you say no? How can you save one and not the other? Please! Please!" My entire body was shaking from the sobs. "Why, Joshua, why?" The enormous lion put its paw on my shoulder and stared longingly at me. From the out of the corner of the lion's eyes I could see tears the size of a jellybean flowing down, wicking up on her fur. I didn't need to read Issy's mind to know what she was telling me--that it was too late.

"I'm sorry, Katherine." Joshua's voice was heavy, "but Issy can only save someone who is still alive. Josephine's heart has stopped. There's no way to pump the serum through her body. She's gone."

Cassie was still administering CPR to Josephine's lifeless body, sobbing uncontrollably. "She's gone, Cassie, stop." Cassie ignored him. She pushed Joshua away and continued with the compressions.

I buried my head into my folded arms. I couldn't look anymore. I wanted this nightmare of a life to end.

A loud boisterous laugh coming from across the room pulled our attention from Josephine. It was a terrifying sound that in spite of my grief stopped me from crying instantly. Reggie, a goofy grin plastered across his sinister face, stood by the hole in the outside wall caused by the explosion. By his side stood Melissa, the woman he had introduced as his fiancée.

Cassie and Joshua stood up, putting themselves between Reggie and me. Nathaniel picked up the sleeping Lindsey and set her down by my side.

"What do you want? Have you come to pick another fight with us or to simply gloat at the destruction?" Joshua's voice was a snarl.

"Oh, I've come to gloat, for sure. I'm pleased with how well my planning has paid off. I'm beginning to believe that I truly am a god."

I was amazed at his perverse sense of humor. "What are you talking about?" Nathaniel asked, bending down to pick up his sword. "How could you have had anything to do with this?"

"Oh, you would be surprised at what I've had a hand in lately. Beginning with the death of Katherine's husband." He paused, letting the admission hang in the air like a bad odor. In the face of my daughter lying dead on the floor beside me, Reggie had my full attention. I stood up, ignoring my buckling knees and Joshua's arm that was outstretched to hold me back. My blood curdled with the anger that had lain dormant over the past two years.

"How could you have had anything to do with Alex's death? It was a car accident." I was barely able to catch my breath as I spoke. In truth my instinct had told me from the beginning that he had somehow been involved. I heard Joshua pull his sword from its sheath and Cassie readied her bow.

"Actually, that accident was fairly easy to arrange, as easy as this." Reggie waved his free arm out in front of him, drawing our attention to the devastation. "Compared to my siblings, Katherine, who insist on sticking to their restrictive diet, I have developed cosmic powers. I sat beside that poor wretched boy and aimed his car in your direction. It was quite an exciting ride!" he said gleefully, not able to contain his bravado. Reggie turned toward Cassie, answering her silent question, "Yes, Arieil, that was the wobble you saw in the passenger seat. I was there, invisible, even to you," he admitted smugly, untroubled by the wail of the approaching sirens.

"Now this little happening...." He reached into his jacket pocket and pulled out a much-disheveled book, the cover dark with age.

Joshua knew what it was immediately. "Where did you find that?"

"While you three have wasted your lives trying to save the world, I've been using mine more productively." Reggie held the book high. "Melissa has been very successful at customizing the Nergal and is now able bring them forth on demand. We're thinking of starting a mail order demon business." He cackled uncontrollably at his own wit. "I have to say I'm impressed at how quickly you disposed of this one. It was the strongest one yet. Of course they still aren't very bright, I had to personally lead it here to the restaurant to find Katherine or it would still have been wandering around the city in circles." Reggie put his hand around his chin and a troubled look came into his eyes. "The weapon is my design also, but I'm having trouble getting them to understand how it works."

A fierce roar rippled up and out from Joshua's chest.

"Oh come now, brother, you should be thanking me. If it weren't for me you and Katherine would never have found each other. We released our first demon in the state park in Townsend. What were the chances that she would be there? Afterwards, I could see how desperate you and Katherine were to be together. She had quite a few adult-rated dreams about you." Reggie shook his right hand gesturing that he had just touched something hot. "Come now, I did you a favor by removing the competition."

I began to burn, a piece of paper held over a match. The weight of the fury was crushing. I glared toward Reggie, wishing that my hatred would scorch him in place, wishing that I could have the strength to tear him limb from limb. Then I watched in confusion as he flew backwards, crashing into the brick wall behind him. The force pulled Melissa to the ground as she tried to keep hold of his hand.

All eyes turned toward me. "What?" I didn't understand what had just happened and why they were looking at me.

"How did you do that?" Joshua asked breathlessly.

"Do what? I didn't do anything."

No one waited for me to answer. Nathaniel and Issy rushed toward Reggie, still down and momentarily stunned, while Cassie begun shooting arrows in his direction. Reggie caught the first few arrows, but the last two lodged themselves in his arm. He ripped them out, grabbed Melissa by the hand and they were gone.

The sirens were just outside the building now and I could hear voices coming from where the dining room used to be.

Joshua turned to Nathaniel. "Get them out of here." With Lindsey in one arm, swords and arrows in the other, he disappeared. Cassie followed them out, the twins in both arms, leaving me with my dead.

I fell to my knees beside Josephine. The tears dropped in a furious torrent from my eyes forming a pool of their own next to Josephine's blood. I couldn't understand how her life could be gone. The life that I had nurtured for nine months, the life that I had given birth to, the life that I had spent endless hours reading to, taught swimming and skiing lessons to, the life that had given me unfathomable joy over the years. I had none of that life left. Reggie had taken it all and Lindsey belonged to Nathaniel. I picked up

Josephine's cold hand to cradle it against my face. In the end everyone had gotten what he or she wanted. I was sure Dante was smiling.

KAREN ANN

Chapter 17
LIFE AFTER DEATH

Love is patient, love is kind.
It does not envy, it does not boast, it is not proud.
It is not rude, it is not self-seeking, it is not easily angered,
it keeps no record of wrongs.
Love does not delight in evil but rejoices with the truth.
It always protects, always trusts, always hopes, and always
perseveres.
Love never fails.

1 Corinthians 13:4–8a

I've had this dream many times before and it's for that reason that I know I'm dreaming. The difference between this dream and all the others is that the monster is in camouflage--dressed in a long white gown. A small bouquet of flowers is clutched tightly in her right hand. Waves lap against the shore. From one of the tents flows the sound of someone playing the Wedding March on a piano. I follow the music in. Everything is bright white, even the perfectly arranged rows of linen-covered chairs. I begin to walk. Two young girls dressed in matching pink dresses skip happily ahead of me, their long blonde curls bounce with each step. I'm aware of figures watching me but I can't seem to shift my gaze from the man up ahead, all dressed in black. My need to be with him overwhelms me and I begin to run. When I reach the place where the man is standing, he turns and I can see that it's Joshua, his amber eyes ablaze with delight. He mouths the words "I do."

*

Noooo...I screamed, gasping for air, looking up at the stark white ceiling. "That is not going to happen. I don't know who you are or what sick joke you're playing, but I'm not going to marry him. I'm not some superhuman with some freaky destiny." I let the empty bottle of Jack Daniels slip to the floor as I grabbed the remote from the night table and mashed down the red button. The TV sparked to life, the volume up at it loudest from the previous day. I fell back and let the tears pour from my empty, broken body hoping the thunderous ranting of the announcer would drown out the images of the dream that I had been having ever since Joshua left, or more correctly, since I made him leave.

Over the past few weeks, I had been unable to lift myself from the dark place that had engulfed me. My family and friends no longer bothered to call or stop by. Not that I blamed them. Not that I wanted any company. Work, that had been a distraction and a comfort for me when Alex had died, was out of the question now. Josephine's presence lingered cruelly in that building.

Reggie's confession that he had had a hand in the deaths of my husband and daughter had pushed me over the cliff that I had been precariously holding on to for so long. I couldn't even find the strength to visit my granddaughters. My heart ached with an unendurable pain that I welcomed. It reminded me of Josephine and so she was constantly with me.

I also knew what Lindsey was going through in transforming to something more than human, but I couldn't face her either. It was a hollow comfort but nonetheless a comfort, knowing that she had Cassie. At least Lindsey would understand what was happening to her. She didn't have to be afraid, as I had been. Nathaniel had stopped by to chew me out for my behavior but after spending a few minutes riffling through my head, he left. I guessed he decided that I would do more harm than good.

Once the fury over the dream had faded, I dragged myself out of bed and headed for the supermarket. I still needed to eat. Starving only made the cravings worse. I picked up a paper at the checkout counter thinking I might find some inspiration to look for a job. I needed exposure to humans because the one thing I was sure of for the future was that I didn't want to turn out like Reggie.

Not one tear escaped as I read the caption on the front page of the Globe. I had already used up my allotment for the day.

LOCAL GAS COMPANY OFFICALS INDICTED FOR NEGLIGENCE IN BOSTON EXPLOSION

Reggie's diabolical plan had caused the death of over two hundred people, including my daughter. I did feel a twinge of regret for three officials at the utility company because I knew the truth—that the accused men had been as much a victim of Reggie's psychosis as I had been. Somehow, he had known exactly where to find us, known the exact spot to lead the monster to, knowing that when it broke through the wall that housed the gas main a tremendous explosion would result. Reggie had also calculated the time that it would take for Joshua and Nathaniel to realize that the demon had left Townsend and was heading for Boston, a crowded city, something the Nergal would never do in the past. Maybe he was a god; his plan had worked flawlessly.

I made myself concentrate on the jobs listing. If I allowed my mind to drift very much from the situation at hand, I might never come back. The local Wal-Mart had several openings, but I couldn't see myself sitting at the front counter happily greeting customers. Maybe if they were looking for a greeter in hell. Now, *that* I could do. I could let people know exactly what they were in store for-- heart wrenching grief and total life devastation. I shook my head. I definitely had to find a job that didn't require any interaction with the general public.

On the last page of the classifieds was an advertisement for kitchen service at a shelter in Fitchburg. The position paid minimum wage but that was fine. Money had never been very important to me when I was human, and it certainly wasn't important to me now. I had had the opportunity over the past year to learn the stark reality of what was important in life.

I called the shelter from my cell phone and was able to setup an interview right away. I chuckled darkly to myself as I hung up. Evidently charity was in my future no matter how much I wanted to distance myself from it.

I decided to hang around in the supermarket parking lot until it was time to leave for the interview. This was as good a place as any. Even though I didn't want to be with people, I didn't want to be alone either. While I waited, my mind wandered unwillingly back to my last conversation with Joshua.

"I need some time, Joshua. I can't be with you right now..." I didn't look at him while I spoke, so sure that fate would turn me to stone for rejecting him. Joshua had, after all, been the most costly gift she had given me.

"Katherine, I know I had no right to take you from your human life, and trust me when I say it is the most regrettable thing that I have done in two thousand years and I know how selfish this must sound to you, but I can't be without you."

"I want to be alone," I pleaded over and over but Joshua wouldn't stop talking.

"You still have Lindsey and you know what she's going through."

"Nathaniel has her now." The bitterness flowed like water. At the time, it had felt like Nathaniel had stolen Lindsey. That somehow he had planned it from the beginning--from the very first day when he knew he could see her mind –believing she was some sort of weird freaky destiny for him, as Joshua believed about me.

I winced now as the painful memory of me pushing Joshua away crept its way into my consciousness. It was wrong for me to have any happiness. I wanted to be punished, as if that would somehow cleanse me of my sins.

"I know you're in a tremendous amount of pain and I'll leave you alone for now, but I'm not going away forever. I promised you that you would never be alone ever again and I intend to keep that promise. You are my future."

That declaration sent me into a rage. How could he even be thinking about us when my daughter was dead? My answering words were so sharp it felt like they cut my tongue on the way out . "Most people think their children are their future and mine are gone. Get out, Joshua. I never want to see you ever again. I have to admit I fell completely for this farce of a life --the fast cars, fancy suits and expensive restaurants but it was all a smoke screen to hide the horrible truth." A thousand glistening shards rained down on the dining room floor as something flew across the room, hitting Joshua's arm. I still didn't know what it was. I hadn't bothered to clean it up because it was a good reminder of my shattered life.

I knew it was illogical to blame Joshua for Josephine's death. He had saved her once. I was really the only one to blame. *If I hadn't gone for the walk. If they hadn't saved me. If we hadn't been in the restaurant. If I hadn't sent her off with Cassie.* The "ifs" went on and on until I thought I must have surely slipped into a higher dimension of madness. But who wouldn't try to push such crushing hurt onto someone else?

I trudged slowly through the front entrance of the shelter, not expecting to find such a clean and inviting the atmosphere. To the right of the entrance were long tables with benches. In a far corner was a set of matching sofas and two coffee tables, piled high with books. Someone very talented had painted a mural depicting a variety of people of different races on the far wall. I couldn't help but notice the bleak difference between this place and the places I had been to with the Stones.

The director, Gary, who appeared to be in his early forties, came out of his office to greet me. He shook my hand and directed me towards one of the tables. We talked for about a half hour.

"It would be great to have you work here, Katherine. You're well qualified, actually overqualified." He paused, hesitant to continue. "I'm wondering though... why do you want to work here? You don't seem like the type of person who usually works in a place like this."

I knew what Gary meant, but I ignored the suggestion that I was the type of person who would have thought that I was above these people.

"Well, I'm out of work for the moment"—no reason going into the ghastly details--"and I want something productive to do with my time."

"Are you looking for solace?" Gary was obviously very perceptive.

"We all need some in one way or another. Wouldn't you agree?"

Gary smiled an all-knowing smile. "Yes, that's true." I watched anxiously as he thought for a moment then said, "We'd be happy to have you then. When would you like to start?"

I took a deep breath, relieved. "Right now!"

That surprised him. "Well...we're getting ready for our lunch shift." I followed Gary into the kitchen where two men and one woman, were busy preparing food for the day's meals. The woman smiled apologetically and handed me a clean apron and a pair of rubber gloves. A normal person might have been overwhelmed by the amount of dirty pots and pans overflowing the stainless steel sink but for me it was great to be able to concentrate on something other than my own self-absorbed misery. As soon as that task was completed, I went to pass out drinks to the "guests," as the shelter referred to its homeless charges.

A large crowd of mostly men wandered in for the lunchtime serving in small groups of twos and threes. Gary explained that I would need to exercise more than average patience, as we were here to offer relief, not to judge.

Of course judging was the last thing they had to worry about from me. I lived in a glass house as big as the Mall of America.

On the ride home that first day, my mind wandered back again to Joshua. I longed for the human days when it was easy to tuck bad memories into the back of my subconscious never to be found.

Joshua was always so sure of his path. I knew he truly believed in it, but I didn't, not now. How could I believe in a senseless world that would take a young woman in the prime of her life and leave me, someone who was at the end of her life, and give her immortality? The universe was a mighty messed up place.

My working hours were from ten to three daily. I became friendly with several of the regular guests, sitting with them during my breaks. After a while, they began to share with me their particular situations. Most of them believed that they ended up here through no fault of their own. It was a perception I could relate to.

Working at the shelter helped me to get through the long days and I came to realize that in spite of their circumstances, many of the guests were happy. They managed to get up every day and go on with their lives even though they had nothing but the shirts on their backs. It gave me courage and I felt myself beginning to crawl out of the hole where I had planned to die.

On my one-month anniversary, Gary promoted me from sink duty to table duty. A f t e r l u n c h , I realized that I was actually looking forward to going home. Rather than my usual routine of drinking myself into oblivion, I was planning to watch a movie and do some stitching. I had gotten halfway through the dining area when I noticed an unfamiliar man sitting at the far end of the room. His clothes where exceptionally ragged, as was his dirty blonde hair and "ZZ Top" beard which fell to his midline.

"Sir, do you need some assistance?"

The man answered without looking up. "No, I just need a few minutes."

"All right." I found it was best not to push the guests into anything until they were ready.

I headed for the kitchen to refill the pail of water. Everyone else had left except Gary.

"Are you done with the tables? It would be nice to close up early for a change."

"I just have two more left. There's still one guest out in the dining room but I'll let him know we're closing."

Gary pulled the plug from the sink and dried his hands. He leaned his head out through the opening in the wall between the kitchen and dining area. "Looks like the place is empty. I'm going out back with the trash, then we can call it a day."

"Okay, I'll be done in a few." A few seconds that is, I thought to myself. Without anyone watching I could move at a much faster pace.

I waited until Gary had disappeared through the back door. Then moving at lightning speed I moved into the dining area but came to an abrupt halt as soon as I passed the threshold, spilling half the water from the bucket. The man was still there. Why hadn't Gary seen him? The last time this happened had been in the bookseller's tent at the racetrack. I dropped the pail and the cloth and bolted for the door, hoping to make it outside before Reggie caught me; then maybe he wouldn't bother with Gary. I had caused enough deaths. As I reached the front door, a hand caught my arm, pulling me back and pinning me against the wall.

"Please...please," I begged, "just kill me, don't hurt anyone else." I still had my eyes closed tightly, too afraid to see what was coming for me.

An unfamiliar voice answered back, "Katherine, please open your eyes. I'm not here to kill you or anyone else."

I did as the voice requested and found myself staring into an unfamiliar pair of bright amber suns. "Who are you?"

"My name is Adid."

I remembered that he was one of the originals---Issy's husband. It was he who had convinced the others to punish her for the death of his son.

"Ah, you know who I am."

"Great, another annoying mind reader."

Adid chuckled unperturbed.

"How is it that Joshua and Issy don't know you're still around?"

"I'm very good at staying out of the hybrids' way. That's not important right now. I came here to set you back on the path that you've strayed from."

I scowled in disbelief. The only thing Adid could do for me at this point would be to put me out of my misery.

"I'm not going to kill you. Please stop thinking that."

"If you don't like what I'm thinking, then stay the hell out of my head."

"Please, come, sit with me. I have a story to tell you."

Didn't these people ever get tired of talking? One would think that thousands of years of telepathy would have shut them up.

"Please, Katherine."

I sighed. "Sure, why not." My head turned towards the kitchen door.

"Don't worry about your boss. He's taking a nap."

"You didn't hurt him, did you?"

"Gary's fine. Human minds are very susceptible to suggestions. I skillfully suggested that a short nap would be delightful after he took out the trash."

I shook my head and sat down across from him.

"Ever since Ishtar, or Issy as you refer to her now, bit you, I've been watching you closely."

"Why? Were you looking for some entertainment?"

Adid chuckled again. "I'm not really sure myself, except that I also had been dreaming of you."

I put my hands over my face and groaned "Not another one." What was it with these people and me? I was like a lightning rod for all things weird. Maybe that was why I was crazy about science fiction.

I looked up and Adid was smiling, obviously amused again at my thoughts.

"My dream is different than Joshua's."

"Well, that's a relief. Because I'm not going to marry him and I'm certainly not going to marry you."

I watched as Adid's brow narrowed. "You're quite annoying. How does Joshua put up with you? Please be quiet for a moment."

I looked down, squeezing my hands together, trying to hold back the tears that had begun to well up at the reminder of Joshua's never-ending patience with me.

"Watching the events of your life has made me come to realize that Ishtar was suffering as much as I was and that it was I who ruined our lives, not her. The dream I've been having that concerned you began around the time of your birth, your human birth. I didn't know who you were, or what the dream meant. We immortals have many dreams that we don't understand." He chuckled quietly as if he thought the whole dreams are our future crap was charming.

I wondered how he would have felt if he had been having my nightmares. I thought about my previous dream, knowing he would see it. Let him chuckle at that one. My sarcasm backfired on me, as the end of the dream became reality. The pain crashed over me like a steamroller. Adid touched my hand, and in a gentle voice said, "Hold on."

I took a ragged breath.

"We never figure out the meaning of many of our dreams. Some of them, like Joshua's dream --" he paused. "I have to say I am very impressed with him. Talk about persistence. Joshua waited over one thousand years to find you. He never gave up or faltered in his pursuit of you."

I fidgeted, not sure how much longer I was going to be able to sit here and listen to this.

"Joshua finding you after all these of years really fascinated me. By some coincidence, of course by now you must have come to realize that nothing happens to us by coincidence--I was in Shelburne Falls on the very same day that you and Joshua were there. I knew instantly that you were the woman in my dream. I've been watching you ever since, knowing I was to be a part of this story and so here I am." Adid seemed thrilled at this realization. Well, at least someone had found something good in the annihilation of my life. He stared at me eagerly but I didn't have a clue as to what he was trying to tell me.

"Katherine, I know what you're going through. Even after all this time, I still mourn my son. No parent should ever outlive a child. The death of your daughter was a tragedy but neither you nor Joshua is to blame. If anyone is to blame, it is I."

I shook my head in disagreement. "If I hadn't been in the woods that day, if Joshua hadn't saved me..."

Adid interrupted me before I could finish with my sob story. "You're wrong. Don't you see?"

"No, I don't." I was sobbing now.

"I set all this in motion thousands of years ago. I not only ruined my own life but yours also. I was hurt and wanted someone to blame. My pride and the opinion of others would not let me forgive Ishtar. You're about to make the same mistakes that I made--going down the same path as me--destroying your life--throwing it all away."

"Well, you're too late. I've already thrown it away." I buried my head in my hands.

"Please, take my hands." I looked up and saw that he had placed his hands on the table in front of me, palms up

I didn't move.

"If you want your life back you're going to have to trust me."

"Fine." What did I have to lose?

My body reacted with a jolt as our hands interlocked and my field of vision was replaced with another. A huge spider web, with me at the center, hung in the space directly in front of me. The essence of my life radiated out in circles and touched every person in my family. Some of the lines had become frayed. Soon my whole family would be floating. I tried to let go. I didn't want to see any more but Adid held me tightly, moving his hands to my forearms, locking me down. I began to shake violently, as a new image appeared

"Please, please, don't make me watch this. I've lived through this once, wasn't that was enough?"

Adid howled at me in a deep voice, rocking my skull. "You must see this. You must understand the complete path of your life if you are going to be able to live your life. I will not let you waste your time on this earth moping in self-pity like I have done."

The drama continued. It stung me to watch, like pouring salt into an open wound. I walked in slow motion toward the back of the ambulance, the young paramedic Neil was hovering over Josephine's swollen belly. He lifted his blood-soaked hands. "I didn't know what to do."

"Please, please, no more," I begged.

Adid let go and I blinked the horrifying image away as he lightly patted my head. "You can see now that Joshua's being with you has saved your granddaughters. All life and death is predetermined. A balance must be maintained. Sometimes the course of a life can be changed for a short period of time, as was the case with your daughter. No course of events can alter a determination permanently."

"I...don't...understand."

"Joshua knows all this and can explain it to you when you're ready to hear it."

I sighed--more stories.

"We had assumed that none of the hybrids could be as powerful as the originals. That the scale of our abilities was directly related to the strength of our blood. There must be some genetic factor we hadn't considered."

"It figures," I mumbled. "I always knew there was something wrong with me."

Adid snickered. "You and possibly your remaining daughter could be more potent than either me or Issy. The hybrids will need your powers or they may not survive the war that's coming next."

I looked at him blankly. There were always so many riddles from these people.

"War? What can I do? I can't even win a fencing match. I don't know what I did that day to cause Reggie to fly across the room."

"You must find your courage. Joshua hasn't pushed you because he doesn't know how strong you are or what Reggie is planning but I do. I've seen the future and it's a future that none of us wants." Adid reached out for my hand again and I instantly saw what he was trying to tell me. The disturbing image lasted only for the brief second that our hands were in contact---long enough for me to understand.

I stared at him, my mouth wide open. What could I do against such a force?

"As far as your telekinetic abilities, I will offer my services in your training. I think it's time that I introduced myself to my relatives and got back in the game."

I nodded and I knew he could see what my next move was. Even if Joshua didn't want me anymore, I had to give him my forgiveness. I had to let him know how wrong I was and more importantly, I had to make sure that my old and new families would be safe from Reggie and his sinister plans.

"Joshua still loves you and always will."

I shook my head, unable to speak past the lump. Losing Joshua would be no more than I deserved in the end.

Then, taking my hands in his again, Adid said fervently, "Thank you."

"Why are you thanking me?"

"For showing me what I need to do to fix my life. I'm going to find Ishtar while you find Joshua. Then she and I will find a way to reverse the spell that imprisoned her."

I stood up and kissed him on top of his head but I hesitated, not sure what to do about my job here at the shelter.

"Just go. I'll make some suggestions for you." Adid smiled smugly. "I'm beginning to enjoy all this intrigue."

Chapter 18
LOVE EVER AFTER

The beauty of life is, while we cannot undo what is done,
we can see it, understand it, learn from it and change.
So that every new moment is spent not in regret,
guilt, fear or anger,
but in wisdom, understanding and love.

~ Jennifer Edwards

Lindsey looked overjoyed to see me as I pulled into the cavernous garage under the Prudential Center. She hugged me tightly as we both wiped away tears. Nathaniel stood behind her scowling. No surprise there.

Lindsey had always been a striking beauty, now she was even more than that. It was sad, though, that she would lose her uniqueness. Her long flowing auburn hair showed streaks of blond highlights and soon she would look identical to Cassie, and me.

"I have been so stupid," I told her remorsefully. "Please forgive me. I'm so grateful you're alive."

I turned to Nathaniel. "I've never thanked you for convincing Issy to save Lindsey's life. It was more than I deserved, considering how I've treated you."

Nathaniel nodded grudgingly. "You're welcome, but I didn't do it for you." Lindsey flashed him a frown.

"I know that, but it doesn't change the fact that I am indebted to you."

"You fix things with Joshua and we can call it even," Nathaniel offered, making peace, I'm sure for Lindsey.

Nathaniel wrapped his arm around Lindsey's waist, pulling her next to him. She stared up at him adoringly. Nathaniel looked back at her with the same look of eternal love that Joshua had had for me. The look I threw away.

I took a deep breath, relieved that this part of the day was over with, although it would not be the hardest part. "I need to talk to Joshua."

Nathaniel frowned. "He doesn't want to see anyone."

My heart sank. Of course he didn't want to see anyone, especially me. "Nathaniel, I need to talk to Joshua one more time. I can't let this end like this. Please."

Nathaniel looked at Lindsey for a long moment and then said, "We'll have to take you there ourselves. It's a long trip. Joshua left his cell phone here and there's no other way for me to get in touch with him."

Where would one go without a cell phone these days? Especially Joshua. He was never out of touch with his siblings.

Nathaniel didn't answer my unspoken question. "I'll make the arrangements. You can stay over in Joshua's place. Be up by seven and ready to leave." His voice was stern, displeased. Nathaniel left Lindsey and me standing awkwardly in the middle of the garage.

"Sorry about that," Lindsey said apologetically.

"It's fine. Don't start anything with him over this, please." The only consolation I could give Nathaniel was that he couldn't possibly hate me as much as I hated myself.

When the elevator came back down, Lindsey and I took it to the penthouse. She made lunch and we sat quietly while we ate. When we had finished, though, I knew it was time to talk about the difficult stuff--Josephine's death and Lindsey's new life.

"Lindsey," I said taking her hands in mine. "You know that you and your sister brought a meaning to my life that was boundless." Fresh tears flowed down my cheeks. Lindsey's face mimicked mine.

"Josephine's death was hard on all of us, Mom. Cassie and I haven't stopped crying for weeks now."

"I'm going to talk to Steven also. I need to be involved with Halee and Hanna."

"I love you, Mom. I'm glad you're back." Lindsey started to say something else but hesitated. After pondering for a few seconds she lifted her chin and in an unwavering voice said, "Mom, Nathaniel asked me to marry him. I love him and he loves me." She held out her left hand for me to see the engagement ring. "It would be great if you could be a part of our lives. I know this is weird and all, with you marrying the older brother."

I doubted I would be marrying the older brother, so the weird part wasn't going to be a problem. "I didn't like Nathaniel very much when I first met him," I confessed. "I can see now how much he loves you and you love him and that's all that matters."

"Time will smooth things over between you. From what Nathaniel has told me about our new life we'll have nothing but time." I liked the way she had said our new life, including me in her future.

"How are you feeling?" I knew Lindsey must still be in pain.

"Just a few aches here and there." She paused taking a deep breath and a few tears trickled down her cheeks. "Do you think it's wrong of me to be happy right now?"

"I think we both know Josephine would want us to go on with our lives."

"I like all the changes," she said guiltily. "The eyes will be a little freaky but I can eat whatever I want and don't have to worry about dieting any more. That's the best!"

I could see it as clear as glass. Lindsey had the same look of awe that I had had when life had first slipped from reality into fantasy. Then Lindsey said something that astounded me.

"Nathaniel told me how you had to go through all this by yourself. That Joshua and Issy wouldn't let anyone explain what was happening to you. Nathaniel said he felt sorry for you. When they changed at least they had each other for support and comfort."

I took in a deep ragged breath, trying to steady myself. I could still feel the sense of dread whenever I thought back to that dark time. "I had Alex and that was all I really needed."

"To tell you the truth, Mom, the whole family knew something weird was going on, with you looking younger and losing weight, and you were always freaked out. What a trip. I'm sorry. I wished I could have helped you."

"I got through it. Joshua and Issy were right to do what they did. Who knows what my reaction would have been if I had known what was really happening. I might have run away and found a cave to hide in for eternity." *Or worse*, I thought to myself.

"Nathaniel told me that you have some kind of extra ability-- that you can move things with your mind. That must be cool."

I frowned. "I'm not sure what it is."

Just then, I heard the elevator door open. Cassie called my name even before she got to the door of the apartment. I took a deep breath, preparing myself.

Cassie threw her arms around my shoulders. "I'm so happy to see you and I'm so sorry about everything."

I grabbed her shoulders and pulled her back. Her eyes were red from crying also. "You're sorry? Cassie, I'm here to apologize to you. I'm the idiot."

"I shouldn't have left Josephine and Lindsey alone. I thought they would be safe in the bathroom. I knew the monster was coming for you. I was supposed to be protecting you. I…"

I put my fingers to her lips. "It's nobody's fault, and you are not to blame. I'm here to make things right. I just need to find Joshua to do that."

"Yes, I know. I'm going with you tomorrow."

"Good. We should get some sleep. Nathaniel was very adamant about the time we need to leave."

Cassie rolled her eyes. "Nathaniel can be so dramatic sometimes." Cassie and Lindsey burst out in quiet glee and I joined them, happy that I could still smile.

Lindsey came to collect me at seven exactly. On the way to the airport Nathaniel and Cassie told me that they had offered Steven a position in their foundation and that upon our return they planned to tell him everything. They also suggested that it was time to let my brother in on the situation also.

For once, I didn't argue the point. I would go along with anything now if it meant keeping my loved ones out of harm's way. Seeing what Adid had showed me, Nathaniel hadn't wasted anytime calling the remaining fourteen hybrids. They would be arriving while we were away.

Nathaniel had chartered a private jet for our flight to Los Angeles. Of course, we couldn't take a regular airplane.

Nathaniel laughed at my thoughts.

"It's annoying. The airport would be put on red alert if we attempted to go through the metal detectors."

We had a two-hour layover in LA before we boarded another private jet for Hawaii. Finally, when the suspense became overwhelming, I asked, "Joshua is in Hawaii?"

"It's just a stop on the way." For the first time I concentrated hard trying to get some look into Nathaniel's mind but I came up blank. He grinned at my wasted efforts. So much for extra abilities!

I had lost track of time and day when we boarded the next plane, which took us from Hawaii to the Marshall Islands.

When we landed in the Marshal Islands, an airport official escorted us to a seaplane that had seats for four passengers. I watched in confusion as our bags were loaded into the small cargo area, wondering where the pilot was going to sit.

Cassie climbed into the front passenger seat and Lindsey into the seat directly behind her.

Nathaniel opened the other back door and motioned for me to get in.

"Who's going to pilot the plane?"

Nathaniel sighed. "Me, obviously."

"You know how to fly a plane?"

Cassie laughed boisterously.

"We partially funded the Wright Brothers," Nathaniel bragged. "We all have our own planes. Jet fighters are the fastest, but for where we're going, this plane will do."

Of course. That's what happens when you have eternity to learn everything there is to learn. I vowed to myself that if ever I did get this straightened out, I would not spend eternity worrying. Joshua had been right--it was time to start enjoying my new life.

We flew at a low altitude over the sparkling blue Pacific. I watched in awe as pods of whales and schools of dolphins broke the surface of the water, swimming happily along with us. Maybe I would try swimming the ocean someday.

"When are we going to get there?" I whined nervously. Maybe it would have been faster to swim.

"Cassie refuses to get wet," Nathaniel commented. He turned to her and grinned mischievously. "Besides, what would she do without her ten pairs of shoes?"

Cassie stuck her tongue out at Nathaniel. "If it wasn't for me, you and Joshua would look like beasts."

During the trip, I recounted the story of meeting Adid because I wanted Lindsey to be able to catch up. I left out the part about vision with the army of Nergal attacking the hybrids. I was sure Nathaniel hadn't gotten around to all the horror stories yet.

Just as the sun began to set, Nathaniel said, "Look, you can make out the profile of Robinson Caruso Island."

I gasped as the shining jewel drifting in the vastness of the ocean came into view.

"We bought it after WWII," Cassie said proudly. "The insect noise can be intense but there are no humans around."

Nathaniel set the plane down as smoothly as landing on a cloud and taxied to the dock. A slight Asian man was there to greet us.

"Hello, Mr. Nathaniel and Miss Cassie. So nice to see you. Please leave bags. I will take care for you."

Nathaniel greeted the man warmly with a hug and a handshake. "Lee, it's nice to see you. I would like you to meet my fiancée Lindsey and her mother, Katherine. Lee is the caretaker here on the island."

"I have everything ready," Lee told Nathaniel pointing in the direction of the thatched roofs that peeked through the swaying palms. "The hot water has been turned on and the refrigerators filled with the food you requested. Will you need anything else?"

"No. Thank you that sounds fine. Umm… I can't seem to locate Mr. Joshua though."

"Mr. Joshua not here."

My breath escaped in a loud huff. "What do you mean he's not here?"

Lee looked at me apologetic. Nathaniel glowered at my outburst.

"Mr. Joshua left three days ago in his kayak. He did not say when he would be back."

Nathaniel tapped Lee on the shoulder. "It's all right, Lee. We'll find him."

I fell to my knees, sobbing. "This cannot be happening."

Lindsey and Cassie each took one arm and lifted me up.

"Come on, Mom, it's been a long trip. We'll find Joshua in the morning."

This was impossible to endure. With the girls beside me, holding me up, I made my way into one of the bungalows and stumbled into the first bedroom I found, ripping off my jeans and falling onto the soft bed, into a deep dreamless sleep.

*

I had no idea how long I had been out but it was pitch dark outside. The insect commotion filtering in was deafening and I suspected that's what had woken me. My thoughts wandered over the events of the last few days ending with the knowledge that I was on the island, but Joshua wasn't. I didn't know how I was going to make it through another day like this. The air in the room was heavily saturated with Joshua's scent making the pain doubly worse. I closed my eyes and let the misery overtake me.

"Hi beautiful," a soft voice said out of the darkness.

I sat up startled.

Joshua touched my cheek with the back of his palm. "I'm very happy to see you, Katherine."

The sound of Joshua saying my name raised goose bumps on my exposed arms. What a huge mistake I had made. I would never be able to live without him.

"I'm so glad you're okay," I said when I could finally speak.

"Of course I'm fine, especially now. I went for a cruise. The Pacific Ocean is phenomenal--plenty of whales and dolphins and sharks…"

I interrupted him knowing I wouldn't be able to keep back the tears for too long. "I have something I want to say to you."

Joshua was still smiling and that gave me hope that maybe we could work things out.

"I lost my mind when Josephine was killed. It was …devastating. I wanted … needed to hurt myself. I know you must hate me for all the awful things I said." I stopped, sucking in a ragged breath, not able to go on--the weight of my wretchedness taking my voice. Joshua didn't say anything. His eyes stared unseeing at the design of the bed sheets. After a long moment of silence he began to laugh.

"What are you laughing about? This is a serious."

"Oh, I know. It's just unbelievable to me that after everything I've told you and everything that you've seen that you could believe that I didn't I love you. For a thousand years I have loved you and I plan on loving you for another thousand."

"You still want me?"

Joshua brushed away a few of my tears. "I will always want you."

"Really?" I asked, relief overwhelming me.

"It was grueling for me to walk away from you but I knew you needed time, time to work through the grief of losing Josephine." Joshua put his face to mine, his tongue tracing the inside of my mouth. I could feel the life being breathed back into my soul.

"I think I need to lie down," I confessed as my head began to spin. Joshua released me and I stretched out beside him.

Something important was scrambling around trying to find its way out of my now fogged up thoughts. "I have to tell you who I met last week or whenever it was." I still couldn't recall what day it was.

Joshua put up his hand to stop me. "The only thing I want you to tell me right now is how fond you are of this shirt?" His dazzling smile had a devious glint to it.

"This shirt? It's just something I threw on. I left in such a hurry."

"Good," he replied, grabbing the neckline. The buttons gave way, flying everywhere.

An unfamiliar sound came out of my mouth and stunned me for a split second. It was a happy relief-filled laugh. The sound assured me that I was finally back where I belonged. "I think you have some kind of a button issue."

"You're right, they interfere with romance." Then his lips were on mine again, his body molding itself to mine. Even though the sound from outside the window was still at a riotous level, I didn't hear anything all night except for the sound of Joshua's heart.

*

The insect noise had been slowly replaced by an ever increasing bird song and I surmised that the sun was probably on its way up. I hadn't slept much during the previous night of bliss, but it had been the first time in a while that I felt rested and whole.

Joshua was awake also, running the tips of his fingers ever so gently up and down my back. I took a deep cleansing breath and turned over, pulling the bed sheet with me. Joshua pulled it back down to my belly button. "Please, no hiding."

"I'm cold," I lied. Too embarrassed to admit how self-conscious I was.

"Liar," he chuckled, not letting me cover myself back up. "Remember you belong to me now, Mrs. Chambers."

I sighed and gave up my hold on the covers. I had something more pressing to talk about. "I want to ask you something, please, if you don't mind."

"All right, we can take a break, if you'd like." Joshua's fingers continued to move methodically across my flesh.

"I can't talk if you're going to keep that up."

"That's all right. What I have in mind doesn't require much talking. " Joshua tried to kiss me but I held my hand up, blocking his advance.

"You're not going to distract me," I told him adamantly.

Joshua pursed his lips---seeming to take my declaration as a challenge. "We'll see about that."

I made a ticking sound with my mouth and continued to concentrate on what I wanted to tell him. "That dream you have of us getting married?"

Joshua's hand froze in place. "Yes?"

"Are you still having it?"

He made no sound.

"Has something changed in the dream?" I asked, automatically biting into my bottom lip.

Joshua frowned deeply. "I hope you won't be too disappointed with my answer."

I swallowed hard.

"Katherine, I've been overconfident and smug. All I thought about these last few years was making my dream come true, while all the time I should have been paying much more attention to what you wanted and to your dreams."

"Well, that's what I want to talk to you about, my dreams. Tell me. Are we still getting married in your dream?"

"Nothing has changed…but I didn't think that was what you wanted."

I sighed in relief. "I want you to read my mind right now and see what I've been dreaming about lately."

"You do?"

"Actually, I'm surprised that you hadn't already seen this." He had been in my head all night.

"Umm…I've noticed that your mind is only on one track when your clothes are off."

"Please, Joshua." I placed my hand over his and concentrated on bringing up the dream memory.

At first Joshua stayed as still as a statue, but as the dream unfolded, he sat up, his expression stunned.

"Katherine, it's exactly the same as my dream."

Before I could speak, his lips were on mine--crushing me into the pillow with the force of an avalanche. The vision faded as Joshua's kissing scrambled my thoughts. Even when he released me, his lips did not leave my body, he continued down my neck and onto my shoulder.

When the dizziness had cleared once again I asked, "Do you know where we are in the dream? I can hear the ocean nearby but the other details are still foggy."

"We're at the house on Nantucket." He mumbled against my neck.

I pushed him back, "You mean the house that you ridiculously bought for me?"

"It wasn't ridiculous to me," he said, not the least bit apologetic.

"How did you find it?"

Joshua shrugged. "It was featured on a real estate website. I took it as a heavenly sign." He looked down away from my gaze. "Time is relentless," he whispered, "even with all our abilities we can't stop it or change it."

I put my hand under his chin. "The past is over and done with. I'm not going to spend eternity in sadness. I have a daughter and two granddaughters to take care of and... I have you to love."

Joshua took a deep breath. I thought I could see water droplets on his cheeks.

"Is it true that if an event we dream about happens, then the dream stops?"

Joshua nodded, his gaze keenly fixed on me.

"I thought that maybe you might be tired of that dream. I mean, a thousand years, really. We should get married once and for all."

I watched as his eyes nearly popped out of their sockets. "Katharine Ann Chambers, are you proposing to me?"

I squeezed his hand tightly in mine. "Joshua Stone, will you marry me?"

"Hey, that's my line," he protested.

"Well, I'm tired of waiting. You know, you never actually asked me to marry you."

"You weren't ready to say yes and I wasn't going to take no for an answer." Joshua started to get up off the bed.

I wouldn't let go of his hand. "Where are you going? Aren't you going to answer my question?"

Joshua kissed my forehead and pulled my hand from his. "I'll be right back." He came back into the room holding something in his right hand and kneeled down beside the bed. With his impossibly long lashes blinking away the remaining tears he asked, "Katherine Ann Chambers, I will love you until time ceases and all life has turned to dust." From out of the small box he produced a bright amber-colored jewel which he slipped onto the third finger of my left hand. "Will you be my wife?"

"Yes." I told him passionately not hesitating for even a fraction of a second. I twirled the ring in different directions trying to catch the streaming sunlight. "It's beautiful."

"My parents gave me a special bracelet when I was initiated into manhood in Assyria. It's one of the few items I have left from that time. I had one of the jewels set into this ring. I thought it was appropriate since it matches the color of our eyes and sparkles like our blood."

"Thank you. What type of stone it is?"

"It's a called a cat's eye. More proof to me that I was destined for this life even when I was young. My people believed this stone would bring the wearer honor, success, good health and …a very long life." We both laughed at the amusing irony of the legend.

"We have a wedding to plan then, really?" Joshua asked, pulling my gaze from the ring.

"Yes, but promise me it will be small." I hadn't seen his dream yet, but if it were similar to mine, it would be a small affair.

Joshua raised one of his eyebrows. "Of course Cassie will be disappointed. It's a good thing the house is small."

"Let's elope then." That sounded like a better idea to me anyway.

Joshua touched his finger to his head. "Sorry, no chance of that."

"Yeah," I sighed, disappointed.

Joshua stood up and quickly pulled his shorts on. "It's too late anyway. Cassie and Lindsey are on their way."

I groaned and begrudgingly got up to meet the girls.

Cassie was so excited she could barely control herself and immediately launched into all her ideas.

I put my hands up to stop her. "Slow down, Cassie. Now, I know you've seen Joshua's dream and we'll let you do all the planning but I want the ceremony to be exactly as Joshua has seen it--nothing extravagant and over the top."

She frowned and turned to give Joshua a pleading look.

"Katherine's the boss."

"Fine, but you'll both be sorry when you see what I'm going to do for Nathaniel and Lindsey's wedding. Thankfully there were no predestined arrangements for that marriage."

"Not yet." I remarked.

Cassie looked stunned. "You're right, we need to have their nuptials right away before someone starts having more dreams and ruins my fun." Her mouth changed from a sour pout to a huge smile as she continued. "You know, we haven't had a wedding since I was married back in the eighteenth century."

I loved Cassie hugely, like a daughter, but she could be too much to take sometimes.

Cassie grabbed Lindsey's arm and dragged her out the door towards Nathaniel's hut. "Lindsey, we need to start planning. Have you thought about where you want to have your wedding?"

I didn't listen to Lindsey's response. I turned to Joshua. "Facing the Nergal might actually seem l i k e a safer p r o s p e c t after Cassie gets done with us."

Joshua wrapped his arms around me. "We'll have each other to get through it."

From behind, I could hear Nathaniel clear his throat and felt Joshua stiffen.

"Yes," Joshua said replying to a silent question from his brother, "I got bits and pieces of the story from Katherine." I knew Joshua was referring to my encounter with Adid.

"We'll decide once we get back to Boston and meet up with the rest of our brothers."

Nathaniel nodded. He turned and followed the girls.

"As much as I would love to stay here forever doing nothing but kissing you, I think we need to head home."

"Yes," I agreed solemnly, "I have other people to apologize to."

"Your son-in-law and granddaughters?"

"Our son-in-law and granddaughters," I corrected. "I also want to go back to work. I owe Josephine that much. She loved her job." I grimaced. "I hope they'll take me back."

"I could have Nathaniel buy the company."

My eyes widened. "Oh that's a good idea! Me working for Nathaniel!" I looked down and mumbled, "He hates me."

Joshua lifted my chin. "You're wrong about that."

"I don't think so." But what had I been right about?

"By the way Joshua, how did you get here? I didn't see another plane at the dock."

"I kayaked from the Marshal Islands." Joshua raised his eyebrows. "My kayak seats two. Do you think you're up for an adventure?"

"You rowed all the way here?"

Joshua shrugged, a look of pain shrouding his complexion. "I wanted to be alone."

I made myself another promise at that exact moment. That I would never cause Joshua that kind of pain ever again and I would do that by keeping my earlier promise. "All right, I'm up for my first adventure."

"Excellent," Joshua beamed.

"When we get back, I want to continue with my fencing lessons and Lindsey needs to take them also. I don't want you to go after those monsters ever again without me by your side." Next time Reggie or a demon came for us, I would be one of their strengths, not a weakness. "And I'd like an outfit."

"An outfit? I'm not sure what you mean."

"Like Wonder Woman or Cat Woman, and a name, something catchy."

Joshua chortled. "Okay, I'll get Cassie on it." He touched my cheek gingerly. "Forever mine, forever yours...."

"Forever ours," I said finishing his sentence. I was looking into my future with eyes wide open and I would never close them again. The ache in my soul would always be there but now it was working to make me stronger. Whatever fate had next for me, I knew my new family would be by my side.

Planning the wedding would keep the girls busy. It was just a formality anyway. The connection that had formed between Joshua and I could not be broken by any force on this earth.

We said our goodbyes, for the moment, but not before Joshua and Nathaniel made a bet as to which o f u s would get back to the Marshal Islands first—the plane or the kayak. I had a feeling this trip was going to be all work and no play.

After filling up with a few provisions, we set off into the vast expanse of the Pacific Ocean. A few hours into the trip Joshua stopped paddling and turned to look at me. "Want to take a swim?

"A swim?" and before I knew what was happening I was wet.

I sputtered as I spit out the warm ocean water. "Why did you do that, Joshua? I'm soaked now."

Joshua held me tightly as we bobbed up and down with each passing wave. I had to strain to look over his shoulder at the kayak that was now floating away.

"Joshua, the kayak..." I began but he interrupted.

"We'll catch up to it later."

My mouth opened as I tried to protest, but Joshua pinched my lips together. "I had the idea from last night that you had made a promise to yourself."

I glanced at the drifting kayak and took a deep breath. "You're right."

"Good, because I want to teach you my favorite swimming technique." I was beginning to wonder if the sun had gotten to him. He knew I could swim.

"It's called the breast stroke."

I laughed. "You know you're going to lose your bet with Nathaniel," I warned as his lips met mine.

Joshua mumbled through the kiss, "Oh the only reason Nathaniel bet me was because he knew he was going to win this time."

"Well then, we should make it worth his while," I mumbled back and we drifted off into our own private dream, safe for the moment in each other's arms.

What awaited us on our return seemed daunting. The hybrids, my new family, would be united, and for the first time in their existence they would be facing a war of their own, but that story would have to wait for the next chapter of my life.

OF BLOOD AND LIONS
BOOK 2: FAMILY MATTERS

I had faced this same death many times before and had survived.
This time it was different. This time it was real. The monsters
came at us in droves, relentless in their quest for our blood. Our
swords, slicing them into pieces, did nothing to deter their lust. I
stared at the one beautiful monster, my absolute attention locked
on his brilliant amber eyes. His grin widened in anticipation and I
knew that he could see what I could see---the Caïna of hell.

In the distance a lion roared

The Lioness and the African

ABOUT THE AUTHOR

Karen Ann, a graduate of Salem State University, has worked for more than thirty five years in the medical device industry. In addition to *Of Blood and Lions*, her first novel, she has authored and co-authored several scientific papers throughout her tenure in the medical industry. Science fiction has been a passion for Karen Ann dating back to the nineteen sixties when the first episode of Lost in Space and Star Trek aired on her parents nine inch black and white TV. Every show and movie since then has been an inspiration for her to finally pen a tale as thought provoking as those 60's TV shows were to that eight year old. Her vocation, which involves an intimate knowledge of chemistry and biology, has worked to her advantage in writing a science fiction novel. Karen Ann is currently working toward a master's degree in biology from Fitchburg State University as well as the sequel to *Of Blood and Lions*. She lives in a small Massachusetts town with her husband and may be reached at www.ofbloodandlions.com.

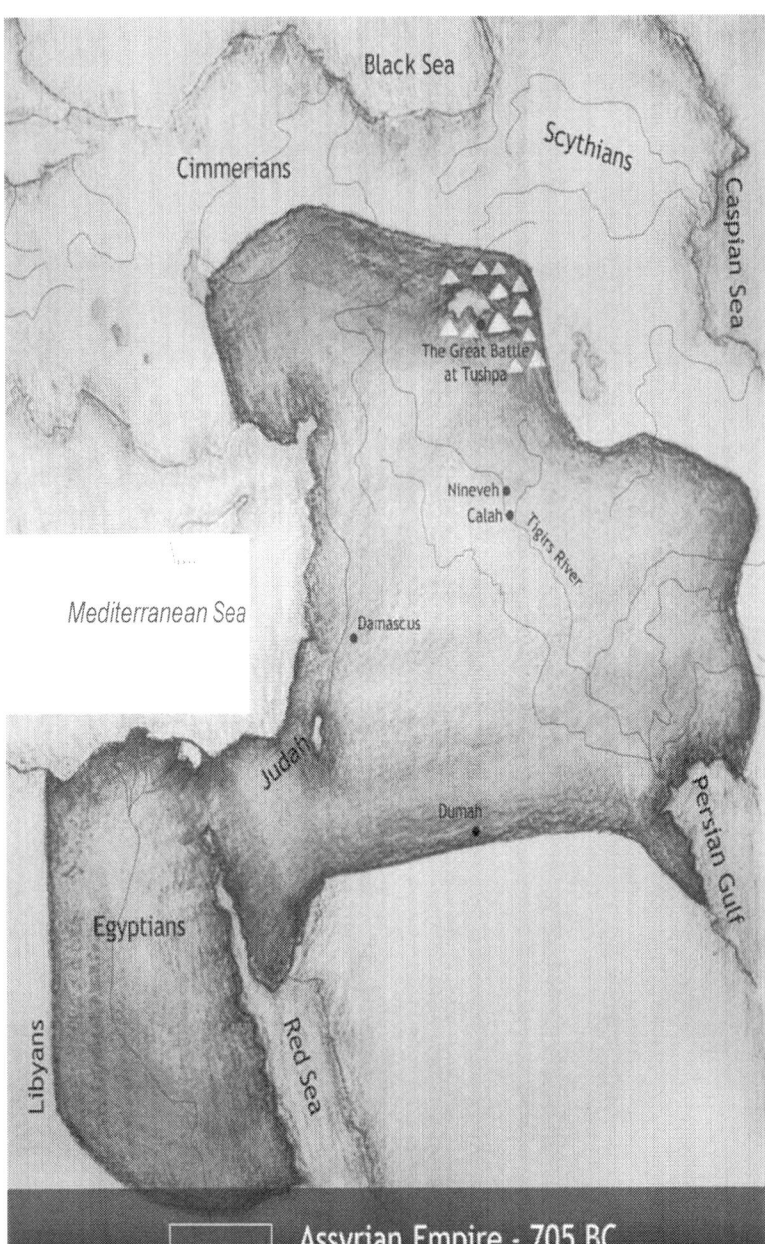

Black Sea

Scythians

Cimmerians

Caspian Sea

The Great Battle
at Tushpa

Nineveh
Calah

Tigris River

Mediterranean Sea

Damascus

Judah

Dumah

Persian Gulf

Egyptians

Libyans

Red Sea

Assyrian Empire - 705 BC

Made in the USA
Charleston, SC
10 August 2013